CC

D0016189

WITHDRAWN

WORN, SOILED, OBSOLETE

THE JANUS REPRISAL

THE COVERT-ONE NOVELS

The Hades Factor (by Gayle Lynds)
The Cassandra Compact
(by Philip Shelby)
The Paris Option (by Gayle Lynds)
The Altman Code
(by Gayle Lynds)

The Lazarus Vendetta
(by Patrick Larkin)
The Moscow Vector
(by Patrick Larkin)
The Arctic Event (by James Cobb)
The Ares Decision (by Kyle Mills)

THE JASON BOURNE NOVELS

The Bourne Identity
The Bourne Supremacy
The Bourne Ultimatum
The Bourne Legacy
(by Eric Van Lustbader)
The Bourne Betrayal
(by Eric Van Lustbader)
The Bourne Sanction
(by Eric Van Lustbader)

The Bourne Deception
(by Eric Van Lustbader)
The Bourne Objective
(by Eric Van Lustbader)
The Bourne Dominion
(by Eric Van Lustbader)
The Bourne Imperative
(by Eric Van Lustbader)

THE PAUL JANSON NOVELS

The Janson Directive
The Janson Command (by Paul Garrison)

ALSO BY ROBERT LUDLUM

The Scarlatti Inheritance
The Matlock Paper
Trevayne
The Cry of the Halidon
The Rhinemann Exchange
The Road to Gandolfo
The Gemini Contenders
The Chancellor Manuscript
The Holcroft Covenant
The Matarese Circle
The Parsifal Mosaic
The Aquitaine Progression

The Icarus Agenda
The Osterman Weekend
The Road to Omaha
The Scorpio Illusion
The Apocalypse Watch
The Matarese Countdown
The Prometheus Deception
The Sigma Protocol
The Tristan Betrayal
The Ambler Warning
The Bancroft Strategy

ALSO BY JAMIE FREVELETTI

Running from the Devil
Running Dark
The Ninth Day

ROBERT LUDLUM'S™

THE JANUS REPRISAL

A COVERT-ONE NOVEL

SERIES CREATED BY ROBERT LUDLUM
WRITTEN BY JAMIE FREVELETTI

GRAND CENTRAL
PUBLISHING

NEW YORK   BOSTON

This book is a work of fiction. Names, characters, places, and incidents are the product of the author's imagination or are used fictitiously. Any resemblance to actual events, locales, or persons, living or dead, is coincidental.

Copyright © 2012 by Myn Pyn, LLC
All rights reserved. In accordance with the U.S. Copyright Act of 1976, the scanning, uploading, and electronic sharing of any part of this book without the permission of the publisher is unlawful piracy and theft of the author's intellectual property. If you would like to use material from the book (other than for review purposes), prior written permission must be obtained by contacting the publisher at permissions@hbgusa.com. Thank you for your support of the author's rights.

Grand Central Publishing
Hachette Book Group
237 Park Avenue
New York, NY 10017
www.HachetteBookGroup.com

Printed in the United States of America

RRD-C

First Edition: September 2012
10 9 8 7 6 5 4 3 2 1

Grand Central Publishing is a division of Hachette Book Group, Inc.
The Grand Central Publishing name and logo is a trademark of Hachette Book Group, Inc.

The Hachette Speakers Bureau provides a wide range of authors for speaking events. To find out more, go to www.hachettespeakersbureau.com or call (866) 376-6591.

The publisher is not responsible for websites (or their content) that are not owned by the publisher.

Library of Congress Cataloging-in-Publication Data
Freveletti, Jamie.
  Robert Ludlum's The Janus reprisal / Jamie Freveletti. — 1st ed.
      p. cm. — (Covert-One series)
  ISBN 978-0-446-53984-5 (regular edition) — ISBN 978-0-446-54718-5 (large print edition) 1. Terrorism—Prevention—Fiction. I. Ludlum, Robert, 1927–2001. II. Title. III. Title: Janus reprisal.
  PS3606.R486R63 2012
  813'.6—dc23
                         2012015902

For Klaus

THE JANUS REPRISAL

1

LIEUTENANT COLONEL JON SMITH opened his eyes to see a shadowy figure standing at the foot of his hotel room bed pointing a gun at him. The red pinpoint dot of the weapon's laser sight skittered up the comforter cover toward his chest, making a wild pattern of loops on the way, as if the shooter were drunk and unable to aim his weapon. Smith rolled to the right, propelling himself off the mattress and onto the floor, hitting the carpet with a thudding sound and landing face down, using his hands to break the fall. A silenced bullet tore into the pillow.

Smith reached up to the nightstand to get his gun but snatched his hand back when the laser pinpoint sight began its chaotic dance over the area near his knuckles. The killer fired again, the bullet narrowly missing Smith's fingers and piercing the alarm clock. It exploded into pieces, and bits of the drywall behind it sprayed into the air.

Smith scrambled farther to the right, and the assassin stayed with him, firing over and over, but continuing to aim in a haphazard, erratic fashion. The bullets cracked into the wall, and he took cover by sliding into the small space between an armoire and a collapsible metal stand that held his suitcase. This position had the advantage of getting him out of the shooter's direct line of sight, but put him farther from his gun and still farther from the hotel room door. The attacker dropped behind the bed, using it for cover, as if he thought Smith had access to another weapon.

Smith crouched in the dark with his back pressed against the wall while he tried to pull together his jangled nerves and think about what to do next. He was in a suburb of The Hague attending a World Health Organization meeting on infectious diseases in Third World countries, an area of expertise of the United States Army Medical Research Institute for Infectious Diseases where Smith, an MD, worked. He was due to deliver a speech the next day on the hazards of cholera in disaster areas. The routine meeting had just turned deadly, and he didn't know why.

Smith's suitcase lay open, containing his still neatly folded clothes; below it were his shoes. He inhaled, grabbed a shoe, and threw it across the room, aiming in the general direction of a lamp that he remembered sat on the desk. He heard the shoe land and then the crash of the lamp falling over and glass breaking. The pinpoint laser sight danced on the desktop. The assassin had taken the bait.

Smith didn't hesitate. He catapulted himself toward the door, moving as fast as he could, fear and adrenaline making the blood pound in his ears. The killer fired again, but Smith was now a moving target and difficult to hit. More bits of drywall exploded to Smith's right. He reached the door, twisted it open, and stumbled into the hallway, blinking in the sudden glare from the overhead lights. He turned, preparing to run to the elevator bank.

Two men carrying assault rifles, their faces covered with hoods, stood about thirty feet away at the end of the hall, facing one of the doors. One turned his head to glance at Smith, but kept his weapon aimed at the room. He returned his focus to the door, muttered something, and both men shot into the panel. The corridor rang with the staccato reports of the automatic fire. The first man kicked open the door, and both disappeared from Smith's sight as they plunged through the shattered entrance.

Smith's mind raced while he tried to understand just what was happening. The shooter in his room obviously valued silence, with his dampened weapon and what must have been a careful entrance into Smith's chamber, but the two in the hall kicked in doors and seemed unconcerned about revealing their positions.

Smith spun left but stopped when he saw the emergency exit door at the far end begin to open. It swung outward, and Smith found himself staring into the eye holes of yet another masked attacker. His own bedroom door remained ajar and he slammed back through it, dropping at once into a crouch. He crabbed to the left, hitting his temple on the corner of the desk and stepping on some broken glass from the fallen lamp. He clenched his teeth as he felt the shard bite deep, followed by a flow of warm blood.

No sound came from the shooter in the room.

The hallway erupted once again in gunfire punctuated by the screams of the other hotel guests. Smith heard an explosion and the floor shook. When the noise died down, he strained to focus his senses in the shooter's direction. No sound. He hovered in the darkness and did his best to slow his breathing, a difficult task because he was panting with a mixture of adrenaline and stress.

His cell phone lit up and began to ring. Smith froze. The phone sat on the nightstand and its display illuminated the area with a yellow color. In the weak glow he saw the shooter slumped at the foot of the bed. The phone's ring increased, getting louder each time. Smith made his way around the desk, past the motionless person and over to the nightstand. He grabbed his gun, pointed it in the direction of the bed, and flicked on the bedside lamp.

The killer remained still. Smith glanced at the phone's screen. The display read "Anacostia Yacht Club" followed by a number that Smith knew was a decoy. His other employer, Fred Klein, head of Covert-One, an organization of clandestine experts in various fields dedicated to fighting terrorism, was calling. Klein didn't call often and never without a grave reason. Another explosion rocked the hotel, punctuated with screams and the sound of sirens from emergency vehicles, still in the distance, but getting louder.

Smith picked up the phone and hit the answer key, keeping his weapon pointed at the motionless shooter.

"It's Smith. What's happening?"

"Get out of the hotel. The CIA just reported that it's targeted for an attack," Klein said. More automatic fire came from the hallway, the noise louder and closer than before and coming from both sides. The attackers were systematically entering each room. "Is that gunfire I hear?"

Smith edged around the bed past the fallen man and moved to the door. He threw the deadbolt and turned the locking bar inward before returning to the body. This attacker wore no mask, and Smith stared into the face of a man perhaps twenty-five years old, with dark hair and the broad, flat, slightly Asian features of someone of Mongolian descent. Smith crouched down and pressed his fingers on the carotid artery, checking for a pulse. There was none. He put pressure on either side of the man's jaw, forcing it open, checking for cyanide suicide pills. Nothing. Smith could discern no reason why the man was dead.

"The CIA is a little late. They're already here. Why are they after me?" Smith transferred his phone to his left hand while he started to search the body.

"They're not after you personally, they're after American and diplomatic targets. This one is just bad luck. Coincidence. The CIA's been warning of an attack in Europe for months, but I just got the report that pinpointed the WHO conference and I knew you were there. Get the hell out of that hotel. Now."

Klein was right. The media had been reporting that certain fringe groups were planning an attack, but Smith hadn't thought much about it. He knew that US intelligence sources received hundreds of bits of information each day and that many led to nothing. Such reports were usually so vague as to be useless, and his business required that he travel to Europe.

"Tell me how many," Smith said.

"They think at least thirty. Two to four on each floor."

Smith heard more screams from the hall. A woman started wailing, the noise cut short by the report of a gun.

"They taking hostages?"

"No hostages. Body count. Get the hell out of there."

The hotel shook from another explosion and the fire alarms went off, making a high-pitched squeal so loud that Smith winced. A sprinkler set high on the wall over his bed began spraying water. Two others came to life, one over the desk and the other near the door.

He rifled the shooter's pockets, finding a spare clip for the silenced weapon and a wad of euro bills. He reached into the next pocket and withdrew a handful of photos. There were three. The first was a picture of a woman, obviously taken while she walked on the street and without her knowledge. She was dressed in a navy suit, carried a briefcase, and her long, dark hair was pinned at her neck. She looked attractive and formidable at the same time. There was no mistaking her serious demeanor.

The second picture was a candid shot of a man Smith knew and admired: Peter Howell, an agent for Britain's MI6 who had retired some years ago.

The third picture was of Smith.

2

S MITH HEADED TO THE WINDOW, still talking to Klein and holding the phone, euro bills and photos in one hand, the gun in the other.

"It looks like they may be after me. Or at least someone is. There's a dead guy in my room carrying photos of me, Peter Howell, and a woman that I can't identify."

"A dead man? Did you kill him?"

"I didn't touch him. He just…died." Smith stood against the wall and used the tip of the gun to slowly pull back the curtains. Emergency vehicles filled the street, their flickering lights sending eerie red flashes that bounced off the nearby buildings. The authorities remained a safe distance from the hotel, but ringed it. "Listen, I'm going to do my best to get out of here, but if I don't, I'm going to put the photos in my pocket. Make sure one of your operatives collects my personal effects, notifies Howell, and then finds this woman and warns her." The door to his room shivered as it was kicked from the outside.

"Get out of there! I'll—"

Smith didn't hear the rest. He aimed and fired into the hotel room door. The 9 mm bullet pierced the wood, and Smith heard the satisfying sound of a man's yell. Bull's-eye, he thought. There was a moment of silence, followed by the report of an automatic weapon firing round after round in response. Ordnance flew into the room along with bits of wood from the door, but Smith was to the right at a 45-degree angle and none of the hits came near. The bullets peppered the headboard and the wall above it with shot.

Smith shoved the phone, bills, and photos into his pocket. He'd worn loose-fitting cotton drawstring pants and a T-shirt to bed and his feet were bare. At that moment he was glad that he'd stuck to his usual, careful habit of booking rooms only on the third floor or below. Fire-truck ladders could reach the third floor, and most hotels had overhangs at first-floor level that could break a fall if need be. Smith always thought that precautions were best when followed each and every time because you never knew when they'd become crucial. This precaution just had.

The hotel was a large, stately stone building built over one hundred years ago on a rectangular lot. The front of the hotel faced the city and the back faced the North Sea and sat directly on the beach. Smith's room was located near the end of the hall, with five rooms on one side, and ten rooms on the other. His room had a view of the city in one direction and one that was cut off by the wall that jutted out in the other. The narrow casement window swung open easily. Smith put his foot on the sill, grabbed the curtains and stepped up.

The attackers began kicking at Smith's door. He fired again, and the battering stopped. He thought the killers must be surprised that one of the hotel guests not only had a gun, but knew how to use it. Smith's military background meant he was trained in weapons and hand-to-hand combat and had learned a smattering of different martial arts moves. In his early forties, he no longer took combat duty, but that didn't mean he couldn't defend himself.

Smith was tall and slender and he had to angle his body to stand on the window's edge. He stuck his head out the window.

A six-inch decorative ledge banded the hotel at least three feet down, with a corresponding band three feet up. A quick glance to the emergency vehicles gathered in the circular front drive told Smith that he couldn't expect any help from that quarter in the time that he needed it. None had ventured closer than fifty feet from the hotel, and most stayed back even farther. The battering began again, and this time the door cracked at the leading edge. It opened, but the safety bar caught. Smith saw a hand reach around the panel. It was time to go.

He put the gun in his waistband at the small of his back and slid one leg, then the other out the window. He lowered himself, face against the brick, until his toes hit the ledge. He held on to the remains of the window and began moving to the right, toward the wall that jutted out at a right angle in the corner. He had almost thirty feet of flat hotel. Once he reached the end of the window, he'd have only the rounded decorative piece above him to grasp.

He reached the window's edge too soon and hesitated. He was sweating despite the cool spring air, and he took a deep, shaky breath. For a moment he thought he wouldn't be able to transfer his grip from the window to the small, rounded piece of stone. Every instinct in him told him not to let go of the solid window edge, and his fingers seemed locked in position. Once he managed to release his fingers, he would be committed to making it around the corner or falling to his death.

Sweat ran down his sides and he swallowed. He heard the bedroom door splinter as the terrorists finally pulled the locking bar out of the panel. With an effort he released his hand, and moved it to the rounded stone piece. His fingertips dug into the brick and mortar.

"Move." He whispered the word out loud, and the action jarred him out of his paralysis. He began inching along to the corner where the walls met. He reached it just as a masked gunman leaned out the window, an assault weapon in his hand.

3

RANDI RUSSELL STOOD IN THE CIA's situation room in McLean, Virginia, surrounded by eight flat-screen televisions mounted on the walls and sixteen computer terminals stationed at desks. At least ten people filled the eighteen-by-twelve-foot room. It was 9 PM Eastern Standard Time, and her entire crew had arrived when the first reports of gunfire near The Hague began. Her best officers sat at computer terminals monitoring the Internet status updates from various networking sites, while others watched the traditional media report live from the perimeter of emergency vehicles surrounding the hotel. Russell herself had been working round the clock to decipher the exact location of the attack and had only just gone home to sleep when her phone rang to tell her that what they had warned about had begun. She'd thrown on a pair of jeans, boots, and a cotton long-sleeved shirt while she raced to her car. For the entire drive to McLean she'd prayed that the terrorists would be thwarted before they took too many casualties.

Now she paced before the screens watching the Dutch police handle an action that was straining their capabilities and plotted how her group could help. The live feed from CNN showed the stately Grand Royal Hotel with fire pouring from a sixth-floor window. Russell could hear gunfire and explosions through the microphones. The CNN correspondent kept pointing out how often shots were heard in a voice pitched high with adrenaline..

"The hotel guests are updating. There appears to be a shooter on every floor." Jana Wendel, a new hire fresh out of Yale, was monitoring a networking site that provided short updates in real time. The site had crashed twice since the beginning of the attack, but each time had been brought back online only to show a continuous stream of heartbreaking sentences. "My husband's been shot, he's bleeding to death, please send help to room 602" was the latest. Wendel set her jaw, and Russell thought she would soon be crying. The man sitting next to her, Nicholas Jordan, another new hire, was in charge of monitoring a second, European version of the site, and he, too, looked ready to weep. Despite the obvious emotion they were feeling, they stayed in position, grimly doing their jobs.

"Where's Andreas Beckmann?" Russell said to the room in general.

"On his way," another officer replied.

"Get him in position. As close as possible to the hotel." Beckmann was a CIA sharpshooter, and one of the few stationed in the Netherlands at the moment.

Russell was temporarily stationed in McLean under a new program instituted by the director of national intelligence. The DNI was an entirely new entity signed into law after the attacks on New York and Washington in 2001. The DNI reported directly to the president and since 2005 had been giving him his daily briefing. The DNI was mainly concerned with correcting perceived intelligence failures of the 9/11 attacks, and the latest program was designed to increase communication between officers in the field and McLean. Russell had proven her competence in the field time and time again, and her last mission had helped destroy a growing problem in Africa, after which the CIA had decided that she was best stationed away from that continent until memories faded. She'd been hauled home to act in a consulting capacity within headquarters and to manage a small cadre of agents spread across Europe. Despite the fact that the job was managerial in nature, she was surprised to find that she enjoyed the broad overview that the role gave her, as well as the power to implement real changes in protocol throughout Europe. Occasionally she chafed at the inactivity of a desk job, even a temporary one, but as an operative she knew just how vital it was to have a command center that could support rather than hinder.

The CNN cameras focused a lens on the third floor, where a man was standing in an open window. After a moment he emerged from the pane, holding on to the building's side. The CNN correspondent noted the man's actions.

"There appears to be a hotel guest desperate to leave the nightmare that is the Grand Royal," the CNN correspondent said. Russell felt her irritation rise. The situation was dire enough without dramatic narration from the media.

The supervisor for her assigned area, the director of European Operations, stepped up next to her. Dr. George Cromwell was in his early sixties and had spent his entire career in the CIA. He'd risen from the ranks during the final days of the cold war and was set to retire in two more years. He wore a rumpled shirt and khaki pants, having clearly just left the comfort of his own home.

"That guy falls and he's a dead man," Cromwell said. Russell nodded. The man clinging to the wall wore drawstring pants in a black watch pattern with a black T-shirt. His feet were bare and he moved along the slender ledge with precision, never looking down. The CNN camera telescoped, and the man's profile came into focus. Russell gasped.

"What is it?" Cromwell said.

"That's Jon Smith." Russell stepped closer to the flat screen. Smith's image filled the forty-two-inch monitor.

"You know him?" Cromwell said.

"He's army, and was engaged to my late sister, Sophia." Both Wendel and Jordan looked up from their computer screens. Wendel gave Jordan a glance, her eyebrows raised, before returning her attention to the monitor.

Russell scanned the room. "Someone get me a list of hotel guests. Didn't we have one?" An officer handed her some papers. She ran her eyes down the first page, then the second, then the third. She pointed to a name that she showed Cromwell. "There he is."

"US Army. He's a doctor?" Cromwell said.

Russell nodded. "And a molecular biologist. Highly skilled." She waved a hand at Jordan.

"Do we have a channel to the fire department? Put me through, could you? But remember to use the cover ID." Russell's cover included a fake name and false picture on the CIA website, and her title was acting CIA director of public liaison. She'd been using it for the past month when sending out communiqués to various European agencies about current threat levels.

Russell resumed pacing while she waited for the fire department call to be connected to the wireless headset she wore. She watched Smith make his way across the wall and felt her stomach twist with tension. While her feelings about Smith were complicated, she didn't want to watch him fall to his death. She stopped pacing when she heard the chief of the fire department address her.

"This is Brandweercommandant van Joer." He spoke English with a British accent.

"Commandant, can you get a ladder to that man? Quickly?"

"I'm sorry, but I cannot. My orders are to keep my men away from the building. They have no body armor, and we're afraid that the terrorists will kill them before they even maneuver a ladder into position. We're waiting for our tactical team to contain the situation first."

"But he might fall at any moment."

"I'm sorry. But I'd like to point out that he also has a gun in his waistband. It's entirely possible that he is one of the terrorists."

"No, no, he's one of ours."

"But he has a gun…"

"Of course he has a gun! He's United States Army."

"What's he doing at a WHO conference with a gun?"

Russell hesitated. She knew that Smith's activity as a Covert-One operative often placed him wherever a crisis was happening, but in this instance his presence at the hotel could have been purely coincidence. His real job also placed him at the scene of disasters and near disasters, and it was entirely possible that he was there in that capacity as well.

"He's an infectious disease specialist. I imagine he was invited by WHO to attend."

"I'm very, very sorry, but I can't risk my men. Again, I'm sorry."

"Ms. Russell, Beckmann's in position. I'm patching him through," Wendel said, and she tapped on her keyboard.

Russell watched the screen. Smith was almost to the corner when she saw a masked man's face appear at the window to his left. The terrorist maneuvered an assault weapon out and trained it on Smith.

"Beckmann, fire," Russell said.

4

SMITH TURNED HIS HEAD to stare into the eyes of the man who was preparing to kill him. He expected some emotion there. Perhaps anger that Smith had eluded him so far, or glee that he finally had Smith where he wanted him, but all he saw was a calculated coldness. A gunshot cracked and the man's head whipped back. Bits of blood shot out of a hole in the man's temple, splattering across the window above the terrorist's head. The bulk of the brain matter that Smith knew would be scattering as well remained contained within the man's hood. The assassin slumped forward and his body hung there, half in and half out of the window. His fingers loosened and the assault weapon fell straight down. It made a clattering sound as it hit the ground below.

"Thank you, whoever you are," Smith whispered the words.

Another attacker stuck his head out of the window.

Stupid, Smith thought. The gunshot echoed again and the second man slumped. This one hadn't pushed all the way out, and his body fell backward, into the room.

Smith heard rather than saw the reaction of the crowds of police and fire personnel behind him. A man's voice on a loudspeaker kept repeating the same sentence over and over in Dutch, and out of the corner of his eye Smith saw the crowds shifting, moving. One camera-toting observer stepped backward, keeping the lens of his commercial-grade equipment pointed at the hotel and Smith, but moving to a new position. The perimeter grew wider, farther away. There would be no ladder for him anytime soon.

Smith redirected his attention to moving to the corner. His fingers ached at each knuckle from the strain of gripping the small protrusion, and his biceps burned. His toes grasped the stone piece well enough, but his calves were in pain from being locked in the same position. He made it to the corner and carefully reached his hand around the point and grasped the section on the other side with a sigh. At least now he could stretch out his arms, which provided some relief to his biceps.

He shifted around the corner and was confronted with another window. This one had a hole in it where a stray bullet had exited. The curtains had been pulled, but Smith was able to peer into the room through a small opening between them. He saw a man's foot hanging off the edge of the bed. The foot didn't move. Presumably the terrorists had already visited this room, and the man was dead.

Smith glanced down, looking for an awning or something below that he could jump into with the hope of a semisoft landing. There was nothing. He wasn't willing to keep going. The burn in his limbs signaled that they were reaching the failure point, and he could feel the beginnings of a cramp forming in his calf. He carefully released one hand from the ledge, balancing himself as well as he could, and reached behind and pulled his weapon out of his waistband. He flipped the gun over and hit the butt on the glass next to the bullet hole, trying to widen it enough to knock out a section. He couldn't get his body at an angle that would allow him to generate any force, and as a result the blows were weak and ineffectual. The pane held.

While not a fitness fanatic, Smith worked out every day to maintain his strength and flexibility, and as a result he knew his abilities. Clinging to the ledge was pushing his muscles to the limit, and he wasn't sure how much longer he would be able to continue inching along. He felt the panic that he'd been tamping down since the start of the ordeal begin to break through to the surface. He swallowed once and prepared to continue forward until his limbs failed completely.

He heard a gunshot crack, and the window shivered as a bullet shot through it, a few inches above and to the right of the existing hole, but this one making an entry pattern. Whoever had shot the terrorists was now shooting at the window. Slivers of glass flew and Smith closed his eyes against the shards. A second crack broke through the dark and another hole appeared, this one completing a triangle. Smith felt hope surge in him. The sniper knew how to shatter a window. A triangular pattern of shots would overcome even bulletproof glass, which this window certainly was not. He heard the double pane start to crack, and long fissures snaked out from the holes. Smith pulled out his weapon and tapped on the glass with the gun's butt to speed it along. The entire pane came crashing down. He moved toward the opening, breathing a sigh of relief as his hand wrapped once again around the aluminum window edge. He swung a leg over the frame and lowered himself into the room on the other side.

Smith fell onto the rug and lay there a moment, breathing hard. He heard a smattering of applause from the police officers at the perimeter, but he was in no mood to celebrate with them. He was back in the heart of the disaster, with a dead man inside the room and no idea what awaited him outside. The terrorists still roamed the hotel.

Water sprayed down on him from the sprinkler system, but the alarm had stopped. The phone in his pocket began to ring and he jerked in surprise. He reached down and pulled it free. The display read "unknown." Smith paused, wondering if he should answer, but decided that it might be Klein calling again from a different phone. He clicked it on and put it to his ear, saying nothing.

"Mr. Smith, this is the man who just shot the terrorists and the window. May I ask a favor? Could you collect any bullets that you find? The two that I used on the terrorists are meant to explode in a manner that renders them untraceable. Not so the two that I used on the window."

Smith rose to standing while he took the extraordinary call. The man's English was inflected with a slight accent that Smith thought might have been German or Swiss, and he spoke in a calm, relaxed manner, as if shooting terrorists dead were a daily occurrence and didn't rattle him in the least.

"Why do you need them?" Smith asked.

"My employer would rather no questions be raised about my role here. I am technically not supposed to shoot people on foreign soil, no matter how despicable they are."

Smith had initially thought that the man worked for Covert-One, but now he knew that was not possible. Covert-One was an organization so removed from governmental checks and balances that Smith doubted it was subject to any rules about shooting undesirables on foreign soil.

He searched around the far side of the bed, looking for the two bullets that had completed the triangle, and found them embedded in the wall. He propped the phone between his ear and shoulder while he used his fingers to dig them out. He dropped the bullets into his pocket.

"I've got them. How did you get this number?"

"My employer gave it to me. I don't think there are any more terrorists on the third floor, but I don't advise that you remain there. I suggest that you make your way down the north stairwell. I'm heading that way and will be prepared to cover you as you emerge. There's a cordon of Dutch police forming, but I saw a second contingent of attackers on the move away from the hotel. This night is far from over."

Smith ran through his mind the people who would have the expertise to shoot with the accuracy that this man had along with the ability to gain access to his private cell number. He decided that the caller was either employed by a European military group or was part of the intelligence organization of another country. His use of the term "foreign soil" meant that he wasn't Dutch.

"CIA, Mossad, or MI6?" Smith said.

"I've been informed that I am to escort you safely out of that hotel if at all possible. You'll be safe with me." The man had dodged the question, but Smith decided to take him at his word. He'd just saved Smith's life, and options were few in any event.

"I'm on my way," he said.

He swept an eye over the dead man on the bed, but didn't bother to take his pulse; the large bloom of blood growing on the man's shirt where the bullet had entered his chest left little room for doubt. He checked his weapon and headed to the door, preparing to face whatever was out there.

5

NATHANIEL FRED KLEIN NODDED to the Secret Service officer manning the entrance to the White House as he passed. About sixty, Klein was medium height, with a craggy, lean face and lanky body. To an outsider, Klein's rumpled suit, ever-present pipe, and piercing eyes that revealed a mind constantly churning with ideas lent the impression that he was either an academic at a nearby university or a member of a Washington, DC, think tank. He stood erect and moved easily, and more astute observers of human nature would have noticed that he carried with him an air of authority. In fact, as the head of Covert-One, Klein managed one of the deepest black operations in the US intelligence community. Covert-One was bankrolled with discretionary funds that were available only to the president and were not tracked by any oversight committee or taxpayer-accountable governmental office. The president alone directed their activities and had formed the unit after an earlier terrorist incident involving a virus that nearly spread a pandemic across the country. Klein ran the day-to-day operation, and now he was headed to a private meeting called by the president. He walked through the White House halls, headed to the Oval Office. Another sentry there nodded him forward.

President Castilla rose from behind his desk and moved around it to meet Klein halfway. In his forties, trim and driven, the former governor of New Mexico appeared young enough for the demands of the job, yet mature enough to have the experience the position required. Klein found him to be a thoughtful and intelligent man, but he noticed that the bits of gray in his dark hair had increased. The presidency had a way of taking a significant toll on the men elected to the position, and Castilla was no different in that regard. This latest bad news from The Hague certainly didn't help.

"Good to see you," Castilla said as he shook Klein's hand. "I suppose you've seen the images from The Hague?"

Klein nodded. "Believe it or not, I have a Covert-One operative on site. He was attending the WHO conference as an expert."

Castilla raised an eyebrow. "Did he make it out of there?"

"He was the man hanging from the window ledge. I haven't had any contact since he pulled himself back into the hotel."

Castilla's eyebrows flew up even higher. "For a moment there I thought we were going to see a terrorist kill an innocent man live on television. I don't have to tell you what a coup that would have been for the attackers."

"I was impressed with the sniper. Was it a member of a Dutch SWAT team?"

Castilla shook his head. "No, he was CIA. He's still on site, but deploying to a new location. I'm told that the terrorists are fanning out." Castilla waved Klein to a seating area with four armchairs and a coffee table in the center.

"That's not good. Has anyone taken responsibility?"

"Not yet. In fact, the main terrorist organizations are denying responsibility."

Klein grunted. "Unusual for them."

"The CIA believes that attacking during a WHO conference is most likely not a coincidence. My concern is that the attackers' real target is either one of the attending scientists or the biological products that several brought with them."

"My operative found a handful of photos in the pockets of one of the attackers." Klein recounted Smith's information about the photos.

Castilla sat back while he listened. "Let's put aside the photo of the MI6 agent and focus on the woman. Could she be an attendee? Maybe one of the scientists?"

"That's a definite possibility. Once I get my hands on the photos, I'll have them analyzed as quickly as I can."

"I have some further bad news, though. I received a call from WHO's director-general. Three of the scientists at the conference brought with them samples of a new strain of cholera, an antibiotic-resistant strain of hepatitis B, and some particularly nasty E. coli. They were to be transferred to a secure site for analysis by an international consortium of biologists. The samples themselves were initially considered small enough to be of limited use to any potential terrorist, but we've just learned that the cholera strain can multiply with astonishing speed. In two weeks that sample will have grown exponentially. If any of these get into the hands of the terrorists, we've got to assume they'll dump it into the water supply somewhere. I don't need to tell you the kind of mass deaths that could occur if such a thing were to happen."

"Are these the only samples we should be worried about?"

Castilla pondered the question. "The rest were 'good' bacteria. Everything ranging from live yeast cultures to a newly discovered bioelectric bacteria that can charge batteries without the need for a separate electrical source."

"Where were they kept?"

"On site in the hotel safe in two different locked stainless-steel coolers. The good bacteria as well as the resistant strains. Because the samples were so small, extra security measures were deemed unnecessary, particularly in light of the quality of the Grand Royal's safe. It's one of the best. Over the years, the jewels of several royal families have been secured there while their owners conducted diplomatic affairs. I'm told it can withstand a blast of the nature of what we're seeing, but the concern is that the terrorists will have found the code that opens it. Covert-One needs to begin tracking down these samples and the scientists that carried them and we need to reacquire any that are taken before they become viable bioweapons."

Klein rose. "I'll get a crew on it. And my first member will be the man hanging from the ledge." He walked to the door. "That is, if he makes it out alive."

6

SMITH OPENED THE ROOM DOOR and peered out, glancing down both sides of the hall. The muffled sound of rapid gunfire came somewhere from above, but this floor appeared to be abandoned. He moved to his former room. He needed a weapon in addition to the Beretta in his hand and he figured the terrorists had no further use for theirs. The door hung lopsidedly on its hinges and he pushed past it, holding his gun high and easing into the chamber. The assassin remained at the foot of the bed and the two terrorists' bodies at the window, one still hanging half in and half out, the other slumped next to him.

Smith moved toward them, but stopped cold when he saw a fourth terrorist's body three feet from the other two. This man lay on his side, still holding his weapon, an AK-47 with a folding stock. Smith approached him slowly, looking for any signs of life or any indication that the man was playing dead, but the body lay there, unmoving. Smith stepped next to it, bent down, and curled his fingers under the attacker's ski mask. He pulled it off, revealing the swarthy features and dark hair of a man possibly of Middle Eastern descent; his face was clean shaven and line-free. Perhaps in his early thirties, no more. Smith checked for a pulse. Nothing. He ran his eyes over the body but could find no signs of a wound. The man wore a hunting vest of greased army-green canvas with several pockets. Smith searched them all, coming up with spare bullets for the AK, and a hotel-room key. He rolled the man over, looking for signs of an entry wound on his back, and opened the man's mouth, once again checking for cyanide pills and once again coming up empty. Neither this man nor the attacker slumped at the foot of his bed had any outward reason to be dead. A part of Smith wanted to analyze the body, figure out why the man had died, but he had no time to spare.

Smith pulled the AK out of the terrorist's hands and collected the extra ammunition. He began to fill his pajama pockets, but they were bulging with the earlier attacker's money, his own cell phone, and the photos. He placed the items on the carpet and moved to his suitcase. The sprinkler system in the room had stopped working, but not before it had doused the army uniform remaining in the case. Smith dug under the top layer and grabbed some underwear, socks, and the shoulder holster for his Beretta before moving to the closet where he pulled a pair of black corduroy pants off a hanger along with a long-sleeved gray T-shirt and a short black jacket in a technical fabric. At least these clothes were dry. He dressed quickly, strapping on the holster and reaching for his running shoes. Smith hesitated. The shoes were also black, a good color for blending into the darkness, but the heels were striped with reflective tape. He took a glance at the one dress shoe left under the suitcase. It appeared dry, but even across the room he could see that the one he'd thrown at the lamp was soaking. He put on the athletic shoes. He'd find a way to obscure the tape when he had more time. He shoved his wallet and passport into a pocket, put the cell phone, photos, and money in another, and grabbed the AK and the spare ammo.

Armed with two weapons, Smith headed back into the hall, moving fast toward the north stairwell. He pushed open the door and stepped onto the landing. Clouds of ash hung in the air. He sucked some in and felt his throat clutch as the acrid soot hit it. He slipped down the metal stairs, slowing at the second landing and placing his hand on the metal fire door. It burned his palm, and he jerked it back at the extreme heat he felt there. His eyes started streaming with tears from the thickening smoke as he continued downward, taking care that his footfalls made no sound. The building shook when he was at the last few steps to the street level, and bits of plaster fell off the stairwell walls. The smoke accumulated to a level where Smith felt as though he was inhaling nothing but ash. He reached a corner and began to move around it inch by inch, keeping his back to the wall and his gun raised. His weapon came muzzle to muzzle on the receiving end of a rifle.

Smith's world stopped spinning for a moment, and he felt his trigger finger tighten as his brain registered the threat. He locked eyes with the man staring back at him. They were green, an inch below the edge of a dark wool cap. Smith saw recognition grow.

"Mr. Smith?" the man whispered.

Smith jerked his head in a quick nod.

"Thank you for not pulling the trigger. I'm Andreas Beckmann. I shot the two men in the window." The building shook again with another explosion.

"Cover me, point to point," Smith said. He moved around Beckmann and kept going downward, swinging his gun in an arc. At the next landing he pressed himself against the wall and Beckmann moved into position again. They made their way to the first floor, taking turns advancing and waiting until they reached the final door.

Smith pushed open the door half an inch. Cool air rushed past him, mixing with the heavy fumes in the stairwell. He was happy to breathe fresh oxygen again. He peered out. The stairs opened into the hotel's lobby. Here the destruction wrought by the terrorists was evident.

The hotel's gleaming parquet floor, marble pillars, and plush velvet furniture had absorbed the effect of what looked to Smith like a hand grenade thrown dead center. The acrid smell of gunpowder hung in the air, and several chairs lay in a jumble where the bomb's force had blown them. A settee, which Smith had noticed when he'd checked in, was shattered. Two of its four legs were cracked in half, and the dark brown velvet fabric smoldered from a stray spark. The pillar at the center of the lobby had sustained the most damage. A ragged chunk of the marble was cut from the side, and the parquet floor below had a deep crater in it.

"Clear?" Beckmann said.

"So far. Let's go."

Smith moved into the far end of the lobby, keeping his back against the wall and sweeping his eyes around to catch any sign of movement. He held the AK up, ready to fire as he continued to slink along the room's perimeter and toward the door and freedom. Beckmann followed, edging around corners with the same silent step. Smith heard a sound in front of him and to the left. He waved Beckmann to a halt. Twenty feet more and the lobby would widen into an L-shaped section recessed to the right that contained the hotel's registration desk. There was no way to see from the perimeter if anyone lurked there. A thick marble pillar five feet from the wall would provide cover yet still allow him to see into the recessed area, but he would be exposed for the few seconds it would take to get there. He gauged the darkness, trying to decide if it, coupled with his black clothes, would camouflage his movement.

"I'm going to the pillar," Smith said. Beckmann nodded.

Smith lowered to a crouch, took a deep breath and slipped out, reaching the column in two long strides. He pressed against the cool stone. Beckmann joined him two seconds later, crouching next to him and placing his back against the pillar. Smith's heart hammered at the risk he'd taken, but one glance told him that it had been necessary.

Three men stood in formation at the head of the recessed area, shoulder to shoulder, their heads turning from side to side as they scanned the lobby. All three wore stocking masks over their faces, and all three held submachine guns at the ready. Behind them the registration desk with its granite-topped counter had been shattered, along with the mahogany-paneled wall behind. A gaping hole allowed Smith to see directly into the offices behind.

"We've got company," he whispered to Beckmann.

"How many?" Beckmann said.

"Six. Three sentries and three others."

Beckmann turned and rose a bit to see over Smith.

The three others were also masked, and they stood in front of what

Smith assumed was the hotel safe. Though it was covered in black dust, the steel container appeared to have survived the blast without sustaining enough damage to cause the lock to fail. The door remained closed. One man held a piece of paper in front of his face, placing it close to his eyes to enable him to read it, and used his other hand to work a keypad. After he had pressed a series of buttons, the door opened with a loud clicking noise. The attacker operating the keypad reached in and removed a small insulated cooler. A decal on one side of it read, *Bioelectrical agent. Handle with care.*

"What's in those containers that they want them so badly?" Beckmann whispered.

Smith shook his head. "I don't know, but there are six of them, two of us. I don't like that they're taking the containers, but I don't like the odds, either."

"Don't even think about it," Beckmann said.

Smith had to agree. He counted five Uzi submachine guns and one AK-47 against his Beretta and AK and Beckmann's rifle. It would be a bloodbath, and all one way. Nothing would be accomplished, except that he and Beckmann would be dead.

"We'll let them go and track them," Smith said.

The men collected two more coolers before backing away from the safe, leaving its door gaping and keeping their guns at the ready; they jogged away from the entrance toward the back of the hotel and disappeared. "How do they expect to leave? The front of the hotel is surrounded," Smith said.

"But the back isn't," Beckmann replied. "It leads onto the beach and they have snipers covering the sides. The Dutch police are staying well away. They're waiting for the Dutch Special Forces."

"Then the terrorist crew must have arrived by boat," Smith said.

Beckmann nodded. "I came from the beach side as well. We should leave that way. I don't want to risk using the front door unless the police are warned that we're friendly."

"Let's go." He crossed the lobby and made his way to the safe, stepping over the branches of an overturned tree in a large terra-cotta pot. He reached the safe and peered into it. The interior contained several shelves, with each shelf divided further into compartments marked with numbers from one to fifty. Nearly all held something placed there for safekeeping. Smith reached out and removed a flat jewelry box from compartment number thirty-six. He flipped it open to find a stunning sapphire necklace with a center pendant stone of several carats surrounded by diamonds. A heavy gold chain also inset with diamonds accompanied the piece. Smith was astonished that the terrorists had left such a treasure trove behind, opting instead for coolers of biomaterial.

"Interesting that they didn't even look at these jewels," Beckmann said. "They're worth a fortune. What was in those coolers?"

"Whatever it is, it's worth more than diamonds." Smith replaced the necklace and closed the safe door, ensuring that it was locked. Whatever had happened to the owners of the valuables inside, he hoped that someone would eventually sort it out and get the pieces to the family members.

"Let's get moving. We don't want them to have too much of a head start." Smith headed to the back and left through a door that led onto a small terrace. After checking for sentries, he took a few steps toward the beach. A trail of footsteps in the sand indicated the attackers' direction and he headed that way. Ten feet from the hotel entrance he was hit with a cool breeze and took in his first full breath of fresh air. Smith thought nothing could smell sweeter.

"Which way?" Smith said.

Beckmann jerked his chin to the left. "There. Toward the train station. Let's cross here and enter that park on the far side. We can stop there and get our bearings." Smith nodded and jogged ahead. He breathed a sigh when they reached the park without any further incident. Beckmann waved him into the darkness of a nearby tree and took out a phone. He dialed a number, said, "I have him" into it, and handed it to Smith. "My employer would like a word with you."

Smith took the phone. "Smith here."

"How is it that if there is any disaster in the world at any given time, you're there?"

Smith heard the voice, which sounded so close to that of his late fiancée, Sophia Russell, yet wasn't, and felt the usual bittersweet emotions wash through him. Relief followed on the heels of that emotion, because Randi Russell was very, very good at what she did, and she was on his side.

"Thanks for the assistance. Was touch and go there for a minute."

"You're welcome. Beckmann says he saw some more terrorists headed toward the train station. Can you find a car? Use it to get the hell out of there?"

"Do I bring Beckmann?"

"I'm afraid I can't spare him. If you can get him close to the train station, I'd appreciate it. He'll move on there. We need to keep tracking the attackers."

"Who's claiming responsibility?"

"No one yet."

"Any ideas?"

"A couple. We think it's tied to the WHO conference, but can't really pin down the target. Do you know anyone there who might be important enough for them to stage such an attack?"

Smith fell silent. Perhaps he was the target. He wondered if he should tell Russell about the first assassin and the photos. She knew Peter Howell, after all, and she would be the logical choice to contact MI6 and deliver a warning, but years of Covert-One activity had made him cautious. She knew of the organization, but he assumed that she was calling on a CIA telephone. Covert-One operatives didn't exist in the usual chain of intelligence hierarchy and no one, not even the CIA, was aware of their existence. He'd tell her more when he was sure they were on a secure phone. He kept his counsel for now and would leave it to Klein to probe into the photos and the possible target of the hotel attack. Instead he ran the other attending scientists through his mind.

"The entire conference is filled with infectious disease specialists.

We've all been at the scene of disasters throughout the world. Any one of us could have angered someone in some of the less stable areas that we address," he said.

"I agree, but something here feels off." Smith heard someone address Russell in the background. When she spoke next, her voice held a world of strain. "Tell Beckmann to forget the train station. Go to the airport."

"Why?" Smith asked.

"A bomb just detonated there."

7

OMAN DATTAR SAT ON HIS BED in his cell in the International Criminal Court's special unit within the Scheveningen prison system and watched the live CNN footage of the attack at the Grand Royal occurring only a few kilometers away. The picture on the small analog television bolted onto a shelf on the wall wasn't ideal, but it was enough to reveal the extent of the damage so far. He chuckled when he saw the flames leaping out of the building's roof and was pleased at the panic he heard in the voices of the English-speaking reporters. They needed to understand that detention of a man like him was not to be tolerated. Crimes against humanity! That the International Criminal Court and the United Nations had the nerve to try and convict him for such activity was infuriating.

It was appalling that the necessary steps he'd taken to rid the Pakistani territory that he controlled of undesirable elements should be designated as crimes against humanity. The individuals he'd ordered killed were not human, so killing them could not be classified as a criminal act. He'd cut off limbs of those who dared raised a weapon against him, yes, but didn't the Bible itself, the West's favorite book, assert that one should take an eye for an eye? Yet they called his action barbarism. They decried his use of child soldiers, but their own gangs used children to deal drugs, and none of the leaders of those gangs stood accused in such a manner. As for the cannibalism, well, he didn't worry about what happened to those already dead, and eating the flesh of one's enemies made one stronger.

He'd paid well for the hotel's destruction and would pay more for the acts that he knew were to follow, and he fully expected the result to be a lesson to the ICC and the countries that had supported it. But he saved his special hatred for the United States and England. The United States was the country that had pushed hardest for his arrest and extradition to the Netherlands, and England had agreed to imprison him on their soil after the trial was completed. Both countries had been instrumental in his incarceration, so both would be punished.

He watched as the camera focused on a man hanging from the ledge. When the image was enlarged, he stood up, unable to believe his eyes. That Jon Smith was still alive and clinging to the outside of the hotel was not possible. Dattar felt his rage rise as he watched the American doctor make his way around the ledge.

The clanging sound of an opening gate caught his attention. He moved to the cell door, peered through the small window and sighed with satisfaction when he was able to see the four prison guards walking toward him. The first two were assigned to Scheveningen and the second were from elsewhere. England, presumably. He'd been sentenced to life in prison and the time had come to transfer him. The Dutch guard opened the cell door.

"Turn around and put your hands on the wall." He spoke in English. Dattar's English was impeccable. He had been educated in America and had been for a while the darling of Washington, DC. He'd told them what they wanted to hear: that he believed in their government and would bring democracy to his homeland. Lies all, of course, and when they'd learned of his deception, they'd moved quickly to arrest him.

He turned and placed his hands on the wall. The door sprung open on the guard's signal, and he entered the cell. He took down each arm and secured them behind Dattar's back with handcuffs. The sound of an explosion came from the small television. Dattar smiled at the man.

"Your country is under attack. Apparently not all agree with what goes on here," he said.

The guard didn't reply.

Dattar's section of the prison was separated from the main building and was accessed by a door dedicated to the wing. Currently, Dattar and two other strongmen from small countries in Africa were being held there. The terms of the leaders' detention differed greatly from that of the regular prisoners, a fact that was not lost on the populations of the varying areas. The people from Dattar's region complained bitterly that Dattar, a war criminal, resided in comfort with amenities such as electric lighting, soft mattresses, and indoor plumbing, while the population that he'd terrorized lived in squalor and with limited access to clean drinking water. Many argued that he should be returned to his province to stand trial, but the United Nations had refused, saying the corruption there ensured that he would be granted a swift acquittal.

They frog-marched him down the hall; one in front, one at his side, and two behind. The small entourage made their way down the darkened corridor and past several interior checkpoints. They reached the back door and an exit sign glowed red.

Dattar gave a glance at a camera placed high on the wall and waited as the lead guard reached out and pushed open the final door. No alarm sounded. Dattar sighed deeply as he stepped into the evening air.

The prison sat in a wooded area in Scheveningen, a suburb of The Hague and not far from the Grand Royal. They were in a small courtyard area, surrounded at the far end by a razor-wire–topped brick wall. The sharp blades glinted in the light thrown by the several large spotlights placed at the far corners of the rectangular area. Two guardhouses perched high in the corners as well. They were covered in satellite dishes and both had pedestal-mounted automatic weapons aimed at the interior. No one would simply walk out of the prison under normal circumstances.

They headed to the main exit, a silent entourage. There was a double-gated security system, with a chain link fence forming a concentric circle ten feet from the final brick wall. The chain link was also topped by razor wire. They reached the second to final exit, and the guard opened it. They hustled through this door and waited for the link gate to close. The double locking system ensured that one door would not open until the door behind it had closed and locked. Dattar heard the snap of the electronic deadbolt as it moved home. They paused in the small area for the lead man to tap in a code to the last and final exit lock, and Dattar was relieved to hear a series of clicks as the second door responded to the input.

The last step was to place him in the transport vehicle. The lead guard opened the panels and assisted him onto the benches. Once Dattar sat down, the guard attached leg chains bolted into the vehicle's base to his ankles and arranged a second attachment to his wrists. When he was done he closed the doors. Dattar listened to the engine start and felt the truck begin to move. He smiled. They were headed to the airport for an early morning charter transport to England. Dattar sat back and waited, quiet and sweating. He wished he'd had a wristwatch to mark the time, but his had been confiscated when he was arrested. It seemed as though something had gone wrong because he felt time ticking away, and nothing was happening. The van bumped over a pothole and drove through the night.

The attack came, but almost twenty minutes later than the time for which Dattar had arranged it. He heard the driver yell and felt the lurch as the vehicle's wheels were shot. He knew that the transport van likely had specialty run-flat tires and it kept moving. Not for long, Dattar thought.

He heard the sound of gunfire being exchanged and saw the flash of an explosive device. The driver fired back, and Dattar heard him yelling into a radio. Dattar did his best to bury his head into his shoulder and faced the wall. When they shot the rocket-propelled grenade at the cabin, he didn't want the shrapnel to hit his eyes.

An explosion rocked the truck and the front of it burst into flames.

Dattar choked in the smoke and waited, his eyes streaming. The armored vehicle was fashioned to withstand the initial blast of a rocket-propelled grenade without exploding into a thousand pieces, but no armored vehicle could take such a hit and remain unscathed. The side wall buckled inward and a gash appeared in the wall between the driver and the back. Smoke began pouring through the hole and Dattar knew it would overcome him soon if he didn't get out. He heard the back panels being opened and cool air rushed into the cabin. His men entered, holding a large bolt cutter, and went to work on the chains.

His first man pulled him out of the back.

"You're late," Dattar said.

The man bobbed his head. "It's true, but could not be helped. The first crew succumbed too quickly, and we were forced to stay and complete their mission as well as our own." The man waved at two waiting Range Rovers then stepped back to allow Dattar to jog past him. They ran together to the cars. Dattar glanced back at the burning transport vehicle.

"We placed a timed explosive underneath it. It will soon be gone," Dattar's man said.

They reached the cars and Dattar grabbed the man by the front of his shirt and shoved him back against the vehicle. Dattar was less than six feet tall and pushing fifty years old, but his stocky body held a lot of muscle. He easily slammed the smaller, thinner terrorist backward. He saw the man's eyelids flutter as he flinched, and his head bounced off the car's window.

"You completed nothing. I saw the television footage, where Smith was using his gun to shatter the windowpane. That footage was live. Jon Smith still breathes and I want to know why."

"We need to go. The hotel crisis has focused the attention of the Dutch police, but not for long. They will be here soon."

Dattar's volcanic temper was legendary, and he gave it free rein. He still had the man by the throat. "Tell me why he lives."

"Ali succumbed too early." The man's voice was strained and he spoke in a rush. "He was ill when he went in, swaying and sweating. He could barely hold his weapon. And there was a gun in Smith's hand. We hadn't counted on him reaching his weapon. He must have shot and killed Ali. Why does a medical doctor travel with a gun?"

Dattar let go of the man's throat. "Smith is a member of the United States Army. He's never far from his gun, as am I. Just be happy that I don't have one now, because I'd use it to puncture your worthless hide. Is Rajiid at the rendezvous point?"

The man nodded.

Rohnen Rajiid was Dattar's vice minister and a cousin. Dattar only employed family members or close relatives to act as cabinet members because all others not related by blood could be twisted or bribed. Many of these kin managed to be both incompetent and corrupt, but all knew better than to steal directly from Dattar.

Dattar crawled in the passenger side of the second car while his crew filled the lead and backup vehicles. They barreled out ahead, staying in formation. Dattar stared out the window. The failure to kill Smith was a problem, but not a dire one. They'd nearly cornered him once, and they would again.

Twenty minutes later they entered a quiet area outside of the airport where a second row of black SUVs idled. Dattar left his and entered the passenger side of another. Rajiid sat behind the wheel and nodded to Dattar before turning his attention to driving. Rajiid was a rare creature in Dattar's world because he had no wife, no children, and cared for nothing. Dattar considered himself to be ruthless, but he often wondered if Rajiid had any heart at all. He was the perfect jihadist, had Dattar needed another one, but Dattar was not concerned with jihad, he was concerned with money.

"Did you bring the notebook?"

Rajiid nodded and handed Dattar a slim tablet computer. Dattar accessed the Internet, typed in his Swiss account's user name and password, and hit the "accounts" link. Six numbered accounts lined up on the screen. Dattar highlighted one and arranged to transfer a portion of the funds to another bank account he maintained in the Netherlands. The words "Unable to Transfer" appeared. Dattar frowned. He clicked on the second Swiss account and attempted the same transaction. Once again, "Unable to Transfer" lit the screen. His heart started pounding and he began to shake with equal parts rage and disbelief along with a slight dusting of fear. His fingers shook with the newfound adrenaline flowing in his system. He clicked on the third, fourth, and fifth accounts; same result. He swallowed as his throat became dry. He worked on the sixth and final Swiss account. It, too, failed to function. He scoured the page to find a reason for the inability to transfer. At the upper right he saw a small envelope icon and a note that said "You have six urgent messages." He clicked the link and read them all. All said the same thing, "This numbered account has been suspended in response to a suspicious activity report (SAR) filed by a member country of the United Nations. Its use is suspended until further notice."

Dattar accessed his portfolio, the one that held over 200 million in currency and various forms of negotiable securities. This account was under a false name. As he had hoped, the account accepted his password and opened to a grid display that should have shown the value of every item within the account. Instead, it displayed zero. Dattar sat there, stunned. He'd taken great pains to hide his funds, moving the money from bank to bank within his own country, and then placing it in various offshore locations. He'd chosen the locations well, using only those countries that would not reveal the identity of the account holders, even if pressured by international authorities. He typed in the web address for a Cayman Islands bank that held a very small portion of his money. Once the account was open, he checked for messages. There were none. He initiated the same transfer. The tiny sand timer rotated while the page worked, and ten seconds later he received a confirmation that the transfer was complete. He flung the tablet against the windshield. It bounced back, clattered off the dashboard and fell on the hand rest between him and Rajiid.

"What's wrong?" Rajiid said.

"The American froze my accounts and somehow moved the securities."

Rajiid looked at Dattar in alarm. "All of them?"

"All six in Switzerland. There are three left in the Caymans, but they don't hold much. The American must be stopped before those are located."

"I thought you neutralized the American threat."

"I thought so too. Give me the phone," Dattar said.

Rajiid got a wary look on his face. "You shouldn't use mine. It can be traced. What do you wish to know?"

"I wish to know why the American isn't yet dead!" Dattar screamed the words at Rajiid, who blinked but didn't remove his eyes from the road. They were on a highway, moving fast.

"The American must be dead. You sent Khalil for that one. The best. He cannot be beaten."

"Like Ali? I sent him for Smith, and he still lives."

Rajiid kept his eyes on the road, but his lips were set in a tight line. "I heard about that. But that was an unusual circumstance. Ali succumbed early. Khalil wasn't part of the suicide crew."

"Has anyone heard from him? Has he reported in?"

Rajiid shook his head. "No, but if there is a job to do, Khalil will do it. If the American isn't dead already, then it will happen soon. Along with the Englishman."

"We'll need to get the freeze order reversed." Dattar stared out the window while his mind raced with ideas.

"To do that you must bring the United States to its knees. And to do that you must continue with the plan."

Dattar nodded. His plan was brilliant. The way to instill respect was to threaten the lives of the many. When they were controlled, the rest would fall into place.

"Do we have the coolers?" he said.

"Yes."

At least something went right, Dattar thought. "I want Smith dead. I won't allow him to interfere with me again. And the American as well. Is that understood?"

"It was always understood. It will be finished."

8

RUSSELL LEANED OVER WENDEL's shoulder and watched the stream of updates. "Which one is the agent?" she asked. Wendel pointed to a sentence from Blackhat 254.

"That's Tyler Biggs. He's positioned at the train station. And here," she pointed to another stream of information, but this one coming from a secure CIA line, "is his personal system. Right now he's transmitting on both, and pretty much the same information, from an aggregating software program. It sends the message to his CIA site, which verifies the sender and then posts it here."

"What if he messes up? Punches in CIA information on the public site?"

Wendel shook her head. "Not likely. He needs to verify his CIA log-in before he can use the aggregator, and that aggregator software is proprietary to us. It's not available to just anyone. He doesn't use it unless he's transmitting public information in any event."

Russell watched as Biggs gave a running description of what he was watching from a street corner in The Hague. His updates matched those of several other Dutch civilians standing around him who were also recording their observations on the public website. The CIA stream, however, didn't match. Russell watched the sentences on a split-screen display.

"Shouldn't his CIA stream and the public stream match then?" Russell said.

Wendel frowned. "Theoretically, yes."

"Then why don't they?" Russell said.

Wendel shook her head. "I'm not sure. Perhaps the ISP system used by the public site is built on a faster platform?"

Russell didn't like the sound of that. She wasn't sure how long it had been since the CIA had updated their cable systems, but she hoped that they could manage to at least match a public-access Internet site in speed and quality. The Internet had become the largest, most lucrative trolling ground for criminals the world over, and keeping one step ahead of the hackers, phishers, and terrorists required that they stay cutting edge.

"That doesn't make a whole lot of sense, though, because the public site is accessed by millions daily, and the CIA site is handling only a tiny percentage of that," Wendel said. "Something else must be causing the lag."

"Maybe the aggregator software isn't pushing out the two windows equally," Jordan suggested.

Russell felt a tap on her shoulder. She turned to see Cromwell with a grave look on his face.

"Can you join me? There's been a new development."

Russell followed him out of the situation room. They moved down a long corridor with gray walls and dark industrial carpeting. Cromwell pushed through a door marked "Conference B." The room contained a large dark wood table surrounded by black leather chairs. A triangular speakerphone sat in the table's center, and a flat-screen television, this one turned off, hung on one wall. Seated at the conference room table was Steve Harcourt, the CIA's Mideast senior operator currently on loan to the New York Police Department, where he was supposed to be providing assistance and intelligence on outside threats. Harcourt had an office in Langley and another in New York and shuttled between them. Tall, with slicked hair, a slender face, and intelligent eyes that swept over Russell in a quick, discreet assessment, Harcourt was only a bit older than Russell, in his late thirties, and had a reputation as a ladies' man. He wore a dark sweater, black pants, and expensive wing-tip shoes that shone from a recent polishing. When the door closed behind them, Cromwell nodded to Harcourt, leaned against the table, and crossed his arms.

"I don't know if you two have met. Steve, this is Randi Russell. She's heading up a test initiative in which we're considering bringing in field officers on a rotating basis to analyze and improve our home base capabilities. With her lengthy field service, she brings critical knowledge to bear on our office operations here."

Harcourt rose to shake Russell's hand. "I've heard a lot about your exploits. It must be difficult to work at a desk."

"Not at all. I'm finding the change refreshing."

"We're here as you requested. You have news?" Cromwell said to Harcourt.

"Oman Dattar escaped from Scheveningen prison."

Russell groaned. "The Butcher? You've got to be kidding. When?"

"An hour ago. He escaped during transfer. The Mideast division got the call first, based on his connection to Pakistan, and contacted me." He turned to Russell. "I work in connection with the NYPD, and New York is considered a first target, so whenever something occurs that involves possible terrorism, I get the call. I told them I'd brief the European Division, since he's stomping around in your area of concern."

"I have to tell you, I'm thinking the escape and the attack on the Grand Royal can't be a coincidence," Russell said. Her alarm was growing; the situation in the Netherlands was fast spiraling out of control. She ran through in her mind the available operatives that could assist in a hunt for Dattar.

"Any idea where he might be heading?" Cromwell said.

Harcourt nodded. "I'll bet any money that his ultimate destination will be the hills on the Pakistani/Afghan border. Once he's there, the UN will never get their hands on him again. He can hide for years."

"Has Interpol been notified?" Russell said.

Harcourt nodded again. "They're working on issuing a red notice." A red notice was the Interpol equivalent of a "Most Wanted" poster. It informed member countries that an individual was wanted for extradition to the country issuing the request. Execution was left to the police force of whatever member country found the fugitive. Some would be quick to apprehend Dattar, but many, not wanting to be involved, would steer clear.

"How do we think he'll get home? The Pakistani border is a long way from The Hague," Cromwell said.

Harcourt walked to a computer terminal located on a credenza pushed against the side wall and punched in a code. Within seconds the flat panel lit up with a map of the world. He placed a small arrow pointer on The Hague.

"He'll want to connect with a country friendly to him, which might include Russia to the northeast," he put a pointer there, "and Cyprus to the south. He's right on the North Sea, but I don't think he'll go all the way by boat. It's a long haul up and over to Russia, and even longer going south to Cyprus. I think he'll fly. All he needs to do is charter a flight under an assumed name. Or, better yet, get a friend to charter one for him."

Russell analyzed the map on the screen. She agreed with Harcourt that a boat north to Russia would be a crazy idea. The logistics were a nightmare. But she didn't agree with his assessment that Dattar would fly.

"I agree that he won't try to sail north, but I don't think he'll fly," she said. "Too risky. The authorities will be expecting that. Plus, we just had a report of a blast in a cargo area by the freight terminals at Schiphol airport. They're on high alert."

"That leaves car or train," Cromwell said. "Both are excellent options. He gets a train ticket, joins the hordes of people commuting every day, and disembarks at a town one or two stops from the border. From there he either picks the busiest checkpoint to drive through, or gets on a second train to cross the border during peak hours."

Harcourt put an arrow pointer on the main train station. "This shouldn't be too hard to monitor. In fact, I'm certain that the Dutch have a contingency plan for security at the train station."

Russell kept her gaze on the map of the region while she tried to put herself in Dattar's shoes. In her years undercover she'd learned a lot about getting from point A to point B undetected. With Belgium to the south and Germany to the north, Dattar had the disadvantage of being in the heart of a cluster of United Nations member countries that had the will to arrest him should they find him. His face would soon be on every television screen in the developed world, along with the details of his escape. His chances of slipping past layer after layer of security on a land journey covering several countries and their border guards seemed remote.

"I think he'll want to leave the continent the minute he can. The quickest way to do that is by boat."

Harcourt frowned. "I thought you agreed that a boat north to Russia was out."

Russell nodded. "I do, but that doesn't mean he won't head south. He's ten miles from one of the largest industrial seaports in the world." Russell walked to the flat screen and reached up to point at Rotterdam. "He'd be nuts to hang around waiting for a train when Rotterdam is so close. The sheer volume of cargo throughput makes it difficult for customs to monitor every single vessel. He gets the added advantage that many freighters head straight toward Cyprus, where we all know he'd find any number of organizations eager to help him." She put her finger on the small island off the coasts of Turkey and Syria. "If I were him, I'd pay a willing ship's captain to take me. Within hours he could be far from the mainland and into international waters."

"I think you're onto something," Cromwell said.

Harcourt, though, looked less than convinced. "Rotterdam's large, I'll grant you that, but he still has to arrange for a freight captain to let him stow away, and then he has to stay put for at least thirty-six hours while the ship sails south. With a train he has the advantage of mobility. If things begin to look like they're headed in the wrong direction, all he has to do is hop off."

"But he hops off into hostile territory."

"Still. If he can blend in, he has the possibility to keep moving, make a run for it."

Cromwell pushed off the edge of the table and looked at Russell. "Can you put agents in both places? Cover the train station and the Rotterdam port?"

Russell hesitated. She'd been to Rotterdam port and didn't think Cromwell understood the sheer impossibility of what he was suggesting. She stepped to the computer keyboard that Harcourt had used and navigated to the Rotterdam seaport web page. From there she highlighted an integrative map with a sidebar listing the port's statistics. They were staggering, even to her, who had seen it in person.

"Four hundred million gross metric tons of throughput per year, 30,000 freighters, and 10,500 hectares stretching 40 kilometers. That's 26,000 acres of land over 24 miles long. I don't have the manpower to cover that effectively."

"Which I think leads us to the conclusion that we should use our available resources in the most efficient manner," Harcourt said. "Let's blanket the train station and leave the port alone. One or two extra men there won't make a dent, but they have a fighting chance to help at the train station."

Cromwell looked over. "Russell?"

A look of slight irritation washed over Harcourt's face. Russell noted the reaction and decided to tread carefully. It was appropriate that Cromwell consult her because tracking terrorists was what she'd done to great effect in the field, but she couldn't blame Harcourt for being slightly put out. Most decisions at Langley came from headquarters to the field, not the other way around. But Russell knew how it felt to be hunted, Harcourt didn't. Until Dattar was caught, he'd be hunted, and Russell knew every trick there was to move undercover. The whole point of the new initiative was to get field experience back into the offices.

"Beckmann's located Smith and they're headed to the airport. I'll divert them and they can watch for anything unusual."

"I know Beckmann, but who's Smith?" Harcourt said.

"He's a doctor with the US Army who was attending the World Health Organization conference."

"What do we know about this guy? Has he been cleared to receive orders from the CIA?" Now Harcourt was frowning, his mouth set in a thin line. Russell saw the objection coming to Smith's acting in any way that might appear to be managed by the CIA, and she strove to head it off.

"I've worked with Smith before on missions where army and agency interests collide. I'm positive that he's had high-level clearance at one time or another, so I don't believe we're taking any risks or breaching any security in bringing him into the loop. As a microbiologist he's there on other business, clearly, but his military skills are excellent and he's already in position. It might be worthwhile to ask the army to loan him out for this emergency."

Harcourt shook his head. "We don't need a microbiologist."

"But we might. It's highly suspect that the attacks occurred during the WHO conference. We think the terrorists may have located some biomaterial on the premises," Russell said.

"I'll defer to your judgment on this Smith character, but then he's your asset to manage. If he screws up, you're going to have to go to the mat for him. " Harcourt gave Russell a slight smile.

"I'll be in the situation room," Cromwell said. "Whatever you need to do, do it." He swung back out the door.

"If you require anything, just call," Harcourt said. He logged off the computer system and followed Cromwell out.

Russell reached for the phone on the credenza and dialed Beckmann. She heard the other end engage, and Jon Smith's voice poured through the receiver.

"Please give me some good news."

"Smith? Why are you answering Beckmann's phone?"

"He's busy hot-wiring a car." Russell heard Beckmann's voice in the background, muffled by the roaring of a vehicle's engine as it revved.

"What's he saying?"

"He's saying I shouldn't have told you that. Apparently he's not supposed to be committing auto theft on foreign soil. I haven't known your officer long, but he appears to break a lot of the CIA's rules. Kind of reminds me of you in that way."

Russell smiled. "I rarely break rules. Merely bend them." She heard Smith's snort of disbelief through the phone. "I'll pretend I didn't hear that. Tell him I've got new orders. Go to the train station after all. Oman Dattar's escaped. We think he may leave by train and we'd like some eyes on the station."

"I'm going with him. Two extra eyes could make the difference."

Russell hesitated. She had no control over Smith, he was free to go or stay, but she knew from Harcourt's pointed question about Smith's status that she wouldn't be able to extend CIA protection to him without at least a tacit understanding between her organization and his military superiors. She decided to let him go and request emergency clearance for him should the need arise.

"Would you recognize him if you saw him? Or should I send a photo to Beckmann's phone?"

"I know Dattar very, very well. I assisted with a UN contingent of doctors to contain the cholera outbreak in the Pakistani region that he controls. He initially refused to allow treatment for anyone that he deemed an enemy. That included infants and small children. I persuaded him otherwise." Russell was intrigued. Few people were capable of persuading Dattar to do anything he didn't want to do.

"Persuaded him? How?"

"A gun, a rotavirus, and duct tape were involved. I'll give you the whole story sometime. He hates me and promised retribution. You can believe that if I see him I'll do my best to detain him."

"But try not to risk blowing Beckmann's cover. Just keep Dattar in your sights and transmit any coordinates to me. I'll arrange for the local authorities to handle the recapture."

"I assume a red notice went out?"

"Any minute now." Wendel stuck her head through the conference room door and waved a hand at Russell.

"Hold on." Russell put her hand over the mouthpiece. "News?"

Wendel nodded. "Two more bombs. One took out a famous restaurant near the city center, and a second at the train station."

Russell pointed to the map on the screen. "Can you switch that up to show them?"

"Of course." Wendel tapped on the computer keyboard and Russell's prior photo of the Rotterdam port was replaced with a detailed map of The Hague. She highlighted two areas.

"Can you send that screen shot to Beckmann's phone?"

Wendel punched a few more keys and the image was copied and sent.

"I'm afraid there's more news." Russell spoke into the phone. "Two more bombs just exploded. One downtown and the other at the train station. I'm sending a map with the locations to you now."

"Dattar's got to be involved in this attack," Smith said.

"I agree. Watch your backs, both of you. He's not to be messed with. He's lethal."

"The next time I get him in my sights, he's going to wish he'd never been born. I'm out."

Smith hung up.

9

SMITH CRAWLED INTO THE passenger seat of the vehicle that Beckmann had managed to start. It was a black Lincoln town car complete with consular plates. The leather seats were remarkably plush and comfortable, and Smith felt his body ease into them.

"Let's see which ambassador's car you managed to steal." He fished in the glove compartment while Beckmann maneuvered onto the road. He pulled out a slim leather document holder that contained several folded pieces of paper.

"With any luck it will be the US envoy to the Netherlands," Beckmann said. "Then it won't be theft. Merely borrowing."

Smith opened the papers. "Drive carefully, it's owned by North Korea. We get stopped driving a stolen North Korean diplomat's car and we'll spark an international incident."

"That explains it," Beckmann said.

"Explains what?"

"The poor maneuverability. This car must be armored. No North Korean diplomat would settle for less."

"Armored. I like that. Just what we need tonight," Smith said. He felt his phone vibrate in his pocket. He pulled it out and checked the screen. Klein was calling.

When he answered, he heard Klein say, "You're alive! Excellent."

"I'm in a stolen North Korean ambassador's car with an officer of the CIA." When Klein didn't respond immediately, Smith said, "Are you there?"

"Yes. I was just considering the implications of that sentence. All I can say is that I'm extremely pleased that you survived, and I have orders. It appears as though the terrorists may be in search of some of the biomaterial and a research report that your fellow scientists brought to the conference. In particular, bacteria stored in the hotel's safe." Smith glanced at Beckmann, who seemed focused on driving. Even so, Smith took care with his response.

"Not anymore. I saw them remove three coolers of biomaterial. I didn't see any research papers, but they could have found them, stuffed them under their shirts or in a backpack and I wouldn't have been the wiser. I checked the safe after they'd left, and only jewelry remained. No reports either. What's in those containers?"

"Various bacteria. Some recently discovered and all antibiotic resistant, as well as a version of H5N1."

"Avian flu," Smith said. "That's a nasty virus with a terrible survival rate, to be sure, but bird flu is not easily transmissible from human to human. Most often bird to human and then in very unique circumstances."

"But we just learned some alarming news. A group of scientists in the Netherlands have managed to mutate H5N1 so that it *is* airborne transmissible, and they acknowledged that one of the attending scientists at the convention was going to make an announcement about the research. They're concerned that he brought the mutated version with him."

"Where is this scientist?"

"He was staying on the fourth floor. They just found his body."

"And the research?"

"His thesis and report were also in the safe."

"What kind of scientist deliberately mutates a virus and then carries a report on it around on his person?"

That got Beckmann's attention. He glanced at Smith with a frown on his face and then swore in German under his breath.

"A scientist searching for fame," Klein said. "I have a question for you. What are the rules for carrying around hazardous biomaterial? Doesn't it have to be locked down in a lab?"

"There are a lot of workplace safety rules for employees that handle the material, but surprisingly few rules regarding security. Avian flu, the nonmutated version, only needs to be kept locked because it's not easily transmitted. The hotel safe would suffice."

"And if it's mutated?"

"Perhaps then it would be considered biosafety-level 4 and the rules would be much stricter, but it's not easy to mutate a virus," Smith said. "If what they say is correct and if they have the nonmutated version in the cooler, it will take some work to alter it, even with a road map provided by the scientist. That should buy us some time," Smith said.

"Let's just hope it's enough. We have to reacquire those coolers just to be sure that the virus isn't the mutated version. I'd love to get our hands on the research papers as well, but I suspect they're copying them as we speak. Unless we can find them quickly. Now, while they're still on the run. Any idea where that crew was headed?"

"I lost sight of them the minute they ran out of the hotel. Randi Russell asked that we go to the train station. Oman Dattar escaped from prison, and apparently the thought is that he will attempt to flee by train. I'm accompanying one of her officers there. I told her and I'll tell you that I think Dattar is involved in some way. It's no coincidence that he managed to escape on the same night as a deadly attack."

"I agree, but my primary concern is the coolers."

"If we find Dattar, I'll lay odds that we'll find the bacteria. If not on his person, then I'll beat the location out of him."

"While you're searching, can you find a scanner and input those photos? E-mail them to me? I want to start some inquiries. Perhaps the woman is a scientist at the convention."

Beckmann pointed through the windshield at a man dressed in black who was staggering down the street. He passed under a streetlight and Smith could see a sheen of sweat on his face.

"That's one of them," Beckmann said. He reached between them where his rifle was propped with its muzzle in the foot well and its stock on the edge of the seat. Smith reached under his jacket and pulled out his gun.

"I've got to go. We've just spotted one of the attackers. We'll grab him and shake some answers out of him."

"Call me the minute you have some," Klein said and clicked off. Beckmann pulled the car even with the stumbling man.

"He looks drunk," he said.

"Pull ahead and then stop. Keep the engine running. I'll corral him."

Beckmann shook his head. "My orders were to protect you, not allow you to get yourself killed in a scuffle with a jihadist. I'll go." But Smith already had the door open. The overhead light turned on, illuminating the car's interior. Smith slipped out quickly, closing the door.

The cool night air felt bracing. He crossed between two parked cars onto the sidewalk and began to stroll toward the attacker, holding his gun down by his thigh and out of sight. They were twenty feet apart, and Smith was closing the distance fast, keeping his strides slow. The attacker continued his swaying, stumbling progress with his head down, watching the sidewalk, his entire concentration on each step. At ten feet apart Smith could see that the man was seriously ill. Smith closed the distance quickly, grabbing the man's arm just as he crumpled, and lowered him to the ground. Beckmann jogged up and crouched down.

"He's been shot?" he said.

Smith ran his hands over the man's jacket, feeling the lump of a weapon in his right pocket. He reached in and removed a 9 mm gun. He handed it to Beckmann, who pocketed it. The man's breath was rasping in and out and his eyelids fluttered. Each time they opened, Smith could see that his pupils were rolled back. Smith continued his search for a wound, finding none.

"Help me lift him. I want to check his back."

Beckmann put his rifle on the ground and assisted in lifting the man from the pavement and turning him to the side. He held him while Smith ran his hands over his back.

"Nothing. But we need to get him to a hospital fast or he's not going to make it."

Beckmann laid the attacker back down. The man gave a last gasp, then stilled. His head lolled to the side.

"Damn," Smith said.

Beckmann made an irritated sound. "There goes our chance at interrogation."

"Two others at the hotel died just the same way."

"Cyanide?" Beckmann said.

"No. I checked. I'd like to get an autopsy done. Perhaps we can find out what's going on here." Beckmann pulled out his phone and sent a text.

"I asked for a team to come collect the body and deliver it to the Dutch authorities. They're on their way, but I think we should continue to the train station. Let me take some photos." Smith moved away while Beckmann took several shots. "Done." He pulled the gun out of his pocket. "Do we leave the weapon? Sig Sauers are my favorite. Not flashy, but solid." Smith cocked his head.

"I like them too, but if he fired it, it could be traced. You sure you want to keep it?"

"I'm lacking a pistol. I think we take it. Just in case."

They returned to the car, which was double-parked with its emergency lights flashing. Smith slid into the driver's seat and was struck once again by the car's comfort. His eyes felt grainy and his body seemed to deflate in exhaustion.

"What time is it?" he said.

"Five AM. Tired?"

"You have no idea."

Beckmann nodded. "There's a safe house two blocks from here. I'll direct you there. Go get some rest."

Smith sat up. "Not on your life. If Dattar shows at that train station, he'll have to deal with me. Again."

"I sincerely doubt Dattar will show. He's on his way to Rotterdam. To the ports."

Smith paused. "Russell think that too?"

Beckmann nodded. "She sent me a text. Said she'd deploy us there if she thought we had a chance to intercept him."

"So he gets away because we haven't enough people available to stop him," Smith said.

Beckmann sighed. "It's frustrating. But it won't be our last opportunity. He may not use the station, but his operatives will. The one we just found was probably on his way there. Let's find another and beat some intelligence out of him. Then we go hunt for Dattar."

"I'll drop you at the station and keep the car. You won't need it there."

Beckmann gave Smith a look full of suspicion. "What do you need the car for?"

"To drive it to Rotterdam port."

Beckmann raised an eyebrow. "You think you'll be able to find Dattar? Where do you expect to look?"

"Wherever contraband is sold. He has a shipping company called Karachi Naman Shipping. When I worked there on the cholera outbreak, WHO had used the company to ship medical supplies. Supplies that never got there. Dattar diverted and sold them to India."

"I thought India and Pakistan hated each other."

"Dattar would trade with the devil if he thought it would bring him more money or more power."

Smith typed on his smartphone, tapping in a search for the company name and a possible address for shipping activities out of Rotterdam. He scrolled through several results, but most contained nothing more than the address for the parent company in Pakistan. Frustrated, he quit the application.

"Forget the port," Beckmann said. "Russell's right, you'll never find him in that vast place. Come with me to the train station. I could use the extra hands."

Beckmann had a point. They had a better chance locating one of

Dattar's minions doing his best to flee the country and prying the information out of him. Smith started the car and headed down the street.

"You can guide me there?"

Beckmann reached out and tapped on the built-in GPS on the dash and within seconds a breathy female voice began giving them instructions in Korean. Beckmann fiddled a bit, but only managed to turn up the volume.

"Sorry, can't get it to switch languages," he said. He peered at the map displayed on the small screen. "Right turn ahead."

Twenty minutes later they approached the train station. Smith entered a no-parking zone and cut the engine. Several police cars idled in front, and he counted at least twenty officers, most in riot gear, stationed at various entry points. They gazed at each person who walked toward the building. Smith watched one officer hold out a hand to a swarthy complexioned young man with a black backpack slung over one shoulder. The young man lowered the pack to the ground and unzipped it. He opened the sack and tilted it so that the policeman could see the contents. With a curt nod, the officer allowed the man to continue into the building.

"He should be stopping them a hell of a lot farther away. If that pack had contained a bomb, it would have taken out the front entrance," Beckmann said.

Smith swept his eyes over the area, getting the lay of the land and counting security and riot control personnel. He shifted the car into gear and pulled from the spot.

"Let's head to the rear. This much heat almost guarantees that these guys aren't going to waltz into the front door." He drove around the building, pulling the vehicle close to its far end. Steel tracks snaked in all directions. Smith watched as a train car appeared, slowly making its way out of the railway terminal. A lone officer stood at the corner, keeping vigil. He eyed the town car with great interest.

"Keep moving. That guy is looking like he wants to stop us," Beckmann said.

He kept going, driving past the officer, whose head moved in tandem with them as they passed, and turned onto a narrow cobblestone lane. Parked cars lined the road, one set of wheels on the sidewalk, the other on the street, their mirrors folded. Even so, the sedan was a tight fit. Smith kept his eyes in front of him, keeping the car in the center with a few feet of clearance on each side.

Two masked men burst around the corner. They ran flat-out, their arms pumping, pistols in their hands flashing; the lead man had a backpack that banged against his shoulder blades with each footfall.

"I'm on it." Beckmann rolled out the passenger door, smacking it against a metal mesh garbage can before slamming it closed. He raised his rifle in a fluid motion and squeezed off a shot, hitting the following man in the shoulder and sending him spinning to the right. The terrorist stumbled and went down between two vehicles, dropping out of Smith's sight.

The lead man didn't hesitate or even flinch at the sound of the gunshot. He sprinted straight at the car, never slowing. Smith kept the car moving as well. They were ten feet apart and on a collision course when the attacker's legs crumpled. One second he was standing, the next he wasn't. He smacked, face first, onto the stones and lay in the harsh pool of light thrown by the town car's headlamps. Smith hit the brakes, skidding to within two feet of the fallen man. He threw the transmission into park and watched as Beckmann flitted past, running toward the man he'd shot and ignoring the body on the ground.

Smith flung open his door and made his way to the fallen man, keeping his gun aimed, but only from an abundance of caution. He had an idea that this terrorist, like all the others, was dead. At three feet away he saw the wires extending from the backpack up and around to the man's collar, disappearing down into his jacket. He smelled the acrid scent of burning Lycra and nylon as the jacket smoldered. Just the sight of it sent a shock of adrenaline through him.

"Run like hell—he's wired," Smith yelled. He leaped over the body and sprinted down the cobblestone lane, Beckmann pounding right behind him. After ten seconds, the explosive pack blew. Smith felt the force of the blast hammer his back, and he flew forward onto the street. When he landed, he curled into a ball, covering his head with his hands. Heat washed over him along with bits of something that he hoped was not pieces of the terrorist's body. The hail of debris ended and he lowered his arms to look back.

The main force of the blast centered on the town car's engine block. The grille was a tangled mass of metal and the hood was bent. Smoke poured from the front, sides, and top of it and the windshield was a crazy kaleidoscope of cracked glass. Smith sat up, his hands hanging over his knees and his right still holding his gun. He watched the smoke billow out into the air. Beckmann rose to a sitting position next to him and gazed at the smoldering vehicle in silence.

"That car's totaled," Smith said.

Beckmann nodded. "I must have been wrong about it being armored. No armored car would sustain that much damage from one small backpack bomb."

"Hard to believe it wasn't, though. Handled like a tank," Smith said. The up-and-down wail of an ambulance Klaxon started howling in the distance. He rose, dusting bits of ash and other matter that he did his best not to look at from his shoulders. Lights had sprung on in the windows around them, and he glanced up to see several people standing on the balconies of the apartments on the third and fourth floors above the ground-floor shops.

"Let's get out of here. The other guy dead?"

"He is. I found this in his pocket." Beckmann handed him an airline folder. "It's a flight to Washington. Leaves tomorrow. This one expected to survive."

"A logical expectation, given the fact that his buddy was wearing the bomb. I wish I knew why the other guys are dying." The disabled car belched out some more smoke.

"Our fingerprints are all over that car," Beckmann said. "The North Koreans are going to be furious."

Smith hesitated. Beckmann had a point. For a brief moment he considered braving the smoke cloud and using his shirt to wipe down the dashboard, but a flicker of flame started to rise from the engine's interior.

"Ahh, perfect. It's going to combust," Smith said.

Beckmann slid his rifle back under his coat, once again hiding it from view. "Good, because I do not want to report this to Russell. I don't know her well enough to predict what the repercussions would be."

Smith pocketed his gun and waved Beckmann away from the car. "Don't worry about Russell. She's blown up more cars than you and I combined, not to mention the time she shot up an entire warehouse filled with Plastique."

Beckmann whistled. "Who was she after?"

"A band of Russian killers out to use it on civilian targets." The wailing sirens were getting closer. Smith turned another corner, putting more distance between them and the burning car.

"What's next?" Beckmann said.

Smith held up the airline envelope. "I'm going to Washington."

10

DATTAR SLID OUT OF THE SUV onto the dock's parking lot. He heard the creaking of metal and wood as the buoys rocked from side to side. The air smelled like engine oil and rotting fish, and one of the sodium lights on the dock fizzed in response to a failing ballast. Dattar stared at the light for a moment, thinking about the mass of electrical power that ran through even such a small device.

"The captain's been paid. He knows to stay on the bridge and not look below," Rajiid said.

"And the coolers?"

"Already on the airplane. I have a sample here, as well."

One of his lieutenants, a man without a history or background known to the authorities, was transporting the coolers via a previously arranged private jet. Dattar wished that he could fly in quick and easy comfort to his destination, but the risk was far too high. He stepped off the planks onto a waiting boat that was to take him to the freighter. The man at the wheel never looked his way. Rajiid untied the ropes that kept the craft in place, tossing them onto the deck before climbing on board. The engine engaged and the cruiser began a slow turn away from the dock.

Dattar felt the muscles in his neck relax as they headed out to sea. He'd contact Khalil from the freighter and impress upon the man the need for quick action, especially regarding the additional assignment. The cargo ship loomed over them when they pulled alongside. Dattar crawled up the metal ladder, stepping over onto the deck. He looked back at the boat and saw the wheel man preparing to return to the dock. The man's head was lowered, so he didn't see Rajiid pointing a gun at him. There was the sound of a compressed bullet, and the man crumpled. Rajiid shoved the gun in his waistband and reached down to grab the body. He hauled it to the boat's side and threw it overboard. Rajiid stepped across to the ladder, releasing the ropes that bound the boat to the larger ship. He used his foot to push the smaller craft free, and it began a slow turn away.

A crew member materialized out of the dark to Dattar's left, and he motioned both Dattar and Rajiid to follow. He led them to a large cabin. A small table was bolted to the floor in the middle of the room, and a steel lamp swung on a chain above it. On the far wall was a bunk, and to the left a long counter held a telephone and a computer with a monitor. A desk lamp bathed the area in light. Rajiid picked up the phone and dialed a number. When the man on the other end answered, he handed the phone to Dattar.

"Smith is alive. Why?" Dattar said without preamble.

He heard the man on the other side breathing heavily into the receiver. "You shouldn't be calling me."

"I paid quite a bit of money to ensure that Smith would die. I'm told that it was the CIA who shot my men. Is this true?"

"Yes, but I'll make up for that. Smith works out of Fort Detrick in Maryland. I've already arranged to take him out once he arrives Stateside."

"How did they manage to get a man in place? That was part of the payment, to ensure that the agency was crippled."

"There's a new head of the European division. Don't worry, she's temporary, and I'll handle it as well."

"You'd better. The coolers arrive in six hours. In twenty-four we go live. I expect no more mistakes."

"There won't be."

"Did you run the test?"

"That will happen in the next two hours. We're not using the actual weapon, but even this less potent version should give an idea of the viability. I'll let you know if it's successful."

"You do that." Dattar hung up.

He heard the freighter groan to life as the turbines began to churn. Rajiid sat down at the computer and logged on. Dattar sat at the table and watched the e-mail program light up.

"Any news?" he said.

Rajiid nodded. "A message from Khalil. He received ours regarding Smith, and he wants to know how hard a target he may be." Rajiid gazed at Dattar, who was taking slow breaths in order to calm himself.

"Tell Khalil that Smith is best handled at a distance, with a gunshot to the head. He becomes more dangerous the closer you get. Also, warn him that Smith is a microbiologist. Khalil should neither eat nor drink anything in the man's presence. He's a coward and will attempt to poison him, as he did me."

Rajiid typed the response into the computer. After a moment a pinging sound indicated that another message had been received. Rajiid opened the link and read out loud.

"He wants to know how much more he will be paid, and when." Rajiid shot Dattar a look full of worry. "Should I tell him that he must wait? Stall him while we work on unfreezing the accounts?"

Dattar shook his head. "No. No one must know about the freeze order. Besides, I consider the problem to be temporary. Ask him first if the American is dead."

Rajiid typed, waited, and the responding ping came quickly.

"He says the American just returned to the United States. He is waiting for the precise moment to do the deed to ensure that there are no witnesses. He says not to worry about the American and to tell him when he will receive the deposit for Smith." Dattar hesitated. He weighed the cost of doubling up on Smith, but his US contact had already failed once. Better have two aiming at the same target than one that continued to fail. "Tell Khalil that he will be paid the same amount for Smith as the others, but his deposit may be delayed due to the fact that I can't access my accounts from this computer."

Rajiid looked doubtful. "He might not believe that."

"Tell him!" Dattar snapped. Rajiid turned to the keypad and typed for a moment. At the return ping he peered at the screen.

"He says that his focus is currently on the American, but planning the attack on Smith will begin immediately and may take some hours. He hopes that you will have access to the money soon," Rajiid shot Dattar a look of warning, "and assures you that Smith is no match for him. He will die."

Dattar smiled. "Yes, that's right. Smith was the recipient of some good luck back at the hotel. His luck will run thin now that Khalil is after him."

"No one beats Khalil," Rajiid said.

Dattar nodded. It was true.

11

RUSSELL CLOCKED THE TAIL halfway through her drive home. It kept a modest two vehicles behind, but turned each time she did, breaking the usual rule of thumb that when you see the same car a third time, it's not a coincidence. She turned again in a direction that led away from her home and stopped at a red light. Four seconds later the black Ford sedan appeared in her rearview mirror. She sighed. She was tired and didn't really feel like a confrontation at the moment, but it was clear she was going to have one. Her gun nestled in the console between the front seats of her car. Russell popped open the lid and pulled out the weapon, placing it next to her right thigh.

While in the States, Russell had acquired a supercharged Audi A4. It had the advantage of being less flashy than some of the more obvious sports models, but it still packed a lot of torque under the hood for those moments when she might need it. At the moment, though, she was in a CIA-authorized vehicle. That auto, a sedan also chosen for its standardized appearance, had half the guts of her private car and weighed twice as much. The agency vehicle came equipped with a GPS tracking system that allowed the CIA to keep tabs on it at all times. What the car didn't have was Bluetooth capability, because the wireless feature left a phone vulnerable to hacking. She put her cell phone's hands-free unit into her right ear and scrolled through her contacts list. She wouldn't call Cromwell to address such a field problem—as a director he didn't deal with day-to-day street operations—but Harcourt had offered his assistance and had the added advantage of perspective because he'd held the position that Russell now filled. She dialed his number, and he answered on the third ring. Russell didn't bother with preliminaries, but jumped right into the problem.

"I'm being tailed. Black Ford four-door. Maybe a Taurus, but I can't tell in the dark. Can you send an intercept and let me know when to expect it?"

Harcourt hesitated a beat. "Of course. Where are you?" Russell named the upcoming intersection.

"That's five miles from here. It's going to take twenty minutes at least. Unless you want me to notify the authorities."

"No, I don't need the jurisdictional hassles right now. I'll keep them on the hook and turn around while you send backup. Can you lock onto the GPS?"

"Will do. Sit tight." Harcourt rang off and Russell took another turn. The Ford appeared ten seconds later. One more turn and Russell was on her way back to headquarters. She watched for the sedan. Ten seconds passed, twenty, then thirty. She kept flicking her eyes to the rearview mirror and back to the road, but the sedan was gone.

"Damn," she whispered to herself.

Three turns again and she picked out the second tail. Her phone rang.

"My guys are behind you in a silver SUV. They don't see a black Ford," Harcourt said.

"It's gone. Followed me one more turn and then broke away."

"That's some bad luck. Sorry. Wish we could have gotten there sooner. Any idea why you might be tailed?"

Try about a hundred ideas, Russell thought. Her field activities had been varied and dangerous, but most had been wrapped up cleanly. The only possible exception would be Africa.

"Has to be from the last mission. I'll keep an eye out and if it happens again I'll let Cromwell know they've found me. We'll have to make alternate arrangements. I'll probably sleep at a hotel tonight."

"Fair enough. Watch your back." Harcourt rang off.

Russell sighed. She really didn't want to sleep in a hotel that night. Instead, she took a winding route to her rented house located thirty minutes from Langley, keeping a sharp eye on the road behind her. The house sat in a quiet, prosperous suburb, where trees lined the curving streets and large homes dominated three-quarter-acre lots. Once there she pulled into the attached garage and waited for the door to close behind her before exiting. She armed the house's perimeter the minute she entered, using a keypad located on the wall next to the side entrance. Still, she held her gun while she did a quiet, thorough reconnaissance of each room. She checked in closets, under beds, and inside the master bedroom's shower stall. Once she was satisfied, she returned to the keypad, disarmed, cleared the old code, created a new one, and rearmed. An hour later she was asleep.

It wasn't a sound that woke her, it was the absence of any. The humidifier in her bedroom had shut off. It no longer made the soft whirring white noise that helped her fall asleep each night. She opened her eyes and glanced over at it. Not only was the humidifier silent, but the clock radio was dark as well. The electricity was down.

She sat up and reached for her gun, which she kept under the pillow next to the one she slept on. The heavy black around her felt ominous, and she slid out of bed and over to the alarm keypad on the wall. The green LED display blinked "Power Failure" in five-second intervals. The battery backup would keep the system functioning, and the phone line connection would allow for a direct call to the local police, assuming that the line was still operative. Russell moved back to the bedside table, where the only electricity-free phone sat. She picked up the receiver and heard nothing. The landline had been cut. Her cell phone was attached to a charging station on a credenza by the front door.

She went to the corner of her window, aligned herself with the wall, and pushed aside the curtain an inch to peer at the backyard. Beyond a brick-paved patio area was a lawn dotted with oaks that were just sprouting leaves after the long winter. The shapes of their branches were black forms in the night, and Russell could hear them shifting and clattering together in the wind. The alarm keypad beeped three times and Russell froze. Someone had disarmed the system. Now even the siren wouldn't blare, but Russell considered that to be of minimal use since the house sat far from any neighbors. She didn't want an amateur stumbling into the situation in any event. What concerned her most was the fact that the intruder was able to disarm a brand new code. These were professionals.

Russell responded the way she always did when in the game, her senses focused, her hand gripping her gun tightly. Her heart beat faster as she headed back to the display. The chime feature would respond each time a sensor was activated, and there were trigger points in each room and one on the stairwell to the second-floor bedrooms. Russell waited to see what location they used to breach the perimeter.

The keypad beeped and the words "front door" ran across the display. Pretty bold, walking right in the front door, she thought. She removed the safety on her gun and settled in with her shoulder against the wall, facing the bedroom door. Whoever was in the house was after her. She expected they'd make their way to her room. The words "living room sensor" came next. In her mind's eye, Russell traced the path they were taking through the house. The alarm chimed again. This time the word "kitchen" lit the device. Russell strained to catch any sound. She heard a rattle of glass bottles: the same sound she always heard when the refrigerator door opened.

What, do they need a beer? Russell thought. The bottles rattled again as the door was closed. Another beep. "Living room" marched across the keypad. One more beep and "front door" appeared.

She heard it close.

She slid into the opening leading to the master bath, keeping back. The walls blocked her view of the hall leading to the bedroom's entrance and, on the opposite side, the window, but kept her safe in case multiple attackers converged on her from both sides. But if the alarm system was correct and if they were once again outside, they'd come through the window.

The small battery-operated clock on the bathroom counter glowed, revealing that it was 3:02 in the morning. Then 3:03. Still silence. She waited until the clock glowed 3:18 before risking a move to peer past the doorway. The alarm pad emitted a loud clicking and the humidifier kicked back on. The electricity was restored.

She crept out into the hallway, tiptoeing quickly down the stairs to the kitchen. The refrigerator door was closed, but she wasn't fool enough to open it. She moved across through the living room to the front door. She wasn't fool enough to step outside and become a target dummy, either. She threw the deadbolt before picking up her cell phone. She dialed Langley, requested assistance, and settled down behind the arm of the living room couch to wait, hoping that the refrigerator's walls would contain enough of the force of any explosion so that she would survive.

Within thirty minutes a large delivery truck pulled into the driveway. The words "Washburn Heating and Cooling" were lettered on the side. The truck idled there, not moving. Russell's phone started ringing.

She answered and a man's voice said, "We've canvassed the area and found no one lurking in the trees. Are you clear in there?"

"Yes. I'll let you in." Two men in coveralls fell out of the doors, keeping behind them while they stared at the front of the house. Russell threw open the door, letting in a gust of cold air that smelled like spring. They walked toward her. Both wore knit caps, and one was Nicholas Jordan, the new hire. The other was a black man in his forties, with hair graying at the temples and a cautious manner. He stuck his hand out.

"Ben Washington. Explosives expert. Should we be standing here discussing the weather when you think there's a bomb?"

Oh boy, I like this one. All business, Russell thought. "I think it's in the refrigerator," she said.

Washington snorted. "So either timer activated or wired to blow when you open the door."

"Or a dirty bomb," Russell said.

Washington shook his head. "Nope, already checked for that. The truck is equipped with some of NASA's spare parts and a jerry-rigged telescope that can scan an area for traces of high-energy radioactive isotopes. A dirty bomb would have left a trail of them in the air. You're clear." He gave her an assessing look. "You sat in that house all that time with a possible dirty bomb? That's either a lot of guts or a lot of stupidity."

Russell shrugged. "I was just playing the odds. Dirty bomb: rare. Attacker with bullets: common. I figured I was safer in the house with the bomb than outside with a sniper in the trees."

She looked at Jordan. "On your basic explosives rotation?" The CIA's training schedule required that each agent learn hand-to-hand combat, basic bomb creation, and disarmament and weapons instruction.

Jordan smiled. "I love this round."

Washington snorted again. "All you young officers want to do is blow things up." He looked at Russell. "Too many video games." He clapped his hands together. "All right, let's figure out if the bad guys put something in the fridge."

Washington sauntered over to the back of the truck and reached in. He removed a metal bomb mask, a Kevlar jumpsuit, a coiled length of rope on a rolling reel, and a white plastic baby monitor. Russell watched with interest.

"Pretty low tech stuff you have there. Not exactly a NASA telescope."

Washington nodded. "Yep. But most bombs are homemade. With the exception of your basic C4 or Plastique, and you and I both know how tough it is to get your hands on that stuff these days."

"What's the baby monitor for?"

"Cheapest closed-circuit television system you can buy. This one's wireless, and while the RF signal can be a problem around some devices, I think the refrigerator's metal should blunt that a bit. Going to set it up so when the door opens we can see what's inside. That is, assuming the door pull isn't a trigger."

"And the rope?"

"I'm going to tie it onto the handle and pull open the door." He waved at Jordan. "Can you help me into the jumpsuit? They're a two-person operation."

"Can I go in?" Jordan said.

Washington shook his head. "You can only disarm after you've completed the written test."

Jordan sighed and held the clothing while Washington stepped into the jumpsuit. It had large Velcro tabs on the back that held it in place, a high collar that stuck up six inches around Washington's face; an additional, thicker Kevlar torso section added another layer of protection. The mask included a ventilator system, microphone, and installed web camera. Jordan lowered the helmet over Washington's head.

"Don't the web camera and microphone operate on a radio frequency too?" Russell asked.

Jordan nodded. "But it can be turned off."

"All right, I'll see you in five." Washington's voice was muffled behind the mask.

Washington grabbed the rope and one half of the baby monitor setup and started toward the house. It was clear from his gait that the cumbersome suit was hindering his stride. He disappeared inside and reappeared five minutes later, walking backward while he unspooled the rope. It extended almost thirty feet from the door, and Russell and Jordan retreated an additional thirty.

"I'm going to pull it," Washington called to them.

"Just like that? What if it explodes? I've got my wallet in there, my car's in the garage, not to mention a brand new laptop."

"Casualties of war. Ready?"

Russell took a deep breath, held it, and nodded.

Washington hauled on the rope.

Nothing happened. Washington lifted off the heavy mask and glanced at his watch.

"Not a trigger. Maybe timer. Let's have a look." He lumbered to the back of the truck, where the two panel doors hung open, and plunked the mask down. Russell joined him, with Jordan right behind. The baby monitor was up and running and the screen gave an excellent view of the open refrigerator's interior. Washington angled it so that Russell could see.

"Anything strange? Different? Condiment bottle where it wasn't before?"

The refrigerator's contents looked untouched. Russell shook her head.

"Nothing that I can see."

"Why break into a house, open the refrigerator, look inside, and leave?" Jordan said. "Absolutely nothing was accomplished. If they wanted you dead, you're not, and if they wanted to blow up the house, they didn't. I don't get it."

"A display of expertise? Trying to make you jumpy?" Washington sounded as puzzled as Jordan.

Russell took a deep breath. "Maybe. But if it's a warning, it's a pretty subtle one, and I'll be honest with you guys: the types of people that could be after my hide aren't known for their subtlety."

Russell stared at the image of the refrigerator. "There is one thing."

Washington perked up. "What?"

She pointed to the plastic cover for the refrigerator light. "The cover is slimy looking. It almost looks like someone wiped it with petroleum jelly." Jordan bent in to take a closer look.

"You sure it wasn't that way before? I mean, the interior of my refrigerator could use a good scrubbing."

Washington tapped him on the shoulder. "You single?"

Jordan nodded.

"Then you'll learn. My wife sees dirt that I don't even notice. Women don't allow slime in the refrigerator."

Russell smiled for the first time since the ordeal began. "You stereo-typing me?"

Washington grinned back. "Yes, I am."

"Well, you're right...*this time*," Russell said. "I'm certain I would have noticed that before."

Washington rubbed his jaw while he stared at the monitor. "Not likely that a bomb is in that small a container. Besides, we'd see the out-line of one through the plastic."

"Perhaps something biological?"

Washington nodded. "That's outside my area of expertise. We'll need a lab tech to come in and take some swabs."

"Now the only question is how did they get the alarm code and once they had it, why did they bother to shut down the electricity?" Russell told the men about the recently installed code.

"Got to be either a camera somewhere or a device implanted into the keypad that tracks your key strikes. I'll check for both," Jordan said. "As for the electricity, maybe they thought it would knock out the alarm sys-tem altogether?"

"Hard to believe guys sophisticated enough to enable a keystroke reader wouldn't know that most alarm systems have backup batteries."

"I think they wanted it dark in case you woke up and targeted them. Harder for you to see them to kill them," Washington said.

Russell followed both men into the house, looking around the front yard before closing the front door. She threw the deadbolt and joined them in the kitchen. Washington was peering into the refrig-erator and Russell joined him. From the closer view the slime on the light cover was even more pronounced. Washington closed the door.

Jordan removed the cover from the alarm keypad and said, "We've got a reader." He removed a small circuit board, clipping the wires that at-tached it to the system and replacing them. The alarm pad beeped. "I'll check all of the pads."

While Jordan worked on the keypads, Russell and Washington

searched the house for anything else suspicious that the intruder might have left. They found nothing. When they were done, Washington and Jordan left.

Russell sat at the kitchen table, her pistol within reach, and watched as the sky lightened with the new day. The refrigerator hummed.

12

SMITH TOUCHED DOWN AT Washington Dulles at three in the afternoon, having hopped a military charter that was scheduled to fly some members of the Department of Defense administrative staff home from The Hague. None had stayed at the Grand Royal, and all wanted Smith's take on the attack. He gave little information, choosing to act the innocent bystander rather than the operative that he was. The terrorist's plane ticket was in his pocket.

He'd faxed the photos and the plane ticket to Klein, and now he sat and worried about the unidentified woman in the photo. While he was sure Howell could take care of himself, he wasn't sure about the woman.

Once he landed he turned on his phone and waited for it to load. As other passengers deplaned, one man, a DOD staff member, tapped him on the shoulder.

"Looks like you have an escort waiting." The man waved to one of the windows. A military vehicle and two MPs he recognized from Fort Detrick waited on the tarmac. Smith stayed in his seat, however, and waited for his phone to load. He had two messages; one from Klein and one from Russell. He called Klein first.

"I've landed. Any luck on the photo?" Smith said. He heard Klein sigh over the phone.

"None. We loaded it into some face recognition software and accessed CIA personnel files for the past five years, Department of Defense, and the World Health Organization's database of scientists, diplomatic envoys for various nations, and as many consular personnel records as we could find. Also, I pulled a search on every present and past judge of the International Criminal Court. Nothing. Whoever this woman is, she's not military, diplomatic, or security. I even accessed present and former Secret Service personnel."

"How about Peter Howell? Does he recognize her?"

Klein coughed. "I'm sorry to say that Peter Howell is missing. We've been unable to contact him through the secure line that he maintains for MI6. They're as concerned as we are."

Smith's dread increased with this news. Howell wouldn't ignore a contact from MI6 unless he was in deep cover, dire circumstances, or dead. Smith shook off the last thought.

"I have a call from Russell. Perhaps she has news?"

"I didn't inform the CIA about the photos yet. Don't need them digging into your status and possibly stumbling over your Covert-One activity. But feel free to follow up with her on the Dattar angle and the coolers. I assume that WHO's director-general has briefed the CIA on the situation by now. Were you able to get any information out of the terrorist you found on the street?"

"Collecting intel from them is going to be a real problem, if not impossible. Each one we got our hands on died. Not from wounds, you understand. They just . . . died. Beckmann promised autopsy results. But for now I want to locate that woman. I think the photos, the attack on the hotel, and Dattar's escape must be related. If I can find her, I might be able to find the coolers."

"I agree, but I warn you, do not return home. And be prepared for what's happening at Fort Detrick. The media is slavering to speak to you, and both areas are surrounded. I've arranged for a short press conference from DOD headquarters at 1600 hours. We'll feed the media beast and hope they move on to other subjects."

"I seem to have an escort waiting."

"That was handled by USAMRIID. After the press conference I've arranged for you to stay a couple of nights at the Four Seasons Hotel."

"Four Seasons. Pretty fancy stuff. Why not a safe house?"

"You're bound to be followed by some overambitious paparazzo. Let's do the unexpected until the media storm dies down. The hotel staff are experts at protecting their guests from anxious journalists." Smith wasn't worried about journalists, he was worried about assassins, but he figured that anything was better than heading to his home.

"Were you able to get a laptop?"

"Yes. It's on hold at the hotel, and there's a car parked there for your use. Are you sure the time you're spending on finding this woman is worth it? You may be chasing down the wrong lead. She may know nothing that will help us recover those coolers."

"My instinct tells me she's in DC or New York. Maybe Chicago on the outside, but nothing smaller and her clothes don't match the West Coast."

"The bigger the city, the tougher it will be to locate her."

"That's why identifying the photo is so important. I'll get on it the minute I reach the hotel."

"I'm willing to let you devote a couple of days to it, but let's not lose sight of the real goal. We need to recover those coolers."

"I understand, but I can't help shake the feeling that Dattar's escape, the attack on the hotel to obtain those coolers, and the photos must be related. I'll keep you informed."

Smith descended the rolling metal stairs from the airplane. He saw the MPs snap to attention at the sight of him despite his casual clothes. For a brief moment he wished he'd put on his BDUs before getting on the airplane, but they were back in the Grand Royal. He returned the soldiers' salutes and nodded to the car.

"Take me to the grilling." The nearest soldier, a young woman with short dark hair and heavy eyebrows, grinned at him, revealing two slightly overlapping front teeth.

"Private Mercer, sir. Won't be that bad, sir."

"You promise to stay by my side?" He smiled at her. Her look warmed.

"Private Warren and I," Mercer indicated the young man with an upright carriage and serious expression standing next to her, "are ordered to protect you, and that's what we'll do."

"Any chance of rustling up a uniform? Mine's back in Europe."

"Yes, sir. There will be one waiting for you at Department of Defense headquarters."

He settled into the backseat, which was separated from the two soldiers by a thick protective window, and hit redial on Russell's missed call. He was surprised to see her private cell phone number run across the screen. He'd expected her to call from CIA offices.

"Are you all right?" she said, without preamble, her voice registering relief. Smith hurried to put her at ease.

"I'm fine and just landed in DC. I used a military charter. No frills and no onboard Internet so I couldn't let you know what's been happening."

"I hope you took the opportunity to sleep since it was clear from your clothing that you'd been trying to when the hotel was attacked." Russell's voice held a tinge of humor.

"I did. Thanks again for Beckmann. Any news on the autopsy?"

"Only a confirmation that they didn't die of any obvious wound. We're going to have to wait twenty-four hours for the pathology report. Beckmann's vowed to find another one before he 'dies of fright,' as he puts it. I hope he does because we need some information and our usual intelligence network has been silent on the attack. Still no takers claiming responsibility." She paused. "On that note, something strange is going on." Smith listened while Russell filled him in on the incident at her home.

"Did they swab the light?"

"They did. It's off to the labs, but I'd feel a lot better if you could have a look at it as well. I know that USAMRIID is on the cutting edge of new bacteria."

"Of course, but I'm avoiding Fort Detrick right now. I'm told it's surrounded by the media, all waiting to snap a photo of me driving through the gates. I have a friend who runs the lab at George Mason University. Can you send it there?" He gave Russell the address. "Any news on Dattar?"

"Nothing. He's just vanished."

It was all Smith could do not to tell her about the photos, and in particular, the photo of the woman. He toyed with the idea of telling her a half truth, that he'd found only Howell's photo and the woman's, but he thought that would be worthless. Russell could spend a lot of time tracking down dead-end leads because she wouldn't have the whole picture.

"I'm in town and staying at the Four Seasons after I give a press conference at the DOD. Let me know when the cultures arrive and I'll check them out." The car turned in front of DOD headquarters, and Smith pressed a button that lowered the window.

"Showtime?" he said.

Private Warren gave him a nod. "Yes, sir."

Thirty minutes later Smith was dressed in a crisp starched military uniform and standing on a raised dais behind a podium, answering questions fired at him from a room full of press. Privates Mercer and Warren were positioned on either side of the room and General Randolph, his supervisor at USAMRIID, stood behind him. He'd run through the bulk of the questions and was nearing the end of the session when a journalist asked about Dattar.

"Colonel Smith, were you aware that Oman Dattar escaped from custody that evening?" Smith tensed but did his best to keep breathing. Just hearing Dattar's name made him grit his teeth.

"I'm aware of that, yes."

"I seem to recall that you were involved in a humanitarian mission in Dattar's region some time ago. Were you scheduled to testify against him in the trial?"

Smith felt the mood in the room darken. "As I said, I traveled to The Hague to attend a WHO conference on infectious diseases. While I'd been notified by the prosecutor that he might need my testimony at some point in the future regarding the handling of a cholera outbreak in the region, I was not scheduled to appear before the tribunal."

"Are you aware that several witnesses were staying at the Grand Royal at the time of the attack?"

Smith glanced down at the podium while he did his best to contain his emotion at this piece of information. The location of testifying witnesses was to have remained strictly secret, and he had not considered that some might have been staying at a high-profile hotel like the Grand Royal. Smith wondered how the journalist had uncovered this bit of intelligence, and he wondered why Klein hadn't mentioned to him that witnesses might have been staying at the hotel. He looked up at the expectant faces staring back at him.

"Are you sure of that information?"

The journalist deflated visibly, and Smith thought his first question was a stab in the dark. He thought of the woman, but dismissed the idea as soon as he had it. Nothing Klein had uncovered revealed that she'd died in the attack.

"I'm asking you," the journalist said in an attempt to parry the question.

"I'm not privy to any additional information about the proceedings against Dattar than is publicly available."

General Randolph clapped his hands. "Thank you all. You can understand that Lieutenant Colonel Smith needs to move on from this terrible experience and reconnect with his family and loved ones. This press conference is over."

Smith felt another pang at General Randolph's words, well meaning though they were. As a Covert-One operative, Smith had no living immediate family, no wife, and no children. He'd always relished the complete freedom that his lack of ties gave him, but for a brief moment, standing there on the podium, he felt a pang of loneliness. He shook it off, straightened, and followed the general out of the conference room.

Smith settled back into the military transport for the ride to the hotel.

Next to him on the seat was a small duffel that contained his civilian clothes. He felt his phone begin vibrating when he was nearly at his destination. It was Klein.

"Saw the press conference. I have a request out to be allowed access to every witness the prosecutor called or expected to call in the Dattar matter, as well as every witness he interviewed when preparing the case. I'll have an answer for you before the end of the day."

"You read my mind."

"I still think it may be a side issue, but I respect your instincts. If you think finding her will get us closer to finding the bacteria, then I'm willing to run down the photo."

The car turned into an alley located behind the hotel and stopped. Smith climbed out, still holding the phone.

Private Mercer pointed to a door located behind a dumpster. "Sir, sorry for leaving you at the service entrance, but we were told to avoid the main lobby and to let you slip in on your own. That entrance leads to a back hallway." Private Mercer whispered the information so as not to disturb the call. Smith saluted both soldiers and stood aside while the car reversed down the alley and drove away. As he approached the door, he noted the closed-circuit cameras that monitored the entrance; his mind was engaged with his phone conversation and his concentration on the problem of the photo. He saw the glint of light that flashed from the bushes at the top of the narrow alley, but was slow to register the danger.

13

A LOUD TRUCK HORN BLARED from a nearby street. Smith jerked his head to look, but kept his hand with the phone in the same position. A searing pain entered his palm, piercing the flesh, and he reacted by dropping the phone. The bullet slammed into the metal dumpster to his right, and ricocheted off at an angle. Smith needed no further incentive to move. He sprinted to the entrance five feet in front of him, yanked the handle to swing open the door and tumbled through the opening. A second shot hammered into the metal panel. Smith kept moving, running down the narrow hallway and deeper into the hotel's interior. The door slammed closed behind him.

Smith jogged through a warehouse area, past pallets of supplies and through another door. This one led to a quiet, carpeted hallway, with soft lighting. He slowed to a fast walk, shoving his bleeding hand into his jacket pocket, still clutching the small duffel with his other. His palm burned and he was sweating freely. He thought the presence of the cameras in the alley would keep the shooter from following him through the back area, but the lobby would be crowded and a perfect location for someone to slip up behind him and slide a knife into him before moving off.

The registration area lay before him, and he headed that way but kept sweeping his gaze around the lobby, looking for anyone suspicious. He scanned the area, looking for more security cameras, but found none.

He figured he had a few minutes before the shooter made his way around the building and into the hotel. That is, if he intended to try a second time. Smith moved fast to the registration desk.

A young male employee smiled at him as he approached. Smith swallowed, and did his best to settle his jangling nerves and affect a pleasant, unconcerned attitude as he stepped up to the counter.

"Jon Smith, checking in. And I understand I have a package waiting for me?"

The young man greeted him, but Smith found it difficult to follow the conversation. He uttered some inane response to the clerk's questions, and retrieved, one handed, a credit card from his wallet. He turned and leaned against the counter, bending his body to once again watch the room, but finding nothing out of the ordinary.

"Mr. Smith? Your keys and your package. Have a nice stay." The clerk's voice snapped Smith back to attention. He gave an absent-minded nod and collected the room key and the small Federal Express box with his name on it. He looked at the room number.

"904? Is that on the ninth floor?"

The clerk nodded. "Yes. It's our concierge level."

Smith pushed the key back across the table to the clerk. "Could you give me a room on the second floor?"

The clerk got a puzzled look on his face. "But you've reserved a concierge level room."

Smith gritted his teeth at the delay. "It's a superstition of mine. Afraid the fire ladder won't reach to the ninth floor."

A look of understanding passed over the clerk's face. "Oh yes. Of course. We saw the images from the Grand Royal. I do apologize. Let me just change that. I'll put you in a suite instead."

"But please use a different name. I don't need a horde of reporters tracking down my room number."

"Our system requires a name next to a room number. Is there any pseudonym you wish to use instead?"

"Robert Koch."

Smith steered clear of the elevator, opting instead to take the stairs. When he entered the room, he crossed to the side of the window and closed the curtains, flipping on a light over the desk. He shrugged out of his jacket, taking care to keep the injured hand steady as he went to the bathroom to check the wound.

It was an angry red slash on the fleshy part of the palm, but not deep and not serious. The pain far outweighed the damage done. Smith washed it with soap and wrapped it in a washcloth. He returned to the desk and ripped open the box, revealing a lightweight laptop and a set of keys along with a valet ticket, presumably to the car. He logged onto the Internet and sent an immediate e-mail update, telling Klein about the attack and that for security purposes he might not spend the night at the hotel. As it was, he would be hard pressed to leave safely. He weighed the idea of taking the car now, before the shooter had time to move into a new position, but decided against it. He was safe enough for the moment, and he needed some time and access to the Internet. He propped the woman's picture next to the screen, typed in Google's webpage and got to work.

For the next hour he stared at the display, tapping in the word "Dattar" with a list of others and reading the first few pages in the search result. He looked into the woman's eyes in the photo. Her serious expression appeared intelligent and powerful. Her clothes—a navy suit, white shirt open at the throat, the hint of a chain around her neck, and diamond studs—gave the impression of understated wealth. Smith worked with medical professionals, biologists, and PhDs every day of the week, and this woman looked nothing like them. The female scientists that he knew had massive brain power matched with a scientific bent. Most donned lab coats for their daily uniform, and as a result they often wore simple shirts and slacks underneath. The woman in the photo was a part of the corporate world, Smith would put money on it, and while her brain power looked as massive, it appeared powerful as opposed to academic.

He picked up the phone, ordered room service, and kept typing, switching it up to Google images every time a woman's name was highlighted next to Dattar's. Another forty-five minutes passed with no success. His conviction that Dattar was somehow involved in the attack at the Grand Royal was faltering. Perhaps the timing of the attack and Dattar's escape was a coincidence.

Frustrated, he started searching for software that could apply face recognition to the Internet. He found a commercial website claiming that it was testing a program that could read an image and then search the Internet for every place in which that image appeared. The software was in the beta testing stage and available only by invitation. Smith clicked the link, asked to be included, and then called the company. When a woman's friendly voice answered the phone, he asked her to speed his inclusion.

"May I ask why you need this information?" The woman's voice now carried a slight hint of suspicion.

"I'm a member of the United States Army looking for a business contact given me by a friend of a friend. I have the photo of her, but not her name, and my friend can't remember her name either."

Smith waited, hoping his white lie would be swallowed. It wasn't.

"I'm sorry, we do have to be careful about who we allow to use the software. We have already had an incident in which a stalker contacted us and was attempting to locate a woman he was under orders to avoid. We never granted him access, thank goodness, but you can see the problem."

"I can, but why bother to have a trailer on the Internet and invite users if you don't intend to allow them access?"

"We're building our subscription list to make the company attractive for a possible stock offering. We're unable to grant access at this moment, but hope to in the next year; those on the list will get priority."

"Would it help if I had a member of the military police contact you? I assume your company could trust them to use the information in a positive manner."

"I'm sorry, but no. We're in negotiations with the Department of Homeland Security to allow them to access the software, but those negotiations are ongoing. The fee has yet to be determined, and until then we are not granting access to any law enforcement authority."

"All right, well thank you for your time." Smith hung up and called Martin Zellerbach, the one man he knew who could hack into any computer, anywhere, any time.

"Hello, Jon, how nice to hear from you." Marty's voice sounded formal, and the sentence was delivered in a stilted voice lacking any real warmth, but Smith was pleasantly surprised. Marty suffered from Asperger's, a high-functioning form of autism. He'd never really learned the social cues that most people took for granted, and if he answered the phone at all he often answered with an inappropriate greeting.

Smith pulled up a mental picture of the small, plump, green-eyed man sitting in the house that he rarely left, surrounded by his beloved computers. Growing up, Smith had protected Marty from the school-yard bullies and taunts that often came his way as a result of his Asperger's and at times was forced to protect others against Marty when he lashed back in a manner far in excess of the perceived wrong. Marty stood too close to others, sometimes thrusting his face into theirs, or made hurtful comments about them. People shied away from him and his strange, intense manner, and the man was isolated as a result. He'd never married, had few friends, and over the years had grown increasingly out of touch.

"You sound good, Marty."

"Thank you. I've been working on a new form of therapy. I saw you almost died in Europe. I'm happy that you didn't."

Smith smiled. Marty recited the words in an almost bored fashion and didn't sound as though he believed what he was saying for a moment, but once again, Smith appreciated the effort.

"How did you see me? I thought television gave you a headache," Smith said.

Marty snorted. "The clip was on CNN's website. I'll bet you got a few hundred thousand views. Do you need my help?" Now Marty sounded eager.

"I do. I'm trying to get access to a software company's beta test. It's an image-reading search software." Smith filled Marty in on the problem, using the same innocuous story that he was looking for a colleague. "Have you heard of this? Can Google images do this as well?"

"I've heard of it, and that company's work is very exciting. And no, Google images won't do that. Google searches the Internet for keywords in text and then shows you where that text is located. So if I put up a picture of us on a blog site and I caption the photo with our names, Google images will read the text under the photo, not the photo itself. But the software you mentioned will read the image's actual pixels and then search the Internet for a pixel match. Great stuff."

Smith felt a small surge of hope. "So it's almost like reverse engineering. If I have a name but no photo I search Google images to obtain one, but with a photo and no name I use this software to locate the photo and then find the name."

"Yes. Is that what you need?"

"That's exactly what I need. Do you think you can do it? I'm sending you a jpeg of the photo that I need analyzed."

"Let me work on it and get back to you."

Smith crawled into the shower, loving the feel of the hot water cascading down his back. He closed his eyes and, unbidden, thought of the woman and her air of determination. She reminded him of another determined woman he knew. He turned and held his face up to the spray. A series of images ran through his mind's eye. Russell grinning at him as they climbed into a vintage car that Peter Howell drove, Howell himself wearing a disguise as he chauffeured them around, Russell standing over him as she fired back at a double agent bent on killing him, Russell piloting a helicopter. The thought came to him, what if the woman in the photo was an agent herself? Perhaps MI6, or other? That would explain the Internet's complete lack of information on her. He switched off the water and stepped out, grabbing at a nearby towel.

Ten minutes later he was back at the computer, keying in "Dattar" and the names of security agencies the world over when his cell phone rang. He picked it up to hear the excited voice of Marty.

"I'm in! I cracked their passwords."

Smith felt a surge of excitement. "And? Did you find the photo?"

"The software is wonderful! A piece of art."

Smith did his best to keep the frustration from his voice. "Okay, but I need to find the woman. Did you run the photo?"

"Yes, but it didn't get a hit. The photo is too blurry. Worthless actually. And the software only scanned 450 million images, though, so only a tiny portion of the Internet. The lag is understandable. They're working on inputting more, but it's time consuming."

Smith was surprised at the depth of his disappointment. The image-search software was his only hope. "Is that software looking for the entire photo?"

"Yes. I told you, it looks for a pixel match." Marty sounded slightly frustrated himself at Smith's ignorance.

"Can you focus it on her face and search for that section alone?"

Smith heard Marty's raspy breathing through the phone. "The software does that already."

"Can you make it search for her photo in areas that aren't already included in their database?"

"Maybe."

"Can you try?"

"Okay, but I'm going to have to alter the registry. That's going to take some time."

"I really need this. I'm afraid the woman is in danger. There must be a photo of her face on the Internet, just not this particular photo."

"She looks like she runs a company or something," Marty said. "I really like her face, but she looks angry."

"Maybe 'determined' is a better word?"

"No. Angry. Like she's mad about something. She's not smiling. Women usually smile a lot." Marty surprised him again. As long as

Smith had known him he hadn't commented on the social aspect of anyone else. Yet he still had it wrong. The woman did not look angry.

"Thanks for helping me."

"I always help you," Marty said, in a matter-of-fact way.

Smith hung up feeling a bit more optimistic than before. He abandoned his search, logged into his e-mail, and read a note from Russell informing him that the refrigerator swab had arrived at George Mason. He called her. "Care to join me? We can look at the swab together."

"You're on."

"Can you pick me up at the Four Seasons? In an armored car? I'm surrounded by reporters all waiting to get my photo."

"I'll be happy to pick you up, but how about I leave the armored car parked and use my own. Last I heard no one needed bulletproof glass to ward off a camera."

"I'd really appreciate it if you came in an armored car."

Russell was silent a moment. "Want to tell me what's going on?"

"I was entering the back door of the Four Seasons when someone shot at me. They missed. I feel the need for more protection."

"If Covert-One's involved, perhaps you should let me know as well. We can pool our resources."

"I'll bear it in mind. But for now, I'm feeling a bit like a target."

"I'll bring a car and an Uzi. Will that make you feel better?"

"You have no idea."

Twenty minutes later Russell called from the lower-level parking lot.

"I'm in a black sedan parked directly in front of the parking garage elevator. The passenger door will be ajar. When the elevator doors open, just jump in."

Smith changed from his uniform back to his black civilian clothes. The different attire might buy him a couple of seconds if the attacker was watching for a man in uniform. He wished that he had a hat and sunglasses to help disguise his face. He grabbed the car key and laptop, and took the elevator to the parking level, bypassing the lobby and emerging into a dank lower level that consisted of concrete and autos.

It smelled like damp earth and exhaust fumes. A black sedan, its door open, idled in front of him. He ducked into the passenger seat and slammed the door behind him. The car started moving the second the door engaged.

Russell turned to look at him. Her blond hair was longer than he remembered and streaked with bleached strands among the golden ones, as if she'd been out in the sun. Her brown eyes were arresting on someone with such light-colored hair, and when she smiled at him, she seemed genuinely happy to see him. His heart clutched a bit at that. Perhaps General Randolph was right. He did have people who cared about him.

"It's good to see you. I'm glad you're all right," Russell said, as if she'd read his thoughts.

"It's good to see you too."

She nodded and directed her attention to driving, pulling up to a gated exit and honking. The gate went up and they drove out of the lot into the late afternoon light. Smith scanned the area, looking for possible snipers, but he doubted he'd actually spot anything. Good snipers wouldn't set up in a place where they could be located.

"Did you bring the Uzi?" Smith said, keeping his voice light. Russell pointed a thumb to the backseat. Smith twisted to look. An Uzi lay there. "I thought you were joking."

Russell shook her head. "I never joke about guns."

"Is this a company car?"

"Yes. One of the fleet we have at our disposal." She gave him a sideways glance. "You want to tell me what's up? The Grand Royal is a long, long way from here and yet you're targeted as you walk into the hotel." He told her about the photos and Covert-One's ongoing attempts to find both the woman and Howell.

"Have you seen or heard from Howell?" he asked. Russell shook her head.

"Not at all, but that isn't unusual. We're not in casual contact."

"I'm not thrilled that Dattar is out there somewhere. Feels dangerous and feels like he's targeting me, both there and here, but to arrange a second hit so far from the first and so quickly would imply that he's a bigger player than I think. "

Russell sighed. "I agree. His sphere of influence never seemed to reach this far, but it's dangerous to have him running free. Half the agencies in Europe are looking for him, but they've found nothing. He's vanished." Smith gazed out the passenger window and thought about the woman, the coolers, and Dattar.

Fifty minutes later they turned into George Mason University's laboratory. Stepping out of the car left Smith feeling too exposed, so he jogged to the modern entrance. Russell caught up behind him.

His friend, Professor Jinchu Ohnara, met them at the entrance to the biochemical lab. In his sixties, slight, with a full head of gray hair, and bright brown eyes, Ohnara was the leading genetic researcher on the East Coast. His research into DNA parsing was praised the world over. Smith had worked with him on a short-term project while a student at UCLA and still relied on him when he needed a fresh perspective on established science.

"Very happy to see you made it out of the hotel alive," Ohnara said as he shook Smith's hand.

"Did everyone see me hanging from the ledge?"

Ohnara nodded. "Everyone."

"My fifteen minutes of fame. May I introduce Randi Russell? She works in the public health sector of the government." Smith delivered the cover identity Russell had suggested.

"A pleasure. I can see why a public health official would be interested in this particular bacteria."

Russell frowned. "That sounds ominous. You found something disturbing?"

Ohnara nodded. "Well, it's something that can be detrimental to the public's health in certain parts of the world." He looked at Smith. "When the specimen arrived, I took a look at it. I think you should too."

He waved Smith into the lab. A slight scent of isopropyl alcohol hung in the air, the smell growing stronger as they stepped inside.

"You didn't open it in the containment lab?" Smith had specifically requested that Ohnara alone handle the specimen and that he do it in a controlled setting.

"I did. When I was done I transferred the sample to a biosafety box, much like a glove box. It has its own airflow system. You won't be handling it, merely looking at it." Ohnara gave him a glance filled with speculation. "I handled it at the appropriate level for the avian virus. Is there a reason to take even higher precautions?"

"I'm not sure what it is. In this day and age..." Smith let his voice trail off.

Ohnara sighed. "You don't have to tell me. Virulent, antibiotic-resistant bacteria will someday be the death of us all, I'm afraid, but I saw nothing that rose to the level of, say, the Ebola virus. You will, though, have to suit up."

All three suited up in disposable suits, gloves, and shoe covers. Ohnara handed them respirators as well. When they were done, Ohnara used a key card to open a locked door into another, sealed area of the lab and waved Smith to the right. Near the far wall was a square island with stools arranged around it. A large see-through cube on the island encased a microscope. Rubber gloves extended into the box through sealed holes and provided access to it, while built-in viewers, one on each side of the cube, allowed several people to view the slide at once. A long tube extended into the box where a scientist could insert a sample, move it into position, and reseal the entrance. Smith could see that a slide was already loaded.

"Tell me what you think," Ohnara said. "Ms. Russell, feel free to look through one of the other viewers."

Smith put his eyes to the viewer and the slide immediately sprang into focus. Several rod-shaped bacteria presented, intermingled with another form that he didn't recognize. He focused on the rod-shaped creatures.

"*Vibrio cholerae*," he said. "It's the bacteria that causes cholera. This other bacterium, the one that's not moving, is floating around with an attached strain of H5N1 virus." Smith directed his last statement at Russell before returning his attention to Ohnara. "Is the bird flu virus mutated in any way?"

"You asked me to check and from what I can see, it's not."

Thank God for that, Smith thought. But even regular bird flu was so virulent that the presence of it in the swab was cause for worry. He watched the sample for a moment. The bacteria moved.

"Still alive," Smith said. While he watched, one bacterium split in two. "They seem to be multiplying."

"They didn't at first, but now they are, and faster than I've ever seen before. Where did this come from?" Ohnara asked.

"A refrigerator light in an outlying suburb." Russell supplied the information.

"Odd place to find cholera bacteria and bird flu. Did they just wash it? Wipe the light down with a wet rag? Cholera needs water to grow."

Russell shook her head. "No, nothing like that. We believe it was placed there deliberately. I've only heard of cholera in hot weather climates. Will it survive in the cold?"

"Oh yes. It can survive several days in freezing temperatures. But warmth really sets it off. When I first loaded a small portion of the swab onto the dish the cholera was dormant, probably from the cool refrigerated air, but since warming up it has really started to multiply."

"And the bird flu virus?"

"It died as readily as the cholera strain. Bird flu isn't readily transmissible through the air, either, though we've confirmed a couple of cases that may have been human to human transmission. They were caretakers and family members all exposed to the same birds that carried the disease in the first place. Avian flu's nasty, to be sure, but encased in the gel as it is, in such minute amounts, and the fragility that I'm seeing makes it not likely to be transmitted to people."

"But it is possible, isn't it?" Russell said.

"Possible, yes. Probable, no. The cholera is the more worrisome factor here. I don't like it."

Smith didn't either. The bacteria became more active even as he watched them. In contrast, the strange species sat unmoving.

"What's the other species that I see? The one with the H5N1 attached to it?" he asked.

"Shewanella MR-1. It's fascinating and quite common in the DC area. A large source is right here in the silt at the bottom of the Potomac River, and we've been analyzing it in our labs for a year now. Let me switch up to the atomic force microscope." While Smith watched, the image changed and the strange bacteria sprang into finer focus. Long, hair-like strands extended from the sides of the creature.

"Ahh, thank you. I see the pili growing from it."

"Are those a type of cilia?" Russell asked.

"Yes, but these are only three to five nanometers in width. Ten thousand times finer than a human hair. The atomic microscope is necessary to see them. We know that these pili are electrically conductive microbial nanowires. Almost like fine wire filament. We've determined that they can conduct electricity even underwater and in anaerobic environments."

"Is it another microbial fuel cell? Like Geobacter?" Smith said.

Ohnara peered into a second viewer. "Have you worked with MFCs?"

Smith had, but only on a superficial level. "Not much. I've heard that there have been some recent breakthroughs in our understanding of how they function."

"Very exciting breakthroughs. We now know that electrons are moving down those wires, but what the bacteria do with the electrons and what their purpose is still remains a mystery. Nevertheless, they're a potential power source and we're extremely excited about the possibility that they can create enough energy on their own to charge batteries. Very beneficial bacteria."

Smith refocused on the cholera. "Will freezing temperatures slow the cholera's multiplication? Can you freeze this sample? Buy me some time to investigate this further?"

Ohnara stepped away from the viewer. "Let's take it to zero centigrade and see."

"Is there a possibility that this came from the kitchen faucet? That someone dumped this into the water supply?" Russell asked the question.

Ohnara pulled over a stool on rollers and sat down. He leveled a serious stare at her. "Cholera is dangerous, no doubt, but it would take a tremendously strong strain to overcome our Western methods of disinfection. Chlorine kills it, and boiling does too."

"What good does it do to wipe cholera in a refrigerator, then?" Russell said.

Ohnara looked perplexed. "I suppose it would spread to a person if the bacteria were placed on the mouth of something one drank. Like a water bottle, for instance, but it's a fairly weak way to injure someone and it's not a way to injure a large number of people. For that you need a contaminated water source that manages to avoid treatment, as we've seen in areas like Haiti. Even then, while thousands can die from lack of treatment, they most often initially contract it through the water source. It's not normally transferred from person to person."

Smith stepped back. "But the rapid multiplication and the viral strain attached are worrisome and unusual. Perhaps this is a form of super cholera?"

Ohnara tilted his hand back and forth. "Perhaps, perhaps not. Some of the sample succumbed as I transferred it to the dish, so it's far from robust. If you like, I can subject it to the standard chemicals that it would encounter during our current water treatment protocols. See if it manages to survive."

Smith nodded. "I'd appreciate that."

Russell looked back into the viewer. "Dr. Ohnara, is it possible to type the strain? Determine where these bacteria originated?"

Ohnara nodded. "I already did that. They match that found in sections of India and Pakistan."

Russell's head shot up and Smith saw the color drain from her face. "Did you say Pakistan?"

"I did. Is that significant?"

"That's a known area of concern for terrorism," Smith said, deliberately keeping his voice neutral. He trusted Ohnara to retain a confidence, but saw no need to draw the lines between Pakistan, the escaped Dattar, and a virulent strain of cholera. He'd ask Klein to get him some more information on the stolen biomaterial. Perhaps this particular strain was in one of the coolers.

Ohnara looked doubtful. "I just don't think it could be an effective form of terrorism. As I said, it's difficult to see how cholera can be used in such a fashion, at least in modern countries like ours. Obviously, if this strand survives some of the chemicals I'm going to subject it to, then my opinion may change."

Smith put out a hand to shake Ohnara's. "Let's hope not."

Smith and Russell walked to the front of the building, but as they reached the door, Smith hung back.

"Still worried?" Russell said. "How about I go out and drive around to the back. You can jump in as before."

He smiled at her, letting the relief show in his face. "Thanks."

"Anytime."

Smith repeated what he now called the "run to the car" game and was relieved when Russell drove away from the campus.

"Well, what do you make of the swab?" he asked.

Russell frowned. "I don't like that it's from Dattar's region, but I guess you picked up on that."

Smith nodded. "I did. Could you be targeted? Have you run into him in the past?"

Russell turned down a street and Smith saw a Metro stop at the end. "No. I've never had any contact with him. It could be completely unrelated, but it doesn't feel like it is." She seemed to want to say something further.

"Yes?" Smith prodded.

She shook her head. "Nothing. Back to the Four Seasons?" she said.

"Can you drop me here? I'll take the Metro. I have some errands to run."

"Certainly. You should be fine. No one tailed us."

Smith smiled. "I'll take your word on that. I know it's good."

She smiled back, but grew serious. "There's a situation brewing with regard to some missing bacteria. I may ask you for some more assistance."

The coolers, Smith thought. "Of course."

He angled out of the sedan, sketched a wave, and headed to the Metro. The minute he was out of sight, he called Marty. There was no answer, but he left a message saying he was on his way over. He boarded the train and settled in for the ride to Marty's house, eyeing the other passengers. Most either read books or newspapers or stared off into space. None noticed Smith. He got off the Metro at Dupont Circle and prepared to walk the rest of the way, making sure to keep moving and giving quick glances behind him as he headed into a quiet residential area. As he neared Marty's house, he spotted the small, rotund man pacing back and forth on the sidewalk. He looked agitated and held an open laptop in his hands. When he saw Smith, a smile creased his face.

"Jon! Jon! I got the message that you were coming! I've been waiting for you. I'm here." He waved a hand excitedly. Smith gave a small groan and glanced around. He wished Marty had waited for him inside the house. The last thing he needed was Marty announcing his presence to the entire neighborhood, but there was no stopping Marty once he was wound up; fortunately the street appeared quiet. Marty closed the gap between them, still holding the laptop. He shoved it at Smith.

"I've found her!" he said.

14

S MITH STOOD IN THE MARBLE and wood lobby of Landon Investments in New York City and wondered anew why Pakistani terrorists wanted Rebecca Nolan dead, why a Pakistani-derived strain of cholera was smeared on Russell's refrigerator light, and how Dattar might have figured into it all. He'd spent the entire train ride from DC reading the documents about Nolan that Marty had amassed and printed for him. What he'd learned about her had impressed him, but also left him returning to the key question about who wanted her dead and why. He'd given her name to Russell, who was throwing the additional strength of the CIA's research capabilities into the project.

Now he gave his name to the front desk clerk, obtained a pass, and headed to the gleaming elevator banks. The elevator was equipped with a television and he watched as a female spokesperson on a financial channel analyzed a complex transaction involving counterbalancing puts and calls in order to gain a dollar spread on a trade. Through it all the screen kept a running ticker tape showing the stock market's performance minute to minute. Smith kept some of his money in the markets, but tended to purchase blue chip stocks through a fund and then held them during good times and bad. The woman on the small screen could have been speaking in tongues for all he knew.

The doors opened with a pneumatic sound and he stepped directly into the Landon Investments offices. A petite woman wearing a telephone headset manned a massive mahogany reception desk. The sheer opulence of the offices attested to the success of Landon Investments. Thanks to Marty's research, Smith knew that the company had over $3 billion under management with a growing private-wealth customer base and a stellar reputation. Rebecca Nolan alone managed over $900 million and was considered a rising star within the company. One article in *Fortune* magazine had described the company as "the finest fund that no one knew." The article stated that managers in the company deliberately eschewed the limelight, preferring to act in a discreet manner that matched the wishes of their extremely wealthy clients. The young Asian woman behind the desk smiled at him as he approached.

"Mr. Smith, I apologize for the lack of a waiting pass, but I was unaware of your visit."

Smith smiled at her. "Please don't apologize. Ms. Nolan is not aware that I wish to see her. It's important that I do, though. Is she available?"

A slight frown appeared on the woman's face. "Did you say Ms. Nolan?"

"Yes."

She shook her head sadly. "I'm so sorry, but Ms. Nolan does not take meetings while the markets are open. Perhaps you can return after four o'clock when they've closed?"

Smith shook his head. "I'm sorry, but no. I must speak to her now. Can you please ring her?"

The woman's frown became more pronounced. "Are you one of Ms. Nolan's clients?"

"No. I'm a member of the United States Army Medical Research Institute for Infectious Diseases and I must speak to her." He handed her his business card.

"Army? Is this about the Wingspan anthrax vaccine? The announcement moved the shares of that company quite nicely." The very idea seemed to make the woman brighten, and he decided to go with it.

"It *is* about bacteria, though not that one."

"Then I'm sure she'll speak to you the minute the market closes."

"I need to see her now, please," he replied.

Smith watched the receptionist struggle to maintain her composure, which he found fascinating. He thought his request was simple enough, yet the woman acted as though he'd asked to see the pope during Sunday mass. The receptionist punched a button. After a moment she announced his presence and said, "he's with the Army," listened and then said, "of course." She switched off the line and returned her attention to Smith.

"Ms. Nolan says that she's sorry, but she can't take a meeting at this time. She asked that I reschedule you after the markets have closed."

Smith was done with the niceties. Behind the receptionist was a frosted glass wall that separated the lobby from the working offices. Smith could see the blurry outlines of people sitting at desks and moving around the room. He started toward the glass doors set into the wall.

"Mr. Smith, I'm sorry, but where are you going?" Anxiety rang in the receptionist's voice and she rose from her chair. She was petite, lovely, and extremely agitated. Smith was sorry to have to upset her, but he needed to do what he must to see Ms. Nolan. He reached the doors and pulled on a handle. It didn't move. He looked back at the receptionist.

"Please unlock the door." The receptionist straightened to her full height, which Smith estimated to be five feet. Despite her small size, she would defend Ms. Nolan's schedule come what may.

"I can't, sir. I would have called security already, if it weren't for the fact that you're with the army. You must come back here. I'll be happy to make an appointment for you promptly at 4:00 when the markets close."

He strode back to her, stepping into her personal space and moving to within inches of her. She didn't shrink back, a fact that he liked— she was no pushover—but he needed to see Ms. Nolan and at that moment she was impeding his progress. He swept his eyes over the desk area and spotted the button that he assumed released the lock.

"Ms.," he looked at her name tag, "Lee. I appreciate your dedication to protecting Ms. Nolan's schedule, but my news won't wait and I'm confident that she will agree once she has heard it. If not, then I'll leave immediately. Either way, I'll be sure to let her know that you did your best to keep the United States Army at bay." He gave her his most winning smile, and after a moment he saw a flicker of an answering amusement in her face. He reached over and pressed the button and was rewarded with the clicking sound as the lock disengaged.

Smith stepped onto the Landon Investments trading floor. Rows of desks, perhaps fifty in all, each equipped with a computer monitor and a corresponding trader, were arranged in a horseshoe configuration with a break in the center to create an aisle. The end of the pattern reached to the windows on the far side of the room to his right and left. The traders all wore headsets similar to the one he had seen on the receptionist in the lobby and most were speaking into the microphone. The noise of fifty different conversations rose and fell around him.

At the center of the horseshoe stood Ms. Nolan. She looked exactly like her photo, except today, rather than the conservative blue suit, she wore a red sheath dress that fit her slender body to perfection. Her hair was pulled back and in her ears were drop earrings with what looked to Smith's untrained eye like yellow diamonds. She stood in front of a semicircle of four computer monitors and frowned at them. He made his way toward her, walking down the center aisle. A few of the traders cast him looks, but the majority stared at their screens, ignoring him. Ms. Nolan, too, ignored him, never taking her eyes off the computers. He noticed that she stood about five foot eight and estimated her age to be in the mid-thirties. She looked up when he was within three feet of the wall of monitors.

She had dark brown eyes that maintained the same serious expression that she wore in the photo. He watched her as she ran her gaze from his face to his shoes and back up again. She raised an eyebrow at him.

"Mr. Smith from the army, I presume?"

He nodded. "I apologize for barging in like this, but it's imperative that I speak with you. It's a matter of life or death."

A flicker of surprise crossed her features. "Life or death? Whose?"

"Yours," he said.

That got her complete attention. Her face registered shock and her body swayed backward. She reached down, pressed a button on a desktop phone and said, "Gerald, watch the pharmaceuticals for me, can you? I need to take a short meeting." When she was done, she removed her headset and nodded to him. "We'll go to my office."

She waved him to the right and they began to make their way past the desks to a frosted glass door that entered into a hallway where muted gray tones on the walls and the plush carpeting underfoot muffled their steps. Smith thought that the entire presentation at Landon Investments was geared to give an impression of great wealth, calm, and competence. The expensive furnishings were easy to purchase, but Smith thought the feeling of calm was much more difficult to accomplish. The world markets were roiling at the moment, and he imagined that there were many millions of dollars slipping through the hands of most of the investment advisors in the world, including Landon's employees. She paused at an open door at the corner of the building and nodded for him to precede her.

The corner office was a study in sleek minimalist design. On the black walnut desk sat another row of three computer monitors, each showing different financial networks with scrolling ticker running along the bottom. Smith saw Nolan's eyes lock onto the screens while she closed the door behind her. The rest of the office was stark. A single-serving coffee maker sat on a credenza behind the main desk, along with a tray bearing black cups, some for espresso and two for coffee. An abstract print on the wall to Smith's right was the only artwork in the room. There were no diplomas, awards, photos of famous people, or even family photos anywhere. Linen blinds were lowered against the morning sun.

"Would you like a coffee or espresso?" she asked.

"Coffee black," Smith said. She walked to the coffeepot and inserted a pod.

"Please sit down."

Smith sat in a black leather chair facing the desk. The machine beeped and she handed him a cup. She took her place behind the desk. The screens sat to her left, but this time she didn't glance at them. "Please tell me about the life-or-death matter."

Smith had spent a great deal of time on the train preparing what he hoped would be a believable story. Now, in the face of her calm, he was afraid he would sound hysterical.

"I have reason to believe that a Pakistani terrorist organization has ordered a hit on you."

Nolan's eyes widened briefly, but she didn't show any of the surprise or fear that he had expected. That, in and of itself, was interesting. Either she didn't believe him or something else was at play here.

"That's a remarkable claim, Mr. Smith. What do you do that you would receive such information? Are you a member of the FBI? Do you have any identification?"

She remained calm, but her voice was tinged with disbelief. Smith could tell that she thought him a bit crazy. He half expected her to call for security to have him escorted out of her office any minute. She gave another sweeping glance at his clothing, as if to assess his mental health, and her eyes came to rest on his military watch.

He handed her his driver's license along with a copy of his business card from USAMRIID. While she read both, he rushed to fill the silence.

"I just returned from The Hague. I was staying at the Grand Royal and was there during the attack. If you watched the reports then you saw me crawl out the third-story window. It was during that time that I learned that you were targeted. Do you have any idea why a terrorist halfway around the world would carry your photo in his pocket?"

She focused on his face, staring intently. "Of course I am aware of what happened at the Grand Royal. I watched the reports. I did see the man crawl out of the window to escape, and if that was you, then I'm pleased that you survived. The attack reverberated across the markets.

The holding company that owns the hotel chain saw its share value drop four dollars on the news."

Smith was dumbfounded and was for a brief moment unsure how to respond to that. He was fast losing patience with her. He'd spent most of his waking moments since the attack thinking of her and how to find her to warn her, and she was only concerned that the hotel's stock was dropping.

"Honestly, Ms. Nolan, I don't give a damn about the hotel chain's financial condition. I'm here to tell you that your life is in danger. I can't give you any more details about how I know this, but I can tell you the danger is real and you need to address it. Now. Not two hours from now and certainly not after the market closes." He pulled another business card out of his pocket and placed it on her desk. "This is the number of a woman at the CIA named Randi Russell. She's prepared to have one of her agents take you to a safe house outside the DC area while they track the intelligence and attempt to find whoever is responsible for the hit. I suggest that you call her now. She'll confirm that what I'm telling you is true."

Nolan picked up the card and rose. "I'll do that. Please, feel free to make yourself another cup of coffee while I verify what you've said."

She left. Smith waited, sipping the coffee and watching the ticker scroll across the computer screens. After ten minutes, Nolan returned. She looked pale but determined, and Smith guessed then that the meeting wasn't going to end as he wanted it to, because she should have looked much more helpful than she did. She resumed her seat behind the console.

"Ms. Russell confirmed your version of events. I asked her this question, and now I'll ask you: How long do you expect it will take to find this assassin?"

Smith hesitated. That was, of course, the dilemma. He didn't know who had hired the man in the Grand Royal, what organization he was working for, or whether he worked alone or with the others in the crew that had demolished the hotel. He didn't have any real credible information to give Nolan, or Russell, for that matter.

"I don't know. It could take days, or even months. There's no way to tell when the attack on you will take place."

She looked alarmed. "Months? The CIA wishes to put me in a safe house for months? No. That won't work. I have a job to do. A life. I'll hire a bodyguard this afternoon. Two, if necessary, but I'm not just walking away for months. If I do, I'll have nothing left when I return."

Smith inhaled. "If you don't go, you may have no life at all. You have to get to a safe place while the CIA works this situation out."

She shook her head. "I have almost a billion dollars of other people's money to manage and an entire office dependent on me to supervise them. I just can't pick up and leave today with no way of knowing when I'll return."

Smith felt his disbelief rising. "Do you ever consider anything else except money in your analysis? Because I've got to tell you, all the money in the world isn't going to matter once you're dead."

She leaned forward. "Mr. Smith, think about what you're asking. You're asking me to simply grab my things and leave." She snapped her fingers. "Just like that. Not tell my clients, my secretary, or my colleagues where I'm going or how long I'll be gone. You haven't given me an opportunity to arrange for my household bills to be paid, my boss to be told, or my client files to be handed over. You're asking me to walk away from my life now, for months, while the CIA attempts to locate some sort of shadowy assassin who may never get caught. Who could do such a thing? Could you?"

He opened his mouth to tell her he could, but paused. As a member of Covert-One he would continue to draw a salary, and his job at USAMRIID would be waiting for him when he returned. He had no close family, no spouse, no lover, and no one to account to before he would disappear. For that moment the difference between his own life and the life of an average person was thrown into stark contrast. He felt a pang and shoved it back. She had to leave. Her life depended on it.

"You have to do this. Money is worthless compared to your life and shouldn't even figure into your plans. Your clients shouldn't expect you to allow their money to play a role in your decision."

She frowned. "My clients care very deeply about the funds that they place in my control. Some care about their money with more devotion than they give to either their health or their families."

"Well then, they certainly aren't going to give a damn about you when you're gone, are they? Especially after you're found with a bullet between the eyes." He'd chosen his words deliberately to shock her. Instead, they seemed to have the opposite effect; they angered her. She stood.

"Thank you for coming to warn me. I appreciate your concern and your candor. Please rest assured that I'll do what it takes to protect myself, and I wish you and Ms. Russell quick success in getting to the bottom of this problem. Let me walk you to the lobby."

Smith stared at her, dumbfounded. She was dismissing him. He'd gone to all this trouble to find her, to warn her, and she was dismissing him. And yet he had a strong suspicion that she was the key to the entire mess, because she was the only civilian in the equation. She was the wild card. Both he and Howell had long histories of dealing with sordid criminals in the international arena and the fact that someone wanted them dead, in and of itself, meant nothing. Unless she too was an operative, but as soon as Smith had that thought, he rejected it. Klein had found no evidence of her in his intelligence agent database. He felt his fury rising at her cavalier attitude. He rose, and though she was tall, he was taller and for a moment he was glad of it.

"You can't be serious. There was a terrorist in the hotel that tried to kill me. He had in his possession a photograph of you, me, and a man I know. The photograph was taken while you were on the street." Smith pointed out the window. "Probably that street. And you had no idea that it was being taken. Bodyguards are not going to help. You need to get to that safe house now. And before you do you can explain why he carried your photo. As one of the other two at risk, I have a right to know your connection in order to protect myself." He stepped toward her, using his superior height to drive his point home. Her eyes narrowed.

"I don't see what you or I could ever have in common that this man wanted us both dead."

"Dattar." Smith said the name without thought. He was too angry to think. A startled look passed over her face, telling him that he'd hit a nerve. "What is it? Is Dattar one of your clients?"

Her expression closed. "Landon Investments maintains the confidentiality of their clients."

"I don't give a damn about Landon Investments!" Smith was practically shouting. Her face became suffused with red, and for a brief moment he thought she'd punch him. Her body practically vibrated with her rage. He watched her struggle to bring herself under control.

"If you're finished delivering your news, then let me walk you to the door." Her voice rang with finality. He stayed next to her, keeping the pressure on.

"Let me tell you one more thing, and then I'll go and leave you to whatever fate these killers have in store for you. Your life has already changed and it won't change back. You're going to be looking over your shoulder from now until either we catch the killers or they catch you. Welcome to the world of the hunted."

She kept her eyes on him, and he could almost see her thoughts as her expression shifted from angry to scared and then back to stern. It was clear to him that she still thought she would control the situation. After a few seconds Smith managed to give a small nod and took a step back. She stalked past him. He followed her down the hall to the frosted glass door and waited as she pressed a button on the wall. The lock clicked open, and she stepped into the reception area. He heard her breath hitch.

"Oh no." Her voice was full of anguish. Before Smith could stop her, she ran toward the mahogany console.

The petite receptionist lay on the carpet behind the desk. Her eyes were open and blood leaked from a bullet hole in her chest.

15

NOLAN GRABBED AT THE PHONE and Smith saw her pound out a number. He bent down next to the body and checked for a pulse. The woman was gone. Nolan still stood behind the desk while she spoke to building security.

"Is she dead?" Nolan said to Smith.

He nodded. "Does this desk have a button that will lock the front doors?"

Nolan pressed a button on the edge of the desk opposite to the one that Smith had used earlier to open the doors behind them, and he heard the entrance deadbolt click home. The desk was ten feet from the doors. Beyond them and extending left was a short hall that opened right into a rectangular area that had elevators on both sides. The killer could be waiting just steps from the door to pick off anyone leaving the offices.

"Get down." He spoke in a whisper and pulled at her arm. She knelt behind the desk while she continued her conversation with building security.

"I just called an ambulance for her," she said. Nolan's voice cracked on the word "her."

"We've got to get out of here. This man's after you. You stay and he'll kill more people to get at you. Either he's making his way through the office right now, searching, or he's waiting in that front hall to pick you off when you leave."

"There are security cameras that record this area. Let me replay the video." She kept low while she pulled out a sliding shelf that held a keyboard. Smith watched her access the security program. Within seconds the screen split into four quadrants and displayed various locations inside the office.

"Wait, before you go back in time, do you see anyone new? Someone who doesn't belong there?" He saw her checking each display. All the hallways were empty. She shook her head.

"Nothing," she said. She switched up the view to zoom in on the reception area, but the screen went blank. Smith looked at the ceiling and saw the round cover that masked the closed-circuit camera. He couldn't discern whether the lens still functioned.

"Wouldn't I see an LED pinpoint if the camera was working?"

"Yes," Nolan whispered.

"Well, there's nothing."

"He did something to the circuit for the reception area only," Nolan said.

"So most likely he's waiting in the hallway. Go back into the interior," he said. She punched the button that opened the door and darted through it. Smith followed, catching the door on the return swing before it closed and locked once again. She was headed straight to her office. It was an amateur's move, because even though she hadn't seen anything suspicious on the video, that didn't mean the man wasn't hiding in there. It was exactly where an assassin would look for her.

"Don't go in there." It was all Smith could do not to shriek through the hall. Nolan disappeared through the door as if she hadn't heard him. He sprinted in behind her.

She was standing at her desk sliding a tablet computer into a black leather attaché case. An electric power cord followed as well as a Filofax with a burgundy cover and a small clutch purse. She zipped the bag closed and headed back out, passing to his left. She shot him a quick look, but said nothing as she raked a short, navy trench coat off a hook on the door. He grabbed her arm before she had a chance to step through the entrance and held her in place while he reached into his windbreaker and removed his gun from its shoulder holster. Nolan's eyes widened in fear when she saw it.

"Relax, I'm not going to use it on you. Though I should," he said in a low voice. "Which way is the exit to the stairwell?"

"To the right. Let go of me." He didn't. He'd had enough and he wasn't about to take orders from her.

"Not a chance. We'll leave together. What about the other employees? How many are in their offices?"

She looked at her watch. "Probably none. They're all in the boiler room and will stay there until the market closes."

"Is that the big room that you were in before we came here?"

She nodded.

"What about bathrooms?"

"The boiler room has two connected to it."

"Good. There's safety in numbers and I doubt he'll approach that room. They should be safe enough until security arrives. I'll go out first and make sure the hall is clear."

"You do that." Her voice was tight with anger. He ignored it.

Smith let go of her, moved to the door and edged out, looking both ways before waving to her to follow. He spied the stairwell exit sign to the right at the far end and started in that direction. He was ten steps closer to the stairs before he realized that she wasn't behind him. He glanced back and saw her vanish around a corner.

My God, I'm going to kill her myself, he thought. He turned and followed, catching up with her as she stood in a small alcove that held a freight elevator. She swiped a key card across the panel and hit the down button. She confronted him and her face held a mixture of distrust, determination, and barely controlled panic.

"I don't know who you really are or why you came here, but the minute you did, you brought death and violence. I neither want nor need your help. Take the stairs. I'm taking the freight elevator. If you follow me, I'll scream bloody murder."

The elevator doors opened. Smith was relieved to see that it was empty. She stepped in and he followed, wrapping one hand around her mouth and the other around her waist, once again holding her still. Once he was sure of his grip he pushed her into the elevator's corner and out of view of the open door. She began to struggle, and he could feel her open her lips as if she intended to bite his hand. He leaned his weight into her, holding her against the elevator wall.

"Now you listen to me," he said into her ear. "There's an assassin out there who intends to kill both me and a man that I like very much. He also happens to want to kill you and even though right now that outcome is starting to sound appealing, I want some answers before you die. Until I get them, I'm not leaving your side. So scream all you want. I'll have Russell at the CIA talk to whatever rent-a-cop Landon Investments hires to protect its employees, and I can assure you the outcome will be that you and I will leave here together." He punched the down key. It didn't light. He hit it again. Nothing. "Use your damn key card and get us off this floor. Now." He lowered his hand from her face and stepped back. She was once again flushed with rage, but now also with outright fear. She swiped her key card across the panel and hit the down button again. The doors closed. He felt remorse starting to creep into his consciousness and tamped it down immediately. This was life or death. She'd have to deal with her distrust on her own.

"When the doors open, what floor will it be?" he said. He sounded harsher than he intended.

"Loading dock." She replied in a calm voice despite her high color and obvious distress. She was cool in a crisis, he had to give her that.

"Do you have a car?"

She shook her head. "Not here."

"Do you have one at home that we can use?"

Her face set. She didn't reply.

"It's to drive to the safe house. Otherwise I have to call the CIA to get us."

She nodded. "Call the CIA. I feel safer with them than you." He found he was actually a bit upset with that statement. He wasn't used to being cast as a villain. Once again he tamped down the feeling. If he'd acted badly, it was not only understandable but necessary. She was alive because he had.

"Fine. I'll do that." He opened his phone but didn't have a signal. He'd get to the street and call then.

The elevator doors opened and Smith stared down the barrel of a gun.

16

SMITH KNOCKED THE GUN upward and spun left. He heard the compressed sound of a silenced bullet. Nolan swung her attaché case in an arc, hitting the attacker dead center in the torso, and he stumbled backward a step. She tripped forward, carried by the momentum. Smith fired, hitting the killer in the chest. The bullet thudded into what must have been a bulletproof vest and the man grunted with pain. A black balaclava covered his face, and Smith could hear the harsh rasp of the man's breathing through the hole for his mouth. The killer sprinted sideways to hide behind a metal garbage can as the elevator doors began to close. Smith grabbed at Nolan to pull her back into the car.

"Get us to the lobby," Smith said. Nolan swiped her key card and hit the button. Her hair had fallen out of its clip, and her knuckles were white on the handle of the case. She pressed herself against the elevator's wall, her eyes wide with fear. Smith flipped the safety on his gun and re-holstered it, pulling the jacket over to hide it from view. "When the doors open, I want you to act with complete calm. Do you understand?"

"There are cameras in the parking lot. Security will have seen that," she said. Her voice was scared.

Smith shook his head. "Doubtful. He managed to mess up the one in your reception area, he'll block the lot ones as well."

"I'm going to warn them. He could kill others." Nolan sounded determined and she straightened. She pulled the clip out and the rest of her hair fell around her shoulders. Smith doubted that the killer would continue his rampage, and he couldn't allow her to take the time to find a security guard, relay her story, and then wait in the lobby for the police. They had to move. The doors hissed open on the lobby level, and he saw several police officers standing at the reception desk speaking to building security. He grabbed her by the arm once again.

"Tell them, but be prepared to run. He's after you and me. I'm not sure why he shot the receptionist, except perhaps to use her as a threat or to create a distraction while he hunted you. I'll let the CIA know that he's lurking in the parking lot." Smith let go of her, pulled out his phone and began texting Russell while he headed toward the lobby.

"Go out the back," Nolan said.

"No. He'd expect that. We're strolling right out the front door. They may want to detain us, so be prepared to talk our way out of here." He hit the door and swung it open. As he expected, the lobby was filling up with police. Three of them looked across at Nolan as she walked to the first one in the main reception area. A male officer swept a glance at them. Smith watched him catalog Nolan's expensive dress, briefcase, and trench coat before turning his attention to Smith. Smith was aware that of the two of them Nolan looked more the part of a Wall Street banker than he did. He hoped she trusted him enough to help him leave the building. If she turned him over to the police, it would be hours before he could leave, and they'd likely hold him in full view while they did it. Smith had no wish to be a target.

"Officer, there's a man in the parking lot waving a gun. I just went down there to get my car and saw him. He's dressed in black and his face is covered as well. Hurry!" She indicated the stairs to the garage. The other officers and the lobby attendants heard her, and everyone seemed to begin talking at once. The officer and three others pulled their own weapons and headed to the stairwell. Smith took the opportunity to haul Nolan across the marble floor and out the revolving doors. They hit the street and Smith turned left, walking fast and moving through the crowd.

"Good work," he said. Nolan didn't reply. She stayed with him, but kept turning around and giving frightened glances behind her. "Try not to look so afraid. It'll only draw attention to us," Smith said.

"Where are you going?" Nolan replied. Smith couldn't help but catch her use of the term "you" as opposed to "we." She still expected to strike out on her own.

"Around the corner to a cab stand. We'll grab one and get as far away as possible."

"And from there?"

"To one of the CIA safe houses." He glanced at her to see if she'd protest. To his relief, she seemed amenable to the idea. His phone buzzed with an incoming text. It was from Russell: *Head to the West Side. Use this location and call me when you get there.* She left an address and instructions. They hit the corner and crawled into a cab. Smith gave the cabbie instructions to an intersection on the Upper East Side.

"That's a block from my house," Nolan said.

"Nice area," Smith said. She didn't reply. Twenty minutes later they pulled up to the address and got out. Smith waited until the cab disappeared around the corner before heading to the park. Nolan walked alongside, saying nothing. He hailed another cab.

"Where to now?" Nolan sounded exasperated.

Smith gave the new cabbie instructions to an intersection on the West Side near the safe house. Nolan gave a loud sigh, but remained silent while they crossed Central Park. Ten minutes later they were standing in front of Russell's safe house. It was one of a series of four-story walk-ups, well maintained and with a realtor's sign on the front. A lock box hung on the door handle.

Smith punched the button on the box, and it opened. A set of keys fell into his palm. He grabbed them and then reached for Nolan, wrapping his hands around her bicep.

"Quit grabbing me. I'm not going anywhere," she said.

"Liar." He pulled her with him, ignoring the annoyed sound she made.

The safe house door was located on the third and last landing. He was thankful for the runner that covered the wood stairs, muffling their steps. There were two doors per landing, but the quiet told Smith that the occupants were gone. When they reached the third landing, "3B" was to Smith's right. Smith put the keys in the deadbolt, shooting it back, and swung the door open.

They entered a foyer that contained a small credenza with a wooden charging station for cell phones. Smith tossed the keys onto one of the felt-covered spaces on the station and walked into the living area, past an open door to his right that led into a kitchen. The living area was furnished with a minimalism that screamed disuse. A leather couch faced a television console that held a flat-screen television and, on the shelf below, a stereo system. A glass cocktail table sat between the two. To the left was a set of stairs that led to the next floor, where Smith presumed were the bedrooms. The entire first level would be considered small by most American standards, but large for a duplex in New York City. He estimated there to be no more than four hundred square feet on the first level, and the same on the second.

Next to the couch an end table held a remote control and a curved, sleek silver telephone on a stand. The phone started ringing. From the corner of his eye he saw Nolan step into the living room from the kitchen. She paused to watch him.

Smith walked over to peer at the small screen built into the handle that revealed the phone number. The display read "Unavailable," which told him it was probably someone from the CIA checking on their status. He picked it up and put it to his ear to answer.

"You made it?" Russell said.

"Yes. Did you catch the shooter in the garage?"

"No. Long gone, or so we suspect. Has Nolan given you any information?" Smith looked at the woman in question, who was still gazing at him with her ever-present serious expression.

"Haven't had a moment to breathe. Will let you know once I do."

"Good. We're still drawing blanks on Dattar's location. Until we find

him, it might be best if you both stayed inside. There's food in the refrigerator and alcohol in the small bar at the corner of the living room.
I stocked it with your favorite drink." Smith spotted the corner wet bar.
For a moment he was confused because, while he had a favorite drink,
he didn't recall filling Russell in on it.

"Which is?"

"Shaken, not stirred."

Smith smiled. "Bond was cool under fire. In contrast, I'll need liberal
amounts while I debrief her."

"Think she knows something?"

"I'm sure of it."

"Call me if you learn anything useful. Anytime. I'm in Manhattan—
Midtown—and expect to stay here at least another twenty-four hours.
We could use a break. Every terrorist has died before we could interro-
gate him, the coolers are still missing, and Dattar has vanished."

"Any news on Howell?"

"Nothing. But no body either, so perhaps he's still alive."

"Who's searching for him?"

"I pulled Beckmann out of The Hague and put him on it."

"Excellent. I like that guy."

"He's the best, albeit a little unorthodox in his methods."

"Keep me posted." Smith hung up.

"Was that Ms. Russell?"

Smith nodded. "They were unable to catch the shooter. She's suggesting we lie low for a while."

Nolan looked around the room. "For how long?"

He put up his hands. "I don't know." He wanted to dive right in and
demand some answers from her regarding her connection to Dattar, but
he didn't think she'd respond well to a blunt question. He decided to try
to build a rapport with her first. "Are you hungry? I'm told there's food
here somewhere."

She nodded. "Very."

He smiled. "Then let's have a look." He shrugged off his jacket, draped it over a chair and stepped past her into the kitchen. He noticed that her eyes were locked onto his gun in the shoulder holster. She followed, which he counted as a win, given that it was the first time she had since he'd met her. It took him no time at all to find the ingredients for a sandwich. He made two, handed her a plate and a bottle of a tea drink.

"No bottled water, sorry."

"Tea is fine," she said. "I'm going to go upstairs to wash my hands first." Smith nodded and settled into a chair by the kitchen table to eat.

Ten minutes later, when she still hadn't returned, he shoved away from the table and headed upstairs to the second floor to investigate. The stairs ended in a long hallway, with two doors placed at the beginning and the end. He slowed and pulled his gun out of the holster. The first door opened into a small bedroom, sparsely furnished with a bed, a dresser with another flat-screen on top, and two nightstands. A door at the back opened into a compact bathroom with a shower and one sink. No Nolan.

He returned to the hallway and headed to the next door, which he now assumed must contain the master bedroom. He opened the door to find just that: a slightly larger room with a king-sized bed, standard dresser, and television. A bank of three separate double-hung windows were to his right, and a cool breeze flowed into the room from the one farthest from the door.

She was gone.

17

STUPID ME, SMITH THOUGHT, and sighed. He placed his free hand on the windowsill and leaned out. The fire escape was empty, the bottom rungs still retracted. She must have jumped from there to the ground. He looked around the area but could see no sign of her. He closed the window, locked it, returned to the kitchen, and pulled his cell phone out of his jacket pocket. He dialed Marty, who picked up on the second ring.

"Jon, I'm surprised to hear from you. Did you find her?"

"I did. And just lost her again."

Marty snorted. "I'm watching breaking news about the gunman in the Landon Investments building in New York. So the dead woman wasn't her."

"It was her receptionist. I brought her to a safe house, but she gave me the slip. Ms. Nolan is not as cooperative as I expected."

"I told you she looked angry. Angry people never do what you want."

Smith paused. Marty's comment was astute, but once again he didn't think "angry" was the right word to apply to Nolan. "I know she's got a telephone on her, as well as a tablet computer. Can you track her through either?"

"What type of software on her phone?"

"No idea."

"Number?"

"Nope."

Marty gave a gusty sigh. "You're not giving me much to go on here."

"I know. Sorry."

"I'm going to have to hack the major carriers, find her number, and then see if I can track her. Some systems have built-in GPS, which will pinpoint her exact location, but others only triangulate her signal from a nearby tower. In the last case I'll only be able to get you a radius. You'll have to canvass for her. How did she get away? Are you losing your touch?"

Marty's comment served to raise Smith's annoyance with himself. Marty was right; he should have predicted that she'd run, but the reality was that he couldn't have held her in the safe house against her will in any event. "I made the mistake of assuming that as a civilian she'd be a whole lot more cooperative than she was. In fact, she's not behaving like a civilian at all." She's behaving like someone with something to hide, Smith thought.

"What's she like?"

"Serious, smart, and obsessed with her job. She reacted to the news that an assassin was after her with a lot less emotion than I expected."

"She sounds like me," Marty said. Smith raised an eyebrow. Once again, Marty was close to the truth. Smith wouldn't be surprised if he was told that Nolan was somewhere on the spectrum for Asperger's. Marty continued, "What are you going to do while I track her, *again*?" Marty seemed to be enjoying himself at Smith's expense.

"I'm going to her home. As an amateur that's probably the first place she'll head."

"You just told me she's not acting like a civilian. Why are you treating her like one?" That brought Smith up short. There came a beep on his phone.

"I've got a call coming through. Let me know the minute you find anything." Smith hung up and switched over.

"It's Randi. I'm coming in the front door so don't blow my head off." Smith still had his gun in his hand. He shoved it back in the holster.

He heard the door open and after a moment Russell stepped into the kitchen. She wore dark jeans topped by a loose-fitting cotton T-shirt and a short blue blazer. On her feet were black sneakers with white rubber soles.

"I lost Nolan," he said.

"What? How?" Russell looked shocked. Smith told her the whole sordid story, finishing with the information that he had Marty tracking her cell. Russell looked down at Nolan's sandwich, still sitting on the table. Smith followed her gaze.

"Do you want it? She didn't touch it."

Russell nodded. "I'm starving." She pulled up a chair and uncapped the tea. Smith thought she looked pale and wan.

"Are you sick?" he said.

She nodded. "Picked up a bit of a virus, which is not surprising. We've been working around the clock in the hunt for Dattar."

"Not from the swab, I hope," Smith said.

She took a bite of the sandwich. "I wondered about that, too. I actually called Ohnara back and asked him, but he said cholera wouldn't present with my symptoms or as a mild illness. If I had it, I would know it."

"Well, that's certainly true. I've seen it in action in Third World countries. It's awful," Smith said.

"What the hell does Nolan have to hide?" Russell said. "And I agree with you, she's headed home."

"Then let's go. We're only a few minutes behind."

Russell pointed at his sandwich. "You haven't finished. Don't worry. I've got an officer stationed at her place. She shows up, he'll lock her down for us. And I need to talk to you about something else." Smith took a deep breath in relief. He should have known that Russell would have all angles covered. He sat at the table, but he found he was too keyed up to eat.

"Ohnara says the cholera sample is mutant, but he doesn't think it poses a risk—at least not in this country. He ran it through our standard water treatment process and it died. In fact, he said it died so swiftly that he thinks the mutation weakened it somehow."

Smith pondered that for a moment. "If that's true, then he should start an experiment to introduce the mutation to the general cholera population. With a little tweaking, he could weaken the disease."

Russell shook her head. "Don't forget, without treatment it multiplied at an astonishing rate. It could just render the disease more virulent."

"Well, that's why you tweak it. Boost what you need and leave the rest," Smith said.

Russell finished the sandwich and pushed the plate away. "My real concern is Dattar. We're getting rumors that a full-scale attack on a major city in America is being planned. We can't be sure Dattar is the mastermind, but I don't like that he's escaped."

Smith stood. "We need to get our hands on Nolan again. She knows something, I'm almost sure of it. I asked her about Dattar and she shut down tight. Claimed client confidentiality. If he weren't a client, she would have had no obligation toward him and could have just said no. The fact that she pulled the confidentiality card tells me that he was." Smith heard the muffled sound of footsteps on the stairs. "Are we expecting someone?" he whispered. Russell shook her head and pulled a gun out of a shoulder holster under the blazer. The steps grew nearer, moving quietly. Smith pulled his own weapon out and pressed himself against the wall on the side of the entrance to the hall. Russell took up a position behind his left shoulder. The footfalls stopped on the landing and a key slid into the lock. The door opened, and a tall man with slicked hair and wearing a suit came into view. Smith put the muzzle of his gun against the side of the man's head. He stilled.

"Colonel Smith?" he said.

Russell lowered her weapon and moved into view. "It's all right," she said to Smith, "he's CIA." Smith lowered his weapon. "You almost got your head blown off," she said to the man. He turned to face her with an apologetic smile.

"Sorry, Russell. I should have told you I was on my way."

Russell holstered her weapon. "Jon Smith, meet Steve Harcourt. CIA's head of the Mideast Division, currently on loan to the NYPD."

Smith nodded a greeting. The man's slick demeanor and expensive tailored suit spoke volumes about his position at the agency. Smith noted a small bump near the suit's arm where he presumed Harcourt's own weapon was holstered. He imagined the residents of New York's Upper West Side would be surprised at how many people were walking around their neighborhood while carrying concealed. A buzzing noise made Russell jump. She pulled out a BlackBerry and read the screen.

"Jordan says that Nolan hasn't returned to her house."

"I thought she was here," Harcourt said. Smith was prepared to once again tell of his blunder when Russell interrupted.

"She skipped. There's a request out to track her by cell phone transmission. I stationed Jordan at her house early this morning just as a precaution."

Harcourt rubbed his chin. "Is that really a good use of an officer? We haven't any information that links her to anything that we're investigating now."

"We have the photos in the terrorist's pocket that I told you about," Russell said.

"I think she's tied to Dattar in some way that may be significant," Smith said. Harcourt leveled a glance at Smith.

"I understand that you're a member of the military branch for infectious diseases? I appreciate your input, and I am glad to see you survived the attack at the Grand Royal, but tracking Dattar is the CIA's job." Smith felt his irritation grow. Harcourt's attitude was that of a pure bureaucrat and his defensive posture was him marking his territory. Smith doubted that the man had actually worked in the field for years.

"It's my job to protect myself. Someone's been targeting me and Ms. Nolan and I intend to discover who."

"It appears as though Ms. Nolan doesn't want your help. Otherwise

I imagine she'd still be here," Harcourt said. Smith took a breath to respond, but Russell stepped between him and Harcourt.

"Let's focus on the facts, shall we?" Russell said. "There's an attack on the Grand Royal the same night that infectious disease specialists are convened there and that Dattar escapes from prison. Photos of Ms. Nolan, Smith, and a former agent from MI6 named Howell are found in one of the attacker's pockets. Ms. Nolan is a money manager who may have done business with Dattar, and her receptionist is gunned down not twenty-four hours after the escape. Currently we have little information on Dattar's whereabouts, and we should be interviewing anyone with any information about him. If that's Nolan, then she needs to be found and questioned."

"By the CIA," Harcourt said. "Not by anyone else." He shot a warning look at Smith.

Jerk, Smith thought.

"Which requires an officer at her home."

"I still think it's a waste of resources. But if you think it's necessary…" Harcourt shrugged.

"I do," Russell said. Her phone buzzed again. She punched the speaker button.

"Ms. Russell? It's Jana Wendel. Jordan's been shot."

18

KHALIL WALKED CALMLY AWAY from his position opposite Nolan's house and passed the car with its shattered windshield and occupant slumped over the wheel. He knew that the agent had survived long enough to call for help, for he'd seen him lift the cell phone to his ear and speak before falling unconscious. Khalil didn't care. The agent should have been quicker, faster. He'd aimed at Khalil, which had forced Khalil to crouch before shooting; as a result, the shot was not a kill shot. Khalil was pushing thirty-five and should have slower reflexes than the young agent. That he didn't revealed the CIA's weakness.

Khalil was only angry that Nolan hadn't appeared at the house. Shooting the agent was small recompense, but it was clear that the agent had noticed Khalil hanging about Nolan's block. Khalil stayed a few minutes more after the shooting to see if Nolan would appear, but that was a risk because he could hear ambulance sirens in the distance. He turned a corner, entered the park, and began to jog. Here his running wouldn't raise a question. Dozens of people ran around him, all getting their afternoon workout. When he was far enough away, he dialed a number on his phone.

"Did you get her?" Dattar said.

"She hasn't appeared at her home. But a CIA agent did. At no time did you tell me that the CIA was involved regarding her."

"I didn't know they were! If anything, that was your mistake. You shouldn't have killed the receptionist."

Khalil stopped walking. "What are you talking about?"

"I'm talking about the receptionist at N— *the target's* office. She was shot in the temple. Your signature style."

"But not by me. Have you paid another to acquire this target?"

"No. And I won't. But that was a foolish move because the police are now swarming the office. If you intend to take her there, you won't be able to without being captured."

"That's of no importance to me. I never intended to take her there. It's too visible. Whoever you paid in addition to me is screwing up, and I'd suggest you request your money back. That's assuming you paid him at all." Khalil's voice dripped with sarcasm.

"I paid no one else. I expect you to get to her. If not, then no money. You understand?" Dattar hung up.

Khalil stared at the phone still in his hand and told himself to stay calm, to breathe deeply. He would eliminate all rivals and acquire Nolan himself. He sat on a nearby bench and called his second, Manhar.

"Did you find him?"

"He's in an SRO hotel in Harlem."

Khalil smiled. "Excellent. Are you sure it's him?"

"I am. Older Englishman. Soft. He's going to be easy to kill. Do you want him shot?"

"Yes, but make it look like something else."

"I'll arrange it."

"Mm. Good. I'm going for Nolan and Smith."

"I heard a rumor about Smith." Manhar hesitated.

"And?"

"He's slippery."

Khalil snorted. "He's American. None are that smart."

"I've heard he's treacherous. He forced Dattar to allow vaccination in his village. Hundreds of children. Mine included."

"Do they live?"

"Yes. When diphtheria raced through the next village, none in ours got it, but Dattar should have stopped it. The village elders are saying the UN brought the disease and infected the neighboring village deliberately to make it look as though their medicine worked. Who knows what the UN really injected them with? Dattar is weak."

Khalil was up and walking again. "Dattar is irrelevant, but his vast utility holdings are not. I want a piece of them. Besides, he's planning retaliation. Don't worry. Soon disease will spread. None will be spared. Just focus on the Englishman." He pocketed the phone and headed back to the East Side.

Dattar dialed the number he needed. When the man answered, Dattar plunged right in, not bothering to identify himself. "Did you eliminate Smith?"

"Not yet. Things were more complicated than I thought. But I know where he is, so it's just a matter of waiting until he's alone."

"Did you shoot the receptionist? That was stupid."

"You let me decide what's stupid or not. Smith's been cooperating with the CIA and is currently under CIA protection. In a safe house, and I can't possibly kill him there, so I had a better idea. The police have been given a videotape of Smith entering the office. In less than three hours every cop in New York will be hunting him."

"How is that better than just putting a bullet in his head?"

"The CIA won't want to be seen as harboring a killer. Questions will arise as to his role in the Grand Royal attack. Suddenly he'll go from a celebrated survivor to a possible co-conspirator. The CIA will want to wash their hands of him. Then I'll shoot him and no one will care. Just another killer eliminated."

Dattar smiled. "Excellent."

"When are you going to pay me?"

Dattar's smile fled. "I'm putting some time between my escape and accessing my accounts. This is better for both of us. You don't want to be seen accepting my money directly after, either, do you?" Dattar gritted his teeth while waiting for the response.

"Fine, but make it soon. I don't do this for free and my creditors are hounding me more and more each day."

Dattar relaxed. "I will." He hung up and exploded. "When I get my hands on that woman, I'm going to string her up and flay her alive. She'll beg for death."

Rajiid turned from his computer monitor. "But they continue to proceed despite the lack of payment?"

Dattar nodded. He moved over to the coffeepot and began to pour himself a cup. The ship rolled and Dattar stumbled back, spilling the coffee. "When do we dock at Cyprus? I can't stand this vile freighter."

"Another day at least. We're working around the storm off the Italian coast." The ship rolled again, but this time Dattar was able to correct for it. The coffee stayed in his cup.

"Tell me about the coolers. When will we be able to spread the disease?"

Rajiid shook his head. "I've received no news on the test. When I do, we'll move quickly. I'm also considering adding a preschool to the target. No o e will question an outbreak under such conditions."

Dattar gazed at Rajiid's placid demeanor. The man lacked any semblance of a soul, that was certain, but Dattar wouldn't be concerned about the children of others, either. Better they not grow into enemies.

"You placed the weapon?"

Rajiid nodded. "In the engine room."

Dattar sipped his coffee and continued to sway with the ship's motion.

19

SMITH FOLLOWED RUSSELL, who ran down the brownstone's stairs two at a time. Harcourt remained behind in the safe house, working the phones and coordinating a response. They hailed a nearby cab and tumbled into it. To Smith the ride across the park took forever, but he thought Russell seemed particularly affected. She was sweating, shaking, and turning pale.

"Have you known this agent long?" Smith said.

Russell shook her head. "Only a few weeks, but he's smart and resourceful. I knew he was a bit inexperienced for a lot of field jobs, but I thought the Nolan stakeout would be fairly routine. All he needed to do was call in a sighting."

Police cars and an ambulance already clogged the street. An officer stood at the corner, waving cars past the intersection. Russell bounded out and headed to the officer while holding her wallet open to show her identification, but closing it before the officer could scan it. Smith stayed with her, looking down the street and checking each window above, searching for movement. Most were empty. Only a couple of faces peered at the scene, and those were women. None were Nolan.

"I've been sent here by Johnson. This is my assistant," Russell said. The officer waved her through.

"Who's Johnson?" Smith said to her in low tones.

"His captain. Harcourt just texted me the name. He gave me the ID, too. It identifies me as a special consultant to the NYPD, just like Harcourt, but with a fake name. Technically I shouldn't be here at all. It may blow my cover. But I can't just leave him."

Smith understood her concern. They moved to the car, now surrounded by officers. A bullet hole marred the windshield and blood was spattered over the glass and covered the top portion of the steering wheel.

"Where is he?" Russell said to a nearby officer.

"In the ambulance."

"Is he alive?"

"So far," the officer said.

Russell jogged to the emergency vehicle, where the EMTs were working on a man lying on a gurney inside.

"What's his condition?" Russell said to a paramedic who stood between the open doors in back.

"We're heading out. Bullet entered his cheek, we think. We can't tell if it exited or is still in his skull. He's bleeding pretty badly." One of the paramedics said, "Let's go" and Russell stepped back while the EMT closed the doors and slapped a hand on them. The siren started to wail as the vehicle began to wind its way through the parked squads.

Another officer, this one older than the first, wearing jeans, a black T-shirt, navy windbreaker, and a lanyard around his neck that contained a large badge and a nametag that read "Manderi" walked up to Russell.

"You know the victim?" He cast a sharp look at Smith before returning his gaze to Russell.

"I do. He works for me."

"ID says he works for a technology company in McLean, Virginia. Only thing I know that's there is the CIA." The officer gave Russell a shrewd look.

"We do some of their... tech work." The way Russell said the sentence left no doubt that she was CIA.

"He had a gun on him. Know why he'd have one as a computer technician?"

"Well, tech work for the CIA can be dangerous." Once again, Russell emphasized the word "tech" and the officer responded with another knowing look. "I'll ask my supervisor to contact yours. Perhaps they can work it out."

The officer nodded. "You do that. I'd be interested to hear the details of that conversation." He directed his attention to Smith.

"You together?"

Smith hesitated. Something in the officer's demeanor made him wary. "Why do you ask?"

"Just heard on the radio that we're looking for a man named Jon Smith in connection with a shooting." The officer stared at Smith. "You look a lot like the photo."

"What shooting?" Russell said.

The officer tore his gaze from Smith's face long enough to address Russell. "Landon Investments. Receptionist shot. Video shows that this Jon Smith was the last one who spoke to her before she died." He returned his gaze to Smith. "You have any identification?"

Smith stilled. "I do not."

The officer raised his eyebrows. "You don't have a license on you?"

Smith shook his head. "No."

"You know this man?" The officer spoke to Russell.

"I'm going to look at the car." She gave the officer a parting nod and stepped away, neatly sidestepping the questions and saying nothing to Smith. The officer watched her go, then turned his gaze back to Smith.

"Perhaps you'd better come with me. We'll go together to find your identification."

"It's not a crime to walk the streets without identification. If I recall my constitutional law class correctly, there was a Supreme Court case that said so."

The officer's brows drew together. "You a lawyer?"

"I'm military. Excuse me." Smith turned and headed toward Russell, his heart rate accelerating. She stood before Jordan's car once again, looking into the driver's side window, then she stepped away and waved Smith to follow her down the sidewalk.

"You have an alibi for the time that you were in Landon Investments? Because it sounds like you're going to need one."

Smith nodded. "I was in Nolan's office. But I have no idea if she'll vouch for me. Especially since she shows every sign of wanting to stay as far away from me as possible."

"And you have to reacquire her first. Listen, I'll arrange to keep your face out of the news for as long as I can."

"How? That guy didn't seem too cooperative."

"Since 9/11 the NYPD has consulted with CIA officers on terrorist issues. Harcourt's the latest guy out on loan. I'm pretty sure he'll help bury the story. We'll tell the authorities that it's a matter of national security. Back them off a bit."

Smith nodded. "Thanks. In the meantime, I'll work on finding Nolan and shaking any information out of her that I can regarding Dattar. Let me know if you locate Howell. I really could use his help right now." He peered at her. "Your flu getting worse? You don't look well."

Russell sighed. "It probably is, and I don't have the time to be sick right now. We have to locate Dattar and those coolers, in that order." She brushed her hair from the side of her face. When she did, Smith could see a line of sweat trickle down her temple, yet the air was cool. Smith looked past Russell in time to see the suspicious officer and another, this one in a suit, heading his way. "Here comes the cop. I'll leave you to handle this."

Smith spun on his heel and walked away, taking care to keep his steps even and his attitude relaxed. He knew that Russell would contain the situation, but he still didn't breathe easier until he turned the corner. Once he did, he started jogging toward the park, heading back to the safe house. The phone in his pocket started to vibrate. A quick glance at the screen revealed that it was Marty calling.

"Give me some good news. I need it," Smith said.

"She's in a coffee shop near the Flatiron District." Marty rattled off the address. Smith turned around and started jogging back toward the East Side and the nearest subway station.

"How'd you find her? Her phone?"

"No. Her tablet computer. I found her phone number first. Figured like most professionals she preferred a BlackBerry to a smartphone. I was right, but that meant that I could only give you a vague idea of her location because that technology is older. However, once I hacked her account, I discovered that she has a subscription for data management on her tablet computer. I hacked into *that* and found that she was online on an open network. She still is." Smith dodged a turning cab as he crossed from the park back into the neighborhood. He was one block from the subway.

"Have any idea what she's doing online?"

"*Of course.* When you hack an open network, you can see every-thing." Marty sounded long suffering. He sighed over the line.

"Marty, don't wear me out here. Just tell me what she's doing."

"She's trading," Marty said.

Smith came to a dead stop. "What do you mean? Trading?"

"Just that. She's trading on the stock market. Buying, selling, you know."

Smith couldn't believe what he was hearing. "Her life is in danger, she just discovered her receptionist lying flat on her back, dead, and she's in a coffee shop trading stocks? Is this woman crazy?"

"I don't think so. From what I can tell she's covering earlier trades and moving investments around. She's way ahead in most of her posi-tions. If she were crazy, I imagine she'd be losing money, right?" Smith started walking again. Leave it to Marty to take his words literally.

"That was, in some ways, a rhetorical question. Listen, I'm headed into the subway. Keep an eye on her. Let's hope she continues for the time it takes me to get there."

"The market doesn't close for another hour. I think she'll stay there until it does. I mean, she's really into this right now. She's moving millions of dollars around in various accounts." Smith heard applause in the background.

"I just heard clapping. Is someone else with you?"

Marty laughed. "No, that was me. I'm speaking to you through a headset. I was clapping at her latest trade. She covered a put with a corresponding call and made seventy-five cents on the spread. That account just gained one hundred and ten thousand dollars. This lady is a genius! A math machine. I can't wait to see what her next trade is." Marty sounded more excited than Smith had heard in a while. "I want her to manage my money. Do you think she'll take me as a client?" Smith reached the subway and swung around the railing, taking the steps downward two at a time.

"Only if she manages to avoid getting killed."

20

SMITH EMERGED FROM THE SUBWAY and headed to the coffee shop, doing his best to appear relaxed while scanning the area for any threats. He saw Nolan through the window and wanted to groan. She hadn't even bothered to get a seat away from the glass. Her hair hung down while she tapped furiously on a small keyboard attached to the tablet computer. He grabbed the door handle and stepped inside.

The rich scent of roasting coffee filled the air. The small shop was shaped like a long rectangle and contained hundreds of tins of tea and coffee arrayed on shelves along the walls. One of the clerks worked a long wooden bar that ran the length of the store and at which several patrons stood and downed espresso. A second door at the back led to an attached hotel. Nolan sat at the corner of a counter next to the far wall, her concentration on the tablet complete. He walked toward her. When he was next to her, she glanced up. He sat down at the free barstool next to her and crossed his legs.

"So, should we just sit here until Dattar or one of his henchmen comes along to kill us?" She had stopped typing, which he took as a good sign.

"You need to leave me alone," she said.

He shook his head. "Sorry, but that's not going to happen until you either tell me what you've done to piss off Dattar or you're dead. Frankly, at the rate that you're screwing up, I expect the latter to be the most likely outcome."

She frowned at him. "I'm taking steps to protect myself, which I told you I'm perfectly capable of doing. You should quit wasting your time with me and get back on the hunt for this assassin that's out there."

"A CIA agent stationed outside your house was just gunned down." That got her attention.

"What was he doing there?"

"The assassin? Looking for you to kill."

"Not the assassin, the agent."

"Protecting you." Smith saw dismay race across Nolan's face.

"I didn't ask for any protection."

Smith leaned forward. "Let's just say for the sake of argument that you, an account executive at an investment house, have enough survival acumen to outwit a paid, trained assassin. If that's true, then kudos to you, but while you're making the world safe for financial advisors, the rest of us need a little information. Like why is Dattar gunning for you?" The computer beeped and Nolan directed her attention back to it. "Touch that device and I'm going to throw it out the window." Smith spoke in a conversational tone of voice. He watched the color rise in Nolan's face.

"You're a regular caveman, aren't you? Threats are your first line of defense."

"Answer the question."

She downed the remaining coffee in the cup and dropped it onto the saucer, making a clattering sound.

"I stole his money."

Smith couldn't help it; he gaped at her. Her computer beeped and she slid her eyes to it, but didn't reach for it. A million questions ran through his mind, but the beep reminded him of where he was, and that where they sat was not safe. They needed to keep moving. He stood.

"We have to go." She shook her head, and the mulish expression he'd learned meant that she was going to refuse settled onto her face. Before she could respond he leaned over, bringing his lips close to her ear. "You're sitting in the window. One shot to your brain and you're dead." Nolan glanced to the pane before returning to look at him. She raised an eyebrow.

"*I'm* not dead, you are. He won't kill me." She folded the computer back into its holder and shoved it into her tote. During the whole maneuver Smith noticed that she remained calm.

Misplaced calm, Smith thought. "What makes you think that?"

She rose and moved next to him, so close that he could see the lighter flecks of brown in her dark eyes and smell the perfumed scent of rose and something else that wafted from her.

"Because only I know where the money is. He kills me, he'll never find it again. And if there's one thing I've learned about people like Dattar, it's that money reigns supreme."

Her audacity astonished him. And her foolishness. But she was right. Dattar wouldn't kill her until he recovered his cash. He would kidnap her and torture her until she told him where it was. Smith decided to fill her in on the breadth of her stupidity.

"You're right, Dattar won't kill you. He'll do to you what he did to a health minister of his who had the nerve to urge vaccination for the helpless children under Dattar's control. He'll arrange for his henchmen to kidnap you, then peel off your skin piece by piece."

Nolan's eyes widened in horror. "I've read everything I can about Dattar and I know he's an animal, but I never heard a thing about any health minister dying. How come the media didn't report such an atrocity?"

"Because the man was rescued before he died. By me. Let me know how long you hold out." Smith snapped his fingers. "Oh, sorry. I didn't mean that. You won't be around to tell me, because once you explain to your torturer exactly where the money is, he'll finish you off."

Smith turned on his heel and headed to the door. He figured she'd follow him now. Even she wouldn't be stupid enough to believe she could outsmart Dattar's assassins now that she knew the full extent of the man's depravity. As he swung the door open, he glanced back and watched her disappear through the door that led to the hotel.

She was gone.

21

SMITH FOUGHT THE URGE to run through the café, charge into the hotel, grab her by the hair and shake her. Instead he pulled out his phone and called Marty.

"I found her right where you said she was," Smith said.

"I know," Marty responded. He sounded peeved. "You made her stop trading, didn't you?"

"You bet I did."

"Two of her calls expired at a deficit. If you hadn't interfered, I bet she would have covered the loss." Marty's voice sounded accusatory.

Smith turned onto Broadway and kept moving, his eyes sweeping the area for suspicious activity.

"Now you're on her side? She needs to agree to protective custody until Dattar is recaptured."

"They won't let her trade from there, you know that. No phones and no Internet so she can't be tracked. What would happen to her positions during that time?" Smith was starting to understand Nolan's confidence in the power of money. Even Marty seemed to think it mattered more than her life.

"A lot less than what would happen if she died. Forget about the trading. She took off again. Can you continue to track her for me?"

"As long as her computer remains on I can."

"That's enough for now. Stay with her. I'll call you back shortly."

Smith hung up and called Russell. "I found her again."

"Great. I'll meet you both back at the safe house."

"But she took off."

There was a silence. "Let me get this straight. You lost her *again?*"

Smith sighed. "I'll tell you all about it at the safe house. Twenty minutes." Once again Smith hit the subway, this time headed uptown. Twenty minutes later he was back at the CIA's brownstone. He found Russell in the living room sitting at the desk against a far wall, typing furiously at the computer placed there. She turned to face him, and he was shocked to see that she was paler than before and her face glowed with sweat.

"You look terrible. Are you getting sicker?"

Russell nodded. "I am."

"I don't like it. That swab must have gotten to you."

She sighed. "I called the bomb detection expert. He was close to the swab while we analyzed the refrigerator's interior and he's fine. I think it's the regular flu. At least I hope it is." She gave him a wan smile and waved him to the couch. "Tell me what happened. How'd you lose her?"

"She bolted and I let her go. Marty's tracking her through the GPS chip in her computer and can continue to do so as long as it remains on."

Russell frowned. "And if she turns it off. What then?"

Smith snorted. "Trust me, she won't. She won't want to miss a moment of stock market activity. This woman lives to trade."

"The market's closed."

"But Japan is opening. She'll leave it on, believe me. And there's more. I know why Dattar's after her. She says she stole his money." Russell remained silent, then a smile spread across her face and she started laughing.

"Oh my God, that's *great.*"

Smith sighed. He had expected a lot of responses from Russell, but her enthusiasm for Nolan's brainless act was not one of them. He was starting to wonder if everyone he knew was losing their minds.

"You know she's as good as dead once he gets his hands on her."

Russell sobered. "Why did you let her go?"

"She refused to cooperate, so I've decided to use her as bait. Track her through the GPS and stay back far enough until Dattar's man makes his move. Then grab him, hopefully before he grabs her."

Russell nodded. "It's a worthwhile idea, but I'd take it one step further. Let Dattar's man grab her and follow them both back to the hiding spot and monitor communications. Eventually the guy will contact Dattar to obtain instructions and we'll be able to follow the transmission."

Smith didn't like Russell's use of the term "eventually." "He could decide to torture her first before calling Dattar. We can't just let that happen."

"Let's worry about that once we're in the situation. Are you going to track her?"

Smith shook his head. "I was hoping one of your agents could take the job. How's Beckmann doing on the search for Howell? I need him more than ever if I'm going to locate Dattar and, frankly, Ms. Nolan and I don't get along."

"I've already put another officer in front of her apartment, but I can switch it up if you'd like. Do you think a CIA officer will have better luck convincing her to come in?"

Smith sighed. "Probably not." He shook his head. "Never mind. I'll track her and try one more time to knock some sense into her. If you hear anything about Howell, let me know. I really need him." Russell stood, swaying.

Smith frowned. "You should rest."

Russell waved him off, took one step, and began to crumple. Smith grabbed her before she hit the floor. He lifted her up and placed her gently on the couch. Her breath came in short gasps and she was sweating profusely. Her body started to jerk and her legs contracted in a spasm. Smith heard the front door open and close and Harcourt stepped into the room.

"Call an ambulance," Smith said. He sat next to her on the couch and felt her head, which was cold to the touch. He checked her pulse.

Russell opened her eyes. "I think I'm going to throw up." She struggled to rise.

"Stay down." Smith ran to the small bathroom off the entrance hall and grabbed the wastebasket. He carried it to the side of the couch.

"You feel sick, just lean over and use this."

Russell eyed the bucket. "This feels much worse than the flu. Almost like food poisoning."

Smith heard the wail of a siren in the distance. Harcourt appeared next to him.

"That ours, you think?" Smith said.

"I hope so." Harcourt crouched down next to Russell's head. "I have an ambulance on the way. Don't worry."

Russell gave a slight nod. The wailing grew louder.

"I'm going out front to direct them here," Harcourt said. Smith heard him run down the hall stairs.

"Hang on," Smith said.

"What if it is the refrigerator smear?" Russell said. Smith didn't want to answer her. If it wasn't the cholera, then it would have been the H1N5. Avian flu was so virulent that he didn't want to consider the possibility. Harcourt appeared at his side.

"It's ours. They're bringing up a stretcher."

"Don't let them see you," Russell said to Smith.

He held her hand, giving it a brief squeeze. He nodded to Harcourt and jogged up the stairs to the same window that Nolan had used. As he climbed out onto the fire escape, he heard the clumping sound of feet on the lower floors. He ran down the stairs, feeling like the fugitive that he was.

22

MANHAR CROUCHED IN THE CORNER of the stinking utility closet and pressed his eye against the small space created by the open door. He'd cracked it an inch in order to see when the Englishman left the hotel room. The closet smelled of industrial cleaner and mold. A nearby washing pail gave off the ammonia odor and the spaghetti mop shoved inside it added the mildew top note. A cockroach scuttled past him in the darkened space, and Manhar reached out and crushed it with the plastic dustpan that leaned against the wall. Manhar hated New York, with its crowding and bugs and air filled with the smell of animal fat stewing in the hot dog carts. He wanted to finish off the Englishman and get on the next flight to Pakistan. He hoped Dattar's weapon would kill everyone quickly. Manhar saw no value to be gained from America's continued existence.

The door at the end of the hall creaked open and a man stepped out. He was slender, rangy, and in his fifties. He had the craggy, thin face of the stereotypical inbred Englishman and Manhar thought that he would be easy to kill. Manhar was the same build, but he was in his twenties and he clutched a gun that made the attack all that much easier. The Englishman appeared to be unarmed. The man turned to lock the door and Manhar rose, crossed the threadbare carpet and reached the Englishman in three quick strides. He shoved the metal gun tip into the man's lower back and felt him freeze.

"Get back inside," Manhar said. The man didn't reply, but turned the key and opened the door. Manhar stepped in tandem with him as he reentered the room. Once inside, Manhar kicked the door shut. The cheap pressed-wood panel shook on impact with the jamb. Noise would travel easily through the paper-thin walls. Whatever he did, it would have to occur quietly or the other guests would hear, though Manhar thought that the types who would reside in such a filthy, dilapidated hotel might be inclined to ignore any criminal activity.

The shabby room held a bed with a sagging mattress, a chair with upholstery fraying at the arms, and a round coffee table with water ring stains. The tiny kitchenette had a small two-cup coffeepot and a toaster oven on its narrow counter. A white range, its burner pans covered with aluminum foil, and a small refrigerator were the only appliances in the room. The gray linoleum floor was grimy in the corners. Manhar saw that the stove was gas and an idea formed.

"May I turn around?" The Englishman sounded calm. Too calm, Manhar thought.

"Stay still and put your arms up." The man did as he was told and Manhar frisked him, checking for a weapon and finding none. "Now get over to the bed." The Englishman walked to the bed and slowly turned until they were face to face. He lifted an eyebrow.

"You're older than I expected."

Manhar felt the first stirring of alarm at the words "than I expected." He decided to finish things fast. Something about the man's blazing, intelligent eyes and detached manner made him seem lethal despite his lack of a weapon. Manhar shook off the thought. The man was old, after all. No danger. No danger at all.

"Shut up. Lay down face-first on the bed." Manhar didn't have a silencer and so would be required to shove a pillow against the man's head and shoot through that. He'd done it before and found that it worked well enough. As the Englishman began to lower himself to the mattress, Manhar shot another look at the range. He backed up to it, keeping his gun trained on the bed. When he reached the stove, he placed a hand on it and pulled. It didn't move. He needed help.

"Stop," Manhar said. The Englishman reversed off the bed and once again gazed at Manhar, who waved at the stove with the gun. "Get over here and pull this away from the wall." The man flicked a glance at the appliance.

"Why?"

"Just do it," Manhar said. He kept his gun at the ready. The man shrugged.

"I'm Peter Howell. And you are?"

"The man who's going to kill you. Now shut up and pull the stove away from the wall." Howell shrugged again and Manhar felt his anger rising at this deliberate display of nonchalance. He watched as Howell placed a hand on the back of the stove, another on the front handle, and strained. The heavy steel body shifted, scraping across the floor. For an old man he was strong, Manhar thought. Howell stopped when the range sat two feet from the wall. "Why are you stopping? Keep going."

"Keep going where? My back's already against the wall." In fact Howell was sandwiched between the equipment and the edge of the opposite counter in the tiny galley kitchenette.

Manhar stepped aside. "Get back on the bed."

Howell slid out and strolled back toward the small sleeping area. "Face-first again, I assume?" His voice was amused.

"Yes."

Once Howell was prone, Manhar focused on the stove, reaching behind it and yanking on the gas line. He pulled it free and instantly smelled the unique odor. He smiled. His plan to cover the crime was good. They'd find a dead guy on the bed in a fleabag hotel that explodes from a gas leak. He returned his attention to the Englishman.

Howell was standing up, with his own gun aimed at Manhar's heart. For a moment Manhar was disoriented by the speed with which control of the situation had shifted. Panic made his stomach clench. He'd never

faced down a man with a gun before because he'd always taken his victims by surprise, sometimes simply shooting them in the back. He felt
himself begin to perspire and sweat trickled down his face.

"A bit of advice: always get your victim away from their mattress.
Untold numbers of people hide their guns underneath. Me included,"
Howell said. Manhar started breathing fast while he gauged what would
happen if he shot Howell first. Howell shook his head. "I can see what
you're thinking and I don't advise it. I'll certainly be able to get my own
shot off as well, and you're near the open gas line. It's entirely possible that a spark from your gun will blow us both up. Now move toward
the door slowly. We're going to leave here and find a nice quiet place to
talk."

"Why? You can't shoot either."

Howell looked unmoved. "Oh, but I can. I'm not as close to the gas
leak as you are and as long as my bullet sinks into your flesh, I'm fairly
certain that the room will hold together long enough for me to leave."

Manhar hesitated. Perhaps Howell was right. He could hear the gas
flowing out of the tube's mouth and the smell was growing stronger, but
Howell stood a good six feet away. Before he could decide what to do,
there was a knock on the door. If Howell was surprised at the interrup-
tion, he didn't show it. He took two steps back, which took his body out
of the direct line to the entrance.

"Who is it?" he said. The door swung open and a man stepped into
the room. Tall, slender, with close-cropped hair and an angular face, he
stood still and took in the scene. Manhar saw a lock-picking device in
the man's right hand and a gun in his left. The man focused on Howell.

"Thank you for not shooting me through that worthless door," he said.

Howell chuckled. "Why, Herr Beckmann, how nice to see you again.
When was it last? Prague?"

Beckmann's lips turned up in a slight smile. "Isle of Man. As I recall,
you were busy depositing money in your offshore account." He looked
around. "But you were considerably better housed there. This room is
depressing. And you appear to have a gas leak."

Howell nodded. "My friend here and I were just leaving."

Beckmann eyed Manhar. "Ah, this one looks healthy for a change. Let's hope he doesn't fall over. I've been searching diligently for a living one to beat some answers out of. Leave it to you to find one that's still breathing."

"He found me. A feat that I doubt he managed on his own."

"Who does he work for?"

"Khalil, I believe," Howell said.

Beckmann frowned. "That's sobering news. Khalil is extremely dangerous."

Howell nodded. "Whatever is going on, it's very big trouble."

The smell of the gas was beginning to overwhelm Manhar and he staggered. In the next instant his legs gave out and he slammed onto the floor. The last thing he heard before falling unconscious was Howell, who said, "First the mattress mistake, then a little gas and he's down. These young terrorists lack any training whatsoever."

23

S MITH CALLED OHNARA the moment his feet hit the ground. He
heard the scientist's voice and plunged right in.

"Ms. Russell just fell ill with symptoms that resemble food poisoning
or worse; cholera or bird flu. My concern is that the swab we brought
you caused it. Any news on the cholera strain?"

"Yes. Our water filtration system handled it beautifully. Not a bit survived. And more good news, the virus died upon contact with the air
almost immediately. I doubt that what Ms. Russell has is from the swab,
but if you're concerned they can run a check on both diseases at the
hospital. Also you might do well to check on what she's eaten in the last
twenty-four hours."

Smith hung up, puzzled, but relieved. Perhaps Russell had a run-of-
the-mill influenza virus. His next call was to Marty.

"Still have a lead on her?"

Marty didn't miss a beat. "Hotel on Park Avenue South." He gave the
address. "She's using their Internet. I can't tell if she's checked in or just
sitting in the lobby."

Well, at least she's still alive, Smith thought. "Trading?"

"No. Japan isn't open yet. She's researching."

"Researching what?"

"You."

"Me? Are you sure?"

Marty chuckled. "I'm sure. She's typed in your name on three different search engines and read everything she can find. Which isn't much, because, as you may recall, *I* was the one who washed the Internet clean of your presence." Now Marty sounded quite pleased with himself. "She's only getting the newest hits that show you hanging from the hotel room window."

"I'm heading her way." This time Smith hailed a cab. He needed a moment to think about Russell and what she could have contracted so suddenly.

He found Nolan in the lobby of a boutique hotel on Park Avenue. What he also saw in the lobby gave him pause. Two men, one reading the *Wall Street Journal* and another at the public computer set up for guest use, gave the definite air of inauthenticity. Neither the men nor Nolan saw him enter, which was for the best. He stepped deeper into a connecting hallway, where he could still watch them but stay out of the open. Watching the three gave Smith an idea. He rang Marty again.

"You there? Do you see her?" Marty said.

"I do. There's a man using a dedicated computer in the lobby for guests. Can you hack into it? Tell me what he's doing?"

"Give me a minute. I'll call you right back."

Smith hung up and continued to watch Nolan. She typed furiously. The man reading the paper turned the page in a leisurely fashion, but as he did, he also made a quick, professional scan of the lobby.

I'm on to you, Smith thought.

His phone vibrated. "Tell me," Smith said.

"Get her and get out of there. Now." Marty's voice sounded strained.

"Why?"

"He's just told a contact named 'Khalil' that a bomb in the hotel is set to go off in seven minutes."

The man at the computer stopped typing, directed his attention to Nolan and removed a gun from underneath his shirt. Smith grabbed his own weapon and bolted into the lobby, heading straight for the computer. The man jerked to standing, knocking over his chair. Out of the corner of Smith's eye he saw the paper-reading accomplice rise. Smith shot the man at the computer in the right shoulder and immediately turned his attention to the other man. He saw the newspaper flutter to the floor, and light glinted off a gun in the man's hand. The desk clerk screamed in the distance, but Smith barely heard it. His senses were dulled while he stared in supreme concentration at the gun. Smith had been shot at before, had been in near-death situations before, and in every instance this single-minded focus occurred. In his peripheral vision he noted that Nolan had risen to her feet. Smith fired again, and this time the newspaper man acted in tandem. Smith saw the muzzle flash and felt the bullet sink into his left arm. Smith's assailant dropped with a bullet in his heart. There were more screams but these were from a group of women sitting in the corner who had escaped Smith's attention. He'd been so wrapped up in Nolan and the men who were tailing her that the rest of the lobby's inhabitants hadn't registered. When Smith glanced back at the computer, the first accomplice was gone.

"Clear the hotel, there's a bomb," Smith yelled at the lone front desk employee still at his post, a wild-eyed young man in his mid-twenties.

"I called the police! You can tell it to them," the man said.

Smith stalked to the counter. "Listen to me very carefully. There's a bomb in this building. Those two planted it. Activate the fire alarm. You need to evacuate. Now. You have," Smith looked at his watch, "five minutes." The young man's mouth was open and he was gasping. He took a step backward.

"Don't shoot me," he said. Before Smith could respond, Nolan slipped past on his right, ran to the wall and pulled at the fire alarm mounted there. An intense shrieking filled the lobby. Smith holstered his gun and started searching the area. He pulled back the leaves of a potted tree next to the counter, found nothing, and moved to an armchair pushed against the wall. He crouched down to look under it. When he stood again he was momentarily dizzy. Blood flowed down his arm and dripped onto the carpeting.

The elevator doors opened and a crowd of people stumbled out of it. So many that Smith wondered how they all fit. He heard the young desk clerk yelling into a phone "They're not supposed to be using the elevator!" The lobby filled with panicked people, all pushing toward the entrance. One caught sight of the dead terrorist and started screaming over and over and a man next to her dragged her away. Smith fought through the line of evacuees toward Nolan, who was moving along the lobby perimeter in her own search. She knelt down to peer behind a sofa against a bank of windows.

Smith grabbed his phone and dialed Klein. He was glad the number was set to speed dial, because he was becoming increasingly woozy. By the time Klein answered, Smith was across the lobby and next to Nolan.

"I need a bomb expert, fast," Smith said.

"Of course. Where?" Klein's calm voice flowed through the receiver. Smith glanced at his watch.

"I have to find it first, but if I do, then I'll have less than four minutes to disarm it. Can you get someone to talk me through it?"

"Stay on the line," Klein said. Smith switched his phone to speaker and joined Nolan in her search. She reached out a hand to move back a heavy curtain. He put his own on her arm to stay her.

"Very gently. It could be motion activated."

Nolan gave him a piercing glance, but paused. She shifted closer to the curtain and slid her entire arm between the window and the fabric. She used the arm as a lever to pull the curtain away. Smith looked down.

An improvised explosive device was nestled next to the baseboard. Smith heard Nolan exhale a shaky breath. He lowered to the ground and put his phone on the carpet to free up his hands. His blood dripped next to it, the loss causing his eyes to blur for a moment, and he blinked furiously.

Three black wires led from the bomb to a cheap cell phone that was set to display an alarm clock. The display was at two minutes fifty-six seconds and clicking downward.

"This is Ben Washington. I'm an explosives expert. Can you hear me over that fire alarm?" Smith almost jerked in surprise when he heard the voice coming from his cell phone.

"I can," Smith said.

"Tell me what you see."

"An IED wired to a cell phone. Three wires, all black. Cell phone is counting down. We're at two minutes."

"Okay. You've got time. Just clip the wires to the phone. All three. Without the spark it won't detonate as long as you are very gentle with it. You understand? No crazy motions. You know if you're being watched?" Smith glanced at Nolan, who looked around the now empty lobby and shook her head.

"Not sure. One got away."

"Because if you are, they can simply call the phone and set it off immediately. It starts to ring and you get the hell out of there. Got it?"

"Got it." Smith looked around for something to clip the wires.

"Scissors," Nolan said. She sprinted across the lobby and Smith heard her demanding a pair from the clerk who was at the door preparing to leave. He didn't watch her though. His wound was a freakish pain that made his entire arm feel like someone was repeatedly stabbing it with a knife. Sweat formed on his forehead and he watched the timer click downward. They'd lost thirty more seconds while Nolan was scrambling for a tool.

Nolan returned and shoved a pair of scissors at him. He positioned the first wire between the open blades and cut. The timer displayed fifty-nine seconds when Smith angled the scissors in order to reach the second wire. This one was short and attached to something that Smith thought was a detonator cap. Reaching this wire was trickier due to its length, and Smith lost twenty more seconds while he maneuvered the tip into place. He snapped the wire. He shifted once again to gain access to the third wire. By now he was sweating freely and a sticky combination of blood and sweat peppered the floor.

The phone shivered on the carpet and the display lit up.

Smith leaped backward, pulling Nolan with him. He staggered with her weight as she stumbled. Smith could hear the phone start to ring over the still blaring fire alarm and smoke poured from the bomb. He turned and ran, holding on to Nolan's arm while dragging her to the entrance.

Seconds before they hit the glass revolving door Smith remembered Washington's warning about being watched. He yanked Nolan to the floor as two holes appeared in the glass right where his head had been only seconds before.

"It's an ambush. Get out the back," Smith said. Nolan nodded and regained her feet and ran to the lobby's far end. The bomb continued smoking, but still hadn't exploded. Smith could hear the scream of fire sirens growing louder. Nolan peeled off to the left and snatched her satchel off the chair, then corrected and ran to the narrow hallway where Smith had lurked not five minutes earlier. Smith hustled behind her through the hallway toward a door marked "Employees Only." When they reached it, Nolan veered left into another hall. Smith saw a door marked "Exit" at the far end. He and Nolan pounded through it, ignoring the warnings that claimed an alarm would sound. The door closed and Smith followed Nolan onto a side street, coming even with her.

"Stay on my left, can you? I don't want any passerby to see the blood," Smith said.

Nolan glanced down. "It's bad. You need to get to a hospital."

Smith shook his head and kept moving. "Can't. Too many questions when a gunshot wound is treated." He moved in close to her, twining his arm through hers and using it to cover the wound on his. To the world they looked like a couple, their arms linked, taking a stroll. In reality he needed her support, because the pain and dizziness were coming in waves and threatening to engulf him.

Nolan snorted. "Afraid of the authorities? I thought you *were* one."

Smith turned left and crossed the street, all the while scanning for the computer man from the lobby.

"Is your tablet in that satchel you're carrying? Was it really worth detouring to get it? The bomb could have gone off in that time." Nolan shot him a quick look, but said nothing. He saw that her knuckles turned white as she clutched the bag closer. Smith kept moving, thinking. His arm needed treatment, fast, he needed to debrief Nolan and discover why she'd foolishly stolen Dattar's money, and he needed to connect with Beckmann about Howell. He silently cursed himself for not letting the computer assailant grab her, as it was clear the terrorist had intended, and then follow them both, but using her as a pawn bothered him. This time he was determined to get some answers from her. He kept walking.

"Where are we going?" Nolan said.

"I'm not sure. Someplace safe. I need a place to rest, work on this wound, and we need to talk."

"We don't need to talk."

"Do you think you could cooperate? For a short while? I just saved your life. I think you owe me." The pain in his arm was unbearable. He wasn't sure that he could take much more and stay upright. He staggered. Nolan grabbed his arm, and he groaned at the pain her touch evoked.

"Give me your phone and tell me who to call for you," Nolan said.

That was a good question, Smith thought. Normally he'd rely on Russell, but she was in no condition herself to help him. Klein would find a safe location for Smith to hole up, but Smith didn't want to call his line too often. If the authorities refused the CIA's request to ignore Smith in response to the receptionist's death, then they would be tracking him the same way he tracked Nolan: through his cell phone. He'd have to toss this one and get a prepaid. Until then, the fewer calls to Klein the better.

"There's no one," Smith said. Nolan gave him a strange look, but Smith was in too much pain to try to analyze what she was thinking.

"No wife? Children? Parents? Siblings?"

Smith shook his head.

Now Nolan stared at him in open disbelief. "Best friend? Colleague at work?"

"I told you. No."

"I don't believe that."

Smith gritted his teeth against another wave of pain. "Listen. We can discuss my complete lack of close personal relationships some other time. Right now we need a safe place to land." They crossed another street, and Smith felt Nolan steering him toward a glass door covered by a red awning.

"Fine. Then let's go here," Nolan said. As they reached the entrance a doorman stepped out and held it for them. He nodded at Nolan.

"Good to see you, Ms. Nolan." He gave Smith a penetrating glance and acknowledged him. Nolan headed straight to an elevator. Once inside she removed her arm from Smith's grasp and pressed a code on a separate keypad on the wall and then the button marked "PH." She stepped aside.

"May I ask where we're going?" Smith said.

"My mother's house."

"Can she keep a secret?"

Nolan shook her head. "Not if her life depended on it. But she's not here. She's in Paris for the couture shows."

"Who's your mother?"

"Grayson Redding."

Smith watched as the elevator lights climbed higher than the third floor. His anxiety rose along with the lift. He pulled his attention away from the display long enough for the name she had mentioned to register. He gave a low whistle.

"Of the railroad and utility fame?"

Nolan nodded.

"If you're a Redding, how is it that you were so difficult to find on the Internet when I was searching for you? I would think the society pages would be filled with your face."

"I told you, Landon Investments values privacy and confidentiality. We have a policy that requires us to be as discreet as possible. As well as an IT specialist who scrubs the Internet on a regular basis. I kept my married name after my divorce and that has helped, too." The elevator made a pinging sound and the doors whooshed open directly into the residence. Smith stepped into a lavish, marbled hall with several doors leading off in different directions.

"Does she occupy the entire floor?"

Nolan tossed her keys into a glass bowl on an elaborately carved antique credenza that Smith figured cost more than his yearly salary.

"She does. And the staff is on vacation as well, so we're alone. Come into the master bath. She keeps the first aid there." Smith reached out and put a hand on her arm to stop her from leaving.

"I assume that an apartment as magnificent as this has an alarm system?"

"It does."

"Set it, please."

"Now?"

Smith nodded. "Right now."

Nolan returned to the wall near the elevator and tapped some keys on a keypad. Smith heard the system give an answering beep as it armed, and he felt a little of the tension leave his body. The pain was steady, but the bleeding had tapered a bit.

"I'll need some tweezers, a bowl filled with a mixture of alcohol and water, a washcloth, and some bandages."

"Who's going to use the tweezers?"

"You."

Nolan sighed. He followed her through a hall lined with wallpaper that looked like silk and past open doors that gave him glimpses of a game room as well as a library. Smith thought the apartment lavish, but was having a difficult time with the fact that it was on the sixth floor and so vast that a man could run through it without being heard. They would not remain long there if he could help it.

He entered a bathroom that gave testament to the long history of money accumulated by generations of Reddings. It was larger than his kitchen at home. Quite a feat in the heart of New York City. Nolan fished around in a linen closet and removed the items he had requested. She pulled up a small stool padded in white leather and pointed him to it, positioning him in front of the first sink in the double vanity. He glanced in the mirror in front of him and was shocked to see that he was pale and drawn, with heavy pain lines bracketing his mouth.

"What's first?"

"Help me out of this shirt. If I can't get out, then we'll cut it off." He started to roll the shirt from the bottom, and Nolan reached over to assist. Some of his blood dripped next to her.

"Sorry," he said. She waved him off.

"I'll be right back."

She disappeared, and Smith continued to bunch up the shirt. He was able to remove his right arm and maneuvered the fabric over to his neck. Pulling it the rest of the way was not as easy, because it strained against the wound. He winced at the first try and decided to wait until she returned. She stepped back into the bathroom wearing dark jeans and a V-neck navy sweater. Her feet were bare.

"Better," he said. "I won't feel as bad when I drip blood on you."

"Let me help." With her assistance, they were able to get the shirt over his head without causing too much pain. He only hissed once, when she pulled the bits of fabric that had crusted to the wound.

"Is it awful?"

"Not yet. 'Awful' will arrive when you start to dig out the bullet."

She took a deep breath. "How do you want me to sterilize the tweezers?"

"In the alcohol full strength. No dilution." He watched as she poured the alcohol over the tweezers.

"Does this kill everything?"

"Everything that reacts to alcohol."

"What doesn't?"

"Biofilms."

She gave him a glance and stepped closer. "What are those?"

"Bacteria that colonize and become so strong that nothing kills them.

Not even bleach. They have to be scraped away. The plaque on your teeth is a biofilm."

"I can see the bullet easily. Are you ready?"

Not at all. "Yes," he said.

She started in. He felt first the cold metal and then a lancing pain that made him groan involuntarily. She moved the tweezers a bit more and he could feel his entire body responding to the pain of this newest assault. The muscles in his arms clenched tight. His ears started to ring and his head to swim. She removed the tweezers and took a deep breath.

"I can't reach it without first expanding the wound around it. Here." She gave him a towel.

"What's this for?" he said.

"You're sweating. Round two. You ready?"

He nodded.

She put the tweezers in and the same lancing pain began. She expanded the tweezers and he felt the entire room spin. He passed out.

24

SMITH WOKE UP LYING flat on his back on the carpeted floor of one of the rooms in the apartment. A pillow had been placed under his head. From the complete darkness he assumed it was night. He heard sounds of the city rolling by outside, but nothing else. His left arm throbbed in a steady pulse to match his pumping heart, but the extreme, ice-pick pain had subsided. Next to his head came the buzzing sound of his cell phone and a small glow lit the area to his right. Smith managed to grab it with his right hand and answer without moving off the floor.

"Mr. Smith? This is Jana Wendel. I work with Ms. Russell. Can you meet me at the hospital? And please, don't tell anyone about this call." Wendel was whispering into the phone. Smith sat up and the small throw that someone had placed over him fell off. He groaned as his left arm reacted with renewed pain. "Are you all right?"

"I'll be fine. Why are you whispering?"

"Just meet me at the loading dock." She gave him the directions and hung up.

Smith hauled himself to his feet. He was shirtless. A white gauze bandage was wrapped around his left bicep. In the gloom he saw that he was next to a billiard table. He went to the wall and switched on the overhead light, blinking in the sudden glare, and was happy to see his jacket and a shirt lying on the ground next to the pillow. He went back and retrieved both. The shirt wasn't his, but was a man's dress shirt in light blue chambray that buttoned up the front.

Thank God I don't have to lift it over my head, Smith thought. He shrugged into it and headed to the hallway. He moved quietly, glancing into each doorway that he passed. He kept going to the kitchen, glanced around, and retraced his steps to the front door. The apartment was dark, quiet, and empty. Nolan was gone. The alarm display read OFF.

Smith hated the idea that he'd been lying unconscious in the vast apartment with an unarmed security system, but he supposed that she had no choice but to disarm it. Either that or leave him a note with the code and instructions. He already knew enough about Nolan to determine that she would never trust him to such an extent. He hit the elevator button and stepped onto it. While he rode the elevator down, he called Klein.

"I know why Dattar's after her," Smith said. "She stole his money."

Klein was silent for a moment. "How ingenious. He was sentenced to life in prison. Had he not escaped, it would have been unlikely that he would have ever been able to regain the funds."

"And now he's gunning for her."

"Whatever he's doing about her, it sounds as though it has nothing to do with the coolers. Do you have any further ideas on where they might be?"

"I still think that Dattar has them. Russell and I are using her as bait to flush him out. When we do, we'll get that information."

"Excellent," Klein said.

"Also, I'm a person of interest in the NYPD's investigation of the Landon Investments killing. I've been able to dodge them so far."

"Let's see if they issue a warrant. If they do, then we'll deal with it. I'll monitor the situation until then."

He found Jana Wendel pacing outside the hospital's loading dock, holding a cigarette that she put to her lips. Smith strolled up to her, doing his best to appear relaxed and nonchalant. She spotted him and took another puff.

"You need to inhale if you intend to look like a real smoker," Smith said. "Are you Ms. Wendel?" Wendel nodded and gave him a rueful look.

"I hate them, but it was the only thing I could think of that would allow me to hang out here without appearing to lurk."

"How's Russell?"

"Sleeping. They have her on an IV drip for dehydration."

"Is it cholera?"

Wendel shook her head. "No. She asked them to check for that first and the avian flu virus second. Quick results showed that it's not E. coli or salmonella, but indicated a possible variant of bird flu."

Wendel's words hit Smith in the gut, but he did his best to keep his face impassive. He must have failed because Wendel gave him a piercing look filled with worry.

"You looked grim just then. I know bird flu is dangerous, but I haven't had time to check the statistics. What are her odds?"

"The average virulent pandemic virus can kill up to fifteen percent of those infected."

Wendel looked thoughtful. "That's bad, but I imagine we're talking about the very young and the very old, right? She's neither, and really strong."

"Bird flu is *not* the average virulent virus. It's like a terrible virus on steroids. It kills fifty percent of infected persons, and the age of the victim doesn't seem to be a mitigating factor."

Wendel swallowed. "So far they're not ready to confirm that it's the bird flu, but she seems to be getting sicker. They're running some more tests, and she's in isolation in the infectious disease area until they figure it out."

"Currently bird flu isn't easily transmitted from human to human." *Unless she has the mutated version.* Smith had the thought, but didn't voice it.

"Where is she?"

"Fourth floor. Room 422. No visitors allowed."

"Why did you need to see me?"

Wendel gave both sides of the street a quick glance. "Come with me into the hospital lounge. I need a Wi-Fi connection to show you."

Wendel tossed her cigarette into a sand-filled ashtray placed against the wall and headed to the hospital's rear door. They entered to a rectangular room with a bank of windows at the far end. The near side contained rows of vending machines offering snacks and drinks. Smith detoured straight to the one that held sandwiches. He fed some money into the machine, grabbed the sandwich that dropped into the vending tray, and joined her at a far table. She had a laptop open to the home page of a software application. He unwrapped the sandwich and nodded for her to begin. She took a deep breath.

"First, you need to know that what I'm going to tell you is confidential. Highly confidential. The only reason I'm showing you this is because Ms. Russell asked me to."

"Okay," Smith said. He watched the screen. It appeared to be a dashboard of a software aggregator for social media sites. Updates for the sites appeared in each column assigned to them. Wendel pointed to the updates for BLACKHAT254.

"These are from one of our agents. This column is the public site, and this column is the proprietary CIA site. I've previously told Ms. Russell that there's something wrong with the CIA site. It's lagging behind the public site." Smith watched the screen and saw that she was correct. BLACKHAT254's updates appeared on the public site but not immediately on the proprietary site.

"Is that a problem? You can always look at the public site."

"It seemed benign, and I didn't really worry until Jordan got shot. After he did, I went back and looked at the feed and saw something shocking. I have a screen shot of it." Wendel switched screens. The same dashboard appeared. She pointed to a line.

"This is what Jordan updated publicly ten minutes before he was shot and this is what appeared on the proprietary site seven minutes later. Moneywoman is our code name for Nolan and 'friend' is anyone that we think may be suspicious."

Smith read the public first. Jordan had written "Watching Moneywoman and see friend on corner of 72nd and Lexington." The proprietary site's line was dated seven minutes later and said, "Watching Moneywoman and see friend on corner of 72nd and Central Park West." Smith stopped chewing.

"They switched up the location. Put him all the way on the other side of the park."

Wendel nodded. "Most of the time on stakeouts the agents will only use the proprietary site. The display is almost instantaneous, so faster than a phone call has the advantage of silence. The agents can update each other without bystanders hearing them. I had asked Jordan to use the public site too until I could figure out what was causing the lag. We had another agent as backup for him around the corner, but he was only screening the proprietary site. Not only did that second agent get the information late, but once he saw the code 'friend' he took off *across* the park."

"And Jordan got shot. Is he still alive?"

"He is. They have him in an induced coma while they wait for the swelling in his brain to go down. Once it does they'll be able to assess the damage." Wendel swallowed and Smith noticed that her eyes gleamed with tears. She blinked them away.

"What did Russell say when you showed her this?"

"She told me that under no circumstances was I to take this to anyone at the agency. She said to find you, tell you about it, and said that you know someone who can search for the source."

She means Marty, Smith thought. "It isn't necessarily happening from within the agency, is it? Can someone from the outside be intercepting the feed and altering it before it gets to your proprietary site?"

Wendel got a dubious look on her face. "That's really doubtful. Yes, we use Wi-Fi, but we have the site encoded and password protected. I think we have to assume first that it's coming from within the CIA, and only then check outside possibilities."

Smith finished the sandwich, bunched up the plastic wrapper, and tossed it into a nearby garbage can.

"Keep Russell's phone on at all times. I'm going to have a man named Marty call you. He's the one Russell knows. He's a genius at computers. He has Asperger's syndrome so bear with his oddities, but he can't be beat for IT matters."

He rose to leave.

"I'll be checking in, but try not to call me unless it's absolutely imperative. Someone is tracking me, and I don't want to help him. I'll be shutting off my phone soon."

Wendel rose with him. Smith was glad to see the teary look replaced with one of determination. Wendel pushed through the exit doors and walked Smith back to the loading dock and smoking station. She put out her hand.

"Thank you for your help."

Smith returned the handshake. "Is there a way you can keep me apprised of Russell's condition? I'm worried about her."

Wendel nodded. "Watch BLACKHAT254 on the public site. I'll have him update on her status. In code, of course. Do you know her CIA cover name?"

Smith nodded. "I do. I'll look for it." Wendel disappeared into the hospital. He watched the door swing shut.

After a moment he headed in behind her. When he reached the lobby he consulted a directory and pinpointed the wing that contained the infectious disease patients. He stepped onto the elevator and hit the button. When he stepped out onto the fourth floor, he was in a long hall with rooms stretching on each side. To his left and twenty feet away was the nurses' station where a lone nurse typed on a computer keyboard. A sign on the wall directly opposite the elevator stated that the floor was secure and asked all visitors to check in. It also listed room numbers in each direction. The nurse looked up.

"Can I help you?" she said. He walked to the counter.

"I'm with the army's infectious disease unit." He handed her his USAMRIID identification. "I need to speak to your patient in room 422."

The nurse looked at his identification and then frowned. "This is the isolation floor. The only visitors allowed are her doctors or any consulting medical professionals."

"Which is what I am. I'm a doctor and I'm here on official business."

The nurse's face became set. "It's late. You'll need to return during regular hours and have the permission of her physician."

Smith leaned over the counter, picked up the phone, and handed it to the nurse. "Please page her doctor. Tell him or her that it's an emergency. That a doctor with the United States Army Medical Research Institute for Infectious Diseases requires immediate access to the patient."

The nurse hesitated. "It's really quite important. It can't wait," Smith said.

The nurse raised her eyebrows, took the phone and punched in a number. After a moment she said, "I have a doctor from the United States Army Medical Research Institute for Infectious Diseases that wants access to Ms. Russell." The nurse listened. "He says it's an emergency. I've seen his credentials." The nurse listened a moment more and then hung up.

"He says it's okay, but he wants you to keep it short." She held a clipboard out to him. "Sign in."

Smith filled out the roster and signed his name. "Thank you. Do I need to suit up?"

The nurse reached across the desk and handed him a flat packet wrapped in thin plastic. "It's a paper gown and mask."

Smith took the package and ripped it open. He shook out the paper gown, put it over his clothes and tied it at the neck. He put on the mask while he walked toward Russell's room.

Russell's small private room was decorated in soft blues and tans, which Smith thought gave it the air of a spa or hotel rather than a hospital. The bed, though, was all business; with metal bars lowered and an attached table that held a remote for the headboard and a television, and a plastic water glass. A nightstand had a small desk lamp. Smith took one more step in and came even with an open door that led into a private bathroom. He caught a glimpse of the sink and the edge of a shower curtain.

A small, glowing bar attached to the wall near the bed acted as a night light for the nurses. Shadows covered large sections of the wall and the only sound was the occasional drip of the liquid from the sink in the bathroom.

Smith walked up to the bed and stood next to a holder that held an IV drip. Russell lay against the pillows, her eyes closed. Smith caught his breath when he got the first look at her face. Her eyes were closed and her cheeks and forehead glowed with sweat. Her lips were cracked from dehydration. Her skin was gray. Whatever ran through her system, it had accelerated since he saw her last. Her eyes opened and she focused on him.

"Hey," she said in a weak voice. He settled next to her on the bed and took her hand. She tried to pull it away, but he tightened his grip. She frowned at him. "You shouldn't be here. I could be contagious."

"I'll wash my hands after. How do you feel?"

"Terrible. Feverish and unable to keep anything down. Even the ice chips." Smith looked at the water glass and saw that it was filled with ice.

"I understand it's not cholera?"

She shook her head. "No, but it may be bird flu. The initial report wasn't conclusive, though. Doctor said maybe a variant. It *has* to be related to that refrigerator swab. There is nothing else. It's connected. I know it."

"I also met with Wendel," Smith said. "She made it clear that you think there's a mole in the CIA."

Russell nodded. "Got to be. That proprietary system is ironclad. Whoever is messing with it has to know the codes."

"Any ideas?"

Russell shrugged. "I haven't been inside long enough to draw any real conclusions. Langley employs hundreds in my area alone, so finding the leak could be difficult. My thought was that Marty might be able to follow an electronic signature. Trace it back."

"Doesn't an internal investigation require you to tell your superiors?"

Russell shifted. "Technically, yes, but I smell a rat here and close by. Jordan only reports to a couple of people in my immediate area, and I think he was deliberately targeted so that Nolan's house would be left vulnerable."

Smith groaned. "You realize then that I can't use the safe house?"

"And neither can Nolan," Russell said.

"What about Beckmann? Can I trust him?"

Russell began to cough, a deep, barking cough. It was an ugly sound and told Smith everything he needed to know about the severity of her condition. She got hold of herself after a minute.

"He's on loan from another department, so maybe he's clean, but it's safest to be careful around him until you're sure."

"That leaves Howell as my best chance to survive this thing. Finding him will become my first priority. I'll get Marty to do his magic, but if he comes up empty, you could be arrested for releasing classified information, you know that, right?"

"I'll cross that bridge when I come to it. There's a mole in my area. I can feel it." Smith could see that she was getting agitated, and he didn't want to upset her any further.

"I agree that something is not adding up. I'll keep on it. Let's see what Marty can discover. In the meantime, you just concentrate on getting better."

She sighed. "I'll do my best."

When her eyes closed again, Smith rose from the bed and left the room as quietly as he had entered it.

Once he was sufficiently far from the hospital grounds, he removed the SIM card from his cell phone, put it in his pocket, and tossed the device. He headed to a drugstore, purchased a prepaid phone, and called Klein. He was inordinately relieved when the man answered on the first ring.

"I have a problem." Smith told Klein about Russell's concerns about a mole and Wendel's claim that someone had tampered with the technology systems inside Langley. "Does the CIA manage the White House configuration? If so, your conversations with the president could be at risk."

"They secure some of the information flow, of course. The president receives a daily briefing and a portion of that comes from Langley onto the White House's data stream. It's not inconceivable that whoever is hacking into the CIA grid could be accessing the president's conversations as well, but I highly doubt it. We have endless redundant systems designed to thwart such an occurrence."

"And Covert-One's? Possible?"

"Again, anything is possible, but I doubt it. And it would be your phone at risk because, while it's encrypted, it still uses the airwaves. They can't be secured as readily as dedicated phone lines. I notice that your number has changed. Did you buy a prepaid?"

"Yes. I'm headed to Nolan to debrief her on the Dattar matter. As soon as I know something I'll check in."

"Don't lose sight of the coolers. Unless she has vital information, debriefing her is a secondary consideration. And frankly, this new information about a mole has me convinced that Covert-One should take the lead on recovering them. Stay with it."

"Understood."

"But watch your back. A compromised CIA is extremely dangerous. The secrets they maintain can put this entire country at risk."

Smith took a deep breath. "Also understood."

25

MANHAR WOKE TO FIND HIMSELF tied to a metal girder that supported elevated tracks above his head. The cold steel chilled him from his neck to his ankles. Plastic handcuffs encircled his wrists, which were stretched behind him around the support. Other ties bound his ankles together, while even more wrapped around his legs just above the knees. There was one around his neck that cut into his throat every time he swallowed. He looked down and saw that in addition to the ties he was bound by rope around his waist and under his armpits. He twitched to test the hold and it was clear that he wasn't going anywhere without assistance. It was night, and the only light was a weak glow from a streetlight nearly thirty feet away. The area was deserted. Piles of trash lay in heaps under the tracks along with the occasional paper napkin thrown away by someone or blown by the wind.

He saw Howell standing five feet away thumbing away on a phone. Beckmann sat on the ground with his back against the metal girder opposite Manhar's. He smoked a cigarette, the tip glowing with each pull, and watched Manhar with a steady gaze.

"He's awake," Beckmann said.

Howell glanced up. "What's your name?" Manhar spit on the ground. Howell rolled his eyes. "Spare me the theatrics. I'm English and Mr. Beckmann here is German. We don't indulge in displays of emotion. Tell me your name or I'll beat it out of you." Howell shoved a toe at a metal pipe on the ground near his feet. The steel looked solid enough. Manhar decided that telling his name would be harmless.

"Manhar."

Howell nodded. "Well, Mr. Manhar, I want to know who hired you to kill me and how you are communicating with him or her."

Manhar snorted. That these two thought he'd simply divulge such things showed their stupidity. He spit on the ground again.

"Hmm. I thought that would be your answer. It really is quite short-sighted of you." Howell kept tapping on the phone. "Got it," he said to Beckmann.

Beckmann rose. "Excellent. Let's leave this one to him." He took another drag of the cigarette and then looked at his watch. "Don't forget to tell him about the pipe. He may want to use it." Manhar did his best to follow their cryptic conversation, but he had no idea what they were talking about. Howell pocketed the phone.

"We're off. Good luck to you," he said.

Manhar was astonished at his good fortune. They only intended to tie him to a post and leave him? He'd get free of the ropes eventually, and when he did he'd come after them. Next time he'd make them pay for humiliating him. He almost laughed out loud at the fools. Howell stepped closer and put up his phone.

"I'm taking a photo. Smile," Howell said. Manhar looked at the back of the device and a small prickling of premonition started at the back of his neck. "I'll send this to your colleague, Khalil, over an e-mail address that I believe he monitors. Of course I'll also give him your location. He'll be furious that you not only failed to kill me, but that you also managed to get yourself caught in the process. Khalil takes failure poorly, don't you think? Knowing Khalil the way I do, I suspect he'll be along shortly. I don't think that you'll enjoy these next few hours before your death."

Manhar felt fear surge through him. He'd expected a beating or worse from these two, but nothing they could dream up could possibly match what he knew of Khalil and his torture techniques. Still, Manhar clamped his mouth shut. Perhaps he could convince Khalil that he'd kept silent. Beckmann finished the cigarette and tossed the butt into a nearby oil drum.

"He'll start in right away. Khalil doesn't allow failures to live long." He looked at Manhar. "If you want to tell us now what you know, we'll untie you. Give you a fighting chance to save yourself." Beckmann shrugged. "I think it's a fair deal, don't you?"

A cool breeze blew and Manhar shivered. In that instant he decided to bargain. The idea of being tied to a post when Khalil started in on him was unimaginable.

"I don't know anything," Manhar blurted out. Beckmann shook his head, a sad look on his face.

"Send the e-mail," he said to Howell.

"Wait!" Manhar said. Howell paused, his eyebrows raised. "I'm telling the truth. Khalil told me nothing. Only that he intended to kill you, Smith, and another American."

"I've heard about the American. Who is it?"

Manhar shook his head. "I don't know."

Howell frowned. "I don't believe you." He looked back at his phone.

"Wait! It's a woman. That's all I know. But Khalil is in charge of Smith. He said he was hard to kill. I was to have you."

Howell looked outraged. "Khalil thinks I'm easier to kill than Jon Smith? I'm appalled."

Beckmann laughed, but suppressed it when Howell shot him a glance. "Sorry. You shouldn't take it personally. I haven't known Smith long but he seemed to be quite inventive in his techniques."

Howell waved a hand. "Well, he's overeducated so that's to be expected."

"Didn't you go to Cambridge before you joined MI6?" Beckmann said.

"Yes, but I had the good sense to stop once finished. Smith just kept going." Howell frowned and turned his attention back to Manhar. "Who's paying Khalil?"

Manhar shook his head. He'd told these fools all that he would. "I don't know."

In an instant Howell had the pipe in his hand and smashed it against Manhar's left knee. The speed of the attack and the shock of the extreme pain caused Manhar to scream. His knee felt like it was disintegrating. Manhar's eyes filled with water, but he still saw Howell swing the pipe backward in preparation for another blow.

"Dattar! He's the one paying." Manhar yelled the name at the top of his lungs. "Please, let me go. If you break my legs I can't run from Khalil."

Howell paused. "What's the plan?" Manhar's nose was running and his knee was in agony. At first he didn't understand the question.

"What do you mean?"

"You heard me. What's Dattar's plan?"

Manhar shook his head. "I don't know exactly. He has some sort of weapon that he's going to use against the US. He's proud of it. Says it's unbeatable."

Howell and Beckmann exchanged a glance. Manhar was trembling in pain. He'd told all he was able to tell, and he hoped they believed him.

"A bomb?"

Manhar groaned. "That's all I know. You said you'd let me go."

"Is it a bomb? Answer that question and we'll let you go."

Manhar shook his head. "No. I don't think it's a bomb. It's something else. Not a bomb."

"When?" Beckmann said.

"What time is it?" Manhar whispered the question. Howell looked at his phone.

"Ten thirty."

"In twenty-four hours," Manhar said.

26

S MITH DIDN'T WANT TO CALL Marty and ask him yet again to track down Nolan, but it was the most efficient way to locate her, so he swallowed his pride and dialed.

"Let me guess, you lost her again," Marty said. Smith felt his irritation rise, but he wasn't sure if it was at Marty's assumption or his own incompetence when it came to Nolan.

"How did you know?"

"She's trading. I figured you wouldn't let her."

"I take it Japan opened?"

"It did. But there's something else. She moved millions of dollars out of one account in the Cayman Islands to another, connected account in Antigua."

"Connected? To whom?"

"It's numbered only, so I can't be sure. I can tell you that it's fairly new. The first transaction was from a month ago and it came from an account of a wealthy individual in Pakistan."

Dattar's money, Smith thought. "Where is she?"

"Restaurant." Marty rattled off an address close to the Redding penthouse.

"I'm there. Call me if she moves."

The restaurant Nolan had chosen was a large eatery and marketplace that sold individual dishes, deli meats, and Italian food and was located in the Flatiron District across from Madison Square Park. He entered off Fifth Avenue and paused.

It was an ideal place for a hit.

The space was the size of a large warehouse and looked like a massive grocery store. The various locations sold produce and meat, and there were several restaurant sections. People, many of them tourists, were everywhere, and all were jostling to get near the section they desired. Smith could hear children crying, dining with their parents despite the late hour, and he cataloged the fact. An attacker could materialize out of the crowd, shoot, and disappear back into the masses of people. Smith wouldn't be able to fire back for fear of hitting a civilian, and the presence of children made any retaliation a greater risk. He scanned the bedlam, looking for Nolan. To his right was a small coffee area that contained red bar-height tables and stools and he saw her there, sipping from a coffee cup with a wine chaser while watching her computer. She still wore the navy sweater and dark jeans. He took a quick tally of the other diners. All looked unremarkable, and he relaxed a bit. He reached the table and when he sat opposite her, Nolan flashed him a small smile, which was unexpected. She slid the wine glass toward him.

"It's for you," she said. "I took the liberty of ordering a heavy red. You don't seem like a white wine type."

"Depends on the meal. I generally drink whiskey neat, but this is fine. You don't seem surprised to see me."

She shrugged. "I'm not. I don't know how you're doing it, but I seem to be unable to shake you. How's the arm?"

"Better. Sorry for passing out."

She grimaced. "It was just as well. What a horrendous job. When I removed it, blood spurted from the wound. For a moment I thought the bullet was plugging an artery and I'd opened it by pulling it out."

"If I'd been conscious, I'd have told you that it wasn't at an artery."

She gave him an amused look. "It was brutal. If you'd been conscious, I doubt you would have been capable of rational conversation." He tipped his glass to acknowledge her, took a sip and then put it down.

"Remember Russell? The CIA agent you spoke with at your office?"

Nolan nodded as she took a sip of her coffee. "I do."

"She's in the hospital. Seriously ill. I think it has something to do with Dattar. You need to tell me everything. Now and quickly, because we have to leave. This place is a security disaster. You can start by explaining why you stole the money."

Nolan stared into her cup. She inhaled and exhaled slowly.

"Actually, I was stealing it back. The money belonged to my family. It was the proceeds of our holdings in Dattar's region. Five years ago he confiscated everything my family had spent years amassing, including a possible new sapphire mine, three utility stations, and a research facility. He claimed that the land and buildings were actually owned by the government, despite the fact that my family had been there for generations when the borderlands region was still considered part of India. We built the roads, train lines, utilities, you name it. Practically the entire infrastructure of the region was the result of the blood, sweat, and tears of generations of Reddings."

Smith refrained from pointing out that the Reddings had made their fortune from the land as well. Some in the early part of the nineteenth century were considered robber barons because they had amassed vast tracts of acreage in India and Africa while crushing any competition. Even so, there was no denying that the family had worked for their wealth and developed the area around their holdings.

"When one of our scientists at the research facility went missing and his papers were stolen, I suspected Dattar or one of his henchmen was involved. Dattar was already making noises that he would confiscate the Redding facilities, and that's when I decided to take the money."

"What scientist? What was he working on?"

Before Nolan could respond, a man slid into the chair next to them. He looked to be in his early twenties, with a backpack hanging off one shoulder and wearing jeans and a light sweatshirt. He shrugged the strap off his shoulder, shook off the pack, and set it on the table. He pulled out a laptop computer followed by a chemistry workbook and placed both next to the pack. Duct tape held the worn textbook's spine together, and when the man opened the book Smith could see yellow marks made by a highlighter pen. Smith relaxed a bit.

"He'd discovered a form of electrical bacteria," Nolan said.

The coolers, Smith thought. He dredged the name of the electric bacteria from his memory.

"Shewanella MR-1?"

"So you've heard of it. Not surprising. I read about you online. Impressive résumé."

"What was this scientist doing with the bacteria?"

Nolan shrugged. "I'm not exactly sure. He had an idea that it could be used as both an alternative fuel source and an efficient delivery system for healthy microbes. Apparently the bacteria communicate with electrical sources and both conduct and create electricity. The utility arm of Grayson Electric was funding the research." Nolan's gaze hardened. "It was after the scientist's body was found that I realized Dattar had to be stopped. I discovered that he had several aliases that he used to hide the money that he extorted from anyone doing legitimate business in the area. A big chunk of it was held by Landon Investments. I moved it out. It was income that he'd derived from Redding holdings and so rightfully ours, anyway. Without his cash he won't be able to hire his killers."

Smith shook his head. "You're wrong. He's hired one of the best to get us. I presume you had an idea that he'd come after you once you took his money?"

She nodded. "Oh yes, I knew he'd try. I scattered the money so that it would take a tremendous amount of time to collect it again. It's not a matter of a single transaction. I was banking on that fact, and the fact that only I can access it. They need me for voice and fingerprint recognition on several of the biggest accounts." She sighed. "You can imagine how happy I was when I heard that he'd been arrested and convicted. I was counting on his imprisonment lasting for the rest of his life. I was concerned when I'd heard that he'd escaped. I knew that he'd eventually try to access his funds, and when he found them missing, he'd come after me."

"Why did, or should I say do, you keep running from me then? I'm on your side."

She leveled a stare at him. "I'm not sure just what to make of you. Something seems off, but I can't put my finger on it. Your refusal to go to the hospital when you were shot just made me all the more suspicious, and it only got worse when you said that you had no one to call. Everyone has someone to call in their life. If they don't, either something is seriously wrong with them or they're lying, or both. Besides, I prefer to act alone. Especially since you told me that you're being tracked by the same killer. It seems to me that we make it too easy for him when we're together."

"You're far too confident in your own abilities to beat this thing. You may be great at financial matters, but survival against a paid assassin requires a set of skills that I doubt you've spent any time acquiring."

She gave him a piercing look. "And you have? I understand that you're military and must have received some training, but your résumé said that you specialize in infectious diseases, not in dodging killers."

He lowered his eyes against her perceptive stare to sip his drink. When he was done, he looked up. "I need to keep moving because I have another mission to complete, and you should move, too."

"And I've decided to go back to the safe house. It's become clear to me from the attempted bombing at the hotel that I'm putting others at risk by staying outside. I was just waiting here for you to find me again so that I can get the code for that lockbox." Smith rubbed his face with his hand. "What is it?" she said.

"You can't go to the safe house."

Nolan snorted. "You've been hounding me to go there and now, when I finally agree, you say that I can't? Why not?"

Smith paused. He wasn't about to tell a civilian about Russell's concerns about a mole, but he also didn't want Nolan to walk into a trap.

"There's been a change of circumstances. The location and security of the safe house may have been breached." Nolan went silent. She sipped her coffee and Smith thought he could see her brain whirring to process the information.

"So we're on our own."

Smith sighed. "For the most part, yes."

"What about the third picture? The man you know?"

"His name's Peter Howell."

"What does Dattar have against him?"

"I'm not sure. Howell's English, and Dattar might be lashing back at the UK for agreeing to jail him after a conviction. No other country was willing to bear the cost of imprisoning him for what most assumed would be a life sentence. England's offer allowed the trial to go forward." Smith sipped the wine again. "Howell's missing. I assume he's still alive, though. Howell's hard to kill." Nolan cocked her head to one side as she contemplated him.

"You've got some interesting friends. Especially for a man who claims to have no close personal relationships."

Smith decided to leave that comment alone. The whole series of events had thrown the stark nature of his life into focus. Right now he preferred action to contemplation.

"We need to keep moving. We've been here too long. It's not safe."

Nolan glanced around the restaurant. "New York's a big city. Hundreds, perhaps thousands, of restaurants. Is this man so good that he can track me the way you can?"

"He may not have the precise tools that I do, but he's been successful without them. You can bet he's watching your home and your office."

"How are you doing it?"

Smith shook his head. "Trade secret. We need to go."

She raised an eyebrow. "Issuing orders?" He nearly bit his tongue. She was right. Something about her brought out the military in him. He was acting like a drill sergeant with a particularly recalcitrant recruit. And it was the exact wrong way to deal with her. He took a deep breath and went for honesty.

"Sorry. Absolutely not. I've learned how useless orders can be when dealing with you. It was a suggestion only." His phone began vibrating in his pocket and he answered when he saw that it was Marty.

"Get out of there, now," Marty said. "Someone's accessing her tablet GPS just like I am, but they're relaying the coordinates to an untraceable prepaid phone. And these hackers are the best."

"Who is it?" Smith said.

"The CIA."

27

W E'VE GOT TO LEAVE. Now," Smith said. Nolan stopped drinking her coffee mid-sip. She swallowed.

"Why? What just happened?"

He hesitated. Normally he'd just try to muscle his way through giving vague responses and assuming that most people would recognize his expertise and take his direction. But Nolan had already proven immune to good advice.

"The group at the hotel is getting information about our location from...a hacker. I give it ten minutes, no more, and they'll be here. Power down your tablet and cell phone."

Nolan put the coffee cup down with a thunk. Her face had turned pale, which was one of the first times that he'd seen her react to the circumstances in an appropriate way. Perhaps she was learning the extent of the precarious position that she was in. Her eyes narrowed.

Well, that's not a good sign, Smith thought.

"Call Ms. Russell's superior. They must have other safe houses we can use."

"That's not a good idea."

"Why not?" Nolan said.

Smith eyed the man with the backpack next to them and the crowd in the aisles. From somewhere in the bowels of the store he heard the shrill laughter of a woman who was on her way to being drunk, and the air was filled with the sound of voices in conversation intermingled with the clinking of glasses, creating a cacophony. From the coffee bar came the noise of milk being steamed; the smell of coffee beans being ground wafted in Smith's direction. Background music overlaid it all. Smith wasn't going to hear the assassin approach; that much was clear. He would have to rely on spotting him before he was able to aim. Smith kept his gaze roaming around the room. His phone vibrated. It was Marty.

"Why are you still there?" he said.

"Just leaving."

"If it is someone in the CIA tracking you both, you'll have to go dark, you know that, right? I mean, for them to be hacking a civilian's computer is domestic spying, which is illegal. There must be a bad seed in the agency for this to be happening."

"I'm not exactly a civilian."

"You're army and on their side, so it's even worse. And she's a civilian. I presume neither the CIA nor you have a warrant."

"Nor do you, for God's sake."

"But what *I'm* doing is just criminal. What the CIA is doing is treason. They're acting like a police state and spying against American citizens."

Smith could tell that Marty was winding up and he didn't have the time to discuss the shades of gray and black that they were engaging in.

"The CIA is good at this. You can't use any technology for any length of time, you understand? That means no credit cards, no phone use, no accessing your bank accounts."

"You're calling me on a burner phone. They already know we're here. I'll send you a text from each new prepaid that I use." Smith checked his wallet. He had three hundred dollars on him. "I'm going to need cash."

Nolan had been looking down, but her head shot up at his comment.

"I have cash," she said. She reached for her tablet.

"Do *not* touch that thing. It's supposed to be turned off. In fact, let's just throw it away."

Nolan shook her head. "I refuse. My whole life is loaded onto this hard drive." Smith wanted to grab it and throw it across the room.

"I'm going to have real trouble going dark while I'm around Ms. Nolan. She refuses to give up her computer," he said to Marty. "Says it's her whole life."

"I think I could love this woman," Marty said.

"Is there a way to turn off the GPS?"

"For the phone, yes. Have her access the GPS feature and switch it off, but that's not a complete fix because the 911 locater remains on and will use tower triangulation, not GPS. I've got to believe that the CIA can access the enhanced 911 feature. Her safest bet is to turn it off."

"And the tablet?" Smith redirected his attention to the room. As he did, the neighbor finished his chemistry work and stood up. Smith shifted the phone to his other ear to leave his right hand free. He moved it into his jacket in preparation. All the while, Marty kept talking.

"For the tablet it's the same. She can turn off the GPS feature, but that only kills one portion of the tablet's systems. Every time she accesses her data package, I can see where she is by following the information flow. She's going to have to turn it off. If she needs to use it, then only turn it on in very small doses."

"Got it." Smith hung up. As he did, he noticed that Nolan was powering down both of her devices.

"Let's go," he said to her. He stood.

"To call the CIA?" Nolan stood as well, but the suspicious look was back on her face.

Smith shook his head. "To get the hell out of here. *Let's go.*"

"Front door?"

Smith nodded. "Fast."

Nolan grabbed her ever-present tote and headed to the door, weaving her way through the patrons. Smith came even with her and gripped her elbow tightly.

"You're grabbing again," Nolan said in a low voice.

"I'm not grabbing, I'm guiding," Smith replied. "When we hit the door we'll split. You head right, I'll head left. Run a circle and meet me at the opposite side of Madison Square Park." They were ten steps from the exit. Nolan's eyes darted back and forth as she scanned the room. Two diners sat at a table and the one facing them, a man, glanced at Nolan and stared.

"Try to calm down. The other patrons are noticing you."

"Calm down, are you serious?" Nolan spoke through clenched teeth. They passed another set of patrons, the last before the front door. They were a large group of men, all in business suits, sitting at a round table to the left. Three of them glanced up and gave Nolan a steady look, two with appreciation in their eyes. Smith realized the men were enjoying looking at her because she was attractive, not because they had divined the stress she was under. They reached the entrance.

"Show time," Smith said.

He stepped in front of her and pulled open the door, reaching under his jacket as he did to remove his gun. He stilled when he came face to face with a couple coming toward them, trying to enter. Behind them he saw the shadow of a man hugging the narrow tip of the Flatiron Building to the right. The man's head was up and his gaze fixed on the restaurant's door. Twenty feet to the man's left another suspicious character was pressed against the wall.

"Reverse," he said in a low voice to Nolan. He smiled at the entering couple, turned and propelled her back into the foyer.

"What did you see?"

"Trouble. Is there another exit in this place?"

"On Twenty-fourth Street," Nolan said.

"Go there."

Nolan turned and race-walked back into the mammoth store. Smith released her but kept his hand in his jacket, grasping the gun but not removing it. He hated to wait—if the shooter appeared, he'd lose precious seconds pulling it free, but the last thing he needed was an entire marketplace in panic as a man with a gun in his hand marched through the room.

They dodged people and passed glass display counters, and Nolan turned right. Smith saw more glass exit doors in front of them.

"This exits onto Twenty-fourth Street," Nolan said. The strain in her voice was apparent. Smith kept at her side, scanning the patrons for any signs of quick movements or unusual interest in them. Nolan kept going. When they reached the door, Smith pulled the gun free of its holster but kept it hidden inside his coat. Nolan gave every indication that she intended to open the glass doors without hesitation.

"Don't. They could be covering this exit as well. Let me do it."

Nolan stepped back. "You should let me go first. They won't shoot me."

Smith didn't reply. He pushed on the bar and the door creaked open, letting in a gust of cool air. Nolan moved behind him. He peered out.

The restaurant door opened onto Twenty-fourth Street. Parked cars lined both sides, narrowing the lane. If they wanted to run across the street, they'd have to dodge between them. Not an ideal situation. His view was limited on either side.

"How long will it take you to run down Twenty-fourth Street until you hit Sixth?" Smith asked.

"Far."

"Give it to me in time. How fast can you reach the corner and turn it? Thirty seconds of running? More?"

Nolan swallowed. A sheen of sweat covered her face. "I don't know. Maybe thirty."

Thirty seconds in the crosshairs of a professional shooter was a long time indeed.

"We'll need to split in opposite directions. When we do, try your best not to run in a straight line. Keep switching up the trajectory. Dodge between the cars and across the street if you can. I'll try to draw any fire from a sentry."

Another set of patrons moved into position to exit and Smith stepped aside to let them leave. He followed them to the edge of the doors and this time he spotted the sentry across the street in the direction of Madison Square Park.

The sentry was young, perhaps twenty-five years old, with sandy brown hair and a lanky body and looked thoroughly American, which surprised Smith. Like most in the Middle East, Khalil generally stuck to using blood relatives, albeit far-removed blood relatives, to do his dirty work. To use an American was an anomaly. He'd assumed that the mole in the CIA was sending his location to Khalil or one of his crew, but this didn't look like the work of Khalil.

Could the CIA mole have his own crew? Was Smith going to have to dodge two attackers, Khalil and someone else? Khalil was a formidable adversary, but Smith was as well. He wasn't afraid to take on the assassin, but two hunting him at the same time was sobering, especially if one of the hunters had access to CIA technology and its network of mercenary assets. There were those who would take any job as long as it paid, even one that involved killing a colonel in the US Army. Howell, where the hell are you? Smith thought. Three people appeared on the street. The man retreated farther into the shadows.

"There's another sentry here," Smith said.

"Should we go back to the front door?" Nolan said.

"Two in the front, one in the back, but with a long run down Twenty-fourth to freedom. Neither situation is good, but I think we try it here. If we move fast enough, he'll have to make a choice about who he wants to kill first." He looked at her. She appeared scared, but focused. "Can you do this?"

"How long do you want me to wait for you at the park?" Nolan said.

"I like your optimism. An hour. No more. Don't turn on your phone or your computer."

"Why not?" Nolan's voice was filled with suspicion.

"Because the hacker I mentioned is breaking into your devices. Both have GPS inside. It's how I've been tracking you and it's how they are as well."

Nolan shot him an outraged look. "You hacked my phone? You tell me you're one of the good guys and you do that? You'd better have a warrant."

"Stealing from Dattar was outrageous. Getting your phone hacked is the least of your problems. We'll talk about it later. Right now we have to sprint to the corner without getting shot. I'm going to go first, you follow." There was a steady stream of single pedestrians passing by the door, but not too many groups larger than two, which is what Smith needed.

"All right, the next move is the toughest. The second that we see another group of pedestrians we're going to run. I'll go first, open the door and try to draw his fire. Whatever you do, keep moving."

Several people flowed past on the sidewalk. He made it to the door in two quick strides, pushed it open, and stepped onto the street. Nolan passed behind him and ran to the left. He stepped out and deliberately caught the sentry's eye, telegraphing his knowledge of the trap. The man straightened. Smith ran to the right, keeping the gun in his hand hidden inside the jacket and banking on the fact that the sentry wouldn't fire with others nearby. Smith could see the CIA asset, if that's who the sentry was, tracking his progress. He began to run parallel to Smith, weaving between the passing sidewalk traffic. They were opposite each other, with only the narrow street and two sets of parked cars between them.

Two more civilians crossed in front of the sentry, who pushed them out of his way in his haste to keep Smith in his sights. One, a young man with baggy pants and a baseball cap, stumbled. He regained his feet.

"Who the hell you think you are?" the man yelled, but the sentry kept moving, ignoring the young man completely. Smith kept his concentration focused on dodging people as he ran toward the corner.

Smith reached Fifth Avenue and darted right, turning the corner and watching for signs of the other two sentries. They were gone, but the one parallel to him kept pace, and Smith kicked into even higher gear, turning onto Twenty-third and running toward Broadway.

He turned again on Broadway and immediately regretted the move. The sidewalk was clogged with slow-moving pedestrians. Smith bobbed and weaved between them. The back of his neck tingled and it was all he could do not to look behind him. He kept swerving, hoping the sudden movements would forestall the sentry from simply shooting him in the back of the head. To Smith the block seemed endless and the flow of people created a human obstacle course. Smith heard a scream and grunted when he felt something punch into his left arm followed by a flow of warm blood. He twisted to look behind him and saw the sentry with a gun pointed in Smith's direction. The attached silencer explained why Smith hadn't heard the shot.

The crowd on the sidewalks reacted to the sight of the weapon. Civilians ran in all directions, cutting across the sentry's line of fire. Smith darted across the street, turned, raised his own gun, pinpointed the sentry, and prepared to shoot.

The sentry darted behind a pedestrian, grabbed him by the neck and used him as a human shield, batting the man's female companion directly into Smith's sights.

"Get down!" Smith yelled.

The woman screamed and knelt, covering her head with her hands. Three other people near her scrambled out of the way and scattered. A man at Smith's right yelled an oath and turned away, bumping into two other people and knocking one down in his haste to flee.

"Get out of here!" Smith yelled at the two on the ground.

Smith heard another woman scream, but he kept his focus on the sentry as he dragged the hostage backward with him. The sentry took stock, let the hapless human shield go, and weaved and bobbed through more civilians back toward Twenty-third. A man pushing a baby stroller with headphones in his ears and appearing oblivious to the panic around him walked into Smith's line of fire. Smith lowered his gun as he watched the sentry hit the corner, turn onto Twenty-third Street, and disappear.

Smith holstered his gun and ran back toward Madison Square Park. At the corner of Twenty-third and Broadway he spotted Nolan across the street, at the park's edge. The two sentries that had watched the restaurant's Fifth Avenue entrance surrounded her. The new attackers held fast to her arms, one on each side as they propelled her across the park. One wore a dark suit and a white shirt that contrasted with his swarthy skin, the other wore dark cotton pants and an un-tucked, short-sleeved embroidered white shirt. When a breeze pushed the shirt against his spine Smith saw the outline of a bulky object. He presumed it was a gun in a holster at the small of the man's back. Nolan marched between them, her tote in her hand and her head up. Smith couldn't see her face, but she stood tall, straight and stiff. He turned on his phone and called Marty.

"Did you get out of the restaurant?" Marty said without preamble.

"Yes, but Nolan's been captured. Are her devices still off?"

"Let me check." Smith dodged around a couple holding hands and past a young man with a backpack talking into his phone while he kept the tail on Nolan. "I'm sorry, but they're off."

A limousine pulled up to the corner and idled. A man dressed in a navy turtleneck, black pants, and a sharp suit stepped out of it. Even at a distance Smith knew who it was. Khalil opened the passenger door and the two men holding Nolan pushed her into it, one man placing a hand on top of her head to help her clear the roof and the other pushing her on the back. When she was inside, Khalil joined her along with one of the men. The other crawled into the front with the driver. The limousine cut back into traffic and shot forward, running a stale yellow and turning at the next opportunity.

"Keep watching, can you? The minute she turns them back on I need to know about it."

His next call was to Klein. "Khalil just loaded Nolan into a limousine at the edge of Madison Square Park. There's a closed circuit camera at..." Smith crossed the street and ran toward a small structure within the park, "the Shake Shack in the park. Can you see if their camera captured an image?" Smith checked his watch. "They must have just closed for the evening."

"I'll run it down. Are you sure it was Khalil? That's very bad news," Klein said.

"I'm sure. I'm going to try to track her again." Smith rang off and started running in the direction that the limousine had gone.

The one time she listens to me and now she's screwed, Smith thought.

28

DATTAR STEPPED OFF THE FREIGHTER onto the dock, squinting against the sun. He wouldn't normally have disembarked in the daytime, but he was anxious to leave the ship and he could see the bodyguards he routinely used when in Cyprus lounging by a large SUV parked parallel to the landing. They were well-trained mercenaries and though they appeared relaxed and held their machine guns downward, he knew they would annihilate anyone who dared to threaten him. Rajiid stood at his right shoulder holding a duffle containing their clothes and fielding a phone call from their contact in the States. The Pakistani captain of the freighter walked up to them both, but kept his eyes on Dattar, his expression grim.

"I just learned that no funds have been wired into my account. I presume this is a simple oversight on your part?"

Rajiid stopped talking and flicked a glance at Dattar.

"I have been maintaining phone and Internet silence while on the ship. It's safer that way." Dattar hoped the lie would calm the man. Instead the captain grabbed Dattar by the shirtfront, bunching it in his large hands and pulling Dattar forward. Before Dattar could respond, Rajiid had a gun out and pointed at the captain's head and the two mercenaries snapped to attention, with their own guns trained on the captain. "How *dare* you touch me!" Dattar's rage, which was never far from the surface, exploded. "I'll have them take you away and boil you alive." To Dattar's great surprise, the captain didn't appear afraid, nor did he release his grasp on the shirt.

"I work for Amir. You harm me and the only one who'll boil alive will be you. Tell your dogs to lower their weapons."

Dattar had a sour taste in his mouth. Amir was a warlord who ruled a vast drug operation from his hilltop villa in Cyprus. Few knew his name, even those who had lived on the small island for years, and the fact that this lowly ship captain invoked it turned him from a mere lackey to a formidable foe in seconds. Dattar glanced at Rajiid, and nodded. Rajiid lowered his weapon.

"Don't shoot," Dattar yelled at his soldiers. They, too, lowered their guns. "Pay him," Dattar told Rajiid.

"But—"

"Now."

Rajiid shoved the pistol back into the shoulder holster under his olive-colored linen shirt and removed the tablet computer from the outside pocket of the duffle. He dropped the luggage on the ground while he tapped on the screen.

"I want to see it," the captain said. Rajiid didn't look up, but simply nodded as he worked. After a moment he walked to the captain and handed him the computer. The captain peered at the screen, moving it out of the sun's glare. He gave it back to Rajiid.

"Don't ever try to rob me again," he said to Dattar. He spun and stomped back up the ramp to his freighter. Rajiid moved in close.

"That was the last of it."

"The credit cards?" Dattar said.

"Frozen by the banks when you were taken into custody."

"The latest from the mine?"

Rajiid shook his head. "Also frozen. And Jain, who regularly siphons from the site, has disappeared."

"Deploy the weapon."

"I'm still waiting for the results of the test, but I expect it will work," Rajiid said.

"Deploy it on the freighter. I want that captain dead."

"It may not work."

"Deploy it," Dattar said.

Rajiid nodded.

Dattar stalked to the SUV, doing his best to ignore the speculative glances from his soldiers. That he had allowed a stinking freighter captain to manhandle him in such a fashion and not retaliated had shocked them. Once he was inside and Rajiid next to him, he had come to a decision.

"Take me to Amir's."

"Why?"

"Just get me there!" Dattar shrieked at Rajiid. The driver threw the car into gear and hit the gas, making the wheels squeal on the pavement.

Twenty minutes later they were at the gates of Amir's high-security compound.

Three guards strolled out, one holding a checkpoint mirror on a pole. He extended the mirror under the car and began scanning for bombs. The second guard indicated that they should step out while the third began a thorough search of the vehicle's interior. The second had a pockmarked face and wary dark eyes.

"You don't have an appointment," he said to Dattar.

"I'll be sure to make one in advance next time so that every one of my enemies knows where to find me," Dattar shot back. "Just frisk me and get it over with. Amir knows me." The guard raised an eyebrow but didn't respond. When the search was complete, the pockmarked guard nodded them through. They drove down a long driveway lined with poplars and past olive trees that opened up to the front of a massive villa. The two-story white stone mansion had a decorative façade, with round medallions bearing the faces of Greek and Roman gods, spaced at regular intervals, plastered horizontally along the center. Statues of the same gods lined the drive. Dattar thought the mansion's design was gaudy and pretentious. To the right the gravel path continued under a portico and disappeared to a separate section of the compound. Stone urns contained flowers that must have been recently purchased because they were in bloom out of season. Two guards carrying semiautomatic weapons stood on each side of the front door and watched their approach. Between them stood Amir's butler, Najon, a man Dattar had met before. The butler opened the passenger door.

"Mr. Amir is in the garden. I'll show you there." Najon headed toward the portico. After a stroll past a long infinity pool, they found Amir sitting at a table shaded by a gazebo. A French press filled with coffee and a platter of small sandwiches were placed on the table before him, along with a smartphone and a tablet computer, their LED lights blinking.

Dattar and Amir had met when Amir was a midlevel dealer in the cartel that he now headed and Dattar was a lowly minister in his country before rising in power. Dattar knew that a rival member of the Russian mafia had ordered Amir's elimination. There had been three attempts already and in the last attempt, a rocket-propelled grenade had exploded under Amir's armored limousine, causing nerve damage to his left arm. Amir held that arm in his lap, using his right to bring a cup of coffee to his lips.

"Your presence here surprises me," Amir said. Dattar glanced at the empty chairs at the table and Amir nodded. "Please, sit, and tell me what brings you to Cyprus and my home so suddenly." Dattar took a seat. Rajiid took one as well.

"I need a loan."

Amir's eyes narrowed. "You? Why?"

Dattar spread his arms wide. "The authorities have frozen my accounts."

Amir snorted. "So? You have many accounts under aliases, I'm sure. Tap into one of those." Dattar had known the moment would come that he would be forced to reveal his failings, but he still found himself swallowing his gorge as he did. That a woman had betrayed him made it all that much worse. He took a deep breath.

"My other holdings have been...diverted." Dattar refused to use the word "stolen." He would recover the funds.

"Diverted? In what way? And by whom?" Amir's gaze was pointed.

"By a thieving investment advisor. But don't worry, I have arranged for the advisor to be shown the error of . . . his ways." Dattar noticed that Rajiid's eyes flicked to the side at the use of the male pronoun, but he remained silent. Nevertheless, Amir seemed to have caught Rajiid's reaction. He shifted in his seat and sipped the coffee.

"Where is this thief?"

"New York," Dattar said.

Amir nodded, as if he had expected that answer. "And the one you have hired to school this person?"

"Khalil."

Amir chuckled. "Ah. I think this thief will soon regret every penny he ever stole. Khalil is the best and ruthless. And so, you require a loan until Khalil completes his mission, am I correct?"

Dattar smiled and relaxed for the first time since leaving the freighter. Amir would loan him the funds and Khalil would find the American. All would be well.

"You are."

"How much?"

Dattar paused. His expenses were building. "Twenty million."

Amir nodded. "And your collateral?"

"Stones from my sapphire mine."

Amir frowned. "I heard that scientists may have discovered a new source of sapphires in your region, but that the yield, if any, would be small."

"Small, but of the highest quality, commanding the highest prices," Dattar said.

"You just told me your assets were frozen. I presume that includes the mine. No. I require something solid. Firm. Nothing that the United Nations can grasp with its greedy hands in the name of international law."

Dattar's mind raced. The Court had frozen it all. He had only his weapon left. He took a deep breath. He needed the money.

"I have something in my possession. It's a weapon that I intend to use against the countries in the international community who dared to insist that I be arrested and tried for crimes against humanity. I will force their hand."

Amir sat straighter.

That got his attention, Dattar thought with satisfaction.

"What is this weapon and how do you intend to use it?"

"I can't tell you exactly, but I'll prove to you it works. In less than twenty-four hours I'll send you a link to a newspaper report that will confirm the results of our first test. Understand that it will be a small test, but it will verify what I say."

Amir looked intrigued. "Is this weapon yours alone? Or do others have it?"

Dattar shook his head. "It's not only mine, but I have the delivery method. I needed additional funding to test it, and so I went to certain key players to receive it. The project is financed by a consortium called 'Janus.'"

"Who else is in this Janus consortium? And don't tell me it's that Russian bastard Rapanov." Rapanov was the arms dealer who had arranged the attack on Amir.

"It's not Rapanov. He's a small player. It's a group of nations that have felt the sting of the UN and their economic sanctions. Of course, they won't acknowledge their role should the plan fail and they be discovered, but they're paying just the same."

"So why not ask them for the money?"

Because I can't afford to show them any weakness, Dattar thought. He wouldn't say that to Amir, though.

"They've paid their share. It's up to me to fund the final part of the plan, the release of the weapon. I'm preparing for that now, but my assets are frozen."

"What nations?" Amir said.

"Why do you care? You sell to them all, don't you?"

Amir nodded. "Yes, but not all pay their bills. Tell me."

"Yemen, Syria, and the Sudan."

Amir snorted. "You're insane. At least two of those countries will devour Pakistan given half the chance, and your tiny foothold on the border will be taken from you. And Yemen contains training camps for at least ten different terrorist organizations, any one of which would be happy to take your weapon from you by force. You're dealing with a group that cannot be controlled."

"You forget that my 'tiny' foothold on the border contains a newly discovered precious gem mine and I control the utilities."

"Everyone knows that you rely on Western technology companies to tap these resources. The royalties they pay you are a fraction of what they take out, and you don't have the know-how within your country to operate the facilities. You need their help."

"I've confiscated the mine and the utility companies."

"And when you did, the West acted swiftly to charge you with crimes against humanity." Amir leaned forward. "A charge that, while true, would never have been made against you had you not taken the action that you did."

"Exactly. But that didn't work, now did it? Because here I am. Free. And when I launch the weapon, they will have no choice but to negotiate with me and the others in the Janus consortium. They'll be falling over their feet to do as we ask."

"If they don't kill you first."

Dattar took a sip of his coffee. "They wouldn't dare. If they try, I'll release the weapon throughout their country and they can watch the rest of their population die."

"And the other snakes in this consortium? What if one of them decides to double-cross you?"

"They won't."

Amir gave him a wary look. "Why are you so sure of this?"

"Because I'm the only one who knows how to deliver the payload. Without my unique delivery method, the weapon won't cause any real harm. Also, they're cowards. They're willing to pay for their dirty work to be done, but none have the guts to actually place the weapon. Listen, I'll pay you back, with interest, once the weapon is released. After it launches, I'll have the leverage to force the world community to not only release my funds, but to pay me more just to stop."

Amir sipped his drink and stared at Dattar. "What will the Janus consortium request if the plan succeeds?"

"For every nation in the United Nations to pay a protection fee to the consortium and to cede control of all of their manufacturing and technology holdings to Janus. We take fifty percent of all profits."

Amir's face held a mixture of surprise and disbelief. "No country would agree to such a thing. It's extortion at the highest level. It would make them serfs and Janus king."

"They'll do it."

"Why?"

"Because they'll die if they don't."

Amir shook his head. "It's crazy. What weapon can force such a result?"

"This one," Dattar said. Amir watched him for a moment. Dattar waited.

"No. You tell me a tale of a terrible weapon but show no real proof that it exists. I need proof before I give you the money. Once I see the link, I'll send the funds, but not before. And I want twenty percent interest."

"That's outrageous!" Dattar said.

Amir shrugged. "No one else is going to lend you twenty million based upon a tale of a weapon. Is it agreed?"

Dattar's coffee suddenly tasted bitter, but he had little choice in the matter. He decided to negotiate different terms if the latest test worked. "Agreed."

"Where will you start after your test?"

"I intend to release it in New York City."

29

KLEIN GOT THE CALL about the freighter from the director general of the World Health Organization while he was at a dinner reception for a major contributor to President Castilla's campaign. He stepped outside the ballroom to take the call.

"Mr. Klein? I've been asked to convey this information to you by the president. We've discovered a freighter floating off the coast of Syria. It was disabled, and aerial reconnaissance revealed that every member of the crew was dead."

"Because you're calling me and not Syrian diplomatic personnel, I presume the deaths were not battle related but disease related?" Klein said.

"We're not sure. The freighter floated into Syrian waters shortly after our reconnaissance. Syria is refusing us access to the ship."

Klein walked farther away from the ballroom, nodding at an acquaintance passing in the hall.

"How many crew members?"

"Thirty-three. Their last port of embarkation was Cyprus approximately six hours ago."

"Were they alive then?"

"Yes. All of them. And they appeared healthy."

"That has to be a mass shooting. What disease can kill that quickly?"

"Our reconnaissance photos managed to snap pictures of at least fifteen crew members scattered on the boat. We've zoomed in on each, and none show any signs of gunshot wounds or blast injuries. Three are lying in pools of vomit."

"Poison?"

"Doubtful."

"Why not?"

"Because while Syria is refusing us access, it's also flatly refusing to send a medical or forensic crew to it. They intend to fly over and drop a bomb on the ship to destroy it."

Klein stopped walking. "They're going to blow the thing out of the water? What in the world is on that ship that they don't want us to discover? Polonium-210?"

"I'm sorry?"

"Polonium-210 is what the Russians slipped to their unfortunate former spy. He died in a London hospital days later. It's highly toxic, but requires a lot of expertise to use."

"I think they're afraid to set foot on it. I'm concerned that this may have something to do with the missing mutated avian flu strain. The freighter began its journey from the port in Rotterdam."

"Ah, now I understand," Klein said. "The attack on the Grand Royal and the coolers."

"Exactly."

"How many can a mutated avian flu strain kill?"

"Avian flu is rare, deadly, and carries a fifty percent death rate. The mutation is new and we're just compiling statistics, but our computer models suggest a mutation that would allow human-to-human transmission could kill up to ninety-seven percent of those infected."

"Do you think it can kill with the kind of speed that you're describing? Can someone go from appearing healthy to dead that quickly?"

"I can't answer your question except to tell you this: During the 1917 Spanish flu that killed over seventeen million people, there was a story of four women in a bridge club who played into the early hours of the morning. They broke up, went home, and three never saw the sun rise."

* * *

Amir learned of his crippled freighter when a member of his crew operating in Syria sent him the intelligence. An hour after that, he received a demand from Dattar to wire the money immediately and without repayment terms. Dattar said that if he did not receive the funds, he would release his weapon in Cyprus.

Amir sent the wire.

30

KHALIL KNEW THAT MANHAR had been captured when the hour struck and he didn't receive the call that he expected, but it no longer mattered now that he had the American in his control. They crossed town, headed west. The woman stayed silent, her eyes fixed in a forward stare and her hands clutching a tote. Khalil thought she didn't appear nearly as emotional as he would have expected from a female. But then he'd read that American women were hardened and this one seemed to fit that profile. The car pulled onto a nearby street and stopped in front of a large construction project. A chain-link fence wrapped in green mesh surrounded a gutted three-story building. Temporary lights placed high on metal poles cast a harsh glare over a small area, while shadows danced in the rest. The door next to her opened and Khalil's man, Ali, wrapped his hand around her arm and yanked her out of the car.

Khalil followed, watching his men hustle Nolan toward the fence. They used a key to open the padlock and swung open a portion of the gate. Khalil followed them inside and strolled to the freight elevator. His men hauled open the metal divided doors and he joined them last. He waved at his third.

"Stay here and watch the entrance." The man nodded and reversed out of the lift. Ali pulled the rope handle to close the elevator's doors.

Khalil was interested to see Nolan flinch at the clanging sound of the metal barriers slamming shut. So she's not as unaffected as she seems, he thought.

They exited at the second floor, where Khalil had set up a battered wooden table, two black aluminum folding chairs, and a light on a tall base that was powered by a long extension cord that snaked to the one exposed electrical outlet hanging from the wall. The developer had run out of money for the project and was currently battling creditors in a bankruptcy proceeding. No further work would happen until after the project was bought in a liquidation sale or the banker convinced a new lender to give him a cash infusion. Khalil paid a minuscule sum for the use of the entire building and the electrical outlet. This was the only floor that had walls and even then only three. One side of the long rectangular room was open to the night air. His men forced Nolan onto a chair. Khalil sauntered up to her.

"You are to die," he said. "I'm paid very well to kill you."

The woman blinked but said nothing. He watched her swallow once.

"I want to know why."

She said nothing.

Khalil waved at Ali, who grabbed her by the arms once again and shoved her onto the floor. She knelt and Ali pushed her head down until she was face-first on the cement and then held her head against it. Khalil reached to the desk and picked up a rattan pole used in caning. He wound up and swung it onto Nolan's back. The pole had been soaked in water to ensure that it wouldn't break from the force and it didn't. Khalil suspected that Nolan's spine would snap before the cane would. Her body shivered after the hit, but her bones remained intact. He didn't really care as long as she didn't die before he got his information. He aimed between her shoulder blades and hit her a second time. This time she moaned.

"Tell me why I'm paid so well to kill you," Khalil said. The woman was silent. He swung the cane again, hitting her on the mid-back. She groaned again and tried to curl into a ball, curving a bit to the side and bringing her knees to her chest. "The next time I hit the kidneys. You may die a short time after in agony. I suggest you talk. Now."

"Money," she whispered.

"What money?"

"Dattar's. I have it."

Khalil wasn't sure that he'd heard right. "How much?"

"All of it," she said.

Khalil couldn't believe his ears. The lying bastard had no money. Khalil was on a fool's errand. He felt his rage rise and he started to breathe in short gasps. Khalil prided himself on being smarter than all the others and now Dattar had tried to use him.

"Where is it?"

"Computer," she whispered.

"I said where is it?" Khalil raised his cane again.

"*Computer.* It's on the computer."

Khalil paused with his hand in the air and the pole poised to smash into her. He used computers to pick up e-mail, surf the Internet, and read the occasional headline. He knew that many banked on them, but he made sure that he didn't. His clients paid him in wire transfers directly into a Swiss account. When he needed funds, he used a traditional credit card issued in a stolen identity to withdraw the funds from ATMs across the world that bore the logo of a famous network. Such transactions were traceable but would be lost amid the massive number of similar transactions.

"Put her in the chair."

Ali pulled her up and forced her into the chair, pushing backward, and she gave a strident shriek. She sat upright in order to keep her spine from touching anything. Khalil reached into the tote that she had clutched in the limousine and withdrew her thin computer in its custom leather holder. He shoved it at her. "Show me," he said, "and don't think you can access anything else. You do and I'll put a bullet in your head." She was pale, and her hands shook as she took the computer from him. He watched her power it on and wait for it to establish a connection. When it did, Khalil watched her type in a web address and wait for it to load. She input a username and password at the prompt, and the account's balance appeared.

Khalil sucked in his breath. The number was huge, but Khalil knew that there must be more. Much more. He glanced from the screen and saw that she was staring at him; once again her face was set, her lips in a straight line. If it weren't for her shaking hands, he would not have discerned that she was in pain.

"Where's the rest?"

"Scattered all over," she said.

"Move it to my account."

She inhaled. "To which bank in what country? Such a large transaction will be recorded. Depending on what country, the bank will have to notify the authorities."

Khalil wasn't sure that what she said was correct. He had experience with moving large sums around in the Middle East, but not in America and nothing as large as this.

"You moved it out of his account. I expect you to be able to move it into mine."

"I did it by taking small amounts each day. Under the limit for scrutiny. The rest I diverted from the beginning by placing it in an account offshore first. It took me months to move it all."

Khalil bent close to her face. "This time it will take three days. Three separate wire transfers."

She shook her head. "It won't work. Part of the requirements for large transfers is that I appear at the bank. In person. I arranged it this way so if Dattar found out he couldn't kill me." She gave Khalil a direct stare and for a moment he was unsure whether to believe her or not. He pulled his fist back to punch her. She watched him do it and he saw her set her jaw in anticipation of the pain. He heard a noise from below and paused. After a moment, when it wasn't repeated, he turned his attention back to her.

"Where is this bank?"

"The Cayman Islands." Khalil had expected the answer. Many hid their money in the Caribbean.

"Transfer the small amounts first. Now. Then we shall go to get the rest."

"I'll need your information," she said.

Khalil waved at the computer. "Initiate the transaction and I'll type it in at the appropriate spot."

Nolan bent her head to the computer. Khalil noticed that her hands still shook but she seemed to steady as her mind focused. He knew that the transfers could be scheduled for a date in the future. He'd have her complete the programming and then he'd kill her. He settled into a chair behind the desk while he waited.

31

SMITH STEPPED INTO A drugstore and headed to the pharmacy section. He needed gauze, alcohol, bandages, and ibuprofen. His arm was throbbing again, from the original wound and now from the second. His shirtsleeve was wet with blood and he could feel it leaking over the back of his hand.

I'm becoming bullet-ridden, he thought. He wished he could purchase equipment to stitch up the second injury, but he didn't want to spend all his cash on medical supplies. His next purchase would be a prepaid phone and he wouldn't turn off his current one until then because he didn't want to miss a call from Marty. His phone vibrated. Smith opened it to find a text from Marty that said, *Nolan back online*, followed by an address and the words *Toss this phone now*. Smith sent Marty a text asking him to notify the police. Then he sent a text to Klein.

His phone vibrated in his pocket and he pulled it out and glanced at the screen. "Unknown number" appeared. Klein, Smith thought. He pressed the call button and put the phone to his ear.

"Jon, you have a lot of trouble." Howell's voice poured through the phone. Smith felt enormous relief at hearing the former MI6 agent's voice.

"Where the hell have you been?"

"I'm in the East Village. You?"

"You're in New York City." Smith's voice was flat.

"Yes. I'm told you're here as well."

"I'm near the Flatiron District. A man just tried to kill me."

"Khalil?" Howell's immediate grasp of the situation and the adversary didn't surprise Smith at all. Peter Howell was one of the best.

"Doubtful. American. I think CIA." The pause on the line dragged out. "You there?" Smith said.

"I won't ask why the CIA might want you dead. Have you asked Russell? Even though she's CIA, I think she'd tell you if they were out to burn you," Howell said.

"Russell's in the ICU. Gravely ill. She thinks there's a mole in the agency who's funneling information outside to a hostile actor. She doesn't know who or why. But I'm not one of theirs, so why hunt me?"

"I'm afraid I have further bad news. I found one of Khalil's lackeys. He says that Dattar has a new weapon he intends to unleash here in twenty hours. Not a bomb. Any ideas?"

"A few. Let me be sure to shake the guy tailing me and we'll meet in thirty minutes." He told Howell about Nolan and gave the address.

"I have Beckmann with me."

Now it was Smith's turn to pause. Beckmann was CIA and therefore suspect. "Can you lose him?"

"If I have to, yes, but I've known him for several years. His adherence to corporate policy can be loose, but he wouldn't turn on the CIA. He's not your mole. I would stake my life on it."

"If you bring him along, you'll be doing just that," Smith said.

He paid for the supplies and left the store, disassembling the old phone as he did. He passed a garbage can and lobbed the electronic components into it before waving down a taxi. Traffic was light and they made it across town in less than ten minutes. The cabbie dropped him a block from the pinpoint location. He walked the block, keeping a lookout for sentries along the way.

The address belonged to a gut rehab of what looked like a former warehouse stuck in between two new square apartment buildings. All three structures were no higher than three floors. The street was tree-lined on the house side, but across from it was a small parking lot. At the end of the street was a massive glass-and-steel conference center building. The area was desolate. Only the occasional car shot down the street, its occupant uninterested in what Smith was doing that early. Smith glanced up and saw a faint glow on the second floor. He moved to the gate opening and saw that, though it was closed, the padlock hung open. It would have been impossible for someone to lock it behind them. The dangling padlock told Smith that they were still inside. He removed his gun and inched the gate aside until he had an opening large enough to allow for a view of the interior. He knelt and put his eyes to the crack.

A sentry stood at the far side of the building's empty shell smoking a cigarette. Smith debated whether shooting him would aggravate Nolan's situation. He assumed that Khalil was forcing her to access Dattar's money in order to return it to him. Once the transaction was complete, Khalil would have no further reason to keep her alive.

Smith opened the door wider and slid in, keeping low. The ground floor consisted of steel beams evenly spaced, and no walls. An elevator in the back looked as though it was original to the building; next to it was a plank stairwell that lacked handrails. There was nothing that he could use as cover. He crept around the edges, keeping to the shadows, and was relieved to see the sentry pull out a phone and dial it. After a moment the man started talking in a foreign language. Smith walked faster around the perimeter while the oblivious sentry was immersed in his conversation. He was within two feet of the man when the conversation ended. Smith rose and placed the muzzle of his pistol at the base of the guard's skull.

"One word and you're dead," Smith whispered into his ear. The sentry froze.

"Show me with your fingers how many are upstairs." The man held up two fingers. Smith was relieved that he was still only dealing with the initial three that he had seen kidnap Nolan. "Lie down face-first." The guard lowered himself to the ground and stretched out. Smith flipped his gun around and swung the grip at the side of the man's head, aiming at the temple. The man went limp.

Smith headed to the plank stairs. As he approached, he heard the murmur of voices. All sounded male. He crept upward, wincing as one board creaked with his weight. When his eyes became level with the floor above, he stretched a bit more and peered into the second floor.

The second floor was enclosed on three sides, one covered in plastic sheeting. The rest of the interior was unfinished. Nolan sat in a chair and Khalil leaned over her. Both kept their attention on the computer in Nolan's hands while a second man stood about four feet away. Before Smith could duck, the second man turned and spotted him. He reached for a gun in his waistband, but before he could draw, Smith shot, hitting the man dead center in the chest. Khalil spun away from Nolan as he pulled a gun from a holster under his jacket.

Smith jerked downward, crouched low and stumbled down the stairs in order to avoid a shot to the head. He jumped the last few risers and headed to the far edge of the building, pressing his back against a steel beam. In the distance came the welcoming sound of an oncoming police siren. To his right he saw motion. The sentry was still unconscious, so it wasn't him. Smith moved around one side of the beam and he felt it vibrate as a bullet clanked off it, but he barely heard the shot. Whoever was making his way around the first floor of the building had a suppressor on his weapon. CIA, Smith thought. His earlier attacker was back.

Smith pressed his shoulder into the beam's side, doing his best to stay in line with the metal, but the span was too narrow to provide complete cover. Smith gasped as a bullet zipped past him. He was breathing hard while he tried to gauge the shooter's direction and angle. The man must be moving around the perimeter, getting in line for a clean shot. With nowhere to run in the gutted and open-air lower level, Smith's options were few. It was the devil below or the demon above. Nolan was above, so Smith raced back to the stairs, taking them two at a time,

heedless of the noise he made. The police siren was near, and the piercing whine had grown loud. He slowed at the floor level and rose into the
room just as Khalil leaped off the back of the building. Smith ignored
him while he went toward Nolan, who had risen from the chair and
stood, strangely hunched over. She seemed unable to straighten. She
threw the computer into a tote. When Smith reached her, she gave him
a look filled with panic. Smith heard the second attacker start pounding
up the stairs.

"We've got to jump like Khalil did. Now," Smith said. He aimed at
the stairwell and fired. The pounding of feet stopped, the sound of the
siren increased.

"He'll run from the police just like Khalil did," Nolan said.

Smith shook his head. "He's CIA. The police won't worry him."

Smith waved her to the building's edge where Khalil had disappeared
and she didn't hesitate. She ran in a stilted manner but still managed to
move. Smith reached the edge, looked back and saw the attacker step
onto the second floor. Nolan jumped and Smith followed her, bending
his knees to soften the impact. He glanced at the plank stairs and saw
the attacker's feet starting back down. Smith fired a round at them. The
angle was off, but the shot had the desired effect because the person
retreated back up.

They had landed at the back of the building, which pressed up
against the neighboring buildings on three sides.

"Through the building," Smith said. "The ceiling will protect us until
we reach the street side." Nolan sprinted next to him, still hunched
over. Smith felt his heart beating in a crazy rhythm. They made it to the
far end without incident, and Smith paused at the perimeter. The run
to the gate would be the most dangerous part. He turned to Nolan. "Go,
I'll cover you."

Smith burst out first, jogging backward and laying down fire in intervals, all aimed at the second floor. Nolan raced by, running in the stilted
manner with her back hunched and her head down. He didn't see the
attacker, but heard a bullet hit a temporary lamppost directly behind

him. The angle was beneficial to Smith, because he was still below and the attacker stuck several feet back from the ledge, but the attacker would get a much cleaner shot when Smith reached the open gate. Smith briefly considered running parallel to the building and climbing over a section of the chain link, but dismissed the idea. He'd be shot in the back as he did. He kept jogging in reverse and firing as he did. He was at the gate when he fired his last round.

He stumbled through the opening. A hole ripped through the mesh only inches from his left shoulder. Smith was relieved at the miss, knowing that he couldn't take many more hits. Eventually an artery would be nicked and he'd bleed to death. Nolan ran on a forty-five-degree angle across the street and through the opposite parking lot. Smith glanced to his left to check the area before he followed. He ran with her through the lot and around the building on the other side. As he hit the corner, he saw the flashing lights of the police strobe flickering off the trees. Nolan was still moving fast, the tote clutched in her hand. Smith was relieved to see a lone cab turn and head toward them. He hailed it. Ten seconds later they were inside, and the cab turned left again, heading north and away.

32

SMITH LEANED BACK IN THE SEAT while he caught his breath. He'd given the cabbie a random address in Harlem to buy some time and to get as far away from the scene as possible. Nolan was sitting at a twisted angle, keeping her body from the backrest. She kept her head down, and her hair obscured her face. In her hand was her tote bag. Nothing, it seemed, was bad enough to make her leave it behind.

"We need a place to land," Smith said.

Nolan raised her head to look at him. The pain in her face was clear, even in the dark of the cab.

"A hotel?"

Smith shook his head. "No credit cards. Perhaps an SRO that takes cash."

"Worried about being traced?"

Smith nodded.

She pulled out her computer.

"Keep it off," Smith said.

"I just need one minute, no more."

"Every minute it's on, they can track us. I don't need them to know which way we're headed."

"Then let's pull over. It will be just a minute, I promise. When I turn it off he'll drive on, and they won't know where we went."

Smith leaned forward to address the cabbie. "Can you pull over for a second? We need to do something." The cabbie shrugged and pulled to the curb.

"One minute only," Smith warned. She nodded, but kept her eyes on the tablet.

"No accessing bank accounts either. Whatever you're doing, it has to be untraceable."

"Don't worry, it is. I'm accessing my kilodollars. They're on the hard drive. I don't even store them in the cloud. The only place they exist is on this computer."

"Is that money?"

Nolan rocked her hand back and forth. "It's a form of currency, yes, but a cybercurrency. No paper bills or gold or silver coins. I store the bits on my hard drive and can transfer them to any other person who will accept them as payment."

Smith had never heard of such a thing. "Are they backed by any government?"

"No. A central computer located God knows where spits them out and scatters them across the net. You download and run a mining program that locates and collects them and offers them to you in an anonymous computer-generated transaction. Then you use them to pay for goods and services. The main computer controls how many are produced so that they can never be devalued." Smith was having a hard time wrapping his head around the concept.

"So you don't earn them or work for them? You just mine them from the Internet?"

Nolan nodded. "The same as if you would mine gold or diamonds."

"Who accepts such a thing as payment for anything?" Smith said.

"Mostly people who want to remain anonymous. Because no central bank holds the funds the accounts can never be frozen, no one can garnish them, and the IRS can't confiscate them."

"So the primary use is for illegal transactions."

Nolan shot him a glance. "That's probably true, but isn't that the same when one uses paper dollars? That's anonymous as well, and cash is the favored currency used to purchase drugs."

"How in the world did you learn about this?"

"It's money." She acted as though that was explanation enough.

"And you love money," Smith said. He kept his voice light to avoid making his statement sound like an accusation.

"I love the *accumulation* of money. The math of it. The puzzle of how to arrange trades that result in a net win. It fascinates me. The kilodollars are just another form of it."

Smith decided he didn't need to understand the details right then; he just needed to be sure she logged off in ten seconds. He was relieved when she did, shutting down the computer. She leaned forward and gave the cabbie a new address north of Harlem. The cab pulled back into traffic and Smith watched behind them, searching for any possible tails.

"Where are we heading?" he said.

"To a house. It's a private club that operates as a type of bed and breakfast, except that one rents the entire house. I paid for two nights."

"In kilodollars."

She nodded. "This owner accepts them on a website, and they'll be transferred from there. The site is anonymous, so untraceable, and the money is as well."

"But the transaction still left a footprint."

She shrugged and then winced. "Yes, but a minor one. I first accessed an anonymous service that blocked my computer's cookies, never mentioned the address of the house, nor did the owner. I've used it once before. Anyone tracking me won't be able to determine where the house is located."

Smith was impressed. "You don't need a CIA safe house, you can arrange your own."

She flashed him a small smile. "Only for two nights. Then we need to move on."

Ten minutes later they pulled up to a square beige brick building on a quiet street as far north as one could go and still be in Manhattan. Smith paid the cabbie and joined her at the steel door. The structure was four stories high and had multiple, evenly spaced doorways along the sidewalk. Each doorway had a small red metal awning with white trim, some with rusted supports as an overhang, which gave the building an old-fashioned air of faded former glory. The window-unit air conditioners that protruded from the façade at various locations only added to the impression that the building had been constructed many decades ago, before the onset of central air. Nolan punched in a code for the second door in the row, and there was a buzzing sound as the lock disengaged.

They entered a narrow foyer that contained a bank of steel mailboxes attached to the wall on their left. In front was another door that separated a small lobby area. Nolan pressed a different code on a second keypad and again the door buzzed. The lobby had an aging marble floor in a white and black checkerboard pattern. A single elevator was on their right. It seemed like an afterthought added to a vintage building. In front of them was a narrow stairway. They hiked up stairs covered in industrial gray carpeting to the first landing, which contained two doors. The door on the left was also steel and had a small round peephole and a keypad in place of a deadbolt. Nolan punched in a code on the keypad and the clicking sound indicated that the door was unlocked.

The duplex's configuration was a shotgun, with a foyer, living room, and kitchen in the back and a narrow stairway on the right that led to a second level. The wood floors gleamed, and a piece of modern art hung above a fireplace on the living room far wall. The disparity between the interior of the apartment and the exterior was marked. Nolan waved him to the stairwell that led to the second floor. At the bottom of the stairs she paused.

"What's wrong?" Smith said.

"I don't know if I can climb them. It was different when we were running away. I didn't really feel it so acutely then. But now, the pain might be too much."

"Would you like me to carry you?"

She shook her head. "Maybe just lend your arm."

He did, and she mounted up the first step, hissing through her teeth in pain. Despite it, she continued and gave a sigh of relief at the top.

"The master's to the right," she said.

He escorted her into a fairly large master bedroom with a king-size bed and a dark dresser against one wall. A flat-screen television rested on a console, and nightstands on either side of the bed held reading lamps. She waved him to a door next to the closet that led to the master bath.

The bathroom was spacious. Smith opened a cabinet and found a hair dryer, toiletries, and, most important, a box containing first aid items.

"I'm glad to see these. I'd just purchased some before I found you. They're currently resting under a bush near that building," Smith said.

Nolan shivered. "I never want to see that building again."

"Looks like I've managed to ruin the shirt you gave me." Smith turned to show her his left sleeve. She gasped.

"Is that a fresh wound?"

He nodded. "Yes. Who first?" Smith held up the alcohol swabs.

"I wasn't shot. You first," Nolan said.

"Could you do the honors once more?"

He unbuttoned the shirt and peeled it off, taking care not to yank at the fabric that was stuck to the wound with dried blood. She opened an alcohol swab and wiped it down. Now it was his turn to hiss in pain. She rooted around in the first aid box.

"No tweezers."

"I don't think the bullet embedded. It's a graze wound only."

"Ah, good, because I honestly don't think I could do that again." She wrapped the second injury in gauze and used some white tape to secure it. She twisted a bit to put the tape back and groaned. Her face turned white. He put a hand lightly on her arm.

"Let me see your back."

"I don't think I can take off the sweater. If I lift my arms would you take it off?"

He nodded. She lifted her arms and he pulled the sweater up and over, taking care not to let it scrape against her back or sides. She was wearing a raspberry-colored bra of mesh fabric that left nothing to the imagination, but though Smith noticed, he was more concerned about what he'd see when she turned around.

She pivoted and he gaped at her back. Huge red welts in straight lines bisected her from side to side. One had split open and oozed blood. More blood ran in a thin line from the steel hook and eye fastener of her bra. Her entire back was swollen and purpling from severe bruising, and he could see where the rod had hit her vertebrae. Smith felt his anger rise. He swallowed it and focused on the spine.

"I'm going to run my hands along your vertebrae—"

"I don't think I can take that," she said.

"Very lightly. I just want to see if they chipped one."

"Okay," she said.

He carefully ran his hands down her spine. She made no sound, but at one point jerked away from him. He was relieved to see that her bones seemed intact. A crushed vertebra would have consigned her to a lifetime of pain.

"I don't think they broke anything." He fished through the first aid box.

"What are you looking for?" she said.

"Some sort of salve, or antibiotic ointment. One of the welts is open." He found an antibiotic gel. He first swabbed the cut with an alcohol wipe and then dabbed on the antibiotic. When he was finished, he put a large bandage on it, taking care to attach the adhesive edges with a light touch.

She turned. Her eyes were large and held a sad look. He wanted to comfort her somehow. He put his palms on either side of her face and kissed her lightly on the lips. He pulled away but kept his palms on her face.

"I'm sorry I wasn't able to find you before they did that," he said.

"You were right," she said.

"About what?"

"What you said at the office. I wasn't prepared for them to kill any-one, and I'm not prepared for this level of viciousness. Any of it. I can't imagine how I thought I would be. Arrogance, I suppose. Once they have their money, they'll kill me without a thought."

He shook his head. "I won't let them kill you." Her sad expression shifted and a glint of light and hope returned to her eyes.

"I believe you," she said.

"So you now think I'm one of the good guys?" He smiled at her.

"After what you just did for me in that building, I'd be crazy to think anything else."

She reached up and pulled him back toward her. This kiss was dif-ferent. She slipped her tongue into his mouth and he felt his body start to hum. She stepped into him and flattened her breasts on his naked chest. The image of her in the red bra rose in his mind. He put a hand on her through the sheer material. He reached an arm around to draw her closer and remembered her injury right before he touched her back. Instead he lowered his hands, grabbed her hips and pressed her into him. She moved in tight and rotated against him. After a moment he lifted his head.

"I don't think you should be on your back," he said. *But God, I wish you were*. She looked at him and the light in her eyes had been replaced with intensity. A bit of humor crept into them.

"I don't think you should hold yourself up with your arms," she said. She rose on tiptoe, sliding her body along his and kissing him again. "I have an idea that might work."

33

RUSSELL WOKE UP AND FELT DANGER. Her nerve endings prickled with it. The hospital room remained dark and the sounds of the city were muted. She shifted and was heartened to note that she felt slightly better, but the feeling of menace was palpable. She glanced around the room, but nothing seemed out of place. The tray holding the cup with the ice cubes remained by her bed, the IV needle still dug into her hand, and the faucet at the bathroom sink still dripped.

She reached out to the cup and shook an ice chip into her mouth. That's when she heard it. A footfall. Stealthy. In the hall.

"Sir, who are you? This is an isolation floor." The nurse's voice rang out. Russell didn't think. She pulled the needle out of her hand, wincing at the welling blood, flung the bedclothes away and rolled off the bed on the side away from the door. What she didn't count on was that her legs wouldn't support her. They collapsed and she hit the linoleum, hard. She lay flat and shifted under the bed. Not hard to do as the bed frame was elevated two feet off the floor. If it wasn't dark in the room, any intruder would easily have seen her.

A pair of men's wingtips appeared in the doorway and took one step into the room. Russell held her breath, waiting.

"Sir," she heard the nurse say again, this time close. Russell watched the shoes turn as the intruder walked out. He paused in the entrance before carefully stepping left, out of Russell's vision. Russell put her cheek against the linoleum and rested there. She didn't think she had the energy to move just yet.

She heard the man's shoes as he went down the hall and the murmuring of voices. After a moment the floor went silent once again. The muted sounds of the city and the dripping bathroom sink returned to her consciousness. There was a pinging sound as the elevator doors opened.

Russell saw a pair of feet encased in women's running shoes step into the entrance.

"Ms. Russell?" Wendel said. Russell was relieved to hear her voice.

"Under here," Russell replied. Wendel crouched down and peered under the bed. She wore a mask on her face to filter out bacteria. Russell inhaled deeply and almost instantly regretted it. The floor stank of antiseptic and dust.

"What are you doing under there?" Wendel said.

Russell rolled back the other way and sat up. Her eyes started to go black and dots appeared. She felt rather than saw Wendel brace her.

"I heard someone lurking outside the room and dropped and rolled to hide. Instinct, I guess. Why are you here?" Russell said.

"Thank God for your instincts. We need to get out of here. Now," Wendel said.

"What's the matter?"

"Your friend Marty says that the CIA mole is feeding information on Smith and Nolan to a prepaid phone that he then tracked here. He called me at the New York office, and I rushed over as soon as he did."

Russell wished she could have seen the face of the owner of the wingtips. When she found out who the mole was, she was going to ensure that he or she never saw the outside of a prison again.

"Please go talk to the nurse. Get a description of the man in wingtips. See if he signed in on the floor."

Wendel nodded. "Can you sit without my help?"

Russell leaned back against the bed frame. "Yes." Wendel left. After a couple of minutes, she was back.

"There is no nurse. And the last person who signed in was over four hours ago."

"There was a nurse only a few minutes ago. She confronted the man."

"Well, there's no one now. Perhaps she went to the coffee room or to get something."

Or perhaps the man silenced her. Russell shook off the thought. There would be no reason to bother with the nurse. The man hadn't signed in, and the hospital didn't have cameras on the floor. He wouldn't be at risk of discovery.

"What does Marty have to say about the time delay?"

"The proprietary system is absolutely being tampered with from the inside. He also says that the mole may be onto the fact that you're suspicious because he tried to counter some of Marty's probes." Wendel waved a hand in the air. "I don't understand the details, but Marty was using your passcode to gain inside access and another person started cyberstalking him." Wendel inhaled. "And that's not all." Russell's eyes cleared and she was heartened to notice that she felt better once sitting.

"There's more?" Russell said.

Wendel nodded. "Your tests came back positive for a respiratory virus related to the avian strain." Russell hated that, but felt a resignation flow over her.

"I can't say that I'm surprised. Can this one be treated?"

Wendel shook her head.

"What's the fatality rate?"

Wendel clamped her lips shut.

"That good, huh?" Russell said. "How contagious am I?"

"It's not easily transmitted human-to-human, but if it is, they say two to five days, depending on the person. Your doctor seems to think that you're no longer contagious."

Russell sighed. "How long have I been here?"

"Thirty-six hours."

"You should leave."

Wendel shook her head. "I'm not worried about catching it."

"You should be. The doctor could be wrong. Especially if I have the mutated version."

"You don't."

Russell paused. "What do you mean?"

"You don't. It's a variant, but not mutated."

Russell almost sagged in relief. Misplaced relief, she knew, because traditional bird flu was deadly enough, but she would have felt worse if she knew that she had been Patient Number One for a deadly mutated virus.

"I think it has something to do with Dattar. All of it. I think he had someone infect you. Maybe this mole," Wendel said.

Russell nodded. Wendel had finally put into words what Russell had feared since the moment she became ill. She gave a weak wave in the general direction of the metal locker across the room that acted as a closet.

"I'll need my clothes and phone."

Wendel nodded and glanced at her watch. "If the night nurse had been here, she would be scheduled to take a fifteen-minute break in two minutes. The second nurse will begin her rounds at the same time. That will last twenty and the main desk will be empty." She left Russell's line of sight. Seconds later Russell heard the locker door creak open. She clutched the top of the mattress and used it to pull herself upright, turned and sat on the edge of the bed. Wendel handed her the phone and placed the clothes next to her. Russell reached for them, but the idea of putting them on felt overwhelming.

"Can you help? I'm ridiculously weak."

Wendel braced her as she dressed.

"Are there any medications you want to bring?" Wendel asked.

"They've had me on a saline drip. Nothing else."

Wendel looked at her watch. "Wait here." She went to the doorway and peered around the corner. She spun and came back to Russell. "It's clear." Russell wrapped an arm around her shoulders. "I don't think the elevators are safe. They all open onto the main floor facing a security station on the lower level."

"There's a stairwell to the left. I'm not sure where it leads," Russell said. Wendel only nodded and helped Russell to stand. Her legs held and they started toward the door, moving in tandem. Russell leaned on Wendel, taking advantage of her strength. She didn't want to waste all her energy walking on her own when she knew a long series of stairs still lay ahead of her. The only sound in the empty hall was the murmuring of a television, volume set low, somewhere to her right. To her left an overhead sign glowed red with the word "stairs." Russell turned that way and was glad to feel the adrenaline begin to percolate in her system. It gave her a boost. They hit the door and pushed it open.

The interior stairwell consisted of metal and cement. The door closed and Russell saw the number four painted in navy block lettering on the back. The idea of walking down four flights made Russell want to groan, but she shoved the thought aside. She was about to start down when she heard a scrape from somewhere below. Wendel must have heard it too, because Russell felt the woman's muscles freeze. Russell jerked her head toward the door. Wendel nodded, and they reversed. Russell opened the door with a gentle push and they were back through it and once again in the ICU hallway.

"Elevator to second floor. Stairs from there," Russell said in a whisper. Wendel didn't reply but started to the elevator bank. Russell pushed faster. Once inside the lift she leaned against the wall while it lowered to the second floor.

"If there's a nurse let me take the lead," Russell said. She waved Wendel off in favor of walking on her own. The doors whisked open and they stepped into a hall that matched the one they'd just left. Rooms stretched on either side and a nurse stood behind a tall counter operating a copy machine. She glanced up, took in Wendel and gave a slight frown when she looked at Russell.

"May I help you?" she said.

Russell nodded. "I'm a patient. I have a friend who wants to see Susan." Russell indicated Wendel. "But she leaves for Europe tomorrow early and this is our only chance. It's just down the hall, room 234. Do you mind?"

The nurse looked about to protest. "Mr. Skorich? He's asleep."

"I'll just have a quick look. I promise to leave if he's asleep," Wendel said. A phone on a nearby desk rang. Hallelujah, Russell thought.

"Please be quick about it," the nurse said. "The time for visitors is long past." She turned her attention to the phone. Russell did her best to stand straight and tall as she walked down the hall. Her eyes locked on the sign for the stairs and she focused on reaching them. Wendel stayed close and pushed open the door, holding it for Russell. The minute they were through Russell wrapped her arm around Wendel's shoulder.

"Go," she said.

They started down, moving fast. Their feet rang on the metal stairs and the sound echoed through the stairwell. Within seconds they heard another set of footsteps running down the stairs from above.

"Faster," Russell said. She was sweating and she began to get dizzy. "Do you have a weapon?"

"A knife. At my calf." Not the worst weapon, and it had the advantage of silence, but if whoever was lurking in the stairwell was CIA, he'd likely have a gun with a suppressor. A quiet and efficient weapon. They reached the bottom and pushed through the door to the parking garage. A sedan that Russell recognized as a company car sat parked in a handicapped spot.

"It's mine. Let's go," Wendel said. Russell got up and staggered a bit toward the driver's side, but she made it there without passing out. She glanced at the parking garage exit. So far, no one burst through. Hauling open the car's heavy door was about as much as Russell could manage.

"There are guns are in the trunk," Wendel said.

"Excellent. Run. Get out of here. Go back to DC. I'll handle this and will call you. I don't want you involved in this any more than necessary."

Wendel nodded and sprinted away. Russell fell into the seat and slammed the door behind her. She drove out of the parking garage and onto the street, where she accelerated at every opportunity, all the while watching the sideview mirror. While it appeared as though no one was tailing her, she wasn't reassured. She picked up her phone and stared at it, wondering if she should risk using it. After a moment she decided that she needed Klein's help badly enough to give it a try. Russell powered it up and dialed Klein. The Covert-One director answered on the first ring.

"We've got a mole in the CIA," Russell said.

"A situation that appears to be depressingly familiar, Ms. Russell."

"Whoever it is, they're after Smith and Nolan and transmitting their location to an unknown assailant. Dattar is in this up to his eyeballs, I can just feel it. And you can bet that he has those coolers. Smith was right."

"That's a lot of speculation. But if even a portion is correct, the CIA can't be allowed to take the lead on the search for them. The mole could undermine each move."

"What if they're here? On US soil? The CIA has no jurisdiction over the investigation then. It has to go to the Department of Homeland Security and FBI. CIA, and its mole, won't know about it."

"You've been overseas for a while. The DHS and FBI are now supposed to receive and exchange intelligence with the CIA when it's required to assist in a national matter."

"Okay, and then the NYPD is out as well. Since 9/11, the NYPD has deployed an intelligence-gathering unit. Its head is a CIA officer on loan named Harcourt. I presume he'll be kept in the loop with the other agencies."

"Are you telling me that the CIA and NYPD are acting in concert on US soil?"

"I am," Russell said.

"That's perilously close to domestic spying, which is illegal," Klein said.

"And Covert-One? What are the rules between that organization and the others?"

Klein paused. Russell waited.

"Covert-One is autonomous." Klein's comment supported what Russell had thought since learning of Covert-One. The idea that Klein headed a covert operation completely free of organizational requirements and reporting duties was astonishing. However, it was just what Russell wanted to hear because she needed to operate free of the CIA.

"I want to bring in Beckmann," she said.

"No others."

"Hear me out. With Beckmann, Howell, and Smith all bases are covered. I know about the inner workings of the CIA, Smith knows about bacteria, Howell knows about staying alive."

"And this Beckmann?"

"Beckmann knows how to skirt the edges and get results."

Klein was quiet on the other end of the line, and Russell bit her tongue while she allowed him to ponder her request.

"I haven't met this Beckmann, but Smith has. If he agrees, then Beckmann can be brought in. If not, he can't."

Russell breathed a sigh of relief. She was halfway home with her plan.

"I'll be sure to keep Smith informed. If he says no, then Beckmann's out, no questions asked." She took a deep breath. "I was hoping for one more favor."

"What do you need?"

"A steady stream of information from the DHS and the FBI in real time, not in weekly reports. Whatever they know I want access to."

"Easy enough."

Russell raised her eyebrows. The DHS and the FBI both weren't exactly forthcoming with the CIA despite their public claims of cooperation. The disconnects between the two agencies were legendary. That Klein could wrap up the disparate reports was a huge advantage to Covert-One.

"Just how connected is Covert-One? What you're able to accomplish is astonishing."

"Do you need anything else?" Klein neatly dodged the question.

"To find Smith. Do you know where he is?"

"He's gone dark. I have little doubt that he is alive, however. A recent police transmission indicated that they had discovered one man dead in a building near the High Line. It wasn't Smith."

Russell didn't bother to ask why Klein was focusing on one dead person in one particular building in New York City. She assumed that he had his reasons.

"And Nolan?"

"Presumably with Smith."

"And not dead."

"Not yet."

"That's ominous."

"She's at most risk. A civilian with the bad judgment to have stolen from Dattar. Her continued existence is not assured."

Russell started coughing. She knew that once she started, it would be almost impossible to stop. She gagged and choked while Klein listened on the other end of the phone.

"Are you all right?" Klein said.

"I think whatever is in those coolers was used on me."

"How contagious is it?"

"Apparently no one's entirely sure. It doesn't seem to be easily transmitted between people, but they don't know how it's contracted. I need a place to rest and I want to speak to a scientist named Ohnara again. He said he'd be here, in New York, for a conference. In Midtown. Which reminds me, I need one more thing. Ohnara's a colleague of Smith's who checked into a suspicious swab on my refrigerator. I think he needs to run further tests."

"I presume they will be costly?"

"Perhaps. The paperwork I'll need to fill out at the CIA would take several days and possibly tip off our mole. I was hoping you could speed things through for me. I guess I don't need to say that I have a vested interest in this. I'm told my chances of beating this thing aren't great."

"I'll authorize it as quickly as possible. Are you armed?"

"I have some CIA-issued weapons," Russell said. "Why?"

"Something tells me you're going to need them."

34

DATTAR STEPPED ONTO A Gulfstream jet bound for New York's JFK and settled in the first seat. Flush with Amir's cash and supplied with a new passport and identity, he now knew that he would have to oversee the return of his money and the release of the weapon himself. Depending on intermediaries never worked. He felt the plane begin to bump along the runway and the video about flight security began to play. His in-flight phone rang.

"You lied to me," Khalil said.

Dattar sat up. "What are you talking about?"

"You have no money. The woman took it all."

Dattar's mind raced. "You're wrong. I have money. Other money. You think she got it all? She did not."

"Then pay me. Now. And the fee just went up because of your lies. I want double."

"Absolutely not. You haven't accomplished anything that I hired you to do. Smith is alive and I presume Howell is as well."

"You either pay me double, or I'll have her transfer it all to me."

Dattar's rage exploded and he stood.

"That money is mine!"

"Double. Now."

Dattar began to pace. Rajiid watched him from a neighboring seat and Dattar thought he saw something close to derision in his eyes. All these problems were chipping away at Rajiid's respect. Dattar took a deep breath to calm himself. He needed to appear as though he was in control, and pacing and screaming would not do.

"Is she in your control?" he said.

"Yes."

"Put her on the phone."

"Not until you pay me."

What a lying bastard, Dattar thought. He didn't have her.

"I don't pay you until you prove you have her. Put her next to you and call me from the computer. Turn on the webcam. When I see her, I'll transfer half the money."

"I do nothing until the money is transferred."

"It seems that we're at an impasse."

Khalil hung up.

Dattar sat back down. He needed to move quickly. If Khalil had discovered Dattar's secret, others might have as well. He stared out the window. The airplane couldn't move fast enough.

Smith woke when a bar of sunlight shot through the white wooden shutters on the bedroom window. Nolan slept next to him on her side. He slid off the bed and padded into the bathroom. A quick look in the mirror gave him some hope. The haggard look he'd been sporting had eased a bit, though the bandages on his arm and the morning beard made him appear disreputable. He noticed that the gauze was stained a reddish brown color from dried blood, so at least he wasn't actively bleeding anymore. He switched on the shower and stepped under the warm water, relishing it. He wet the gauze in order to be sure that it wouldn't stick to the wound and then unwound it in the shower. He took care to cleanse the wound gently. When he was finished, he used his teeth to hold one end of a clean piece of gauze while he rewrapped the wound. He tied a decent knot on the field dressing, wrapped a towel around his middle, and headed to the kitchen.

The house was well provisioned with shelf-stable food and drinks.

Smith was interested to see that the pantry contained UHT boxed milk, the type normally found in Europe that could be stored indefinitely without refrigeration. It gave Smith a small clue about the nationality of the house's owner.

He placed a coffee pod in a maker and checked in three cabinets until he found cups. He placed one under the spout and pressed the start button. From upstairs he heard the sound of a bath being drawn. While the coffee cup filled, Smith rooted around in the kitchen drawers, looking for a telephone book in order to find a big box store where he could purchase a prepaid phone. His search turned up nothing. Apparently phone books were too low tech for the house's owner. He heard footsteps and Nolan walked into the kitchen.

She wore oversized men's gray sweatpants topped with a large white undershirt, also a man's. She smiled at him and Smith was glad to see that it was one of her first real smiles, not a half effort. He smiled back. She walked over and gave him a quick kiss on the lips.

"Nice outfit," she said.

"It never occurred to me that there would be clothes available for our use. Those look like they'd fit me a whole lot better than you. Want to switch?"

"Sure. There are some other choices up there, but most look too small for you. First, though, that coffee smells delicious."

He pulled out a kitchen chair for her. "I'll make you some. Take a seat."

She settled into the chair, pulled her feet up and wrapped her arms around her knees. Smith noticed that the position had the advantage of keeping the most injured part of her back from touching the furniture. The coffee cup filled and he placed it in front of her. "Milk or sugar?"

She shook her head and took a sip. She eyed his bandage. "A new dressing? Looks a little rough. Want me to fix it?"

He nodded. "I needed a shower and I didn't want to wake you." She began to rise and he waved her back into her seat. "Doesn't have to be now. Finish your drink." He opened the pantry door. "This place is well stocked. What kind of person needs a house like this and accepts kilo-dollars for payment?"

Nolan's eyes held a knowing look. "People like us."

Smith held his cup up in a toast. "Touché." He swallowed the rest of his coffee and placed the cup in the sink. "I'm headed out in search of a prepaid phone."

She nodded. "I'll let you wear these clothes. I threw ours in the washing machine and now they're drying. By the time you get back they'll be clean. Although that shirt of yours will still have a tear in the sleeve."

"As long as it's not covered with blood, I'll be happy."

Twenty minutes later Smith was in the sweats and T-shirt, which on him were slightly too small, and walking to an electronics store that Nolan had suggested. He purchased the phone and fired it up with a charged battery that the clerk had offered. He dialed Klein.

"Glad to hear that you're alive," Klein said. "Ms. Russell left the hospital and is working on the bacteria angle."

"Left the hospital? So she's recovered?"

"Apparently enough to leave. She's concerned about the CIA mole finding her and is keeping on the move."

"Did they type the virus that she had?"

"It was a variant of avian flu. Nonmutant."

Smith heaved a sigh of relief. "So not the strain we're searching for. Still bad, but it sounds as though she's recovering."

"She seems as convinced as you are that Dattar is behind everything."

"I heard from Howell. He confirmed it. Told me about some sort of weapon."

"I think it's in the coolers," Klein said.

"I have to agree. But how in the hell are we going to find them?"

"I thought you were intending to use Nolan as bait," Klein said. Smith had not been thrilled with the idea when he'd had it, but now he found that he detested it.

"Initially I thought we could contain the risk, but after last night's near fiasco, I'm reconsidering it. I almost didn't get to her in time. She nearly got killed."

"It may be our only option." Klein's voice was calm. Smith didn't reply. He was nearing the building and slowed. "She's always at risk of being killed until Dattar gets his money back or is neutralized," Klein continued. "She's got to know that and just might be willing to assist. Why don't you tell her what you're thinking? Give her a chance to make the decision?"

"She's a civilian. She doesn't understand the risk and is not trained to protect herself."

"She put some of this in motion when she stole the money. She may be at risk, but she seems perfectly capable of understanding the danger we're facing. I'd like you to explain it to her." Smith didn't reply. "You seem to have changed your mind on this tactic. Is there something I'm missing here? Something you're not telling me?"

"No. I'll address it with her."

"Good. Where are you staying? I'll tell Howell and Beckmann."

Smith turned onto the street and spotted two men leaning against a tree opposite the apartment building. "Never mind. They're here." He rang off and strolled up to them. Howell watched him approach, but Beckmann was intent on watching two aging men who sat next to him on wooden crates and played dominoes. He glanced up as Smith came near.

"How did you find me?"

"We found the cabbie that drove you here. Beckmann and I were just coming around when you and Ms. Nolan jumped into it," Howell said.

Smith snapped to attention. "Did anyone else see that cab drive off?"

Howell shook his head. "No. We canvassed the area after you left. There was no one. You're fairly safe for the moment. Happy to see that you handled the situation so well."

Smith grimaced. "Khalil and the CIA mole both got away."

"A pity," Howell said. "But not surprising. Khalil has a way of staying alive."

"Come on in. I want to hear all about the guy you found."

He punched in the code, and both men followed him into the kitchen. Nolan was at the counter eating orange slices. A bag with the logo of a grocery chain was on the counter next to her. She was back in the jeans and navy sweater and her feet were bare. Smith made the introductions and noticed that she regarded the two men with a wary look in her eye. The men took chairs around the table, and Smith started coffee.

Howell ran down what he and Beckmann had learned.

"Russell seems to think the weapon may have something to do with the missing bacteria coolers," Smith said.

Beckmann nodded. "I agree. There's the attack on the Grand Royal; Dattar escapes; the coolers are stolen; and now a foot soldier of Dattar's says he's planning an attack. It seems to be a logical conclusion."

"But now he has no money to launch the attack." It was the first time Nolan had spoken.

Howell raised an eyebrow. "Why is that? Dattar is thought to be quite wealthy."

"I stole it."

Smith watched Howell and Beckmann over the rim of his coffee cup and was pleased by their shocked reactions. They were as surprised by her announcement as he had been. Beckmann gave a soft laugh.

"Just like my ex-wife," he said.

Howell shot him an amused look. "One hopes you didn't give her all of it."

Beckmann just shrugged. Howell glanced back at Nolan with new respect.

"Your audacity surprises me, but it concerns me as well. Dattar is not one to be stolen from. Also, are you quite sure that you got it all?"

"As of two days ago I was."

"She can't access the Internet. It's how they're tracking her," Smith said.

"Is there no computer here?"

Smith pushed off the counter. "Actually, I hadn't gotten that far when I bumped into you."

"There's a Mac in the living room. It should be clean," Nolan said.

"Would you mind checking?" Howell said.

"Not at all." They followed Nolan into the living room and waited while she accessed various sites. After a moment Smith heard her suck in a breath. "Twenty million dollars was deposited in one of his Cayman accounts twenty-four hours ago. It's a functioning account that the authorities must have overlooked."

"Can you find its source?"

Nolan worked the keyboard, keeping her focus on the screen. "It came from a wire. I can't access the routing numbers. I'm sorry."

"Seems as though Dattar has arranged some interim financing," Howell said.

Smith began to pace. "So he's back in the game. We need to flush him out." Smith focused on Nolan. "It has occurred to me, as well as to Russell, that dangling you and his money might encourage him to come out of hiding."

Nolan sat back in her chair, a thoughtful look on her face. To Smith's relief she didn't appear outraged or betrayed by his suggestion. He watched her think the proposition through. Howell raised an eyebrow at Smith but refrained from commenting, and Beckmann shifted forward in his seat. After a long pause she looked up at Smith and her usual determined expression was back.

"Would all three of you gentlemen be present to take Dattar down once he appears?"

"Yes," Smith said without hesitation.

"I'd like nothing better," Howell replied.

Beckmann nodded. "Of course."

"Then let's do it," Nolan said.

35

WENDEL DROVE INTO THE parking lot near CIA headquarters, killed the engine, and sat back with a sigh. She'd driven through the night, gone to her house for a short nap, and come straight to the office. She collected her things, along with her keycard and a briefcase, and headed inside. Marty was due to call in thirty minutes. He needed her help from within the compound in order to continue his search for the mole. Russell had given him her password and access codes, but now that the stalker had found him through that patch, he wanted hers as a new entry point. He also wanted both women's computers turned on so that he could delve deeper.

The building was beginning to bustle in the morning. She passed through the security checkpoints in a tired daze. She made her way to her office, keeping her face neutral for the benefit of the security cameras that lined the halls. Inside, though, she was shaking. Turning on the computer was of minor assistance, but if the agency discovered that she'd helped an outsider to breach their network, she'd be charged with aiding and abetting treason. Yet she knew that it was necessary. The delayed transmissions had nearly killed Jordan and were compromising God knows how many other missions. Her office was past Russell's. As she got nearer to Russell's office, she saw that the door was closed, which was odd. She was almost sure it had been open when she'd last seen it. She slowed, not sure that she wanted to confront whoever was in the office. She knocked once and opened the door.

Steve Harcourt sat in Russell's chair and George Cromwell sat opposite. Harcourt was typing on the computer keyboard, but paused when he saw Wendel.

"We've been preparing to speak to you, Ms. Wendel," Cromwell said. Wendel's already sick stomach gave a wrench that made her want to bend over in pain. Instead she took a deep breath and stood straighter.

"Why is that, sir?"

Cromwell gave her a grave look. "Someone's accessing the CIA database from the outside. They're using Russell's passcode. We're not sure how much damage was done as yet. Luckily her computer is offline, and the IT specialist says that unless it's open there are only a few areas that can be accessed from outside, even with the passcode. We're monitoring the threat. Letting him use the code for the moment. Trying to trace the hacker back to the source."

Wendel's mouth was dry. She managed a nod but didn't trust herself to speak. Harcourt stood, and she looked across the desktop at him.

"We just called the hospital and were told that she was gone. The night nurses described the woman who was with her and the sign-in sheet. Your name was on the sign-in sheet. Then we had hospital security check the security camera feed. You were seen smoking outside when Russell's asset, Jon Smith, appeared and spoke to you, and later you were found on the parking lot security tape with Russell."

Wendel swallowed, which was of little use to her parched throat. Her hands were shaking, but she clasped them in front of her to control them.

"I understood from Ms. Russell that Smith was assisting in this investigation."

Harcourt nodded. "She suggested that he be involved in the investigation early on and agreed to manage him. Why were you at the hospital?"

"I was with Ms. Russell."

Cromwell pointed to an empty chair. "Perhaps you should tell us everything you know. In particular, we want to hear everything you know about Smith. He's been implicated in one shooting at an office building in New York and another at an empty construction site where a body was found."

Wendel had no trouble looking shocked at this statement. She knew so little about Smith, but watching him hang from the wall of the hotel during the attack and then his instant grasp of the technology breach along with his access to a man with Marty's talents left her with little doubt that he was capable of protecting himself. One only had to speak to the man for a few minutes to tell that his survival skills far surpassed those of most civilians. Whether or not he was truly on the right side of things was something that Wendel couldn't know. All she had to rely on were her instincts and Russell's confidence in him.

"I'm sure he had nothing to do with that, sir."

"Just tell us what he said to you," Harcourt's voice was harsh.

Wendel sank into the empty chair. Her mind raced with possible explanations for her conversation with Smith, but she decided to stick as close to the truth as possible. Russell had already coached her on what to say if Marty's activities were discovered. She was to be forthcoming and lay it all on Russell.

"Ms. Russell asked that I speak with him. She had concerns about the CIA."

Cromwell leaned forward. "What type of concerns?"

Both men stared at her. Wendel hesitated. Even with Russell's insistence on taking the blame, fingering Russell felt as though Wendel were throwing her under the bus. She swallowed again and then plunged on.

"She thought there was a mole. On the inside. Feeding information to the outside." Harcourt and Cromwell exchanged glances.

"Did she say who?" Cromwell said.

Wendel shook her head.

Harcourt snorted. "Well, it's her passcode that's compromised. I'd say she's the mole. And I don't like that Smith is receiving information from her. He's supposed to be an asset, not a confidant. What is she thinking?"

Cromwell nodded. "So much for bringing in field officers. Clearly she's gone rogue and he's assisting her." He stood. "We need to bring them both in."

"I suggest that we use the FBI for this one. Send out a bulletin. The New York City police are already looking to speak with him about the Landon Investments killing, but Russell managed to back them down."

Cromwell looked surprised. "She did? How?"

Harcourt frowned. "I'm sorry to say that she asked me to call one of my contacts on the force and get him to sit on the Smith connection for a little while. Refocus their attention away from him. She said she needed Smith's expertise to assist in the search for Dattar and the coolers." Harcourt held out his hands, palms up, and a contrite look passed over his face. "I thought it was a good idea at the time."

Cromwell waved him off. "You acted appropriately. Nothing wrong with assisting another officer and Smith was her asset to manage. Call the FBI. Get them on it now. I want Russell found, and I want Smith dragged off the street."

"Unharmed?"

Cromwell got a pensive look on his face. "Her, absolutely. Him? I'd like to bring him here and get some answers, but they should know that he's armed and dangerous and if he puts up a fight then they should use their own judgment. If he responds with deadly force, they shouldn't hesitate to do the same." Wendel did her best not to gasp out loud. Harcourt reached over and shut off Russell's computer.

"I'll be sure to have this office sealed and let the IT department track the hacker for a little longer before inactivating her passcode." Cromwell walked to the open door.

"Ms. Wendel, come with us. I'd like you to prepare a formal statement for inclusion in the file." Cromwell stood at the door and indicated that she should precede him out. She gave one glance to the darkened computer and left.

36

MANHAR WATCHED DATTAR's limousine pull into the gated drive of a house in Long Island. True to their word, Howell and Beckmann had let him go, and he had spent the first few hours holed up next to Khalil's base camp. He'd been unable to decide what to do. To return home without having accomplished his goal meant death; that was certain. To admit failure to Khalil meant death by slow torture. He had huddled in a dark corner watching the half-finished building for any signs of his boss, and it was then that he saw Khalil's limo pull up. He'd seen them push the woman into the construction site and later watched Smith stroll down the street and disappear inside. It was to his great dismay that he saw Khalil run away. He'd hoped that Smith would kill him.

He'd kept his ear to the ground during the entire mission and had heard a rumor that Dattar was flying into the States to stay at the home of a Pakistani nationalist who lived in Long Island. To the neighbors, this man was a Turkish import-export entrepreneur, but he was actually an arms trader. The rumor was that Dattar was renting the house for his own use.

Now Manhar stepped out of the bushes and ran behind the car in an awkward, limping motion due to his injured knee, and slid into the compound before the gates closed completely. The driveway was not long, perhaps fifty feet. He walked slowly toward the house, trying to stay calm as Dattar's bodyguards climbed out from inside the limousine. Dattar himself stepped out next. Both he and the three bodyguards pulled weapons and trained them on him. He put his hands in the air.

"I'm unarmed. I just come to give you a proposition, Mr. Dattar, on how to recoup your stolen money."

Dattar looked Manhar up and down. "Who are you?"

"Manhar. Khalil's man. He plans on double-crossing you, and I thought you should know."

Manhar was pleased to see the two bodyguards exchange a glance. Dattar raised an eyebrow but didn't move. It was clear that Manhar had his attention.

"Why should I believe you?" Dattar said.

"I also know that he managed to let Howell slip out of his hands, and Smith nearly killed him one day ago. Smith *did* kill his first lieutenant."

"And?"

"And I know where you can find Khalil. I know all of his safe houses. I'll give you the information."

"In exchange for what?"

"Safe passage home."

Dattar shook his head. "Not enough. Leaving me with an address gets me nowhere, as I still have to get Khalil. And that will not be easy. You want to go home? You'll have to assist me in catching him."

Manhar didn't like this development at all. He would rather never see Khalil again. Dattar must have noted Manhar's hesitation because he frowned.

"You're either in all the way or out. Make a choice. Now." Manhar's choices had been taken from him the minute he'd screwed up on killing Howell, this much he knew. He sighed.

"I'm in. Tell me what it is you want me to do."

Dattar waved him forward. "In the house. We'll lay it out for you."

Manhar followed Dattar into the spacious home and through the main entrance to a kitchen filled with dark wood cabinets, granite countertops, and a large central island. Manhar had never seen such a kitchen. It was all he could do not to stare, his mouth open. He did his best to act nonchalant and took a seat at the table while Dattar reached into the refrigerator and removed a bottle of water. Dattar poured himself a glass, but offered nothing to Manhar.

A second, thin man entered the room and flicked a glance Manhar's way. Dattar jerked a chin at him. "That's Rajiid." A third man appeared and placed a laptop computer on the island. He stared at the screen. "And that's Nihal. My lead strategists. You will listen to them. This one," he waved the glass in Manhar's direction, "wishes to bring us to Khalil. He says Khalil is intent on taking my money from the American and pocketing it himself."

Rajiid frowned. "Is Smith dead? Khalil was to have killed him days ago. He said it would be easy."

Manhar shook his head. "Not only is Smith alive, but it was *he* who nearly killed *Khalil*."

"And the American?"

"She's with Smith."

Dattar stopped drinking in what looked to Manhar like mid-swallow. He put the glass down.

"Smith has her? How did he know about her?"

Manhar shrugged. "I don't know."

Dattar started to pace.

"How he knows of her is unimportant," Rajiid said. "What is important—"

"What is important is that she lives long enough to tell me where the money is!" Dattar's voice carried an intensity that made Manhar sit up straighter. Rajiid inhaled.

"What is important is that we can still go forward with the plan," Rajiid said. "After we do, you'll have all the money and power you need."

Dattar leveled a stare at Rajiid. "No one steals from me and gets away with it. Especially not hundreds of millions whisked away while I rotted in jail."

"She won't die immediately. We can begin and still have enough time to find her."

"And who will stay when the weapon is placed, huh? I won't be coming back here to die from my own weapon, will you?"

Rajiid shifted in his seat.

"I thought not," Dattar said. "This is why I wanted Smith dead and her captured before we began, remember? I hired the best in the business to kill him, and now I'm told that Smith not only lives, but he survived an attack."

"But—"

Nihal barked a laugh. It was such a strange reaction that Manhar stared at him. Both Rajiid and Dattar looked at Nihal as well, and the fury on Dattar's face was evident.

"I think our troubles are over," Nihal said. He sat back, a smirk on his face. "I have an e-mail from the American. She wants to cut a deal."

37

SMITH WALKED WITH NOLAN down the street in front of the apartment and crossed Broadway. Despite the early hour, they had passed bodegas with men sitting on flimsy wooden crates drinking from bottles kept in paper bags. They continued east of Broadway and to Smith it seemed like they'd entered an entirely different neighborhood. Instead of neat but dated buildings, they saw trash strewn across the sidewalks and collected against the curb. Closed storefronts were covered by protective grates secured with padlocks. A currency exchange on the corner offered legal services upstairs that advertised divorces for $500.

Smith indicated the sign.

"Beckmann should have hired this guy. Would have saved him some money."

Nolan smiled. "It's that cement building across the street."

They were headed to a Pakistani gold merchant who Nolan said would gladly exchange her dollars for gold bullion. They expected Dattar to demand his money in full by wire transfer, but they needed him to appear in person for the plan to work. Also, she was hesitant to fire up her tablet and tip off whoever was watching her at the CIA. It was Nolan who had suggested tempting Dattar to appear in person with a good-faith offer of gold bullion.

"What's a Pakistani doing in this neighborhood? Seems mostly Spanish."

"Dominican, actually. But Bilal has been here for years."

"Do they know that he trades in gold?"

Nolan smiled again. "Take a look." She pointed to an ugly two-story square building with a neon sign with the word "Pawnbrokers" across the top and another, smaller neon tube light sign that said "We Buy Gold." They stepped into the street and across to the other side. Nolan headed to a side door made of steel and guarded by a closed-circuit camera mounted at eave level. She pressed a button on the intercom, and Smith heard a buzzing sound somewhere deep in the center of the building. Within seconds the door gave an answering sound, and Nolan pushed it open and stepped inside. As Smith crossed the threshold, he heard a beeping noise and the door closed behind him with a decisive click. The only light came from an open door at the end of the hallway.

"Miss Rebecca, back here," a man's voice with a heavy accent called to them. Nolan stepped into the office. A Middle Eastern–looking man with salt-and-pepper hair and mustache and dark eyes, and dressed in a white T-shirt and faded jeans, stood behind an L-shaped green metal desk. He pointed a gun at Smith.

"Your friend here has a weapon," the man said, then turned to Smith. "Put your hands in the air."

"It's all right. I'll vouch for him," Nolan said. "Bilal, this is Jon Smith. He's trustworthy."

Bilal didn't lower the pistol. "Interesting name, Jon Smith. Quite common."

Smith kept his eyes on Bilal. "Someone has to have it."

"Miss Rebecca, please remove your friend's gun from its holster and put it on the table."

Nolan stepped up to Smith, and he smelled the fresh scent of shampoo that came from her hair. She unzipped his jacket, glanced up at him, and ran her hands along his chest until she reached his gun in the shoulder holster.

"Is the safety on? I'd hate to shoot you accidentally."

Smith nodded. "It's okay. You can remove it." She pulled out the weapon and held it muzzle down while she took the few steps to Bilal's desk.

"How did you know it was there?" she said after she placed it on the desk.

"I have a metal detector at the door."

"Ahh, that was the beep I heard," Smith said.

Bilal nodded. "I have a lot of expensive items stored on the premises and, as I'm sure you saw while walking here, the neighborhood is sketchy. Are you police?"

Smith shook his head. "Military."

"Here to sell gold?"

"Here to be sure that Ms. Nolan remains safe."

Bilal gave Smith a speculative look. "Miss Rebecca and I are old friends. She is always safe with me."

"So I've been told. But one can never be too sure," Smith said. In fact, Nolan had explained to him that most of the traders in the city knew of Bilal, and many routinely converted their cash to either Kruger-rands or gold bullion there. Apparently Bilal was known for his honesty in an industry where that commodity was scarce.

Bilal turned his attention to Nolan. "Are you here to sell gold?"

"To buy it, actually. I'd like to exchange some cash for bullion."

"Wire transfer your account to mine?"

Nolan nodded.

"Then please take a seat." He included Smith in the offer but reached out and put Smith's gun on a small desk behind him.

"May I use your computer?" Nolan said. Bilal nodded and opened a drawer in front of him and placed a laptop on the desk. She scooted her chair forward to access it.

"It's on," he said. Nolan started tapping away, and Bilal turned to a second PC to his right. After a moment he rose and opened a closet door to his left, revealing a massive safe. He kept the door tilted so that neither Smith nor Nolan could see his hands, and after a moment Smith heard the sound of a lock disengaging.

"Is it there yet?" Nolan asked.

"The computer will give a signal." A moment later, Bilal's PC pinged.

"Let's see." Bilal held some bars of gold in his hands while he walked back to his monitor and peered at it.

"Just so." He placed one bar on the back desk next to a scale. The second bar he put on the scale's pan. "You wish to verify the weight?" Nolan got up and stood next to Bilal, watching as he placed bar after bar on the pan.

"The London fix?" Nolan said.

"Down a bit. Here." Bilal reached to the computer and tapped on the keyboard. From his location across the desk Smith couldn't see the screen, but Nolan watched it for a moment before returning her attention to the scale. When Bilal was finished, he reached below and opened the cabinet, removing a black briefcase. Nolan gave a soft laugh, and Bilal turned his head to smile at her. "You recognize it?"

"I wondered where it had got to."

Bilal looked over his shoulder at Smith. "See? Everything is safe with me."

Smith waited patiently while Nolan finished her transaction, rising to carry the briefcase. He estimated that it weighed close to sixty pounds. If Dattar expected to ambush them and steal the gold, no one who had it would be able to run away. Or at least not very fast. Bilal locked his safe and gave a short bow to Nolan.

"Always a pleasure doing business with you, Miss Rebecca," Bilal said. He handed Smith his gun. "Mr. . . . Smith."

Smith slid the gun back into the holster. "Thank you." They left by the side door, and Smith blinked in the sudden sunlight.

"That was an extraordinary transaction. What's the London fix?"

"London banks are the primary gold traders. Twice each day they set the settling price for their contracts. The price is called the London fix." Smith carried the case as they walked to Broadway.

"Do you know what type of precautions he takes to protect the shop? Besides the metal detector, of course."

"I know he has a gun as big as a cannon taped under the desk. That metal front is perforated for a reason. There are solar roof tiles for electricity that will kick on and keep his security system running should there be a blackout. They feed excess to the grid. Bilal's quite proud that he often gets paid by Con Ed for electricity rather than the other way around. And I've heard that his car is armored, and the office loaded with every type of weapon imaginable."

"I still find it hard to believe that no one has tried to rob him," Smith said.

"Oh, there are rumors that some have."

"And?"

"And they were never seen again."

38

MANHAR STOOD IN THE BACK of the magnificent house on Long Island and watched as Dattar's men started to outfit two large trucks with square trailers. First went in a long fireman's hose, several reflective vests, steel poles, and canvas along with several three-foot-long metal wrenches. On the outside of the first vehicle two men were affixing a large decal that read MTA.

Manhar stopped one of Dattar's men and pointed at the logo.

"What's it mean?"

"Metropolitan Transportation Authority."

"What's that?"

"Runs the New York subway." The man walked away and Manhar gave a low whistle. He'd heard that some wanted to attack the New York subway the way the terrorist organization in Japan had attacked Tokyo's, but he would not have believed that Dattar had the guts to do it. Dattar went up several notches in Manhar's esteem. At that moment Dattar waved him over.

"You're blowing up the subway?" Manhar said.

"No. How's Khalil tracking Nolan?"

"He's had a man watching her every moment for the last month. He knows her schedule, favorite places, everything."

Dattar's face turned red. "Are you saying he's had a month to take her out and he didn't? Why?"

Manhar didn't like the direction the conversation was turning. It was simple: Khalil hadn't taken out Nolan because Dattar hadn't yet paid him. But Manhar didn't want to tell Dattar this bit of information. Dattar tended to kill the messenger. He tried to change the subject.

"You're using sarin gas in the subway. Like in Japan?"

"No. *Why didn't Khalil take out Nolan?*"

Manhar saw no way around the question. Rajiid and the other men had stopped outfitting the truck and were all staring at Manhar.

"He claimed he was waiting to get paid."

Dattar's face worked and his breath came fast. Rajiid slid his eyes sideways, noticed that the men had halted, and barked an order. They began working again, and Manhar felt the tension subside.

"Get in the truck. You're going on the mission with the others," Dattar said.

Manhar did as he was told, but his stomach was twisting. He crawled in the rear of the truck and joined the others sitting on the floor with their backs to the wall. Rajiid appeared and started handing each man two small pills and a bottle of water. He handed them to Manhar.

"What's this?" he said.

"A drug. It will make you strong."

Manhar hesitated.

"Take them," Rajiid said.

Manhar made an elaborate show of tossing the pills in his mouth. He shoved them under his tongue as he swallowed some water. Rajiid watched the entire maneuver before nodding and walking away. Manhar spit the still intact pills back into his hand and tossed them onto the steel bed. He wasn't so foolish as to take any pills given to him by a viper such as Rajiid.

He suddenly had an overwhelming urge to know what Dattar had in mind with the false trucks. Manhar's goal in coming here was only to arrange for Dattar to kill Khalil. With Khalil dead, Manhar would never have to look over his shoulder, wondering when retribution would come.

What Manhar didn't want to do was die like a jihadist on some elaborate suicide mission. He couldn't imagine any scenario in which Dattar's men could bomb, gas, or shoot up a New York City subway and survive the inevitable aftermath. He sat in the back of the truck and did his best to keep calm as they began the drive to the city. After ten minutes Manhar turned to the nearest man riding with him. He was able to see his face in the illumination from a high window. The light flickered each time they passed a light pole.

"Will we get away before the gas is released?" Manhar said.

"We're not using gas."

Manhar pointed to two small canisters. "That's gas, I know it. I saw it used in Iraq."

The man shook his head. "That's only a backup. It's not the main plan. And why do you care? Our families back home will be well compensated for our deaths and we will bask in greater glory."

"Will the plan work?" Manhar said.

He heard the man chuckle in the dark. "Oh yes, it will work. In three hours most of Manhattan will begin to die. And no one will be able to stop it."

"Will Dattar die too, then?"

"No, he will not. He must live, of course, to pay our families."

"And us?"

"In the kingdom of the everlasting life."

Manhar wanted to shake him. The only kingdom he wanted to experience was in Pakistan, with multiple women and a large house with many rooms. He needed to get away from Dattar's crew before they put their mission in place. The only problem was, he needed to know which way to run, and to learn that, he needed to know what Dattar had in store for the city.

"What is the plan, then?"

"I don't know. We will be told what to do by Nihal when we arrive."

Manhar didn't believe him. "You don't know? Then how can you be so sure it will work?"

"Nihal told me it will. I believe him."

Manhar sat in the back of the truck and began plotting his escape.

Dattar rode in the lead car and ran through the plan a final time with Rajiid.

"You have the bacteria?"

"We have the coolers in place," Rajiid said.

"And the guns?"

Rajiid nodded. "Ready. If there are any disturbances, or a too curious police officer, the men know what to do."

"Killing an officer is to be a last resort. Try to talk your way out first. We just need enough time to place the bacteria." When Rajiid didn't reply, Dattar began checking the pistol he kept in a holster at his waist.

"Will you kill Nolan?" Rajiid said.

"Yes. After she tells me where the rest of the money is located."

"And Smith?"

"Him too."

"He is savvy, so you've always told me."

"He is nothing against me," Dattar said. "And besides, I will have Khalil with me."

"And Howell?"

"Khalil must have already killed him. I've heard nothing."

Rajiid pressed his lips together.

Dattar was no longer worried. After learning that Nolan wanted to meet to "end this thing," as she'd put it in the message, he'd called Khalil back. He'd pretended to be calmer, and cajoled Khalil into joining him. "Together we're stronger than alone," he'd said. Khalil had agreed.

Dattar had already contacted his informer at the CIA to ensure that the plan went his way and only his way.

Dattar sat back and watched the lights on the expressway whiz by.

* * *

Smith stood at a street corner back at the CIA safe house on the Upper West Side and watched as a van embossed with the logo of a well-known cable company pulled alongside the curb. The driver's window lowered and Howell stuck his head out.

"Climb in back and see what we've got." Smith swung open the rear panel doors and was greeted by clouds of smoke and Beckmann, who sat on a short stool in the middle of a neatly arranged row of wires and technological equipment, puffing on a cigarette. A television system, complete with multiple screens and several computer towers, was packed into the interior. The air was stale from the cigarettes as well as the fumes of several PCs running at once.

"Quite an operation," Smith said. "Are you sure it's safe to smoke in there? I can practically feel the electromagnetic waves. One spark and something's going to blow up."

"Without a cigarette that something's going to be me," Beckmann said. "What organization can produce a setup like this on such short notice?" Beckmann indicated the machinery all around him. "It would take me several days and a stack of paperwork to complete before I could obtain it at the CIA. And the FBI doesn't even have equipment this new."

Smith had called Klein first, for procurement, then Marty, for assembly. In fact, the interior held the stamp of Marty all over it, from its perfectly arranged PC consoles to the wires encased in color-coded cable organizers. Not a thing was out of place and each item hummed with precision. Smith had asked Marty to man the vehicle as well, but he'd refused, preferring to continue his search for the mole at the CIA.

"No one else can hunt this man the way I can. The CIA's systems are proving ridiculously difficult to crack," Marty had said. The gleam in his eye made it clear to Smith that Marty was actually enjoying the challenge. Engaging in a stakeout couldn't compete.

Smith handed Beckmann a long-nosed rifle. Beckmann put the cigarette in the corner of his mouth while he inspected the weapon.

"Nice. What is it?"

"A dart gun. It's for big game, but the theory is the same for humans. We need him alive to tell us what it is he's planning on doing." Beckmann transferred the gun to one hand while he resumed smoking.

"I'd rather just shoot the bastard."

Smith nodded. "Me too."

"Howell has one of these as well?"

"And a regular sniper rifle. He's going to get into position now. Good luck."

Beckmann saluted Smith and grabbed a panel to close it. Smith swung the other and secured them both. As he did, he checked them. Each had what appeared to be a secondary logo in the form of a black circle with spirals, but in reality they were two-way mirrors engineered to allow a man from the inside to see out. A flick of a lever and they would slide out of the way, giving Beckmann enough space to aim and shoot without opening the back doors.

Smith strode across the street and up the stairs to the safe house apartment. They'd picked the exchange location after some discussion. They needed a spot that allowed them to cover the position from above as well as below. The safe house had the added advantage of being empty of neighbors; the CIA owned the entire building. The "For Sale" sign was a ruse by the CIA to allow the nearby apartments to remain empty without raising suspicion. Howell had canvassed the street thoroughly before they re-entered the apartment, and they figured it was as safe as it was going to be for the few hours that they needed it. Smith hoped to be long gone by the time the CIA mole discovered they had returned to the original safe house that he and Nolan had used. Howell was in the kitchen inspecting the sniper rifle.

"He all set?"

Smith nodded. "As good as he'll ever be." Smith picked up a vest as well as the wire transmitter that Nolan would wear for the meet. "She upstairs?"

"Yes. She said she'll wait for you."

Smith headed to the master bedroom. He found Nolan in the bathroom wearing only jeans and the bra while she inspected her wounds using a hand-held mirror to view her reflection.

"I didn't want to get dressed until you arranged for the wire," she said. He held it up for her to see. "That's small."

"Has to be if it's going to be concealed. It's wireless, and should easily transmit to Beckmann and me in the van. Anything happens, we're right here."

"What's the other?"

He held up a vest. "Bulletproof. Nice and slim, isn't it?"

Nolan nodded. "Looks nothing like the kind the police march around in."

"It's a dense weave of silk and other fibers. Don't let the thin profile fool you, it will stop a bullet as well as Kevlar."

"From Ms. Russell at the CIA?"

Smith shook his head. "From a friend." Klein had arranged for the vest.

He clipped the tiny microphone to the edge of her bra strap and ran the wire to the transmitter no larger than a deck of cards and attached that to her waistband. He held the vest open while she put her arms through the armholes. He stopped a moment and caught her looking at him intently.

"Don't look so grim. He won't kill me until he has access to the money."

"So you say."

"So I *know*. How did you get to this stage in life and not realize that it's all about money?" There was a puzzled look in her eye. For a moment he felt the gulf between his experiences and those of the average person get even larger. He'd long ago lost confidence in the idea that money could solve the evils of the world.

"Because I've seen many whose ambitions revolve around power and righteousness and just plain craziness. You think it's about money because you live on a small island and are surrounded by people in the pursuit of it. But Dattar and others like him don't think the way you do.

If he shows the first sign of killing you in a rage or before you've given up all of the accounts, I want you to say the code word and I'll take him out." Her face took on its usual set look.

"You can't. Howell told me the truth."

Smith frowned. "What did Howell tell you?"

"That if it came down to me or Dattar, your orders were to let me die. Dattar can't be killed until he reveals his plan. Howell said that your superiors were clear on this."

Smith wasn't sure how to respond. He *was* given orders: One may have to be sacrificed to save many. He, Klein, and Howell agreed in a private conversation that the stakes were too high. Dattar had to be stopped before he used his weapon. While Smith knew this to be true, an image of them together from the night before flashed through his mind, and all his instincts recoiled against the idea of letting Dattar harm her.

"I don't usually make love to a woman and then feed her to a dog like Dattar." He focused on securing the straps on the vest. He could feel her eyes on him as he did and he didn't raise his own until he was done.

"I stole his money and by doing so brought this on myself. I've told you time and again that I'll take care of myself. What happened last night doesn't change that."

He felt himself getting angry with her. That she thought him so mercenary.

"I don't use civilians as shields, no matter what my orders."

She held his gaze a moment and then reached up and brought her lips to his in a soft kiss.

"Don't worry. I'm right. This one's about money. I'll be fine." Smith wished he could believe it, but in his experience everything and anything could go wrong. His only hope was that whatever occurred, it wouldn't be something catastrophic. He picked up her sweater and helped lower it over her head, taking care not to touch her injuries.

"I'll be happy when we have Dattar."

Nolan nodded. "Let's go."

Smith followed her down the stairs past the kitchen. Howell was gone.

The plan was simple. Nolan would sit on a wooden bench that wrapped around the trunk of a tree with the bag of bullion next to her. Its weight ensured that whoever appeared and took the bag would be slowed; this was an added security measure to counteract any possible grab-and-run attempts. She'd negotiated by e-mail with Dattar and arranged a series of these drops every day over the course of a month, each physical drop to be followed by a million-dollar wire transfer from one of the hundreds of accounts that she'd set up to hide the money. In this way, they hoped to keep Dattar on the hook and returning time and again. If they missed taking him down on the first round, they'd get him on the second.

Dattar had insisted that she keep her computer on and ready to accept e-mails. None of them had liked that aspect of his demands, but he refused to appear unless she did, so they had Marty watching the data stream and prepared to relay any message that Dattar sent. For her part, Nolan had emphasized that she would give the account numbers and passwords to Dattar only. If an intermediary appeared, the deal was off. When Dattar appeared, they would close in.

They continued out the front door and down to the street where she headed to the bench where the bag was already arranged. He walked to the van, rapped twice and opened the doors. He found both Howell and Beckmann inside.

"She's in place, I see," Howell said.

"She told me that you gave her the worst-case scenario. I wish you hadn't."

Beckmann stopped fiddling with a walkie-talkie and glanced in Howell's direction. Howell grabbed his gun with one hand, rose to a crouch and jumped off the back of the van, stopping to stand next to Smith.

"I thought she should know the parameters of our assistance. I've learned that it doesn't pay to lie to a woman."

Beckmann snorted and Howell shot him a quelling glance.

"I'm not going to let Dattar kill her."

Howell didn't look surprised at all by this statement.

"The orders were clear. If she were a man, would you go so far? If she were Russell?" That question gave Smith pause. He would go very far for Russell, but the two couldn't be compared.

"Russell's a soldier. She isn't. And if she were a man, we wouldn't be having this conversation because I wouldn't have gotten so close."

"Exactly," Howell said. "You're letting your emotions get in the way of your good sense."

"Maybe I'm just tired of living on the fringes. Fighting animals like Dattar by crawling into the same pit." He sighed. "I need to get into position." He turned to go, and Howell put a hand on his arm.

"The fact that this is bothering you so much shows that you're not the same. You've got me and Beckmann behind you. We'll get him and do our best to keep her alive."

Smith knew that there was nothing left to say on the subject. He headed back to the building and into the apartment. He opened the bay window and settled in, facing the street. He liked the high angle for viewing purposes, but it had the disadvantage of keeping him far from the action. If anything went awry, he would have to descend several sets of stairs to reach Nolan. As one of the youngest and most fit in the group—Beckmann's smoking made him a poor choice for an extended sprint—Smith was stuck with the perch. Smith picked up a sniper rifle and settled in to wait.

Dattar reached the corner of the street near the rendezvous and stopped to check his weapon. In the next instant he felt the muzzle of a gun press against the back of his neck.

"I take half," Khalil said. Dattar knocked the weapon away.

"We'll talk about it once we have her. In the meantime, keep your threats to yourself." Khalil's eyes were hard, but Dattar noticed that he didn't raise his weapon again.

"It's an ambush. It must be," Khalil said.

Dattar nodded. "Of course." He handed Khalil a small set of binoculars. "We're more than a block away. Take a look."

Khalil looked through the lenses. "In the van. And probably from an upstairs window. It's what I would do." He returned the binoculars to Dattar.

"The bag at her feet contains a million in gold bullion."

Khalil whistled. "Heavy. How do you intend to get your hands on it and her? They'll shoot you the moment you get close."

"I'm not going to get anywhere near her."

"So how do you get the money?"

"I'm going to make her come to me," Dattar said. He tapped on a smartphone. "I just sent her an e-mail."

"What did it say?"

"That she is to pick up the bag and come to the end of the street. If she does not, I send a signal to my men and she will be responsible for what happens next. I suggested to her that money was not worth the number of innocent lives that would be lost if she didn't comply."

Dattar put the binoculars to his eyes and watched as Nolan consulted her tablet. She typed something and sat back. Dattar's phone beeped. He opened the reply, read it, and hissed through his teeth.

"What did she say?"

"That money is worth a lot and people die every day."

Smith saw movement at the end of the street. Seconds later the shadows formed into several men making their way toward both Nolan and Beckmann's van. When Smith put his eye to the scope they came into focus. Six men in dark uniforms, combat boots, Kevlar vests, and sniper rifles. All wore communication headsets. Smith placed his sight on the first and waited as the man drew closer to Howell's hiding place. Nolan sat over fifty feet away and they had to see her. None targeted her, though, a fact that gave Smith pause. Howell's voice came over the speaker of the phone that Smith had placed next to him.

"You see this crew?" Howell's whisper sounded soft in the darkened apartment.

"I do. Dattar's?" Smith kept his sight trained on the first. The man slowed and as he drew even with Howell's hiding place, he turned back to speak to one of the team. For a moment the letters on his shirt became visible in Smith's sight.

"Beckmann, Howell, don't shoot. They're FBI. Probably a SWAT team."

"Who the hell called them?" Howell said.

"I have no idea, but they're going to blow the plan sky high. Dattar sees them, he'll run for sure."

Smith's phone beeped. "Hold tight, everyone." Smith switched the line. It was Marty.

"He's contacting her. He told her to come to the corner or he'd unleash his weapon."

Smith was on his feet and headed to the door with the phone at his ear and the rifle in his hand. If she walked to the corner, Dattar would get her.

"What did she say?"

"That money is worth a lot and people die every day." Marty made a noise between a laugh and a snort. "She's calling his bluff."

"He's not bluffing," Smith said. He opened the apartment door and stared into the eyes of Harcourt and the barrel of a gun.

39

P UT DOWN YOUR GUN AND walk into the apartment or I'll put a large
hole where your forehead used to be," Harcourt said. Smith lowered the rifle to the floor. It dropped with a clattering sound onto the
wood.

"What are you talking about? I'm on your side," Smith said. "We're
using Nolan as bait. Dattar is close. You're interrupting a mission here."

"Shut up," Harcourt said. He tapped out a text.

"Jon, they're lying to her. Dattar just told her that he has you and de-
manded she move to the corner. She's doing it." Marty's voice held a
manic tone and it startled Harcourt, who twitched.

"Who the hell is that?" he said. Smith felt his blood pressure spike.
Because of him, Nolan had surrendered. Bitterness welled up in him and
then anger washed over him. He kept his hand that held the phone still.

"Howell. MI6. He knows I'm up here. You kill me and he'll kill you."
Smith hoped the lie was effective, but Harcourt shook his head.

"Forget about lying to me. The FBI has surrounded both of your buddies. Or should I say both of Russell's buddies? CIA knows she's a mole
and we've requested that the FBI pick up her, you, and Beckmann.
Everyone she brought with her when she came inside. They'll detain
Howell long enough to transfer him back to England and into the loving arms of MI6. Give me that phone." Smith tossed it at Harcourt's
feet and tensed, waiting for the moment Harcourt would glance down.

When he did, Smith would make his move. It didn't work. Harcourt kept his eyes on Smith and his gun pointed.

"Pick it up and hand it to me," Harcourt said. "You don't think I'm that stupid, do you?"

Smith reached down to the phone, all the while hoping that Marty had kept listening to the open channel and had the good sense to remain quiet.

"Russell's not a mole. You've got to know that." Smith spoke loud enough that Marty must have been able to hear. No sound came from the phone, but the screen lit again as Smith handled it. The connection was still live. He handed it over. Harcourt powered it down.

"It's Russell's password that's being used to hack the system. Lie on the floor, face down."

Harcourt glanced at the phone and in that instant Smith took a fast slide step, raised his leg at a ninety-degree angle, knee bent, and extended it out as he kicked at the other man's face. The blow was backed by the rage that consumed him. Harcourt sensed the action, but moved a split second too late, and Smith's foot hammered into Harcourt's chest, knocking him backward. The gun went off and fired dead center into Smith's breastbone. He grunted as he felt the bullet's punch into the protective vest, and he stumbled with the force. Harcourt lost his footing and landed hard on his lower back. Smith kept coming on, his fury eclipsing his good sense, and he aimed another kick at Harcourt's face, connecting with his nose at the same moment that Harcourt fired again. The second shot whizzed past Smith but his foot hit its mark. He felt the man's nose shift to the right with the blow and a plume of blood sprayed with it.

Smith grabbed at the gun and yanked it out of Harcourt's hand with his left while he delivered another punch to the man's nose with his right. Pain reverberated through his knuckles when he hit Harcourt's hard cheekbone instead of the soft cartilage of his nose. Harcourt swung a fist that managed to land on Smith's injured left arm, but the resulting sting hurt far less than the bullet to the vest had.

The sound of pounding feet on the stairs told Smith that the SWAT team had heard the shots and were coming to Harcourt's rescue. Smith leaped over Harcourt's prone body and ran back up the stairs to the room with the fire ladder that Nolan had used days ago. The window was still open and Smith clambered through it, not bothering to check whether the team had shown enough foresight to cover the rear of the apartment. If they had, then he would be forced to surrender. He jumped on the stairs to release them and held on as the bottom ladder portion swung downward. He heard rather than saw the men above him. Their voices got louder as they reached the window. Smith didn't look up at them or down at the street. He kept his focus on the ladder and the left-right motion of crawling lower as fast as he could. Above him a man's voice yelled.

"I got him. On the fire stairs. Hold tight." In the next instant Smith heard the sound of a compressed air shot fired from a rifle. They had either Beckmann's or Howell's gun.

The dart hit him in the back of the neck. A small part of Smith's brain, the one that was in charge of his logical thinking, informed him that the dart had missed his vertebrae and hit his upper shoulder where the neck met the collarbone. It sank into his flesh and he winced from the rush of tranquilizer that pumped into his system.

His legs kept moving despite the fact that several milligrams of a powerful animal sedative was pouring into his bloodstream. He made it to the corner before the real effects hit him. Each step was becoming an uncoordinated mess and his vision started to blur. He stumbled forward, functioning on adrenaline more than anything else.

He turned the corner and a silver car jumped the curb and slammed up onto the sidewalk. It came to a halt five feet away from Smith, which was a good thing, because Smith was in no condition to dodge out-of-control cars. Simply walking was becoming a feat unto itself. The car's window lowered and Russell stuck her head out.

"Get in."

Smith lurched to the passenger's side, wrenched open the door, and collapsed inside. His feet weren't off the ground when Russell slammed the car into reverse. She hit the gas and the car shot back, bouncing off the curb, the front swinging into place as she twisted the steering wheel. The rear window on the passenger side cracked and Smith heard the bullet whiz past. Smith was still wrestling with the door when Russell shifted into drive and the car jumped ahead. She drove down the street and turned at the first corner. Despite all the motion around him, Smith was having a hard time staying awake. He tried to thank Russell for saving him, but his lips wouldn't follow his brain's command and form the words. She seemed to deform in front of his eyes, her body undulating like a flag in the wind. He knew it was the tranquilizer setting in, but he couldn't bring himself to care at that particular moment. He decided to let the languor take him and he closed his eyes.

40

MANHAR EMERGED FROM THE truck near the 191st Street subway station. They'd dropped off a first crew at the 72nd Street subway entrance and now the rest filed out. Manhar wore a reflective vest and a hardhat. It was ten o'clock at night, well past rush hour. Rajiid was laying out orange street cones in a circle around the truck and added a horse with a sign that said "Men at Work." Next to that he placed a yellow plastic model of a man holding a red flag. He went back to the trailer and began giving orders. Soon the men had used the poles and canvas to create a large cube that screened the area from prying eyes. They arranged the cube to hide the grates over the subway.

"You." Rajiid waved at Manhar. "Get the tool to open the hydrant. The others will get the hose." Within minutes they had attached a fire hose to the hydrant. They removed one of the grate portions and stuck the end of the hose in it. Rajiid waved at Manhar. "Open the hydrant." Manhar did and the hose inflated as gallons of water ran through it.

"What now?" Manhar said.

"Now we wait."

Manhar was confused. "Wait for what?"

Rajiid smiled. "For the water to flood the station and the MTA to shut down the power to this track." Manhar looked at the hose as it pulsed and listened to the water as it gushed downward.

"Will that work?"

Rajiid nodded. "The infrastructure is old and this and three other stations are vulnerable to flooding. We're flooding two stops in a row in addition to Seventy-second Street. It won't take long." Manhar listened to the water flowing.

"I can hear it, it's true, but you're thinking they'll shut down the whole station?"

Rajiid smiled. "I've been planning this for two years. They'll shut it down. Go get the poles and canvas. We'll need to screen off a portion of the platform downstairs."

One hour later an employee of the MTA drove up to the truck. Rajiid slipped a gun into his waistband, covered it with the edge of the reflective vest, and strolled out to greet him before he could walk behind the barrier. The employee waved at the canvas.

"The station is flooding." The man pointed to the sky. "But there's no rain."

"Water main leak. We're working on it. Have them shut down the power. Should only take twenty minutes at the most."

The employee sighed. "I'll let the Rail Control Center know. Give me a little time."

Rajiid shrugged. "We'll wait. Water will short out the switches."

The man sighed. "I'll let 'em know to send out a crew."

Rajiid nodded. "Good enough."

The man walked away. Rajiid stepped back into the barrier. "Get the coolers. You," he indicated Manhar, "come with me. The rest stay up here and keep pumping that water."

Manhar watched as the flunky he'd ridden with in the back of the truck grabbed two coolers and followed Rajiid into the station. Manhar paused. He couldn't decide. Run now? But to where? In which direction? He still had no idea what Rajiid was planning. After a moment he headed downstairs. The station smelled of wet mud overlaid with the scent of old garbage. Water pounded from the grate above, the deluge hitting the third rail in a stream. The area around the track was filling fast. Manhar looked up at a camera.

"What about those?"

Rajiid shook his head. "We knocked them out."

"Turned off the electricity?"

"No. That would raise suspicion. Just disconnected the cable line at a source that feeds into the station."

"Why is the water rising so quickly?" Manhar asked.

"We also knocked out two sump pumps. This will overload the track." Rajiid smiled. The water kept pouring down. Portions of the stream let off a rising vapor.

"Is that steam?" Manhar said.

Rajiid nodded. "Six hundred volts in the third rail. It's heating the water, which will eventually start to boil. When it does, the switches will short out." He looked at his watch. "An hour at the most. Less if that rail employee does his job and arranges to shut down this section."

He waved at the flunky. "Put the coolers there and set up the screen. Help him," he said to Manhar.

The flunky dropped the cooler and began to arrange the poles. A train rumbled into the station, driving right through the flow of water and splattering it in all directions. The doors opened with a swish. Several people got off and hurried to the exit, barely sparing a glance at Manhar. The train doors closed and the car rumbled away. The screen was up, the coolers stashed behind it, and Manhar headed to where Rajiid was watching the waterfall.

"But if you're going to use sarin or mustard gas, shouldn't you do it while the station is full? It won't be if it's shut down." Manhar hoped his question about sarin gas would prompt Rajiid to tell him what he really had planned.

Rajiid raised an eyebrow. "What makes you think we're using gas?"

"I saw containers of mustard gas in the trucks. And then you have these." Manhar indicated the coolers.

"We have the gas, yes, but only for an emergency. If we used that, they'd shut the subway once it was discovered and most would flee. We'd end up killing only a few. This is much more efficient. It will kill thousands. But the electricity to the rail has to be turned off first. So, we wait."

Rajiid walked to the far end and crouched down, watching the water flow. Manhar crouched next to him, sweating as he watched the water rise.

41

DATTAR HAULED BACK HIS FIST and punched Nolan in the face. Khalil was holding her in place by grasping both of her arms behind her back. They were in the rear of a van, heading toward the 191st Street station where Rajiid waited for the subway tracks to short-circuit.

"Give me the location and access to my money."

Nolan's head hung down and she remained that way. For a moment Dattar thought that perhaps she was unconscious, but Khalil wrenched one of her arms tighter behind her and she gave a moan. Dattar took out a knife from his boot.

"Put her hand down." Khalil switched up his position and held Nolan's palm against the bottom of the van. Dattar stabbed downward, and the knife pierced the meat of her hand between the first finger and thumb. The point went clean through. She jerked, but didn't make a sound.

"I want my money. You have ten minutes to tell me where it is. If you don't, we kill Smith."

She looked up.

Ahh, so that's what gets to her, Dattar thought.

He could see the enormous effort that she was exerting not to react to the pain from the knife. The van lurched to a stop. Dattar yanked the point from her hand.

"Get out." He waved at her and Khalil opened the back doors and dragged her from the vehicle. Her hand bled profusely but she ignored it.

Dattar was pleased to see that the canvas screen functioned well, shielding the work area from prying eyes. He stepped behind it and found a man sitting on the fire hydrant and smoking a cigarette. He snapped to attention when he saw Dattar.

"Where's Rajiid?"

"Down. Waiting for the short."

"Any civilians on the platform?"

"None."

"What about the elevators?"

"We've strung some more tape on either end. They break so often, no one seems surprised."

"And employees?"

"One. We disposed of him already."

Dattar waved at Khalil.

"We'll enter off Broadway. Bring her. She can plant the bacteria."

He headed to the station entrance on Broadway. His men had strung yellow caution tape across the entrance. Few people were on the street and none used the subway entrance. Those that came close took one look at the yellow tape and veered off.

Dattar climbed over it and headed down a short stairway, ignoring the connected ramp, and into a long, narrow, dark tunnel with arched ceilings and dirty yellow walls marked with graffiti. The walls were marred by gang symbols, crudely drawn flowers and words, including a long quote by some writer that Dattar didn't bother to read. Fluorescent light fixtures spaced evenly along the tunnel's ceiling created pools of harsh illumination followed by sections in shadow. The tunnel continued for three city blocks. His shoes rang on the concrete floor. The tunnel smelled musty and felt damp.

Dattar reached the turnstile and clambered over it. The air was heavy with humidity, and steam hung in the area around the tracks. The entire group walked to the edge and looked down.

The platform stood about four feet above the bottom of the rails. Water filled the tunnel, most of it simmering, and some nearest the third rail was beginning to boil. Dattar glanced left and saw Rajiid at the platform's end crouching next to Manhar, the one who was so quick to sell out Khalil. This should be interesting, Dattar thought. Out of the corner of his eye he saw Khalil straighten. He'd spotted Manhar. At the same instant Manhar looked up and an almost comical expression of dread crossed his face.

"What are you doing here?" Khalil said.

Manhar stood. "Helping." He looked at Nolan's swelling black eye and mangled still-bleeding hand and his face turned an even lighter shade. "I'm glad to see you survived Smith's attack," he said to Khalil, almost as an afterthought.

"No thanks to you," Khalil said.

Rajiid looked at Nolan, and Dattar saw a small smile cross his face.

"As you can see, Rajiid, all our problems will soon be solved," Dattar said. "She's going to return to me what is rightfully mine, and then I think she should be the one to place the bacteria. Along with that one." He pointed at Manhar. "Since you are so busy *helping*." Manhar looked sick, and Khalil snickered.

"What's happening at Seventy-second?" Dattar asked Rajiid.

"MTA shut down the rail. It flooded fast, just as I predicted. Our crew said that the MTA is there already, crawling all over the station, removing passengers from trains. That should keep them busy for a while." Rajiid smiled.

"So? When does this one go off?"

"Soon. It's almost flooded. When it does, I expect a second, much smaller crew to be dispatched here, but I think we'll have time. Twenty minutes at the least."

Dattar heard a small, explosive sound and the station signals blinked off.

Rajiid stood with a triumphant expression on his face. "The third rail is down. Tell them to shut the hydrant and bring the pump."

Khalil waved at Rajiid. "Let him do it."

"Not unless you want to place the bacteria, eh?" Dattar said.

Khalil frowned and sauntered off to deliver the news. Through it all Nolan stood to the right of Manhar, her eyes downcast and her shoulders hunched. Dattar walked over to her.

"Tell me where the money is."

She raised her head. He could see the pain on her face, but also something else. Dattar had chosen her as his investment advisor due to her single-minded focus on all things financial. She'd come highly recommended as a market wizard, one of Wall Street's finest. It was said that she had nerves of steel and remained composed even as the worldwide markets gyrated wildly. She would trade her way out of a morass that sucked others down with it. Now he saw her preternatural intensity at work and it made him nervous. So, he did what he always did when someone made him nervous; he hit her. His fist landed in the same place as before and her body swayed back. She stumbled and fell. Manhar stood to Dattar's right and watched. Rajiid, looking slightly bored, returned his gaze to the third rail.

"I said, tell me where the money is."

She raised her head.

"No," she said. Manhar's mouth fell open and he gaped at her. Rajiid shifted on his feet so that he faced them, but remained in a crouch, staring. "Not until you prove to me that Smith is still alive."

Dattar felt a slight thrill at the idea of using some of his torture techniques on her. No one, male or female, had ever held back on information after he'd started and no one survived them. He took a step toward her.

"Before you start, let's place the bacteria," Rajiid said. "I know she'll be in no condition to do anything afterward." Dattar reined himself in and nodded. Rajiid went to the first cooler and opened it. He sucked in a breath.

"What is it?" Dattar said. Rajiid pulled out a flask containing a cloudy, viscous liquid.

"The color is off. This batch could be dead." He reached across and opened the second cooler, removing another flask.

"And?" Dattar said.

Rajiid shrugged. "This looks better. Obviously I can't be sure without a microscope, but I assume it's still alive."

"Is there enough in the one cooler?"

Rajiid nodded. "It will have to do. And remember, once it starts, it spreads. Rapidly." Rajiid pointed to Manhar and Nolan. "Put on some gloves."

Nolan looked grim. "I won't put your bacteria anywhere except down your throat," she said.

Dattar was done with her. He pulled out his knife and stepped in, getting close. Rajiid grabbed his arm before he could stab her.

"Leave off," Rajiid said. Dattar paused, but he could feel a vein in his head pulsing. Rajiid looked at Nolan. "Either place the bacteria or we kill Smith."

She shook her head. "'Either place the bacteria or we'll kill Smith.' 'Tell me where the money is or we'll kill Smith.' Sounds like you are both planning on killing him no matter what. Do you expect me to believe anything you say? I won't help you. You want to implement some grand scheme to kill thousands, you'll have to do it yourself and die along with them." Dattar jerked toward her and winced as Rajiid tightened his grip.

"I'll kill *you*," Dattar said to Nolan. She looked him straight in the eye. Her own was turning purple with some black edges.

"And I'll die with all your money safely tucked away. Then who's going to pay for the guns and ammo and that huge estate in Pakistan? For all the wives? You forget that I know what it costs to be you."

"Once this bacteria is placed and my plan is working, I'll have enough money to buy and sell the world. The accounts will be returned to me as well as my country. My mine alone has enough stones to pay for all that and more."

She snorted in derision. "*If* it works. You've emptied the *Redding* mines, so there won't be any more coming from that quarter, and you managed to kill the only man who knew how to operate the utility facility. Your men can't get it to work. I don't know what plan you have going here, but it had better be simpler than running a utility company, or it won't work either. Whatever happens, you'll be out your two hundred million. Kill me and it will take a long while to replace that sum. You need me, Dattar. And I'll make you a trade."

Dattar swallowed the building rage. "You despicable money trader. What makes you think you're in any position to deal?"

She laughed in his face.

He broke away from Rajiid and lunged at her, slashing with his knife. He sliced at her right shoulder and slit open a long line along the sweater. Blood poured from it. He moved in for the kill, and Rajiid grabbed at him.

"Help me hold him back!" Rajiid yelled at Manhar. Dattar felt the younger man wrap an arm around his neck and pull. Nolan was against the wall. She looked over his left shoulder and her gaze locked there.

Khalil stepped into view. He held his own knife and walked calmly to Nolan. She pressed back against the wall as he approached. He placed the knife against her neck, right under her left ear, and turned it so that it cut her. Yet more of her blood ran. He moved the tip of the knife to the edge of her right eye.

"The money that you retain is interesting, yes, but if you continue to anger me, I'd just as soon kill you. Don't push me over the edge. Understand that you have nothing that I need so desperately that I'll put up with you. Get to work on the bacteria or this will be the first to go. Say one more word and I'll take both. If you don't place the bacteria we have several more that will, so your resistance is worthless and will accomplish nothing except your blindness." He stepped out of her way.

She stared at him. After a moment she dropped her gaze, took a deep breath, and walked to the coolers. She picked up a pair of rubber gloves and slid them over her damaged hand, wincing as she did. She went to the coolers and lifted out a tray that held several flasks, each filled with a yellow liquid.

"What do I do?" she said to Rajiid. He let go of Dattar, walked to the cooler, and removed a tray that held six flat jars, each filled with a gelatinous base.

"Pour the bacteria into the substance." Nolan grasped the first jar with her good hand, but gasped when she tried to unscrew the lid with her bad one.

"I can't do it."

Rajiid reached over and unscrewed the jars, then dumped the contents of each flask on top of the gelatinous base.

"Now we need to test the water temperature."

Khalil jutted his chin at Manhar. "You. Get moving." Manhar let go of Dattar and headed to the coolers. Rajiid handed him a thermometer. Manhar looked at it with dread.

"Are you sure the third rail is off? Is the water electrified?"

"For the moment the rail is off. You keep wasting time, and it will eventually turn back on." Rajiid waved him forward. Manhar crawled down onto the tracks. Dattar moved closer, watching.

"How hot do you need the water to be?" he asked. Rajiid once again crouched by the tracks' edge.

"It's not how hot, but how cold. The bacteria die if the water is over thirty-five degrees centigrade. Since water boils at one hundred, I presume it hasn't yet cooled enough, but we will see." Manhar stuck the thermometer into the water and waited. Sixty seconds later it beeped.

"And?" Dattar said.

"Eighty."

Rajiid hissed. "Too hot. Khalil, tell the men upstairs to turn the hydrant back on. We'll add cooler water." Khalil left. Manhar started back to the platform, his booted feet sloshing through the blackened water.

"If they turn the third rail back on, will we be able to place the bacteria?" Dattar asked.

Rajiid shook his head. "No. So we'd better get this water cooled fast. Eventually someone at the MTA is going to appear and try to fix the problem."

Dattar snorted. "If they do, then someone at the MTA is going to die. I didn't come this far to be stopped." He looked at Nolan.

"You're a thief. We punish thieves by cutting off their hands. You give me the money, then you live, but without your hands. If you don't, you die."

42

S MITH WOKE TO FIND RUSSELL and Ohnara leaning over him. Russell looked dreadful as opposed to near death, which was actually a gain. Ohnara looked pensive and frightened. Smith shifted his head to gaze around the room. It appeared that he was flat on his back on the floor of a lab. Something soft was bunched under his head as a makeshift pillow, but it wasn't even close to comfortable.

"Where am I?" Smith said.

"In the Medicon Corporation's laboratory," Ohnara said. "Ms. Russell brought you here. How are you feeling?"

Smith rose to a sitting position and groaned. His head pounded, and the world went dark for a moment as the blood failed to rush upward.

"Aspirin," he managed to croak. Sixty seconds later, a hand holding a cup of coffee was thrust in front of his nose.

"That's not aspirin." He inhaled deeply, taking in the heady smell of roasted coffee, and then breathed out. "But I'll take it. What time is it?"

Russell consulted her watch. "Midnight."

He sipped the coffee, thought about Nolan, and felt a welling sadness, but he shoved the feeling away. He wouldn't assume that she was dead. She had her trump card to use against Dattar, and he hoped she'd play it well enough to stay alive until he could find her.

"Thanks for showing up when you did," he said to Russell, who sat on a stool facing him. "How did you know where I was?"

"Marty called me, as did Klein."

Smith raised an eyebrow. "Klein?"

"I asked him to keep me informed about any actions taken by the FBI or DHS. He said that Harcourt had asked the CIA to pick you up on suspicion of terrorist activity, and his monitors heard that they had located you and were sending a SWAT team. Marty told me where you were."

"And Howell and Beckmann?"

"Beckmann is in FBI custody. Howell managed to escape. We don't know where he is."

Smith eyed a stool to his right that he would have loved to sit on, but he wasn't entirely sure that his legs would work yet.

"Need help getting up?" Ohnara said.

Smith nodded. "Yes." Ohnara lent an arm while Smith struggled upward. When he was on the stool, he leveled a look at Ohnara. "Talk to me."

Ohnara sighed. "I can't determine if the avian flu that Ms. Russell contracted was the same that attached to the Shewanella in the swab. It's extremely difficult to get bird flu without close contact with an infected animal. Ms. Russell's distance from the refrigerator swab seems to rule that out as a factor. Also, the cholera died, and Shewanella MR-1 does not cause illness."

Smith looked back at Russell. "Despite all that, you have a hunch that the swab was involved in some way, don't you?" She nodded. Smith kept sipping the coffee, thinking. "Let's approach this thing from another angle." He addressed Ohnara. "Tell me again about the Shewanella. Gram negative, lives underwater in an anaerobic environment, and conducts electricity."

Ohnara nodded. "It not only conducts electricity but it actually feeds off it. We're not sure how, but its nanowires attach and communicate with metal or an electric source. And I can't emphasize this enough, but it doesn't, as far as we know, cause any disease or illness of any kind."

"What if it were weaponized?" Russell asked.

Ohnara shook his head. "I don't see how it could be. Most weaponized substances have, at their core, a toxic capability. Since it doesn't, it's a poor candidate for such a use. In fact, it is actually the opposite. It can create energy and because it feeds off metals, it's used in rivers in a beneficial manner."

"DMRB bacteria," Smith said.

"English, please, for the one who's not a microbiologist in the room." Russell swung her stool to face Smith. He gave her a small smile and she smiled back.

"It stands for dissimilatory metal-reducing bacteria," he said.

"Oh, well, that clarifies things," she said.

"It can be used to reduce heavy metals in water. Iron, things like that," Ohnara said.

Smith's head was clearing. He looked around the lab and saw a series of flasks and petri dishes along a counter.

"What's that?" he said.

"I asked for some more testing," Russell said.

"It's the bacteria. I'm growing it both aerobically and anaerobically."

Smith slid off the stool and stood. He was pleased that his legs felt normal again. He walked to the bottles and stared at them.

"When it's communicating through the nanowires, what is it doing?"

"Colonizing. It forms a biofilm. We think it breathes without the need for oxygen by using the wires to communicate, one to the other, until finally the portion of the biofilm that is in contact with the air transmits the oxygen down to the lower levels. The nanowire electricity is the conduit that the O_2 travels along."

Smith took another sip and stared at the flasks. What was he missing? The sound of a ringing phone filled the room. Russell checked the screen.

"It's Klein. I'll put him on speaker."

"Ms. Russell?"

"And Ohnara and Smith," Russell said.

"Smith? You're awake?"

Smith shrugged more out of reflex, since Klein couldn't see him.

"Russell gave me some coffee. It's helping."

"I've been monitoring both the FBI transmissions as well as the New York City police band and I've learned something interesting. The NYPD considers both you and Russell to be criminals: Russell a CIA agent gone rogue who is acting as a mole within the agency, and you a killer of the woman at Landon Investments. A warning has gone out that you are both armed and dangerous. Needless to say, I found this surprising."

"I have a pretty good idea who started that rumor in motion: Harcourt."

Russell's head snapped up and she looked at Smith. "You've got to be joking."

Smith shook his head. "Didn't Marty tell you? I was staring down Harcourt's gun minutes before you showed up."

"All Marty said was that the FBI was mistakenly trying to arrest you."

"No mistake about it. Harcourt pointed them to us both. He discovered that Marty was using your passwords to access the CIA system. He says the agency assumes that you're a mole. I think he's utilizing his close contacts with the NYPD to encourage them to see us as persons of interest; me in the shooting incident at Landon, and you for allowing the CIA system to be hacked."

"Please ask Mr. Ohnara to step out of the room. I'd like to speak with you both on matters that require clearance," Klein said.

Ohnara nodded. "I'll get some more coffee." He left, closing the door behind him.

"Has he left?" Klein said.

"Yes." Smith took a sip of his drink.

"This is a sticky situation. I can't very well explain to the CIA your status with Covert-One, and while I can warn off the FBI with some vague argument about international security and 'need to know' claims, I expect that the CIA will quickly countermand that order."

"So we're on our own," Smith said. "Not the first time."

"And not entirely. Two can play this game. I'll do my best to suggest that it's Harcourt that's the mole and request that he be detained."

"Anything in those transmissions give us a clue as to where Nolan and Dattar may have gone?"

"Nothing. Only real news is that a subway station on the Upper West Side and now another near Inwood have been shut due to flooding. Apparently some brand-new sump pumps stopped working."

"Is that so unusual? The New York subway often floods. Old infrastructure," Russell said.

"It's dry outside," Smith said.

"Which doesn't mean much," Klein said. "Water is always an issue for the subway. On a daily basis those pumps remove thirteen to fifteen million gallons of water. Now that they're down, water is accumulating fast. And the sump pumps were brand new. Perhaps it's nothing, but I thought you should know. Both the electric grid and subway stations are considered prime targets for terrorist activity. I usually keep a close eye on both."

"Did they close the station?"

"Not only that, but they shut down the third rail. The electricity is off."

An idea fell into place. Smith put the coffee cup down so fast that liquid sloshed out of it onto the white Formica counter. Russell gave him a piercing look.

"My God, I think I've figured it out."

There was a knock and Ohnara returned, holding a cup of coffee. "May I come in?" he said.

"Absolutely. I have a theory."

Ohnara stepped closer. "What?"

"The Shewanella isn't the weapon, it's simply the conduit. Whoever stole the coolers figured out how to make it pass not only oxygen but a virus through its nanowires. That's why the avian flu strain is attached. The Shewanella is feeding it upward."

Russell stood as well. "We just learned that the third rail of a subway line was shut down."

"What if the bacteria was added to the metal rail? What then?" Smith said. He looked at Ohnara. "How fast can it colonize and how quickly will it travel?" Ohnara turned so pale that Smith thought he would faint.

"On a third rail? In a subway line?" Ohnara swallowed. "I can't be sure, but under ideal conditions it could double every forty minutes. With a live electrical source as powerful and limitless as a train line, who knows?"

"Where does the line terminate?" Klein's voice on the phone sounded strained.

"That's just it," Smith said. "The bacteria feeds on both metal *and* electricity. The subway train rail terminates, yes, but the electricity feeding to it continues out to the grid."

"Where it then continues to every house and building that's connected to it," Klein said.

"And the nanowires push the virus up to the air," Ohnara said. "The mutated version, so that it can be easily transmitted by humans."

"You have any weapons?" Smith said.

Russell grabbed a set of car keys. "An Uzi, a knife, and a Beretta."

"That'll work. Let's go."

43

MANHAR CRAWLED DOWN FROM the platform to the third rail, sloshing through the brackish, stinking water as he did. He plunged the thermometer into the stream for the second time. He waited, heard the beep, and pulled the stick out.

"Forty-two." He called the words to Rajiid, who swore in Urdu at the number.

"More water!" Rajiid yelled into the handset of a pay phone on the wall. The hose resumed pouring the fresh water into the stream. Manhar stayed where he was and watched as a dead rat floated by. He wanted out of this despicable country, away from Rajiid, Dattar, and all of the others the moment he could flee. He glanced at the Nolan woman. She bled continuously, but seemed oblivious to her wounds. Manhar hated women who controlled their emotions; it was unnatural. To be stoic was a characteristic of men, not women. At that moment, Dattar erupted in anger, yelling at Rajiid and waving his arms around to emphasize his piercing shrieks.

Well, maybe not that man, Manhar thought. Dattar was ten times more volatile than most. He excelled at instilling fear. Manhar had heard that Dattar had once skinned a European alive in retaliation for some affront or another. Manhar had no wish to be next. For the moment he was stuck cooperating.

"Check again," Rajiid said. He yelled over the cascading water. Manhar reset the thermometer and shoved it back into the stream. Sixty seconds, a beep and a reading.

"Thirty-eight."

"Almost there," Rajiid said.

Manhar slogged to the platform and hoisted himself back onto it. As he did, he heard the sound of steps running down the stairs. A man wearing a hard hat and a reflective vest stepped into the room. He held a walkie-talkie and stopped when he saw Rajiid, Dattar, Manhar, and Nolan.

"What the hell is going on here?" he said. "This station is gonna be closed for the next three hours. You all have to leave."

Khalil stepped into view behind the man, raised a gun with a silencer attached and shot the man in the back. Manhar watched the body drop. Nolan made a small, moaning sound.

Rajiid looked annoyed. "I would have talked my way out of that. Told him that we were with MTA. Now when he doesn't respond to their calls they'll send someone to check on him."

Khalil shrugged. "And how long do you think that will take? They'll call, he won't answer, they'll assume he's busy, and by the time they send another, the water will be cool, the bacteria placed, and we'll be long gone." He waved at Manhar. "Toss his body into the tunnel. Far enough in so that he can't be seen from the platform."

"And out of the way of any trains. I want the subway operating at full speed during the rush hour, not closed while they remove a dead body," Dattar said.

Manhar rose and headed to the construction worker's corpse. The man was at least six feet and had a stomach the size of a basketball. No way was Manhar going to be able to move the body alone.

"I need some help. This guy's too big."

"Get up and help him," Dattar said to Nolan. She hadn't made any noise other than the moan and Manhar noted that her face once again held the closed expression that she commonly wore. She rose and joined him. He hooked his hands under the man's armpits and she grabbed his feet by the ankles. Together they hauled him to the platform's edge and left him there while they jumped down onto the tracks. They grabbed the corpse and started down the tunnel past the water flow. As they walked, it became increasingly dark, and when they left the lighted platform area and entered the tunnel, the only illumination came from the sporadic lamps attached at the ceiling and the signal stands. About fifty feet in, a recessed area allowed for someone to step inside. Manhar nodded at it, and they arranged the body there in a sitting position, being sure to keep the arms folded so that the train conductor wouldn't see anything on approach. Manhar reached into the man's pants pocket and removed a wallet. He flipped it open, took the money, and tossed the wallet on the ground next to the man's feet.

"Come on," he said. Nolan glanced down the tunnel. It wasn't difficult for Manhar to read her thoughts, despite her expressionless face. "Forget it. They'll catch you."

Nolan turned and followed him, keeping to her usual silence. At the station opening Rajiid shoved the thermometer back at Manhar.

"Check," he said.

Manhar snatched the device from Rajiid and bit his tongue to avoid snapping "check your own damn water" at him. He dipped it into the stream and pulled it out at the beep.

"Thirty-five," he said.

Rajiid smiled. "Showtime. You," he said to Nolan. "Carry the flasks to the edge. Then get on the rails and start applying the gel. I want it applied directly to the third rail, not the cover, so you'll need to find each slide, where the rail is left exposed, and work the gel through it."

"Will the water wash it away?" Dattar said.

Rajiid shook his head. "The gel will allow it to be placed despite the water. The bacteria thrives underwater, so it's not a problem."

"Should we be here?" Dattar said.

Rajiid waved him off. "It won't get to you unless you're standing over it. Now, after the rail goes back on you'll want to be on your way out of New York City."

Nolan shuffled over to the cooler and grabbed the metal basket that held four flasks. As she did a drop of blood plopped onto one of the flasks.

"And don't contaminate the flasks with your blood!" She stood up straighter. Manhar sloshed over to meet her and grabbed a flask.

Manhar smeared the substance in the flask over the third rail, moving into the tunnel to search for the next slide as he did. Nolan worked next to him, keeping her head down and her eyes averted from the area where they'd hidden the body. Manhar worked as fast as he could. The cooling water would allow the third rail to be electrified again, and he didn't want to be standing in the stream and touching it when it resumed. When the signal lights blinked, Manhar started to sweat.

Nolan worked as feverishly as he did. They both wore rubber gloves and scooped out the gelatinous substance with their fingers. Then they smeared it on the rail. The worst part of the job was moving into the tunnel. Every so often Manhar would hear a splash as a rat jumped in the water and all manner of dead bugs and bits of garbage floated by. Plunging his hand into the water was also disgusting. Once he pulled out some twisted mass of hair and blackened grease on his fingers. He shook his hand, but it clung stubbornly to the rubber glove. Nolan made a surprised sound as a small rat jumped up onto the third rail and hustled away, running along the narrow metal track with precision.

Manhar kept smearing the gel and trying to work a plan that would get him as far away from New York as soon as possible. Dattar hovered at the platform, watching. Manhar had long figured out that Nolan had stolen some money from the man and that he wasn't going to let her out of his sight until he retrieved it. They finished and kicked through the stream to the platform and scrambled back up. As they did the water near the third rail shivered.

"Electricity's back on," Rajiid said. He consulted his watch.

Khalil came into view. "Three of your men just dropped dead."

Rajiid shrugged. "The suicide pills are kicking in. They're time release."

"Will they all die at once?"

"No. It'll be staggered," Rajiid said.

Manhar felt a chill. All this time they thought he would die with the others. He'd lied for them, killed for them, and now they wanted him to die for them. Well, he wouldn't. He'd never signed on for a suicide mission. He was a soldier, not an idealist. Let the other young men with fire in their eyes and nationalist fever in their blood die for a cause. He didn't die for freedom. He killed for money. He would take matters into his own hands.

Rajiid glanced at his watch.

"Let's get out of here," Dattar said. "I don't want to stay while those bacteria grow. The helicopter waiting?"

Rajiid nodded. "And the plane at the airport."

Dattar looked at Nolan. "Upstairs. We'll transfer the funds." Nolan limped toward Dattar. Manhar thought that she had little fight left in her. He knew that once Dattar cut off her hands, she'd die from the blood loss. It's what happened when the vessels weren't immediately cauterized. He'd seen it in Africa. But she wasn't his problem. His problem was getting as far away from them all as possible. Rajiid closed the cooler and shoved it in a corner behind a trash bin. Dattar, Khalil, and Manhar started toward the exit.

44

KLEIN STEPPED INTO THE situation room where the president and a secret service agent waited. A large conference table dominated the rectangular area, and flat-screen televisions, turned off at the moment, lined the walls. The president nodded and the agent left, closing the door behind him.

"Tell me your urgent news," Castilla said.

"I think we've figured out why the terrorists stole the bacteria." He laid out Smith's theory and told him about the subway malfunction.

Castilla shifted. "I think I should inform you that the DNI briefed me on the situation involving Russell and Smith. He said that the CIA believed that she's gone rogue, and he's one of her more questionable assets."

Klein wasn't surprised. The director of national intelligence usually gathered information from a broad range of agencies before preparing his daily report. The CIA would have notified him of the action against Russell and Smith.

"And the DNI? Did he believe it? I mean, technically, placing field officers in responsible positions within the CIA was his policy decision. The CIA didn't like the idea from the start."

"Actually, that was my decision. I thought we needed to close some of the disconnects that I was seeing between the knowledge of the officers in the field and that of the officers Stateside. At the time the DNI agreed with me." Castilla shook his head. "He, too, thought that Russell was a convenient scapegoat. However, he said that he wouldn't interfere with the CIA and their handling of the situation unless it became clear that they were trumping up false charges against her."

Klein sat down in a chair opposite the president. "I'm convinced that Smith is solid, of course, but I'm also fairly certain that Russell is as well. I haven't known her that long, but I know she's very good at what she does. I think there's a mole in the CIA, but I don't think it's Russell." Castilla stared at Klein and said nothing. Klein let him think it through.

"Let's put the question aside for the moment. Tell me about the subway. Did you send the NYPD to check it out? Along with an FBI officer responsible for the region?"

Klein shook his head. "Neither yet. Smith was concerned that they'd fill the station with personnel and, if he's right, all will get infected with the virus. That's a concern of mine as well. I'm afraid the Seventy-second Street station has already been swarmed with MTA personnel because it malfunctioned first. The good news is that they've done a routine check of the rail and reported to the NYPD that they found nothing unusual. With regard to the 191st Street station, I've agreed to give him some time to verify his theory."

"Have the NYPD called in hazardous incident teams?" Castilla said.

Klein shook his head. "The NYPD is currently under the mistaken impression that Smith is a killer and Russell a mole, and I'm concerned that they'll tip off the real one to our knowledge of the plan and he'll get Dattar out of there before we can nab him. Especially since they have a CIA officer working in their intelligence-gathering arm. His name is Harcourt, and he has a direct pipeline to the agency. Whatever they discover might immediately be transferred to the agency and, by extension, the mole. This problem is best resolved by Covert-One operating alone."

"Dattar is the least of our problems. Let's secure the subway from the top and let Smith do the initial reconnaissance. After that we can send in the NYPD to sweep the area and flush any suspects," Castilla said.

"With all due respect, I don't think we can afford to let Dattar slip through our hands now. What if Smith's theory is wrong? Then we'll be back to square one, and Dattar will be long gone. We need to buy Smith some time to check it out."

Castilla paused and again Klein let him consider all the angles.

"Okay. We'll do it your way. Give me worst-case scenario."

Klein inhaled. "Assuming that Russell and Smith don't find the source and stop it?"

"Yes."

"The Shewanella multiplies rapidly and begins to communicate through the nanowires feeding the virus upward. It travels along the electrical current through to the grid and outward. To everywhere the grid touches, disseminating the virus throughout the New York City region. Then nature takes its normal course and everyone who is infected becomes a carrier. The New York subway has over five hundred miles of track and five million riders each day on a weekday. Once the bacteria starts pumping the virus into the air, those five million will be exposed."

"So a flu pandemic. Survival rate?"

"We believe it's a mutation of H5N1 or avian flu. Regular avian flu has a fifty percent death rate. This one kills ninety-seven percent. No treatment or cure."

Castilla was up and pacing. Klein could sympathize with his agitation. It was all Klein could do to deliver the scenario in a calm voice.

"How about turning off the third rail at the affected station? Can the MTA shut down in sections? Then the bacteria will lose its transportation source."

"Yes, the rail control center can shut down individual sections of track, and that will slow the progress, definitely, but the bacteria can also generate its own electricity that will be conducted through the metal rails. Given enough time, it will reunite with a live section."

"How much time?"

Klein shook his head. "I've heard it can reproduce every forty minutes. How far down the track can it get in that time without an outside source of electricity? I don't know. And there is the additional problem that we may have the wrong station."

"Or the wrong theory entirely," Castilla said.

"Agreed. This theory could be wrong. But if it's right, the most effective way to stop the bacteria is to shut down the entire subway system."

Castilla stopped pacing. "That's a massive undertaking. Not pulling the plug, mind you, but ensuring that after you do, thousands of people on every line remain safely inside the trains. Plus, if I make such a drastic call, it's likely that someone in the NYPD is going to learn of it. If they do, then that information will be shuttled to the mole, and Smith is at risk and Dattar takes off."

"I thought of that as well. NYPD often deals with the rail control center," Klein said.

"I think we roll the dice and shut down the affected station. It's an occurrence that won't raise too many eyebrows, and we'll keep it short enough to ensure that the riders stay put, and long enough for Smith to determine whether his theory is solid."

Klein nodded. "Agreed."

"I'll give Smith half an hour. That enough time for him to make his way through the station with the malfunction?"

"I think so. And at this time of night there's a fifteen- to twenty-minute headway between trains, which should buy him a bit more if we time the shutdown right. Can you black out the area around the suspected subway station? Target a small section on either side? Maybe just the electric substation that handles the neighborhoods in question?"

Castilla thought a moment. "Probably, but why?"

"Two reasons. The signals work on an AC circuit separate from the track, and Smith wants it dark in there. Also, some stations have cameras. Fifty percent don't work anyway, but I've made inquiries and can't get a straight answer on whether those at the affected stations are functioning. I don't want one catching Smith and Russell on the job. Another chance that a cop could get ideas and interfere."

"Done. And if they find that it's already spread? What then? Tell everyone to turn off their lights? Shut down every appliance? At least then they won't be drawing the stuff into their homes, and it can buy us some time to address how to destroy the bacteria."

"Even if we could ensure one hundred percent compliance, there would be the televisions to consider," Klein said.

Castilla resumed pacing and frowned. "What do you mean?"

"Your television is never really off. The power switch just makes it appear so."

Castilla rubbed his forehead. "Okay, total blackout. We shut down New York City. No power whatsoever."

Klein nodded. "Yes, that's what I keep coming back to. The bacteria can double every forty minutes under ideal conditions, but destroying just that should be manageable if Smith gets there in time."

Castilla sat down. "So we'll start slow. First, shut down a section. Half hour maximum. Give Smith some time to reconnoiter at the affected station. He finds it, fixes it, we're done. He doesn't, we shut down the entire city. What will he need to eliminate it? Bleach? Alcohol wash?"

Klein inhaled again. And Castilla put up both hands.

"Whenever you do that, I know you're preparing to give me more bad news."

"I'm sorry, but I am. Shewanella can form a biofilm. One of a few found in nature. It can't be killed with any substance. Even bleach won't get to it. Heat will initially kill the individual bacteria, but once it's formed the biofilm, it will be immune. It needs to be scraped away manually. So now you see the problem. If it's allowed to spread, there's no way we can conceivably scrape over five hundred miles of track effectively."

Castilla headed to a phone. "I'm making the call now."

45

SMITH FOUND HIMSELF once again in a drugstore, though not the same one he'd been in the last time when he bought first aid. He moved through the aisles collecting flashlights, batteries, and two pairs of rubber gloves, one for Russell and one for him. Russell was in a separate aisle looking for water bottles and aspirin. They met in the middle.

If anything, Russell looked worse under the drugstore's fluorescent lights. Her skin remained pasty and slick from sweat, her lips were chapped, and her hair lank. She had pulled it into a ponytail and wisps fell around her face. She'd insisted on coming despite her weak condition, and Smith knew better than to try to stop her.

"What's the tape for?" she said, indicating the duct tape in his grocery basket.

"To tape the lights to our waists. Allows for freedom of movement."

She nodded. "Think Klein will be able to come up with some more weapons?"

Smith shrugged. "Maybe, but we can't wait for it. Every minute that goes by, the bacteria spread."

"If we're right."

"If we're right, yes. And I've got to hope that we are. I don't want to be the one who missed the ball so completely." She turned toward the cash registers and he followed.

"We have it right. I can just feel it."

He didn't reply. The clerk behind the counter didn't seem to notice Russell's condition, or perhaps working the late shift meant that he was used to seeing dreadful-looking people buying aspirin. They left the store and climbed back into the rental.

Ten minutes later, Russell pulled within thirty feet of the 181st Steet subway stop and killed the engine.

"Klein's going to orchestrate a partial blackout," Smith said. "We'll have thirty minutes from when it starts." He had his bulletproof vest on, but Russell had none.

"We need better equipment. You take the vest. I'll take the rifle."

Russell shook her head. "Not a chance. You're the one we need to address removing the bacteria. I'm just the hired muscle."

"I hardly think of it in those terms."

"Well, you should. We need your expertise to get through this thing. Mine, not so much."

"I'll make you a deal. When we get closer to the target, you walk in front. You draw their fire while I work on the track. For that, you'll need the vest."

She held out her hand. "Fine. Give it to me."

They both opened their doors and slid out of the car. Smith shrugged out of the vest and handed it to her. As they did, a shadow emerged from behind two buildings. It was Howell.

"Out for a stroll?" he said.

Smith clapped him on the shoulder. "Glad to see you. Klein fill you in?"

Howell nodded. "All the gory details. Where's Beckmann?"

"In FBI custody."

"Shame," Howell said. "So what's the plan?"

Smith turned to the subway stop. "This is the next station down from the target. We go in, jump down to track level, and make our way to the 191st Street platform."

"Subway crawling."

Russell nodded. "Beats dying."

"That it does," Howell said. He showed them his sniper rifle. "I'm armed and ready to take someone out. Lead on."

Before he did, Smith spotted a black man in his early thirties with long braids and a soft-sided guitar case slung over his shoulders like a backpack. He kept a steady eye on Smith and Russell as he walked toward them. He stopped when he reached Smith.

"Nice night for some rat hunting. Special delivery. My friend, Mr. Klein, asked me to give you this." He shook one shoulder out of the pack's straps and then the other. Smith took it from him and nearly dropped it in surprise at the sudden weight.

"Heavy for a guitar," Smith said.

The man smiled. "I agree but it's the best. Good luck." He nodded at Russell and Howell and sauntered off.

"What's in it?" Howell said.

"My weapons, I presume. I asked for an AK-47, two Berettas, and some tear gas bombs. You know, just in case."

Howell nodded. "Of course. May I suggest a pincer movement? I will approach from the Dyckman station, you approach from this one. They try to run through the tunnels at least then we'll catch them. Drive them toward me. I'll be up on the platform ready to ambush them when they come even."

"Good. We'll give you twenty minutes to get into place. That work?"

"Yes, it does."

"The streetlights will go dark first. Remember, that doesn't affect the third rail, which is on a different system. I'll wait until you're in place and then give the signal to cut power to the third rail. Good luck," Smith said. Howell jogged away and as he did, the streetlights went dark. Smith kept a close eye on his watch. After twenty minutes, he sent a text to Klein.

"Thirty minutes," Smith said. He headed down the stairs.

Smith was surprised at the depth of the blackness, both on the street and in the subway. He dodged a woman heading upstairs and mumbled an apology that he doubted she heard. Two more people slogged up the stairs with resigned looks on their faces. A young man wearing skater pants and a graphic T-shirt and carrying a backpack with a skateboard lashed to it waved at him.

"Lights went out. Don't think the trains are coming."

"I'm MTA and you're right. Many people waiting?"

"Nah. Only me, those two, and that lady."

"Good. Hope you don't have too far to go to get home."

"I got the board. It'll be cool."

Smith joined Russell at the bottom.

"New Yorkers are a resilient group, aren't they?" he said.

"Yes, they are." She headed to the turnstile and vaulted over it. Smith followed, jumping up onto the support, swinging his legs, and landing on the other side. He switched on his light and kept moving. The light was taped to his belt at his hip and faced forward, throwing a beam that was easy to follow. The platform was empty.

"Let me get the AK out of this guitar case." Smith carefully removed the case from his back and unzipped it halfway. He felt around inside and his fingers closed on a metal weapon. He pulled out an AK-47 with a carry strap. He felt around again and found a pistol that he shoved into his waistband. He reached back inside and pulled out a small bulging nylon bag. It had carry ropes to make it a backpack. He ran his fingers over it, found the opening and pulled it wider so that he could put his hand inside and figure out what was there. He felt a cylindrical portion that held the filter of a gas mask. He smiled when he realized that it contained two. He transferred the tear gas from the larger pack to the smaller and left the guitar bag on the ground. He put the smaller nylon bag over his shoulders. They jumped down onto the tracks, and water splashed upward.

"The flooding's going to slow us down."

"Wish we could fan out. I hate to be stuck single file if we come upon Dattar and his crew," Russell said.

"I'm equally afraid of the third rail. It's mostly covered, but there are small open sections. If somebody gets the idea to switch the electricity back on, I don't want to be anywhere near it," Smith said.

He continued forward, with Russell behind him. The tunnel smelled of mildew and dust, but overall it wasn't as foul as he'd expected. The tunnel's ceiling was made of jack-arch concrete and the walls were tiled. The sound echoed, as if he were in a shower, so they maintained silence.

Smith figured it would take them 15 minutes to walk it. The water, with its tendency to splash and make noise, slowed them a bit, but they still kept a brisk pace. Smith felt the dirt beneath his feet begin to suck at his shoes, and his feet and calves were soaked. He felt something squish under his sole. It felt dense, like the body of a small animal.

Mouse or rat, Smith thought.

After ten minutes they came upon a recessed opening. Smith turned his hips so that the light shone into the area, but he found nothing. He waved Russell on. After another five minutes, he thought he heard a sound ahead of him. He stopped and switched off his flashlight; Russell did the same. Smith stayed perfectly still. The sound of another soft splash, this one closer, made his skin crawl and his heart start racing. Someone or something was in the tunnel with them.

46

Dattar, Khalil, Manhar, and Rajiid had taken three steps toward the exit, when the lights went off.

The blackness shocked Manhar and, for a moment, he thought the world had come to an end. He heard shuffling and a smothered oath from Khalil.

"What did they do? Shut the rail down again?"

"The lights are on a different system." Rajiid's voice came from Manhar's right. "This is more extensive than just the station."

"You have a flashlight?" Dattar's harsh voice grated on Manhar's ears. He thought he heard a soft splash from behind him, and it made his skin crawl. The rats were jumping in the water.

"There's one in the cooler. Let me get it." Manhar heard Rajiid making his way to the trash bin. The total dark was disorienting. He heard the sound of a siren far in the distance and the steady drip of water that still fell from the hose. A hollow sound and then another oath, this one from Rajiid.

"What's the problem?" Dattar's voice came through the dark.

"I stubbed my toe on the damn cooler."

I hope it's broken, Manhar thought.

After some scratching noises, a light blinked on. Rajiid ran the beam over the area, highlighting Khalil, Dattar, and Manhar.

"Where is she?" Dattar said.

Rajiid moved the light all around the platform. Nolan was gone.

"She has my money," Dattar shrieked. Manhar couldn't see Rajiid's face, but he heard the man make a small, irritated sound.

"She must be in the tunnel. Khalil, could she have gotten past you and up the stairs?"

"Not at all," Khalil's voice came from the area near the stairs.

"Find her. Now. She has my money," Dattar said. "Manhar, into the tunnel." Manhar tried to think of any possible reason not to enter the tunnel.

"We don't know which way she went. You need two, maybe more, to go in both directions. And flashlights."

"She's in there in the dark and if she can go there, you can too," Dattar's voice was harsh. "Rajiid, give him the flashlight. Khalil, go with him. Find her." Manhar started toward Rajiid, who still held the flashlight. When he got to the man, Rajiid handed it over with a grimace.

"How long before the bacteria sour the tunnel?" Manhar asked.

"Forty minutes if the rail is off, less if the rail is still on."

"And then?"

"Ten minutes will see it double. At that stage you'll still have to stand directly over the areas where you applied it. At twenty, it will reach fifteen feet in every direction. At forty it will reach ninety feet each direction."

"What does it carry?"

"Mutated virus of H5N1. Pandemic strength."

"Does anyone survive it?" Manhar said.

"Three percent do. Ninety-seven percent do not. If you get it, don't bother going to the hospital. They can't help you. Only time will tell if you survive or not."

"Get moving!" Dattar yelled.

"I will, but first I need a weapon."

"I want her alive, you idiot," Dattar said.

"Give me your knife. I won't kill her."

Dattar made an irritated sound and shoved the knife and a gun in

Manhar's direction. He took both, and snatched the flashlight from Ra-jiid. Cowards both of them, Manhar thought. They won't go into the tunnel to do their own dirty work.

Khalil walked up. "Let's go. I'll use this." He turned to Dattar. "You'd better not leave. Anything happens in the tunnel and I'll expect you both to jump in and provide backup."

Dattar waved a second gun in the air. "I'm not leaving without her. I thought I made that very clear."

Khalil grunted and switched on a stick lighter. The flame flickered. Manhar thought it was ridiculously weak, but Khalil was an expert tracker and huntsman and he presumed the meager light was enough for him. He jumped down onto the track, splashing water as he did. He focused the flashlight down to his left, in the direction where they had discarded the body, and saw nothing. He swung it right and again saw nothing.

"We both go left," Khalil said. "She's headed that way."

"How do you know?"

Khalil pointed to the edge of the platform. A few drops of red glistened in the light beam.

"Ah, you're right. I'd forgotten she was bleeding."

Khalil shot him a smirk. "You first," he said.

Manhar didn't want to go first. He didn't like the idea of Khalil at his back with a gun in his hand.

"We walk together," he said.

Khalil shook his head. "I'm not walking near the third rail. Who knows when it will switch back on?"

"Then I'll take that side."

"As you wish."

They started forward. Manhar didn't bother to cover the sound of his feet splashing through the water. Let her hear him coming, he thought. As he trudged, he flashed the light from side to side, covering the area. There was nothing. No sign of the woman and no noise of her either. In the distance he heard sirens. They came even with the dead body. Khalil didn't glance at it. They took a few more steps and Khalil stopped. He held up a hand and Manhar stilled as well. From somewhere in front of them came the noise of splashing. For an instant, then all was quiet.

Khalil stepped to his left and hugged the wall.

47

S MITH AND RUSSELL KEPT MOVING. She tapped him on the shoulder. "Me first," she said. "When they start shooting, you need to be behind me. Remember?"

Smith backed off, and she slipped past him. He lined up behind. Every so often the tunnel wall was cut away, either with a narrow archway that looked like a window that had been cemented up, or to a small alcove with a metal staircase that led upward. Graffiti covered the walls. The taggers must have run into the tunnel between arriving trains. Russell slowed before each opening, making sure that no one was waiting to ambush them before taking the risk of stepping even.

They had advanced twenty feet when Smith got the overwhelming sense that someone was in front of them. He put a hand on Russell's shoulder. She paused. He put his mouth to her ear.

"Someone's out there."

He felt her nod. She turned her head to whisper into his ear. "I'm going to lay down rifle fire. Let's head to an opening and get low." He crouched down with Russell, moving in tandem.

"I'm ready. Tell me when. I'll switch on the light." He moved flush against her left side and prepared to flick on his flashlight.

"One," she whispered. "Two. Three."

He turned on the flashlight and Russell started firing the Uzi. He felt her body vibrate with the weapon's recoil and the noise pounded his eardrums. The light gave a gray glow and her shots pierced through the tunnel. Smith saw bits of her muzzle flash and two men standing about fifty yards into the tunnel.

Seconds later they returned fire. He could see muzzle flash only from the one on the right. The plaster in front of Russell's face exploded and he heard her grunt as bits hit her face. He switched off the light and used his body to push her into an opening to the right. A bullet winged past his ear.

"How many did you see?" Russell said.

"Two. But only the one on the right was shooting."

"Let's continue to lay down fire in spurts and take it in sections. This time run to the left and when we reach the next opening get inside. We need to get to the bacteria. The station is behind them."

Russell nodded. "One, two, three." She stepped back into the tunnel and laid down some more fire, racing across to the left side. This time Smith didn't turn on the light but kept with her, firing the AK-47 on semiautomatic to conserve bullets. The return fire was quick and raked to the right. Russell jogged forward and Smith did as well, firing and praying that a stray bullet from the two in front didn't hit him dead on in the chest. He kept looking for a recessed section, but couldn't find any.

"One, two..." Russell wasn't letting up. Smith didn't either. She started moving right again. This time Smith didn't see any return fire. He kept shooting. They jogged ahead. He breathed a sigh of relief when the muzzle flash revealed another opening, this one without a ladder, but deep enough to provide cover for both him and Russell. They'd managed to reach this section without seeing any return fire. Right before they stepped into the tunnel, Smith thought he saw motion from inside the recessed area. He put an arm out to hold Russell in place, moved his back against the wall, inched his way forward, and led with his gun, arm stretched out. He stepped into the opening and flicked on his light. His muzzle was three feet from Nolan's face.

"Don't shoot, it's me," Nolan said.

Smith swallowed as relief went through him. She stepped up to him and put her arms around his waist. He placed an arm around her neck, felt her temple at his lips and kissed it. She moved in close and gripped his waist harder. He could feel her shaking and, because she'd never shown fear before, he knew that it meant the situation was dire.

"How many are there?" he said.

"Four. And a crew upstairs."

"I'm Russell. Are they all armed?" Russell's voice came in a whisper through the darkness.

"Likely, yes. Khalil and Dattar for sure. I don't know about the other two."

"Did they hurt you?" Smith asked. She was silent. His anger spiked and his face felt hot as he flushed.

"I'm alive," she said. "And still in one piece." She sounded a bit more like herself, but she still gripped him tightly.

"Did he get the money back?" Russell said.

"Not yet. They wanted to set up their attack first."

"Tell us," Russell said. "But make it quick. They're out there."

Nolan ran down the story, and as she did Smith was both relieved and sickened that the theory he'd reached was the right one.

"How much time?" Russell asked. Smith touched the glow button on his watch.

"Seven minutes."

"What happens then?" Nolan said.

"The third rail switches back on."

"Do you know how many more recessed areas there are before we hit the platform?" Smith said.

"Only one. And there's a body in there." Nolan's voice cracked on the word "body."

"Whose?" Russell said.

"An MTA employee. He stumbled into this mess."

"Ready?" Russell said.

"We're going forward. You stay here. When you think it's safe, run in the other direction." Smith reached into his jacket and pulled out the Beretta. "Take this. It has a full magazine and a laser sight. Do you know how to shoot?"

"I'll figure it out."

"And take this." He handed her his phone. "As soon as you get a signal, call the Anacostia Yacht Club from the contacts list and tell the man who answers that Smith's theory was right. Tell him Dattar's here and to send in the police to surround the station, but under no circumstances should they descend into it without face mask protection."

"How far down on the third rail did you place the bacteria?" Russell asked.

"Twenty feet at least. That means it's at least one hundred feet from where we're standing. One of Dattar's crew thought some was already dead, though."

"We've got to move," Russell said. "One." Smith felt Nolan's palms on either side of his face. One was warm and the other held the gun. The metal was cool against his cheek. She brought his head down and kissed him.

"Two," Russell said.

"Please don't die," Nolan whispered.

"Three." Russell stepped out with Smith right behind her.

They fired in unison, jogging ahead. Smith reached out and tapped Russell on the back. When she stopped, he pulled her down into a crouch next to him.

"No return fire. I don't like it," Smith said.

"I agree. They're cooking something up."

"Ideas?"

"None."

"Then just keep it going," Smith said.

"One, two, three."

Smith and Russell started in again. Smith estimated that they were halfway to the next alcove when Smith saw a row of three muzzle flashes of return fire. This time he heard Russell grunt. She staggered back and he grabbed her around her waist with his left arm while he continued to fire with his right. He dropped to one knee, dragging her with him, and felt bits of stone and shrapnel rain down on his head. In front of him and to the far left he saw muzzle flashes from a new shooter targeting their attackers. Howell, Smith thought. He heard a scream as one of Howell's shots hit home. Russell rolled out of his arm and regained her feet.

"Retreat," he said. "Aim to the right. Don't hit Howell on the left." He fired round after round while he crab-walked backward. Russell was to his left and slightly behind him, and she fired along with him. They made it back to the alcove where Nolan had been hiding. She was gone.

"You hit?"

"Yes. Vest stopped it. Still hurts like hell when they land, though. Knocked the wind out of me for a moment." There was a fizzing sound. Smith thought he could hear the harmonics of the third rail as the electricity poured through it. He looked at his watch.

"Time's up."

48

DATTAR HEARD THE THIRD RAIL come to life and he moved back behind a small portion of wall that jutted out from the stairwell. Khalil, Manhar, Rajiid, and two others from his crew, one bleeding from a shoulder wound, huddled in the space. While he wanted to keep firing, the addition of the shooter from the right as well as the two from the left required that they all take cover.

"The rail's back on," Rajiid said. "Let's go."

Dattar could barely make out the man's features in the dark, but it was clear that Rajiid expected him to agree.

"Who do you think is crawling through that tunnel and firing at us? It's Smith."

"You can't be sure," Rajiid said.

"I saw his face for an instant. I think it was Smith," Khalil said.

"If he's here, then he knows about the bacteria. He'll derail the plan."

"We need to go."

"Not without my money. We get Nolan."

"Forget the money! It's lost. The rail is back on, didn't you hear me? The bacteria will start multiplying. Soon you'll have ten times more than she stole. We need to get out of here. Now."

Dattar couldn't believe his ears. "Forget the money? Are you insane? Smith is a microbiologist. He'll know how to neutralize the bacteria. The plan will fail and I'll have no money at all."

"What good is money if you're dead, I ask you?" Rajiid said.

"What good is being alive without it?" Dattar shot back. "I have to pay back Amir, or did you forget? I'm a hunted man. *You* are a hunted man. Do you have any idea how much it requires to drop out of sight?"

"Is what she said about the sapphire mine and utility company true?" It was Khalil who asked, and Dattar paused, his mind racing to find the right answer. Finally he decided on the truth. Perhaps if he told Khalil that he needed Nolan to be able to pay his debts, Khalil would stay and assist.

"Yes. The mine is depleted. And the utility company manager is dead."

"I'm staying," Khalil said. Dattar felt the tip of Khalil's gun against his skull. "I expect to be paid." Dattar knocked the muzzle away.

"You'll be paid."

The two crew members were silent through the whole exchange, and for a moment Dattar was concerned that the suicide pills had taken them, but just as he had the thought, one of the men shifted.

"We'll need to hold this platform if we expect to find her," Khalil said. "She's in the tunnel."

"Rajiid?" Dattar said. "Are you staying?"

Rajiid's watch lit up as he checked it. "We have twenty minutes. No more. By then the bacteria will have filled this station. There will be no turning back."

"Who are we facing, do you think?" Khalil said.

"Smith for sure. Probably Howell as well. The third could be anyone. I need to get upstairs and acquire a signal on my phone."

"Where are the police?" Manhar said.

"That's what I need to find out. Stay here," Dattar said. He felt Khalil's hand wrap around his bicep.

"You take off and I will hunt you down."

Dattar shook him off. "I'm not leaving without my money."

Khalil let go and Dattar jogged up the stairs. The air above felt fresh and cool after the humid atmosphere in the subway. Dattar's phone acquired a signal. He called a number and heard his informer answer.

"I'm under attack at the drop location. Three shooters. Why aren't the police coming?"

"What are you talking about? I heard nothing about this."

"What the hell am I paying you for, if you can't complete the simplest job? I'm being attacked at the location. Three shooters. I think two are Smith and Howell. Are you telling me that the CIA hasn't heard a thing about this? I thought you had contacts in the New York City police and the FBI."

"I do. If there were a mission at the tunnel, I would know about it."

"I'm telling you there's a mission at the site. Get on the phone and call your contact at the NYPD. Tell him to get some officers here, now. Tell him to kill them. Make up some story that they were resisting arrest. I don't care what you say, but get them gone. And make it fast."

"Hold on. I'll make a call."

Ten minutes later Dattar's phone rang.

"My contact knew nothing about it as well—"

"He lies!"

"Wait! I'm not done. He started calling around. Seems there's been an order, from somewhere, for the police to stand down." Dattar wanted to reach through the phone and strangle the man.

"Countermand it. We'll hold them in place until the police come and then get out of sight while they're arrested. I need the tunnel cleared so that I can track Nolan."

"I can't countermand it. The order came from someone powerful in the government, I'm not sure who."

"You lie! You're the CIA. If the order came from anyone else, your organization has the power to reverse it. Do it. Now."

"I'd love to, but I can't. Listen to me. The order had to be from the top, or as near the top as one can get. You know what that means? If not the White House, then a cabinet member. I'm not going to get that order reversed."

"Yes, you are or you're going to die, because if I don't get my money and get out of this hellhole in the next twenty minutes, I'm going to come after you."

"I'm coming myself. I'm near and I'll bring some backup. We'll do it fast, before the bacteria light up the subway. Whatever happens, we'll be sure to get our hands on Nolan. We can always bring her to where you are."

"How long?"

"Ten minutes, no more."

Dattar switched off the phone and headed back down the stairs. He worked his way through the darkness to where he had left Khalil and the others.

"And?" Khalil said.

"We're getting some backup. And my contact at the CIA is coming personally. Any movement?"

"None. But they could be upon us, and I wouldn't know in this darkness."

Dattar ran the plan down.

"That's a bad idea. First, if the NYPD comes, there will be some that may recognize you. That means we have to get out of here now. Second, even if they do secure the station, there's still not enough time to get our hands on Nolan and get away before the bacteria colonizes."

"My contact's going to bring her to me. We'll leave before the twenty minutes are up and be far enough away to be safe until that happens. Good enough for you?"

"Better." Khalil's voice sounded grudging. Dattar heard a man from his crew groan, followed by a thumping noise.

"He's dead," Rajiid said.

"Great." Khalil's voice sounded disgusted. "Why in hell are you giving these men a suicide pill?"

"Dead men can't turn on me."

"They can't fight, either."

Dattar didn't bother to respond. In the distance he heard sirens, growing louder.

"Rajiid, time."

"Twelve minutes."

The sound of pounding feet came from the stairwell.

"Dattar, it's me."

"Just in time," Dattar said.

49

W E CAN'T LET UP," Russell said.

"I agree, but I'm concerned about Howell. I don't want a stray bullet to hit him."

"We'll throw the tear gas first. It's formulated to create black smoke as well. Once they deploy, we'll lay down some more fire in the platform's direction, avoiding the left wall, where he was last."

Smith slid the pack off his shoulder and took out the bombs. He fished around and removed the masks.

"Put this on." He shoved one at Russell, donned his own, and removed the remaining pistol. Moving the pack out of his way, he hefted the bomb in his hand. "Howell's going to hate this," he said. "He doesn't have a mask. Ready? One, two, three." He pulled the pin on the bomb, stepped into the center of the tunnel and threw it as far as he could. There was a clanking sound as it landed on one of the rails, followed by a fizzing. He pulled the pin on the next, tossed that one, and then switched on the flashlight.

Smoked belched upward from the bombs, billowing into a black cloud. Smith jogged forward, his rifle aimed to the right. He began firing and Russell joined in with her Uzi. They were effectively blinded and Smith clenched his teeth on the thought that while they couldn't see him, he couldn't see them. One lucky shot and he was a dead man.

They kept moving, foot after foot, getting closer to the beginning of where Nolan said she'd placed the bacteria. Smith kept the outer edge of his left foot against the second rail, using it as a guide to keep him on track. It was all he had. He reached the beginning of where the bacteria should be and was thankful for the mask. He breathed heavily, sucking in air. Russell was near and kept a relentless pace, stalking ahead. Water dripped on his head, and he jumped at the cold contact. A second drop hit his back.

When the return fire came, it felt as though it was from all directions. Smith heard the higher pitched sound of the reports from the rifles and he dropped to the ground, doing his best to keep his weapon high. Water splashed up on his face and he felt it soak through his clothes. He crawled to the first rail and over it, keeping his gun pointed up and firing. A click told him that it was empty. Even on semiauto, he'd fired a lot of rounds. He pressed his back against the platform wall and felt in his waist pack for fresh ammunition.

While he slammed the magazine home he noticed that Russell, too, was out. She'd stopped firing. From somewhere farther down the tunnel he heard the report of a new shooter. Howell was back and firing high, a fact for which Smith was grateful. The smoke bombs caused severe facial pain along the lines of tear gas and the enclosed space would intensify it. Smith's mask smelled of rubber and stale air, but at least his eyes and throat didn't burn. He could only imagine what Howell was experiencing. The way the chemical made one's eyes run, it would be tough to fire on a target with any real accuracy. The best Howell could do would be to blanket the area, just as Smith and Russell were doing. Smith kept low, among the rails. They were right where the bacteria began, and Smith was thankful for the mask for another reason. He wasn't breathing in the toxin.

He bent around and resumed firing, keeping the shots high. He saw Russell's muzzle flashes in his peripheral vision and was grateful that she had more ammunition. This was his last magazine.

A fresh onslaught of gunfire from the platform caught him by surprise. It was as though the number of attackers had doubled in the last few minutes. The noise in the tunnel became deafening. Smith's heart was racing and his ears rang continuously. The smoke was beginning to clear and Smith wished he had another bomb. He focused on the muzzle flashes, firing directly at them in a staccato byplay. He heard Russell give a short yell, and her gun clattered at his feet. She stumbled against him.

"I'm out and hit. Right arm."

Smith didn't take his eyes from the target. "Get back in the tunnel. Howell and I will cover here."

"Not on your life. You have another pistol?"

Smith fired two more rounds. Ten left, he thought.

"Yes. Shoulder holster."

"That leave you with one?"

"No, that leaves me with none. I gave Nolan the other one."

"Then I *am* heading to the tunnel. I'm not going to take your last weapon."

She was gone before Smith could ask how badly she was injured. He kept shooting and started to count: eight, seven, six. Howell shot as well, but Smith couldn't help but worry that Howell would also be down to his last few rounds. The attackers, though, with their renewed numbers and zeal seemed to have been given a fresh lease on death, firing round after round. As the smoke cleared, their muzzle flashes became sharper. Smith saw one shooter moving toward the ledge.

Four, three, two, Smith counted. Time to go, he thought. He bolted across the tracks, bent over, keeping between the first and second rail, but this time running in Howell's direction. He saw a last flash, heard the report, and he knew it was Howell.

Smith fired his final round, slung the AK carrying strap over his shoulder and yanked the pistol out of his holster. The smoke had dissipated enough that he could once again see the blue signal lights glowing halfway into the tunnel. The attackers emerged from the blackness, appearing as darker shadows amid the smoky atmosphere. He ran forward, holding his breath until he cleared the wall and was protected from the shooters. Howell moved up flush with his left shoulder. Smith was inordinately happy to see the man.

"No more ammo?" Smith said.

"Correct," Howell replied. He wiped the tears that streamed from his eyes. "You?"

"AK's out, but I have a pistol. How'd you slip past them to get to me?"

"The heavy smoke helped."

"Any idea how many are on that platform?" Smith kept jogging forward while he spoke. He kept glancing back to see if any additional attackers would crawl onto the tracks and shoot straight down the tunnel. When they did, he wanted to be safely inside an opening. The next alcove couldn't come soon enough.

"Six at least. It was down to four but I think two joined in the last five minutes. You managed to drive them backward, so that's a gain." Howell stumbled and Smith grabbed his arm.

"Watch out, the third rail's hot."

"You sure?"

"I have no doubt."

"Why?" There came a rumbling from in front of them, and a train's headlights came into view.

"That's why," Smith said.

50

RUSSELL FELT WEAK as she worked her way back down the tunnel. She reached the dead man and took a break, breathing heavily in the face mask. Sweat ran down the sides of her face and accumulated near her chin and at the bottom of the mask. Her fever had spiked again. She supposed she should feel regret at pushing herself so hard when she was newly recovered, but she couldn't muster any.

She listened to the exchange of gunfire with rising dread. The shots from the direction of the platform had increased substantially, which told Russell that some additional muscle had joined the attackers on the platform. She'd seen four men at least. Some more with fresh ammo and renewed purpose would be enough to overcome Smith and Howell. She needed to get to street level fast so that she could ask Klein for reinforcements. She pressed on, leaving the safety of the alcove and keeping low, crawling through the tunnel. Water saturated her shoes, and her shirt was soaked with sweat under the bulletproof vest. The tunnel seemed an endless dark path that would go on forever. The glowing signal stands gave her some minimal illumination, but it failed to show her the small holes and debris that appeared on the tracks. She rose to a crouch, tripped over a small box and gasped when her foot fell into a hole and threw her off balance. Three steps later she kicked something that flashed bits of silver as it jumped into the air and then landed. She reached it and kicked it again. It was inanimate, whatever it was. On the third encounter with it she grabbed it with her hands. She felt the spokes and nylon covering. It was an umbrella. She tossed it out of the way, against the wall.

She heard the rumbling of a train coming from behind her and panic started to rise. She tried to stay rational; she could always step into an alcove and the train would simply sail by, but the idea of being on train tracks when an actual train was in sight made her palms start to sweat. She could hear the rasping of her breath in her ears, the sound magnified in the mask's close confinement. A quick glance back told her everything she needed to know. A train was headed into the station. The smoke bomb had cleared completely, and the subway car's headlights and signals were lit. The train was directly in her path. She increased her pace, looking for the next alcove. She found it and jumped inside with a sense of relief.

The rumbling grew louder, and she pressed her back against the wall. The train flew by, illuminating her hiding place in regular bursts of light. The noise was loud, and she winced at the sound. It never had seemed so loud when she was waiting safely on a platform.

The last car passed and she leaned out a little to watch the taillights recede. Soon her ears readjusted and she strained to hear whether the fight continued after the train had gone, but there was no sound that she could identify. She found the silence almost more ominous than the shooting. At least while the two factions were battling it out, she could be assured that Smith and Howell were alive.

Russell pushed that thought aside. In all the years she had known Smith, he had prevailed, sometimes against steep odds. She wouldn't bet against him now. She heaved herself to a standing position only to have her eyes lose focus; black settled over her, forcing her to lower back down. She used the wall as a support, sliding down along it to avoid falling over. When she was seated, she put her head between her knees.

Exhaustion clawed at her. Her skin was clammy, and she could feel rivulets of sweat pouring along her sides and from her hair. The mask was stuck to her cheek. She would pass out soon. She only hoped it would be after she reached the surface and spoke to Klein, but the way her body was collapsing made her realize that she might not make it out of the tunnel.

She couldn't imagine living this long only to die of an unknown virus in a subway tunnel, but a part of her recognized the irony. She'd become a CIA officer in order to protect her country in the international arena. She'd always thought that if she died on the job, it would be in some exotic locale and at the hands of an enemy agent. Now she realized that the enemy was a virus so small she hadn't seen it coming. For a moment she thought about all the men, women, and children who would go about their day unaware that this virus had entered their bodies and was working its way through.

Her sister Sophia had died that way. In her sickened haze Russell felt her heart constrict at the thought of Sophia. She'd been a researcher at USAMRIID and died from a deliberate stick of a deadly bacteria. Russell suspected Smith had never really gotten over the loss of Sophia. They'd been engaged to be married, and he'd never allowed a woman to get that close again. Russell remembered Nolan kissing him in the alcove and wondered if Nolan had managed to break through Smith's reserve. She hoped so, for his sake.

The mask sputtered, and she no longer could inhale oxygen through it. She pulled it off her face. A bit of the rubber coating stuck to her cheek, and she winced when it yanked her skin before releasing. She took a breath, stood up, and vowed to continue forward. All her speculation was getting her nowhere. She needed to move.

Her legs felt heavy and her head spun as she walked, but she set her teeth together and continued. Deep-seated chills started at the base of her spine and flowed outward, the skin on her arms puckering with it. She felt waves of cold followed by heat. Her teeth started chattering, and she clenched them to stop it. She had counted alcoves during her walk in and now calculated that she had two more to go before she reached the next platform. Her foot hit yet another piece of detritus and she stumbled against the wall. As she did she leaned her cheek against the stone, relishing the chill. She pushed off and staggered ahead. The wall disappeared and the platform was there. Even better, this platform was lit.

She got to the edge, and it took all her strength to lift the Uzi and put it on the platform. When she placed both hands on the yellow treads at the edge, she found she was at least four feet lower. It was going to take some physical strength to haul her body up and over. Physical strength that she wasn't sure she had after more than two days fighting the virus. Both her hands were in view and for the first time Russell noticed how dry and desiccated they looked in the bad fluorescent lighting. They were the hands of someone beyond dehydrated. Another chill took her, but this time she wasn't sure if it was from her existing illness or from the mutated version placed on the rail.

A volley of shots came from the tunnel in the direction where Smith and Howell still fought. They echoed through the cavern and galvanized Russell. She took a deep breath and hauled with her arms while using her toes to inch up the wall. She made it over the edge and flopped onto the floor, panting. She rolled onto her stomach, then to a crouch and finally stood. She staggered to the stairs. As she turned a corner, she found Nolan facedown on the ground, her hands tied behind her back. Blood pooled on the ground next to her head, but Russell saw her body move as she breathed. A man stood over her, pointing a gun at the prone woman's head. He turned around to face Russell and smiled a triumphant smile.

"Hello, Russell. Looks like I've managed to round up all the thieves this evening," Harcourt said.

Russell swayed, but managed to stay upright. "You're the thief, not me." She wobbled as the blood once again threatened to leave her brain:

"Lie down, face-first, just like your friend here."

Russell swayed. She wasn't going to stay upright much longer, and she had no energy to fight Harcourt. She decided to threaten him with someone who could.

"Smith is headed this way. You'd do best to get the hell out of here before he does."

"I'm not worried about Smith. The NYPD is on its way and will make quick work of him. Or did you forget that I have influence there?"

"Not with them all."

"Do as I say or I'll kill you here. One less traitor to worry about."

Russell knew that her condition made it impossible to overcome Harcourt. The better plan was to go along and survive to fight later. She lowered to the ground next to Nolan, who didn't move. Harcourt tied her hands with plastic handcuff strips.

"Now we go."

"Where to?" Russell said.

"To a place where I can be rid of you."

51

SMITH PRESSED HIS BACK against the alcove wall with Howell next to him. The train had passed without stopping at the 191st Street station.

"They're bypassing," Howell whispered. "That has to be Klein's work. An extra precaution because he hasn't heard from you."

Smith hoped that Nolan would get his message to Klein soon and the trains would stop altogether. He knew it was only a matter of seconds before the attackers would jump onto the tracks and start firing. Smith glanced back and saw some motion in the blue glow of a signal light.

"They're in position," Smith said. He swallowed, but it did little to wet his throat. He checked his watch. They had six minutes before the bacteria would reach twenty feet on each side of the drop location. His mask had shifted, covering one eye, and he moved it back into place. It was then that he got a good look at Howell. The man's face was swollen and turning red from the combination of the tear gas effects and exertion. In the fitful light thrown by a signal Smith could only make out the sheen of sweat that covered Howell's face.

"How bad do you feel? Is it from the tear gas?"

Howell shook his head. "I've been gassed twice before. This is something more."

"The virus?"

"I believe so."

Smith yanked on the ripped portion of his shirtsleeve. He worked the tear until the sleeve fell free. He handed it to Howell. "Wrap this around your nose and mouth. If they toss some more bacteria, it will help."

"I also found a discarded plastic bag. It's foul, but I'll not hesitate to put it over my head if it is required."

"I'm sorry to tell you this but I'm the one who threw the tear gas."

"Ah. I see," Howell said.

"But it's still advisable to cover your mouth and nose." Howell placed the cotton around his face, tying it in the back.

Smith peered down the tunnel. He could see the men scrambling onto the platform.

"They're taking off, let's go." Smith burst out and started running toward the platform. When he reached it, he saw three of the attackers as they vaulted up the stairs and disappeared around a corner. He pulled himself onto the platform and followed.

There were two stairwells about ten feet apart. Smith pressed his back against one and waved Howell to the other. He peered around.

"This one's clear. Yours?"

"Clear," Smith said. He ran up the stairs, meeting Howell on the first landing where the two stairs met. They repeated the maneuver and kept going up. Smith made it to the next landing. He caught sight of one of the attackers, who lobbed something at him. Smith dodged and it flew past him, rolling on the ground and then tumbling down the stairs.

"That sounded like a grenade," Howell said.

"They wouldn't risk it. It would destroy the third rail. They need it to spread the virus."

"Then it's filled with something other than explosives, because I've heard grenades being thrown and that was one."

Smith listened to the attackers' footfalls as they ran away.

"Strike that. They're taking off, it must be a..." Before Smith could finish, he heard a small pop and then a fizzing noise. With it came an overpowering smell of garlic. "Gas. Hold your breath and run like hell," he said.

Smith turned another corner and stared down a long tunnel. The attackers were already at the far end. The first group pounded up the short stairwell and disappeared into the night. Smith sprinted down the tunnel. He pulled the mask back over his face completely as he did. It had no more oxygen, but covering his face with the rubber was better than nothing. Howell was next to him. Graffiti images and drawings flashed in his peripheral vision. The tunnel felt endless. He felt his lungs start to burn from holding his breath, but he knew better than to inhale. After a moment he noticed that Howell had fallen farther behind. He backtracked to grab him, wrapping his arm around the man's bicep and dragging him forward. Howell had the plastic bag over his head. They reached the stairs and Smith pushed Howell ahead of him. While the oxygen mask was out of air, it still contained a filter, so Smith thought he would be spared the worst effects. Howell's makeshift mask would be far less effective. Cotton was useless against gas and while the plastic would help, the best antidote would be to get out of the subway and get clean.

Smith couldn't hold his breath much longer.

He ran up the stairs, taking them two at a time. He reached the top and stumbled into a man standing at attention with a gun pointed at his head.

"Bloody hell," Howell said.

A quick glance told Smith all he needed to know. Sheets of sweat ran down the man's face and the gun wobbled a bit. Nevertheless, Smith stayed still, not wanting to provoke him into firing. A temporary canvas screen surrounded them, blocking the subway entrance and creating a ten-foot-wide area. A makeshift work light clipped to a pole threw a harsh white glare in the small space. The light's cord snaked into the back of a panel truck and Smith could hear a generator humming. At their feet was a large hose that had one end attached to a fire hydrant and the rest fed into a subway grate. Next to the hydrant lay two men, both dead. Then the man with the gun collapsed.

"The hydrant. Fast," Smith said.

"Ricin?" Howell said. He pulled the plastic bag off his head.

"Mustard gas. Smelled like garlic, which is a marker. Mustard gas is heavier than oxygen, so it sank. Running upstairs to higher ground helped, but we need to get this hose out of the grate and ready to use, fast. We need to wash it off." He shoved his own pistol into his waistband and pulled on the hose, retracting it from the subway grate. Howell worked next to him. The hose was heavy but the water wasn't on, making it easier to remove. When the end appeared, Smith dropped it next to the body of the collapsed man and reached for a two-foot-long heavy-duty wrench that was still attached to the nut on the hydrant. It wasn't until then that he noticed that the hose connection to the hydrant was not complete. The men must have been in the process of disconnecting it when they took ill.

"Slow," Howell said. "There may be a lot of force."

"We can't afford slow," Smith said. "Step back." He hauled on the wrench and was rewarded by the sound of gushing water. He jogged backward, watching the hydrant. Within seconds the force of the water unseated the hose and water exploded into the air. Smith stepped into the stream and shivered as the water washed over him. He fought to keep standing while being pummeled by the open hydrant. Howell stood next to him, with his face up to allow the water to rinse it. He started to tear his clothes off and Smith followed suit. The stream hit the canvas screen and drenched it. The aluminum frame rattled from the force of the pummeling water, but the supports' feet were held down with sandbags and the screen stayed upright. Too late Smith remembered the pistol in his waistband. He placed it out of the main stream of water before stripping off his pants, but it was probably soaked already. So be it, he thought. Better than having two-thirds of his body blistered with third-degree burns from mustard gas exposure. He stood naked in the shower of water and shivered at the cold of it. He stepped past the screen and spotted a pharmacy, closed at the early hour, across the street.

"Wait here," he told Howell.

He reached down and ripped the clothes off the collapsed terrorist, putting the pants on as quickly as he could. They weren't his size but Smith didn't care. He removed the wrench from the hydrant and ran across the street, dodging a lone car that drove past.

The pharmacy was a small independent, with minimal square footage and inventory. The partial glass door was recessed between two glass storefront displays. Smith stepped into the recessed area and swung the wrench at the side of the glass display. The pane shattered and an alarm went off. Smith hit it again, knocked out a section large enough for him to fit, and angled through into the store.

It was his third visit for first aid in less than twenty-four hours and he had the fleeting thought that he hoped it was to be his last. His clothes dripped and the floor was cold under his bare feet. He snatched at a plastic bin and carried it with him, heading to the baby section and tossing three big bottles of baby shampoo into the carrier. He found the contact lens supplies and snatched two bottles of saline off the shelf and headed to the pharmacy area. He located the Betadine and tossed in four bottles. He worked his way back to the front door, crawled through the glass and ran back to Howell, who was still standing in the water. He shoved a bottle of baby shampoo at him.

"Mustard gas has lipid qualities. This will dissolve some of it."

"Excellent," Howell said. "I put the clothes in the plastic bag and tied it. That should help contain the off-gassing of the vapor."

Smith nodded. He pulled his clothes off again, uncapped a bottle of baby shampoo and poured it over his head, arms, chest, and legs. He scrubbed his skin, letting the soap run down his body. Howell was busy flushing his eyes with the saline.

"Here." He handed Smith the bottle. "Don't delay."

"Use the baby shampoo in your eyes as well," Smith said. He flushed his, though he thought that perhaps the mask had spared him his eyes. His major exposure would be to his body, because clothes wouldn't be any protection against it.

Howell picked up the Betadine. "Why this?"

"It's been shown to help. It's the same thing that we used to wash our hands in the ER, so it makes sense. Can't hurt. Done?" Smith indicated the water spray. Howell nodded.

Smith went to the hydrant and shut it off. He grabbed the Betadine and started to smear it over his skin. Howell did the same. They worked in silence. Smith's mind raced with clinical observations; that they'd gotten their skin rinsed within one minute of exposure, washed in three, and flushed their eyes within five. One minute was good. Five, not so much.

"How long do we have to wait before the symptoms appear?" Howell said.

"Earliest would be one hour, four hours at the latest. First your eyes will swell and itch. Then the itch will spread to your entire body. After that the skin will start to blister from the exposure to the gas, which can create second- or third-degree burns." Howell rubbed the Betadine on his face while he listened. Smith couldn't help but notice the grim expression there.

"Painful?"

Smith nodded. "Horribly so. But we acted fast, getting into the water and washing it off. I'm hoping the skin eruptions will be lessened. It's the eyes and lungs that I'm worried about. They're particularly sensitive."

"Will it blind us?"

"Temporarily, yes. After a while, though, it should clear. While people can die of severe exposure, many recover completely."

"How long for the eyes to clear?"

Smith hesitated. He didn't want Howell to worry. There was nothing more to be done for them that they hadn't already done. Even a hospital could do no more. There didn't exist a shot, pill, or antidote to halt the symptoms. One just had to endure them. But Howell had taken a far worse hit than Smith had. His symptoms would be severe.

"How long?" Howell pressed for the answer.

Smith sighed. "Thirty days."

52

KLEIN SAW THE INCOMING CALL from Howell.

"Peter, what happened?"

"It's Smith. I'm using his phone. Did Nolan call you?"

"No, she didn't."

"What about Russell?"

"No. What's going on?"

"Switch off the third rail. My hypothesis was right. And block all traffic to the target stop and one stop in either direction. Dattar threw mustard gas. The NYPD is going to have to send in a decontamination crew."

Klein was on his feet and headed to his second secure phone.

"On the rail shutdown. Station only? Or system-wide?"

"System-wide. I don't think we can take the risk. The rail's been on for twenty minutes while I was in the tunnel."

"Do you have Dattar?"

"I'm sorry, but no. He got away."

"Does he have more of the bacteria? Can he spread it elsewhere?"

"I don't know. It's still imperative that we get him." Klein heard the screaming of sirens in the background.

"What's that?"

"Probably the NYPD. I just broke into a pharmacy. I needed something to wash off the gas."

"I'll ask for a hazmat crew to be sent to the location."

"I'll stay here until the hazmat team comes, but then I'm going after Dattar," Smith said. "Can you call Ohnara? The clean-up crew may need his expertise."

He hung up and handed Howell the phone. The sirens were increasing. Howell was busy putting on the clothes of another dead terrorist. Smith dressed as well. His shoes were only slightly wet, and Smith wondered how many gas molecules were embedded in them, but decided that the protection from the soles outweighed any risk from the gas.

When Howell was finished, he wore green cargo pants and a gray T-shirt, both two sizes too big for his slender frame. His eyes were still red and his cheeks raw looking. "I'm going to go get Russell. There's no gain in my being here. You can handle the NYPD. Staying here will just blow my cover."

Smith nodded. "Can I have the phone?" Howell handed it back.

"I'll pick up another," Howell said. "Russell's one station away?"

"I hope so. Neither she nor Nolan checked in with Klein. I don't like it."

"I'm on it." He slapped Smith on the shoulder and took off, cutting around the corner of the screen. Smith waited in the screened-off section for the NYPD. The canvas walls turned red with a flashing glow as the spinning lights threw their color.

The first police car blew by without stopping. The second and third followed suit. Smith picked up his gun and stepped out from behind the canvas just as a fourth car went screaming by. Two ambulances followed. All drove by. Smith dialed Klein.

"They're not stopping. Do they know the gas is here?"

"They know exactly what to do. The president called the governor and he briefed the antiterrorism unit, but they received a call from Harcourt, the CIA's liaison with the NYPD. He said that he received some intelligence that Dattar is at the 215th Street station. That's where they're going."

"Is the subway off?"

"We're doing it in sections, with the stations closest to the infection point shut down, and those farther away allowed to enter a station and unload before turning them off. Too many people would be trapped in the cars if they shut the entire system down. It would be a nightmare to evacuate. They've cut power to four stations on each side of the 191st Street station." Smith ran a hand through his hair and started to pace.

"What about a hazmat team? They need to get down there and start scraping away the biofilm and figure out a way to stop it from spreading. I can't go back down without a suit, the bacteria are active and so is the mustard gas."

"It was notified. It's not there?"

Smith looked up and down the streets. Only four cars and two cabs were on the road. The pharmacy alarm still shrieked.

"I don't see anything."

"I'm going to check. Hold tight."

Klein rang off and Smith went back behind the screen. His left eye felt itchy and he rubbed it, relishing the feeling. He paused. In the distance came another siren, growing louder. This time he stepped out to greet it, waving his arms as the boxy emergency vehicle from the Fire Department of New York approached. It pulled to the side and two men stepped out.

"What's going on? I'm Carter and this is Rolly." Carter was a large, paunchy forty-something with a sharp nose and a buzz cut. His arms were huge. He wore a uniform and standard-issue shoes that squeaked as he walked. Rolly was the exact opposite, slender, with graying hair and a hawklike nose that took up a ton of acreage on his face. Smith pointed to the subway entrance.

"Mustard gas. Thrown twenty minutes ago. The entire station is contaminated."

"Who are you?" Carter said.

Before Smith could answer, an NYPD patrol car came screaming around the corner. It angled halfway into an open area at the curb before coming to a halt. The officer catapulted out of his car with his weapon drawn, and Smith saw that it was Manderi, the same suspicious officer Smith had spoken to right after Jordan was found shot in his car.

"Down on the ground. Now!" he said.

Smith stood his ground. "I'm Lieutenant Colonel Jon Smith of the United States Army Medical Research Institute for Infectious Diseases."

"I know who you are, asshole. You're the one who killed the lady at Landon. I said get down!"

Smith felt his fury rising. He pointed a finger at the cop. "You get on the phone to your superior, now. Because every minute you delay, the gas is filling the tunnel."

"Get down or I'll shoot you down," Manderi said.

Smith kept his eyes on Manderi while he lowered himself to the ground. The grit from the asphalt bit into his cheek. He felt Manderi jerk his arms behind him and seconds later the cold metal of handcuffs tightened around his wrists.

Manderi glanced at the canvas screen. "What's that?" He walked around the canvas and Smith heard him give an oath. He came back in sight. "There's three dead guys here!" Carter and Rolly went around the screen. The squawk of a radio came from inside Manderi's car.

"Watch him," Manderi said to Carter when he came out from the screen.

Smith could see the car from his prone position, and he watched as Manderi crawled back inside. Manderi slammed the door and began a conversation on the radio. The words were unintelligible. After a moment he emerged.

"I'm taking him in," Manderi said.

"Wait a minute, I want to ask him some questions." Carter lowered himself down next to Smith's head. "Tell me why you think there's mustard gas in the tunnel."

"I was there when the canister was thrown. An overpowering smell of garlic came with it," Smith replied. "I got hit with it."

"Funny, you look all right to me," Manderi said.

"The symptoms don't appear right away," Carter told Manderi.

"You see anything? A smoke cloud?" Manderi said.

"Mustard gas is colorless. Stop wasting my time," Smith said.

"Carter, that true?" Manderi said.

Carter nodded. "I was National Guard. Did a stint in Iraq during the Gulf War. He's right. Mustard gas is colorless, and some guys can't even smell the garlic when it's thrown. That was the real danger because you didn't even know you'd been exposed until the burns show up later. I wouldn't mess around. It's a bitch that they threw it in the deepest subway stop in the system. The stuff is heavier than the air and sinks. Ventilating the area is gonna be tough."

A second vehicle pulled up to the patrol car. Smith lifted his cheek from the ground and craned his neck to see the new arrival. This one, a heavy American-made sedan, black with dents on one side, was an obvious undercover patrol car. A light on the dashboard circled in the dark. The door opened and the same black man in the long braids who had appeared from the darkness and given Smith the guitar case emerged. This time he wore a lanyard that displayed a large badge. He took in the scene, glancing at Smith on the ground and at Carter and Rolly.

"Hello, officers. What's the status?" he said.

Manderi took a step toward the man.

"I'm Officer Manderi," he said. "I got this under control. You are?" Manderi squinted as he tried to read the man's badge.

"Agent James Brand. FBI. You've got a possible gassing and you're standing around? Get moving."

"Back off. This guy," Manderi pointed to Smith, "claims someone threw mustard gas in the subway. I've seen him before, though. He's a suspect in the Landon Investments killing and there are three dead guys behind that screen. I'm betting his claims are bullshit."

Brand pointed at Smith. "That's Lieutenant Colonel Jon Smith of USAMRIID. Get those cuffs off him. Now. We're going to need his assistance in clearing the gas."

"Alleged gas," Manderi said. "And maybe you don't get it. I'm with the NYPD. A special operations terrorism unit. The NYPD has jurisdiction over hazmat incidents in the subway. We decide what gets cleaned up, and the Fire Department does the rest. *We* got jurisdiction here."

Brand stepped closer. "If you're with NYPD terrorism, why aren't you at the 215th Street station with the rest of the unit? They're up there battling a possible terrorist incident."

"Who do you think you are, questioning me?" Manderi said.

"I'm with the Department of Homeland Security. The DHS trumps you when it comes to a domestic terrorism incident. While NYPD should be handling hazmat incidents, it's clear that you're screwing up. If Colonel Smith says there's mustard gas down there, then there is." He turned to Carter.

"In addition to the gas, there's a bacterial agent that's been applied to the third rail. A man named Ohnara is on his way to assist. He's an expert."

Carter nodded, looked at Manderi, gave a slight shrug, and he and Rolly headed to the rear of the truck.

Brand pointed at Manderi. "I don't know who or what this special operations unit is that you claim to be a part of, but you'd better get those cuffs off that man now or the only special operations you'll be handling will be at a desk in a file room. Get it?"

"I'll be checking on you, too. Then we'll see who runs this operation," Manderi said.

"You do that. But I want those cuffs off him."

Manderi was breathing heavily. He looked down at Smith with loathing, but Smith was relieved to see him pull the cuff keys out of his pocket. Smith breathed a sigh as the tight metal bands fell from his wrists. He sat up, rubbing them, and looked at Brand.

"Thanks," he said.

Brand nodded. "How bad is it?"

Smith stood up. For a moment his head began to swim and a slight chill ran through him. The chill felt like the beginning of a fever.

"The gassing?"

Brand shook his head. "The bacteria."

"Bad. The subway lit up again for twenty minutes. Long enough to give the carrier bacteria a hefty boost. You'll need to get a crew down on the rails. Have them bring brushes and start brushing every inch of the third rail. The biofilm colonizing activity needs to be disrupted."

Brand frowned. "Wouldn't a chemical wash be better?"

Smith shook his head. "Won't work. Biofilms are like plaque on your teeth. When you brush or floss, you are really disrupting the activity. Some washes help, sure, but the plaque can survive it, and once it colonizes, it becomes impenetrable."

"Tartar."

Smith nodded. "Exactly. Tartar on your teeth is a hardened biofilm. Let's not let it get to that stage. And if the rail is still surrounded by water after you're done brushing, you can turn it on and heat it up. The bacteria that haven't yet colonized will die in the heat. That's a risky move, though, because the bacteria will start to feed off the rail."

"I'll get on it. Anything else we can do?"

"The FBI has a friend of mine in custody, Andreas Beckmann. Can you spring him?"

Brand nodded. "Yes, Klein's already contacted me about that. Sorry, we were unaware that you were running an operation, or we wouldn't have interfered. I'll handle it."

Smith waved at Manderi. "And can you make him get lost?"

Brand snorted. "That, my friend, is too much to ask. But you want to suit up and join?"

Smith shook his head. "I need to hook back up with Russell and find Dattar. For all we know, he could be placing more at another location. I sent her back in the tunnel. I'll go to the previous stop. Can you take me there?"

Brand opened the driver's side door of the sedan and waved Smith to the passenger side. "Get in."

Smith hesitated. "I've been gassed. These pants are from one of the dead guys, but I'd feel a whole lot better with some fresh clothes. I put these on before I completed washing off the vapor."

Brand nodded. "Get in. I'll call ahead and have someone meet us there with some clothes."

"And a gun," Smith said.

"Definitely a gun," Brand replied.

53

HARCOURT KICKED NOLAN in the shoulder. "Get up," he said. Nolan moaned and rolled over. Russell shook from head to toe but did her best to keep focused and stay conscious.

"She's bleeding," she said.

"That's her fault." Harcourt kept his gun pointed at Russell. "Get up."

Russell rose and stumbled.

"Bacteria get to you?" He smirked.

"Call the NYPD. I'll go in with them," she said.

"Maybe you don't get it. You're not going to get out of this one."

At that moment Russell's mind settled. She needed to get away from Harcourt, and she needed to be strong to do it. She settled her shaking limbs, but only succeeded for a second. They started up again the moment she turned her attention back to Harcourt. She moved until her back was against a wall and bent her knees. The knife that she kept in a holder was at her ankle, but it was of no use while her hands were cuffed behind her back.

Nolan moved and Harcourt kicked her again.

"Get up. Time to move some money around."

Nolan sat. Her left eye was blackened and dried blood stained her upper lip and chin where her nose had bled.

"It will be traced to you," she said.

"Gold bullion won't. You're going to get some more."

Nolan glanced at Russell. "Is he alive?"

Russell nodded.

Relief washed over Nolan's face. She put a hand on the wall and rose unsteadily. When she was upright, Harcourt waved to the stairs with the gun.

"Move," he said. He turned his weapon on Russell. He was going to kill her.

Her heart began racing, and the chills that were racking her body actually stopped for a moment as the adrenaline in her system overrode everything else. She looked up and spotted a security camera high above his head and behind him.

"There's a camera. You shoot me here and the whole world will see it."

He glanced back at it. "Dream on. That camera's not working. MTA's security team is way behind schedule and overbudget. I should know. As special liaison to the NYPD, it's my job to know where the security weaknesses are. I know a lot."

He smirked at her and aimed at her heart. She scrambled for another excuse to stop him from shooting.

"Smith knows that I wasn't shot. They find a bullet in me, they'll trace it to you," Russell said.

"Say goodnight," he said. She heard the noise of a siren, coming fast. Or maybe it was the roaring of her own ears as the blood rushed to her head. The light dimmed and she battled against passing out. The blackness deepened, and she thought with relief that at least she wouldn't see the bullet coming.

Harcourt shot her, point blank.

It was the second hit the vest had taken, and she could feel the punch but also heard the vest shred with the impact. She flew back and her head hit the ground. A wet liquid started at her shoulder and spread across her chest. Blood, she thought. The vest must have allowed the bullet through. She lay on the cold stone. Harcourt was hauling Nolan up the stairs when he looked back and aimed again at Russell. He's going to finish me off, she thought.

She heard a noise on the platform behind her and looked over to see Howell, his face covered in oozing blisters and the skin around his eyes bulging. He swayed a bit as he aimed a weapon at Harcourt. He fired. Harcourt winced as bits of the wall near his face broke off and sprayed him. He turned and hustled up the stairs, dragging Nolan with him. Howell fired again, but the only visible part of Harcourt was the back of his legs. The shot didn't land.

"Russell, are you alive? I can't see," Howell said. Russell nodded and then realized that Howell probably couldn't see the motion. She tried to formulate a thank-you, but she couldn't get her lips to move. Howell took a step nearer to her and then dropped to his knees. "Smith said it would be bad, but I'm afraid he underestimated it."

Howell slowly slumped to the ground.

The rushing noise filled her ears and she floated in the space between full awareness and unconsciousness. She wasn't sure how long she hovered in that state before she felt a warm, live human arm wrap itself around her shoulders and pull her to her feet. She opened her eyes again, expecting to see black, but was rewarded with a view of Smith's face as he lifted her off the cement. He looked like hell and she wanted to tell him that and about Harcourt and Nolan, but her voice failed to function. Or maybe it did function and she just didn't hear it, because he said, "You don't look so good yourself."

"You're right. Harcourt's the mole," she said.

"Can you walk?"

She was too tired to respond. She started walking. Each step required her entire concentration. She leaned on Smith's arm and kept moving.

"I'm going to get you into a car, and Agent Brand is going to get you to a hospital."

She shook her head but couldn't tell if he noticed, so she stopped to get his attention.

"Howell."

Smith nodded. "I saw him. Klein's arranging to quietly remove him

from the platform and get him to a hospital. Which is where you're going as well."

"No hospitals. I could have contracted the mutant virus and this illness could be the flu starting all over again. I could be contagious. Take
me someplace where I can be alone."

He frowned. "You need a hospital. They can quarantine you."

"No," she said. "Did that already. It's not safe."

"Yes," he replied. "I'll get someone to guard you."

"Take me where I can be alone. Or let this Brand person take me.
But go after Harcourt. Now. He's the mole and he has Nolan." Smith's
face took on a vicious look, which was not a word she would normally
have applied to him. Russell stumbled against his side and spotted a
gun stuck in his waistband. "Do you have another weapon I can use? I
hate being unarmed."

"Brand may have one in the car."

They were at the stairs, and Russell directed her attention to climbing them. As she rose, the air became fresher and she inhaled. At the
top of the exit, Smith pulled her toward a large, unmarked sedan. Brand
stepped out.

"This is Agent Brand of the FBI," Smith said.

"The guitar man," Russell said.

Brand smiled. "Yes."

"I could be contagious," Russell said.

Brand nodded. "I know."

She looked at Smith. "You could be too."

"If I find Harcourt, I'll be sure to spit on him," Smith said.

"He said he's going to force her to get some gold bullion. I don't know
where or how." Smith lowered her to the sidewalk, then turned to Brand.

"If they're getting gold bullion, then I know where they're headed. I'll
need a car to get there."

Brand waved at the sedan. "Take it. I'll help Ms. Russell."

Russell fought the waves of nausea as she waited for the ambulance.
Then the blinking lights returned and she passed out.

54

SMITH KEPT THE LIGHTS and sirens going as he barreled uptown. He used the car radio and asked for backup for a possible kidnapping at the pawn shop. The response he received heartened him.

"We already have officers at the scene."

"You do?" Smith said. Perhaps Bilal's security system had clocked Dattar and Harcourt, and Bilal had called for help.

"Thank you for your report," the dispatcher said. She clicked off.

Sweat poured into his eyes and he wiped it away. His lids started to itch and he rubbed them lightly. Then his arms followed suit and he ran his nails up and down his bare skin. The gas was starting to do its work.

Ten minutes later he shut down the siren, removed the strobe from the dash and switched off the headlights. He coasted into a spot at the curb and killed the engine. Smith watched a bum stagger down the sidewalk, and cars drove by, but little else moved on the street. The lights in the predominately business block were dark and the stores' doors were barred and locked. The pawn shop's neon signs, though, still flashed, and a light glowed through the one window that was still glass, though it was glass block rather than a pane. Bilal's solar panels were still working, pumping electricity, Smith thought. Bilal was taking no risks with his gold stash.

All of the other windows in the building had been replaced with metal sheets and overlaid with metal. The glass block corresponded to where Smith thought Bilal's office had been. Smith crawled out of the car, holding his gun down where it wouldn't be seen. He hitched up his collar and did his best to move slowly. Brand had given him some standard uniform pants and a man's white undershirt with a dark uniform shirt to wear over it. Smith did up the buttons, hoping to blend better into the darkness. He moved closer to the building, approaching with as little noise as possible.

One lone police cruiser was parked in front, confirming what the dispatcher had said, but Smith thought it was a pathetic response in light of the potential capture of an international terrorist. He stepped into an empty doorway and called Klein.

"I'm in front of a pawn shop in Inwood. Harcourt is the mole and he's in there with Nolan, moving around Dattar's money. I called the police, but got one car. Can you get them to send more?"

"The report I'm getting is that the NYPD can't find anything wrong at the 215th Street station and are heading down to 72nd Street, where a new report claims a sighting of Dattar and two others. They've got thirty cruisers and FBI on the scene."

"Why would Dattar head into the subway? He'd get infected."

"It's an anonymous report, but it sounds promising. There's a dead man name of Manhar who appears to be of Pakistani origin at the top of the stairs, and they received an eyewitness report that someone matching Dattar's description and two others hustled down the stairs. Dattar was carrying a cooler."

Smith hesitated. It all sounded correct, yet he still doubted that Dattar would be anywhere near a subway station after the bacteria were placed.

"You're aware that we think Harcourt is a mole and he's got a connection to the NYPD? The report could be a plant."

"We're aware, but it's clear that they've been pumping water into the 72nd Street station for a while, and it shut down first. Add a dead man's body and they're duty bound to investigate."

"I see your point. It sounds like there's not much I can do to help down there, but the situation here is bizarre. Only one car when a possible kidnapping is called in? Once Harcourt strong-arms Nolan into handing over the money, he's going to kill her. He needs to be stopped."

"I agree, but who called in the report? Perhaps you should confirm that before you go in there with guns blazing."

"I have no idea who called it in. Where's Howell?"

"Off to a place where he can recuperate. He's in bad shape, but the dispatcher told me that he should be dead. Seems the measures you took helped him."

"Here's hoping he's okay. And I agree that going in with guns blazing isn't the way here. Harcourt will only hold her hostage. Let me reconnoiter. She told me this Bilal has an entire arsenal in there. Maybe he's already disposed of the Harcourt problem."

"Fine. Proceed with caution. And remember, they're going to need you to assist with the decontamination once Dattar is contained." When Klein rang off, Smith called Marty.

"Can you track Nolan's computer?" he said.

"It's off. I'm sorry, Jon."

Smith's right wrist began to burn, and he gritted his teeth to stop groaning with the pain. His right eye itched, but he resisted the urge to rub it, since it might increase the swelling that was already occurring.

"What about her accounts? Can you see if there's any activity?"

"I've been only able to access one main offshore account. I'll pull it up. Hang tight."

Smith remained silent, listening while Marty typed on his keyboard. The burning in his wrist progressed to his elbow and he felt the nerves on his arm begin to react. Then the vision in his right eye began to blur. The blindness was setting in. He felt the beginnings of panic, both at the idea of the pain that he knew was coming and at the thought that he might be completely blind before he could assist Nolan.

"Hurry. I'm in bad shape and getting worse. Dattar used mustard gas on me." He heard Marty gasp.

"Where are you?"

"At the northern tip of Manhattan. Outside a building that I think has Nolan in it."

"I've got it. Yes, the payments and transfer page is being accessed. Someone's filling in an online wire transfer form."

For a moment Smith was distracted from his injuries. "Can you access the source computer?"

"I'm tracking back the cookies now. Hold tight."

Smith held his breath. In contrast he heard Marty's heavy breathing through the phone.

"It's coming from a PC located in the Inwood area of Manhattan."

"The minute she finishes that transaction, they'll kill her. Call this in. Get me police backup. Tell them silent approach—there's a hostage and I don't want Harcourt to know we're on the way and possibly kill her, but also warn them that a member of the military is inside so they don't shoot me."

"I'll…"

Smith didn't wait for the rest. He started running toward the building, shoving the phone into his pocket. His arms burned and his eyes were blurring. He felt the skin of his lids puffing and saw the edge of the blister that was forming at the corner of his right eye. Through all the scorching heat in his arms he still shivered as a chill passed through his body. He was ten feet from the entrance when the staccato sound of gunfire came from within the building.

He hit the door and it swung open, making the same beeping noise that it had when he'd come the first time. The interior hallway was dark and the building silent. There were four doors on either side of the long hallway and at the end Bilal's office door was open, with light pouring onto the carpeting. He ran to the first entrance and crouched behind the door. He put his eye to the crack at the doorjamb and saw a man's figure in the hall. He paused in the room's doorway for a moment and then continued down the hall.

Smith felt a hand wrap around his ankle. He froze and looked to his right. He saw that it was Bilal, lying on his side with a gun in his right hand. The man's harsh breathing sounded loud in the room.

"Are you hit?" he whispered.

"Side. Miss Rebecca." He made a slight coughing sound that Smith didn't like at all. As a medical doctor, he'd heard it too many times right before someone died.

"Where is she?"

"Office. Go armed. They're guarding the entrance. Cowards won't come down the hall to fight me. They have all my gold," Bilal said. "I can't let them take it."

Smith laid his gun on the carpeting and began to run his hands over Bilal. He found the wound and heard Bilal's sharp intake of breath as he probed it.

"My gold," Bilal said.

"Forget about the gold. I'm calling for an ambulance." Smith pulled out his phone and prepared to text Marty.

"Those stinking sheepherders aren't taking my gold," Bilal said. Smith tried to send the text, but it failed. He had no service. "My phone isn't working." Bilal made a sound that Smith thought might have been a chuckle, if the man hadn't been near death.

"Roof is metal. It's safer," Bilal rasped.

"Is there a phone in this room?"

"On the desk, but I called the police. Told them they have her as a hostage. They caught me doing it and shot me. Bastards think they've killed me."

Smith began to rise and Bilal grabbed his sleeve. "Be careful. It's a business phone, many lines. If you pick it up, they'll see the light and know someone's using it." Smith lowered back down. "They sent the skinny one to pour their chemicals on my solar panels."

Smith stilled. "Were the chemicals from a cooler?"

"Yes. Kill them. Get me my gold." Smith wanted to tell the man that the gold would be worthless if the entire city was dying from a pandemic. He also wished he knew how often the panels kicked back electricity to the grid.

"How many?" Smith asked.

"Four." Bilal made a choking sound. "One is Dattar. I know of him from the old country. The skinny one is on the roof. There's an Uzi in the cabinet here. Back right shelf. And a flamethrower in the safe across the hall. The one on the right. The gold is there as well, but not enough to satisfy them. I emptied the rest three days ago and moved it to another location. There's fifty thousand dollars' worth left here. Combination six–twenty-five–six for the weapons safe. Burn the building down. The gold will melt, but it will survive."

"What about Rebecca? Is she alive?"

"They have her. They beat her," the man choked, "bad. So bad. Her face is…" He closed his eyes and shook his head. He grabbed at Smith's arm. "The large picture near the safe swings open. There's a two-way mirror. You can see into the office. My bodyguards would watch while I made transactions."

"Are the bodyguards here?"

"No," he said.

"How did the skinny one reach the roof?"

"Drop-down stairs. In the safe room." The man inhaled. "My son is Malik. You give him the gold. You tell him I love him." Bilal's head lolled and the rattling sound came from his throat. Smith watched the man die.

Smith swallowed and immediately regretted it. His throat flared in pain as he did, and his arms continued to burn as if heated. His eyes blurred and watered. He glanced across the room, and the cabinet that Bilal had pointed to swam in his vision. He looked to the rug to find his gun and was horrified to realize that he was unable to see it. He ran his hand along the industrial carpet till the cold metal hit his knuckles.

The cabinet sat on the opposite wall. Smith's vision readjusted again. It was as if his eyes were warring with the effects of the gas. He grasped the gun and headed across the room. Once he reached the cabinet, his vision again blurred. As the mustard gas symptoms progressed, they would cause blisters to erupt on his corneas. He presumed that they were forming now and that his eyes were reacting.

He opened the panels and ran his hands along the cool wooden shelf. Encountering a mesh strap, he followed it to the Uzi's handle, collecting the gun and feeling for a magazine. An elongated one, already loaded, jutted from the handle.

He moved back to the doorway, peered down the hall toward the front door, and froze. Khalil stood there, with the door slightly cracked open, watching outside.

The burning on Smith's arms spread to his torso, and he felt as though he were a walking torch. If this is what burn victims experienced, he couldn't understand how they could bear the pain. His skin started to crawl and for a brief moment he thought he heard it crackle as though cooking to a crisp. His eyes kept up their crazy wavering, first focusing, then failing.

The safe room was opposite the one he was in, directly across the hall. The floor was carpeted and Smith gauged how quickly he could cross the distance. Khalil stayed where he was, staring out. Smith took a breath and stepped across to the next room, immediately moving against the wall near the doorway, and waited. No sound came from the hall.

There were two five-foot-tall metal safes on the opposite wall. Next to them, drop-down stairs led to the roof. Smith wrapped the Uzi's strap over his shoulder and headed toward it. An electronic keypad glowed on the front panel. He punched in the combination and was rewarded with a clicking noise as the door disengaged. It swung open on well-oiled hinges.

In the safe was an arsenal. Several pistols, two AK-47s, a rocket-propelled grenade launcher and three shelves of ammunition, several grenades designed both for the launcher and to be thrown, along with two small canisters of fuel attached to a flamethrower. Straps allowed the canisters to be carried on one's back. Smith once again put his weapons on the floor while he ran his arms through the flamethrower's straps. The flamethrower hose and nozzle were attached to the canister's side with a clip. Smith left it there. He wanted his hands free to use the Uzi and the pistol first. He left the safe door open.

Loud thuds came from the back office. Smith heard a woman's voice cry out. Above his head he heard someone walking on the roof. From the office came the unmistakable sound of a fist against flesh, and Nolan cried out. Smith fought the urge to leap in there with the Uzi firing full bore. His duty was clear; first he needed to stop the man on the roof from spreading the bacteria. The solar panels would feed it directly to the main grid and from there into every home in the northeast region. He needed to get to it quickly before it colonized and while the heat from the flamethrower could still kill it.

He lowered to a crouch and nearly groaned as the burnt skin on his legs stretched. His vision was fluctuating in an erratic pattern, and he could feel his index finger sweating around the gun's trigger. Through it all he felt the beginnings of a fever, but he couldn't tell if it was a reaction from being gassed or if he had contracted the virus. A large landscape painting with a frame that was easily three feet square hung on the wall near the safe. Smith pulled on the frame's edge. It swung away, revealing the two-way mirror into the office. Bilal's paranoia had paid off. Smith was watching the participants in the office.

Nolan sat in front of the second of Bilal's computers on the credenza, typing furiously. Her face was a mass of bruises and contusions, and it appeared that her nose was broken. Finger marks imprinted on her neck gave testament to the fact that she'd been strangled, and her bare right arm bled from long slashes of a knife.

Around her stood Harcourt, Dattar, and Manderi. Smith's rage flared at the sight of Manderi. If he was the "officer on the scene," it was clear that no others would be appearing. All the men peered at the computer screen. Three black bags sat on the desk behind Nolan. One was unzipped, revealing bars of gold. Dattar was leaning over Nolan's shoulder with a bloody knife in his hand. He held the knife to her neck and a line of blood ran from the place of contact with her skin.

Smith turned away and started toward the stairs, climbing them slowly. When his head became level with the roof, he glanced around. He saw a slender man kneeling in front of the solar panels' conversion box. A cooler sat open next to him. The man was using a scoop and a painter's brush to apply a gel-like substance to sections of the panels, moving fast.

Smith heard the sound of his phone announcing a text message and froze. His location at the top of the roof must have enabled a signal. The man, though, didn't hear it. Smith pulled the phone out of his pocket and did his best to read the text, hoping that it would be Klein telling him that the NYPD was on its way.

It was Marty. The text read, *Erasing her keystrokes as she types. Buying you more time.*

Smith swiped the phone face, set it to vibrate, and replied, *Where the hell is my backup?*

Smith angled the pistol over the roof's edge and took aim, but paused. Once he fired, he would reveal his position, and he fully ex-pected both Khalil and Manderi to come after him. The silence of a knife would be ideal, but he would have to crawl back down the stairs, into the weapons safe, find a knife, and retrace his steps. He would have done it, but he didn't recall seeing any knives in the stash. His phone vibrated. Smith looked at the text.

Brand and Beckmann here silent approach there are no windows to shoot through if we storm the building will they kill the hostage?

Smith typed back, *Yes.*

His phone vibrated and Brand wrote, *High angle view of building await your instructions.*

Smith's vision began to blur, his eyes were watering. He blinked, but it didn't clear his vision this time. It was now or never. He put the key-pad up to his eyes and squinted at the lit screen. He typed, *Shoot the guy on the roof.*

Beckmann's gunshot wasn't as loud as Smith's would have been, but it wasn't as quiet as Smith had hoped, either. He heard a group of voices raised as the crew in the office reacted to the shot. Smith watched the man slump, then collapse backward. Smith vaulted up the rest of the stairs and ran to the coolers. The dead man lay sprawled over them and Smith rolled the body off. Inside he saw a tub of the gelatinous substance that the man had been working with, as well as several capped test tubes. Smith grabbed a test tube, shoved it in his pocket, and stepped back. He unclipped the flamethrower's nozzle and opened the ignition valve. He felt around for a button to engage the spark plug, finding it on the gun's side. A small flame appeared at the end of the thrower. He aimed it at the coolers and pressed the fuel-release trigger.

The resulting flame shot forward, engulfing the cooler in flames. Smith could see the fire, but not much else as his vision contracted even more. He worked his way around the panels, running the flame along every access wire. The smell of burnt rubber and wire filled the air along with a toxic brew of melting plastic from the cooler. He angled the column of flame onto the panels and the fire whooshed along the flat surface and fell off the edge. The edges of the ducts on the roof began to burn, and he felt the metal growing hot under his feet. He heard shoes pounding up the stairwell, and he turned in the direction of the noise, keeping the flame on. He shot it at the doorway.

The heavy canisters hampered his movement. His vision was contracting down to one small pinpoint before flaring wide again. When it contracted, the column of flame was just a small orange line.

The solar panels were burning at various wire access points, and the roof was heating up to a frightening degree. He kept dodging and pivoting, keeping his soles from burning while trying to make himself a tougher target to hit in case someone attempted to shoot through the roof. He ran to the stairs and angled the flame down them before turning and descending. The Uzi was in his other hand. He leaped down the stairs two at a time, missing the last few and staggering into the room. A body lay on the floor next to the picture frame. When he got close, he saw that it was Khalil. Blood pumped from a bullet hole in his chest.

Smith looked into the office and saw Harcourt, a gun in his hand, zipping up the bullion bags. Nolan still worked at the computer and tears ran down her face. Dattar, his face red with his fury, kept her there, screaming into her ear. What he said was unintelligible, but Smith had little doubt that it had to do with the erasing letters.

Smith shrugged the Uzi strap off his shoulder and aimed at the glass and at an angle that would hit Harcourt. He pressed the trigger. The resulting shots shattered the glass and a hit sent Harcourt spinning against the wall. He dropped out of Smith's line of vision as bits of glass rained into the room. Dattar straightened and Nolan slammed the chair backward, catching him in the stomach and pinning him against the desk. Smith aimed and fired several bullets into Dattar. Nolan screamed over and over and covered her ears with her hands. Smith knocked out the remaining glass in the frame, grabbed the side wall and jumped up to sit in the opening, twisting to swing his leg over and dropping into the room. Harcourt was gone, but a smear of blood streaked the floor from where he had dropped, indicating that he had managed to crawl out of the room. Manderi was missing. The bags of gold remained on the desk.

"Get behind me," Smith said. Nolan staggered up and limped as she walked toward him. She still cried. Smith could see her trying to regain control of her sobs. "Where's Manderi?"

"He went with Khalil to check out the gunshot."

So he killed Khalil and was still in the building, Smith thought. He wouldn't leave without eliminating all the witnesses. Nor would Harcourt.

"Did Bilal tell you if there were escape routes in this building?"

"Only the doors. The windows are glass blocks. He had a secret escape, but he never told me its location."

"We can't leave through the hall. Manderi could cover that too easily, and we'll have no room to maneuver. We're going to crawl through that opening and go up to the roof on an access stairway. The building is only one story, so you'll have to either find a fire escape or jump down." He moved to the opening, angling his legs over. Nolan followed. He kept the flamethrower aimed at the door, providing her cover. He jutted his chin in the direction of the stairs.

"Take my phone. When you get to the top of the stairs, access my last text message and reply to say that you're going to the roof and not to shoot. When you do, run like hell. Find a safe place to hole up for a while. Get a message to me when you can."

"Aren't you coming with me? I'm not leaving if you don't," Nolan said.

"I'll come after you." He delivered the half truth with as much sincerity as he could, but he could tell that she wasn't buying it. He leaned closer to her. *"Go."* He watched her climb the stairs, but before she made it to the top, his vision contracted. He didn't see her disappear.

He headed back toward the open door, inching along until he could see down the hall. If Manderi and Harcourt were there, he couldn't see them, but he had an excellent idea about what they might do. He took a deep breath and darted to the door, hiding behind the open panel. His vision was down to a pinpoint and from the tight feeling in the center of his eye he could tell it wouldn't expand again. He paused, listening. After a few seconds he heard an expected sound. A small cough. Harcourt, he presumed. It was a rare man who could maintain complete silence after getting shot.

He heard the stealthy footsteps coming down the hall. A form flitted past the open door. Smith saw Manderi's shoulder appear in the corner of the broken two-way-window frame.

"Hurry," Harcourt said. Smith couldn't see the other man, but he recognized his voice. They'd done exactly what Smith thought they would. They'd gone back for the gold.

Smith rose, moved to stand in the doorway, pointed the flamethrower in the direction of the open safe, and pulled on the fuel trigger. The flames easily covered the twelve feet to the container and engulfed the inside of it. The ordnance exploded.

The resulting fireball knocked Smith off his feet and slammed him across the hall and against the opposite wall. He shrugged out of the backpack in a panic, fearful that the fuel on his back would be the next to explode. He rose and ran down the hall in the direction of the front door. A second explosion rocked the building and pushed him to his knees. He thought he heard a man's screams, but the roar of the fire blotted out most sounds.

He moved forward, keeping one hand on the wall as a guide because he had no vision. Smoke choked him. He heard gunshots, and a bullet hit the wall next to his head, but he didn't flinch or stop his flight.

The third explosion took out the rest of the hall, and he felt the suction pull on him as the blast created a vacuum. He reached the front door and tumbled out of it. The cold night air hit his face and he sucked in a breath of fresh air. Something sharp pierced the side of his shoe and sunk into his foot, but he barely noticed the pain. He ran forward, tripped over a curb, and slammed his knee into what he supposed was a parked car.

"Smith?" Smith heard Brand's voice and felt a hand on his elbow guiding him. "You're at an open car door. Watch your head." Brand put his hand on top of Smith's skull to help him clear the door panel. He crawled into the vehicle and sat back. The car door slammed, and Brand knocked on the car's side. Someone put the car in motion.

"Air conditioning. My skin is on fire," Smith said. His voice came out as a croak. "I can't see."

"The mustard gas?" It was Beckmann's voice. "Hold on, I'm heading to a hospital."

"You steal this car?" Smith said.

Smith heard Beckmann's low laugh. "It's the FBI's. Even I'm not crazy enough to hot-wire a department vehicle."

"Forget the hospital. Get me to an Army doctor with experience in mustard gas injuries and when he's done get me home."

55

SMITH SAT IN FRONT OF his computer screen in the quiet of his kitchen early on a Sunday morning. The sores on his arms had healed within three weeks thanks to his rapid cleansing of the mustard gas, but his eyes were still mending. Bright light bothered him, and he wore sunglasses continuously when outside. He'd received word that Howell was recuperating as well, but at a much slower pace due to a higher level of exposure. Wendel told him that Jordan also was healing well, but wouldn't return to active duty for at least another three months, and Russell checked in periodically. The decontamination of both the bacteria and the gas had gone well thanks to Ohnara, who had stepped up to assist with cleanup once it became clear that Smith could not.

He logged onto his e-mail and left the laptop whirring while he made a fresh pot of coffee. He heard the sound of his Internet phone ringing and headed back to the computer. It was Russell calling. He turned on the web camera.

"Good morning," she said. She had been recuperating at an undisclosed location. In the past three weeks she'd gained back some of the weight she'd lost, and her skin was less pale. Smith held up his empty coffee cup.

"Good morning to you. How are you feeling?"

"Very good, and you?"

"Better. My eye doctor seems to think I'll heal just fine. It'll be nice to be able to walk around in the sun without getting a migraine. How's Howell?"

"He checked himself out of the hospital and returned to his house in the mountains. Said he couldn't take all the interruptions. I guess they woke him up late at night once too often."

"Beckmann?"

"Back in Europe. And Brand says hello and to tell you that the man on the roof that Beckmann shot was another of Dattar's crew. A man named Rajiid. And they were finally able to identify the bodies in the building as Bilal, Manderi, Dattar, and Harcourt."

"Why'd he do it?"

"Harcourt?"

"Yes."

Russell sighed. "Cromwell's keeping a lot close to the vest since the news broke of the CIA and NYPD liaison. Seems as though the agency's lawyers are screaming bloody murder. They claim the sharing program with the NYPD was never approved by them, and they're afraid that it appears as though the CIA was engaging in domestic spying. The most I could get out of Cromwell is that Dattar had promised Harcourt and Manderi hundreds of millions of dollars and large tracts of land back in his country. Both men were deeply in debt. Apparently there's also some evidence that Harcourt was intending to pull a double cross and turn Dattar over to the agency before the bacteria was placed. He'd then look like a hero."

"Like the fireman who starts the fire so he can put it out?"

Russell sighed. "I guess so. And we've received intelligence that a group of countries may have been bankrolling Dattar. They call themselves the Janus Consortium. All of the countries deny it vehemently, of course."

"Of course," Smith said.

"And the large tracts of land that Dattar was promising actually belonged to the Reddings. Their utility holdings have been returned to them. Have you heard from Nolan?"

"Nothing."

Russell shook her head. "For a civilian she does a pretty good job of dropping out of sight, doesn't she?"

"That she does."

"Well, enjoy your Sunday."

"You, too." Russell smiled at him and logged off. Smith went to the coffeepot to refill his cup. The pinging sound of an incoming message brought him back to the table.

The screen contained a picture of a stylized "KD" logo. Beneath it were the words:

"This is an automated message. Please do not reply. You have been sent 23,500 kilodollars mined from various points on the web for your use should you ever need them. Please click the link below to download them to your hard drive." There was a hyperlink below the notice. Farther down was one word:

SAFE

AUTHOR'S NOTE

My first experience with Robert Ludlum's novels was through my mother, who came home one day with his book *The Matarese Circle* and proceeded to read it while making dinner and preparing for work. She was a jazz singer in Chicago at the time and would vocalize in the early evening before heading to the clubs. Not so that day. That day she was silent, reading. She finished it in twenty-four hours and then raved as she passed it to me. From that novel, our mutual love of thrillers was born. My favorite was, and still is, *The Bourne Identity*. A nearly perfect plot for a thriller.

When I was asked to write this novel, I thought about what made Robert Ludlum's books so fascinating. Pacing, certainly, and plot, yes, but also characters. You really cared if Jason Bourne would discover his true identity, and you worried along with him that what he would discover would be abhorrent to him. I wanted to write about Jon Smith with the same humanity, and I wanted to give him a high-stakes plot that also fit within our current worldview. I also wanted to add some interesting tidbits from the real world, and so while this book is fiction, there are two aspects that are not.

First, the "electric" bacteria Shewanella MR-1 is real and does colonize, conduct through metal, and breathe through tiny wirelike pili. The Navy has been testing it to determine if it has the ability to generate electricity. It does, and from what I could gather, testing appears to continue. I didn't find any studies regarding weaponizing it as described in the novel, and I hope there never will be.

Second, Nolan's mining and use of "kilodollars" are actually based on a currency system called "Bitcoins." I read about Bitcoins in a Forbes article some time ago, and I find the idea of a virtual currency that can be mined from the Internet fascinating.

However, the hotel under attack in the beginning of the novel is fictional and its architecture is a mixture of several hotels in The Hague and in the suburb of Scheveningen. If you're planning on visiting either location, you can sleep without worry.

I'd like to thank Mr. Kevin Ortiz of New York's Metropolitan Transportation Authority for his assistance with some of the aspects of the New York subway system. While security considerations made it impossible for him to answer all of my questions, he helped me with facts and figures when he could. Any mistakes are mine.

I'd also like to thank my agent, Barbara Poelle; the Estate of Robert Ludlum, for giving me the opportunity to create a story using Mr. Ludlum's characters; Henry Morrison, agent for the Estate; and everyone at Grand Central Publishing, for guiding me through the process. Thank you to my editor, Jaime Levine, for her astute insights and suggestions; my second editor, Mitch Hoffman, who picked up the reins so seamlessly; my production editor, Kallie Shimek; and my copy editor, Georgia Maas. As always, thank you to my family for their support and enthusiasm.

And lastly, to the late Mr. Robert Ludlum. It's been an honor to play a small role in continuing his legacy. This book was a pleasure to write, and I hope that you enjoy reading it.

Jamie Freveletti
May 8, 2012

ABOUT THE AUTHORS

ROBERT LUDLUM was the author of twenty-seven novels, each one a *New York Times* bestseller. There are more than 225 million of his books in print, and they have been translated into thirty-two languages. He is the author of *The Scarlatti Inheritance*, *The Chancellor Manuscript*, and the Jason Bourne series—*The Bourne Identity*, *The Bourne Supremacy*, and *The Bourne Ultimatum*—among others. Mr. Ludlum passed away in March 2001. To learn more, visit www.Robert-Ludlum.com.

JAMIE FREVELETTI is the internationally bestselling and award-winning author of *Running from the Devil*, *Running Dark*, and *The Ninth Day*, which was named one of the "Best Thrillers of 2011" by *Suspense Magazine* and "Best of Chicago" by the *Chicago Tribune*. A trial attorney with a diploma in international studies, she is an avid distance runner and holds a black belt in Aikido, a Japanese martial art. She lives in Chicago with her family.

D0016218